The Children at the River's End

James Steven Clark

For more info on James' novels, visit:
Jamesstevenclarkauthor.com

In Memory of my wonderful Granny Vena

who provided the perfect haven

2

3

Chapter 1

A summer's day, sometime in 1983

My memories of summer are halcyon. But in many ways… exceptionally strange.

I remember boys were invited to the village to beat me up. Actually, invited! Friends, who I would loosely describe as 'part-timers', would call to me from across the other side of the road, and I, unsuspectingly, would cycle to greet them. A pal from yesterday, previously remiss of bad intentions, was now a gangster with a new heavy. This big brooding heifer from a neighboring village would - frequently right there and then - punch me straight in the face. Just as I was leaning forward on the handlebars, saying "Hel-".

Smack in the gob, or cheek.

No warning.

It was a very public thing; finished in a second. Other kids would watch on, possibly gasp, but life would reset its 'normal' trajectory almost immediately. Then, the perpetrators cycled off together, under the lusty sun, and I'd maybe see them later at the park. I'd be wary, but there was seldom more trouble. Sure, there may be a little bruising, but young kids learned that punching hard was surprisingly painful. You'd never get thumped more than twice in a single session.

Location was important for these acts; outside a bus stop, the local school, or the small village shop. Never the pub because dads were drinking on the tables outside.

Never by the river either. The river was different. Nobody ever went there to fight.

This place captured our minds in some kind of collective utopia; a real treat - a place of escape. The thugs stayed away because they could neither absorb, nor understand the joyous emotions it evoked. Far too many screaming kids, perpetually overwhelming their limited neuronal highways - any aggressive physical action would be lost, inappropriate - and they knew it. If they did 'happen' upon it, they'd frequently lob bottles into the waters and then cycle away - bored by the sight of true, uninterrupted happiness. And for five small souls, this was our *go-to*.

A special place, a place replete with mystery.

Of course, it wasn't really a river at all. It was a *beck*. I guess, based upon observation, a beck was one up from a stream, and maybe one down from a river, but the very definition, in turn, was subject to local dialects, and subjectivity. At the point where we would gather and chatter, it was simply a quiet and secluded body of water at the end of a farm track, with reeds of varying lengths sticking out of the sides, and a small cattle bridge connecting one side to the other. A large bramble bush attached itself to a wooden post on the south side, and we would readily consume blackberries to the point of belly-ache sometime in July and August. Despite the bush's size, we were always disappointed with the scant fruit it would produce. But, hope and optimism were aplenty, so it didn't matter.

You could easily step down tiered bank into the shallow beck itself, and the earth around always seemed dry. More importantly, our parents had played there when they were younger, so it always seemed to carry a timeless quality of generational love, and appreciation. The sandy bottom was visible and the water seldom rose above mid thigh. At its widest part, it was no more than seven feet across.

It was cool but never cold.

On sun-baked days, within the warm treasure troves of our minds, you never shivered for long when you departed the calm waters. Joy masked the memories of shivering… always.

The sun was yellow, and the sky was always blue.
My first memory of this place was formed back in 1983.

It's hard to recall the exact point in the year we first ventured there.

Certainly, our massive games of tag in the small village consumed a lot of our time, and they were certainly fun, as were games of football in the fields. Likewise, the farming community were generally very generous to us kids, letting us play on the safer parts of their expansive land; acre, after glorious green acre.

But, the river we loved was further away, right on the outskirts of the village, nestled away at the edge of Hislop's farm. It was popular with every child - for the space of about a week - but for the five of us, it was a secret preference; our hallowed haunt. We knew that when the fair-weather and fickle crowds dispersed, we were the ones who always remained, savoring its majesty.

Robert would tenderly maintain the tree house he'd cobbled together in the branches of an old birch tree, jutting out from the northerly bank. Effectively, it was two boards of wood tied together with some rope, but it made for a sturdy perch. I remember belly-laughing the first time he jumped from the highest bough into the beck (and being jealous of his bravery). As did Hazel and Scarlett; rolling around in hysterics. Water had never been displaced to that extent ever, not in this part of the river. It was a bit of a heroic thing; that's how I remember it. Jumping off the side of a swimming pool was a brave enough endeavour for me.

I also remember, in that moment, Scarlett laughing but then strangely crying, upset over the river somehow being hurt. Or perhaps she believed the ambiance of this magical place had suddenly and temporarily become unsettled.

They were quite a queer pair, in hindsight, those two girls. At first I thought they lived near a village on the other side of the dual carriageway (which cut straight over the beck due west). There was another primary school serving this particular village, and we *never, ever* really mingled until June came around. To be fair, the initial tentative stand off - girl and boy - occurred at the start of every holiday, taking less than an hour to thaw, before normal service resumed.

Apart from Robert and the girls, the only other regular attendee was Ishaq. I liked Ishaq. He was polite and inquisitive. Always staring at you through those wide-rimmed spectacles, ready to deliver a 'logical' observation about whatever you were discussing. They were pretty interesting statements, too. He was renowned for his contraptions, and he'd drag them absolutely everywhere. Combustible engines, go-karts or rockets; he'd have a right good crack. He never succeeded, but he did have heart. Ishaq was a rational kid - his parents being respectable doctors in the area - but he also had an organic appreciation for the river. So, one day, when Scarlett claimed she saw fairies dancing across the surface, Ishaq wasn't dismissive in the least. Instead, he sought to fetch a device that would verify her claims. And the next day he did, and it was a real thing - a microscope. Round peg for square hole, of course, but the investigation was on, and I was impressed with the science. Ishaq brought huge reams of paper too, one with annotated lines pointing to a large hypothesis emblazoned at the top.

It simply read: "I, Ishaq, propose to study the behaviour and distribution of Jinn in the river."

We had *no clue* that Jinn were evil spirits in Islam, and roundly wound him up about his mis-spelling of gin, told him he was getting drunk on the river bank. He didn't like it. Eventually, we stopped because he teared up quite a bit. As a kid, you know no such concept pertaining to alcohol and haram, and his was a very real fear attached to spirits. The river was a totally *inappropriate* place for upsetting people, and I regretfully remember teasing him there, even to this day.

Looking back...

It's as if our parents purposefully directed us there.

Of all the things they encouraged us to do in the holidays, the river was the number one spot in their eyes. Get us out of their hair. A safe location for them, automatically became a safe location for us; innocently white-washed with their rose-tinted seal of approval.

Their mischievous story-telling about yesteryears down the beck was eye-opening. Long-winded yarns, as always, covering a different reality; an alternative time. Their youth to me - neither medieval nor Victorian - was some whimsical blend between. Beyond question, the vivid recounts, somehow, matched what I *always* remembered, namely, forever-blue skies stretching over endlessly verdant fields. *But* - far more infuriating - was the dearth in concrete details about one particular claim; that there was something truly 'magical' happening there. That always got me. Intangible, almost ethereal. Could never get to the bottom of it. I'd bend an ear to the mysterious tales, but it was difficult to discern - what, if anything - our parents were referring to: some kind of rock-dwelling sirens; troubled ghosts from distant days gone; time-travelers displaced in a different land. Each and every anecdote, was distinctively woolly, like they were recalling legends passed down by great, great, grandparents; increasingly diminishing returns when it came to accuracy and elegance. But, the same enchanted themes remained, and I gladly settled for a sense of something 'other' always residing in those waters. Whereas Ishaq would be all out for empirical evidence to prove or disprove, I was happy not to push too hard for the smoking gun.

Trails of smoke in themselves could be very interesting.

One evening, as I sat at our kitchen table eating my two meaty Findus crispy pancakes, each bathed in a sea of freshly washed garden peas, I'd listen, (or even imagine listening) to mum telling me more stories about the children at the end of the river. When I asked, she always obliged. I'd place myself at the scene, visualising past events; far more alluring than my real life.

All this would change, of course.
We were the first generation to discover the secret.

Chapter 2

A summer's day,
sometime in 1984

It was the beginning of June, exactly a year later.

After a telling-off, I'd finally got round to fixing a puncture that was closing in on its first year. A neglected birthday gift. I guess I resented my bike, purposefully not tending to it, because it wasn't the blue and yellow BMX Burner I royally pined and begged for. This hadn't stopped me from performing stunts anyway, and now the handlebars were slightly sagging forwards. I figured if I kept being boisterous, they'd eventually snap off, and I'd force my parent's hand. As yet, this increasing curve (with smatterings of rust) hadn't been noticed by my folks... the flat tyre had.

Our flecked, green garage door stood permanently open, itself, too rusted around the hinges to close. Whilst cursing my feeble attempts at inserting spoon ends in the wheel rim, Robert cycled up our drive. He stopped, watching me prise out the inner tube.

'We should be the first at the river this year. Claim it. It's ours.'

I liked what he was saying, and I agreed. 'How?'

'Ishaq says something about creating defenses.'

'Defenses?'

'Submarine defenses.'

I smiled as Robert stooped down to help. Despite going to the same school, we'd only been friends for a couple of years. A mistake ruined our initial, blossoming acquaintance. Having both reached a table tennis final at a youth event (which I'd won, but only just), he'd accidentally been declared the winner. The distracted host (who bore a comb-over, and winked at women) invited him up on stage to receive the star-shape winner's award. I couldn't believe what I was hearing. As the blue and yellow ribbon was placed around his neck, he stared down at me... but didn't say a word.

The following Monday morning, as I arrived at school, he was there waiting by the stone wall. He tried giving it to me, but I was sulky, refusing to even acknowledge him. In the back of my mind, my vengeance would be my soon-to-be-owned blue and yellow BMX; far more worth than his *poxy* blue and yellow ribbon! But nothing blue or yellow came my way... not for quite some time. And even though I knew it wasn't his fault, it set the tone for our first few years together. Only gradually did we reconcile through the healing balm of time and the commonality of childhood.

Now, he was one of my best friends.

And this is how our river-summer of 84, started.

In fact, this time, Ishaq had gone one better. This small boy (with his impeccably posh English accent and his measured, gentrified manners) had already boldly approached the farmer who owned the land the river coursed through. He'd requested 'limits' and 'crowd control'. And, the friendly farmer gruffly replied that if Ishaq could, "Round up them there sheep in tawd field yonder," he could have whatever the hell he wanted. (He didn't care.)

Ishaq gave it a go.

Failed.

~ ~ ~

By the time we arrived one warm, sunny morning, the girls were already there.

Of course.

Hazel and Scarlett, standing side-by-side, like they were waiting for a dance at a school disco. Asking a girl to do that was the most terrifying thing a boy could do; but not as bad as playing with their dolls. The awkward stand-off ensued. I was amazed that they never brought bikes, and there was never a need it turned out. Here, within half-an-hour (with them instigating conversation), I learned they came from two nearby farms and didn't even *live* in the village with the suspected primary school. It was far easier for them to reach the river than us, and this genuinely intrigued me. All I saw, from beyond the cattle bridge, was a winding farm-track, culminating in a small forested copse. It headed - I assumed - in the direction of their village. However, their farms were actually only a stone-throw north of the beck. I was startled! I couldn't visualise them living so close, let alone walking here. When they told me it took less than five minutes, I was flabbergasted. Place, and perspective are a weird thing, when you're a kid.

Two girls, living exceptionally close by, who don't even *come* to *your* school! That stuff thoroughly messes with your head as a kid. So, all they had to do was scoot across the periphery of fields to reach us. They won the race every time, and this irked me.

Regardless, we were soon in advanced discussions about notable changes since last year. They were actually lovely girls. We all had a lot in common, and both were endearing: Homely Hazel, a true earthy lass; a caring, perceptive soul. And Scarlett, who could equally enchant and annoy with her airy-fairy nature. Hazel would bring ice-cream cartons full of freshly baked butterfly buns. Her mum must have liked us because she would appear with a new ice-cream carton nearly every day. We were exceedingly grateful for these wonderfully succulent gifts. Honestly, you'd lick the crumbs the off cake-case - they were *that* good - and I'm sure I once saw Robert, turn away, and secretly devour a whole one.

Hazel seemed to enjoy looking after us all.

Although more restrained and quieter than Scarlett, her goodness was evident for all to see, even at an early age. She had the warmest smile and her kindness would certainly feature in my top twenty-five, or maybe even, top twenty, memories of growing up.

Scarlett, on the other hand, would bring something unique to the beck... on *every* occasion.

Her insight; as good as the buns, but contrastingly so. And this year, like last, her ideas steadily clamped hold of my imagination. Every time. On a night, I would muse over the new pieces of the jigsaw puzzle she'd present, incessantly weaving them together in my mind, blossoming and exploding with endlessly mystical scenarios and sagas. However, at this point, it was still only a river. To us, anyway.

It was our beck.

It was isolated, and that was it.

Nothing truly magical here.

~ ~ ~

On that particular summer's afternoon, I considered both sky and water, and the peace they held. Early June, was late spring, of course - which I didn't actually realise - subsequently securing myself a losing position with Scarlett as the debate became as heated as the day. Scarlett won, obviously. I remember this June-thing being a bit of a revelation, to be honest; I was seasonally incorrect and puzzled. All was quickly forgotten. Wispy clouds hung high over our youthful heads. We'd been there for hours, complete and content in one another's company.

My arms had turned pink, and I lightly prodded white marks over skin with dusty fingers. Bees carelessly glided and gathered on flower heads, and sheep called out their nonsense to one another in the surrounding fields. The indescribable smell of the surrounding nature - innocent and fresh - complemented by a vividly lush world at its very vibrant best. This had been a really good day; my soul being soothed by the afternoon's rays. I'd laughed with friends. We'd adventured. We'd splashed. We shared triangular, potted beef-paste sandwiches my mum had provided. That beef paste was *great*.

In the distance, I eyed the dual carriageway that crossed the beck due west. An eye-sore; sure. But it had always been there, certainly for us. Part of the furniture. Nobody travelling along this busy stretch of road would ever know they'd crossed an overpass; seamlessly blending into road below. And, it was far enough away to not trouble us. The underside of this bridge possessed two deceptively steep slopes, each converging down, allowing the beck to flow through the middle.

Grey, smooth concrete.

And last year we got as far as the southern ramp, even making it a few feet along; cars, and trucks rumbling overhead. Despite the noise, and the fumes... it was the stillness of the river, and shadows bleakly cast, that coalesced to halt our intrepid brigade. Something felt prohibited and amiss, even then. A sacred border of sorts - to a land - fools dare venture. Beyond the pale, on the other side, was a stretch of impossibly dense trees. Forbidden. An invisible line separated the far side; coaxing you forward into a willful transgression; a trespasser in an unknown world. I wanted *out* straightaway. As soon as I clambered onto the acute slope, I chickened out. Despite my desperation to see the origin of our beck, the vegetation was inhospitable; the path, entirely unnavigable. It was darker and cooler, with the complete absence of any wholesome sun.

And the water - and by that I mean its depth - uncharted. It may as well have been Lake Baikal. If you tumbled in, you were sinking into the Mariana. Not been able to deduce any of this, of course, especially as we stared at the strangely calm currents, frightened the most steely of our frightened hearts.

Inevitably, during our first attempt - right on cue - Ishaq slipped, losing his footing, part-rolling, part-sliding down one of the underside slopes, straight down and in. He got trapped, submerging in the reeds at the bottom, halfway in, and halfway out. I remember his wide-eyes. Sea serpent fodder. He knew this too. His fearful squeaky cries cemented our collective sense of foreboding. It was Robert, of course, who bravely slid down on his back, and yelled, "Grab my ankle." And then he - somehow - shimmied, using his natural strength and guile, pulling a stricken Ishaq to bank-side, away from concrete and the clamour up above.

Sack *that* off.

We never went back.

In fact, we didn't enter any part of the brook for the rest of the summer, not even our special spot much further back from the dual carriageway. That was the first trauma; next level. Lesson learned. Not least, because Ishaq's subsequent and pointed claim didn't help matters *at all*. Said he'd been startled; relinquishing his hold in shock at what he beheld… at the sight of seeing clothes and boots on the far side. His voice quivered, as he explained, 'Logically speaking… a dead body.'

No thanks.

Enough was enough.

But, there was another big reason for being apprehensive here. As yet, we'd had no direct, nor personal experiences. Parental tales of mysteries - here, in and around our river - were *firmly* sealed in our heads, and expectancy can cloud the mind, and negate sound judgement, especially when they're the type of story a child never forgets. Tales passed down, to terrify - although embellished, and largely in jest - because the passage of time dulls and coats fear in the solace of rational thought. For the adult mind, anyway. A good ol' yarn. That's all.

I know now, maturity causes you to resist, and lose the *true reality* you experienced in your youth. Concerns, responsibilities; all assisting the process. Time helps you postpone the unseen. It comforts you as you reclassify your experiences over time, clutching for common sense, confounding the possibility of the paranormal. This complacency is a form of neglect. And this - definitely for our parents - and certainly for the five of us… turned out to be a grave mistake.

Chapter 3

The first half of the June school holidays

At the very end of the first day back there, while sitting on the dry and parched bank, our conversations finally turned to the folklore. Over the course of the year, there'd clearly been a gathering of information, of sorts.

Robert tied a stopper knot to the end of a rope, now hanging from the birch tree's lowest lying branch. Caught in a light summer's breeze, it delicately skimmed the surface of the water, swaying lazily from side to side. It was here, now hanging upside down, that he informed us about two huge rusted hinges on the inside wall of the cattle bridge. His, was an observation with no real conviction. Easily brushed aside. No response either, from the other four - lost in the feel-good reverie - of an outstanding day. There'd be plenty more to come; I was sure. Youth was lost on the young.

'Maybe it had doors once.'

Robert's tone bordered on lazy self-disinterest at his own flippant comment, but we all politely looked in the direction of our inverted friend. That's a daft thing to say, I thought. Who would put doors in water? Around us, Red Admirals and Peacocks fluttered out of the long grass, delicately dancing past us. The day had left us tired, but happy. Without words, we watched the polka dots of vibrant reds and blues and whites as they fluttered in the near and far.

'My Great aunty once said they heard the children playing in the river at midnight.'

That was Scarlett, nonchalantly volunteering her thoughts while rubbing her reddening knees; her pale skin, particularly prone to abundant rays.

I was skeptical. Immediately so. 'How? She'd be too far away to see.'

'They watched them walking through the fields, from their bedroom.'

'Which fields?' Ishaq said.

'The one behind us.'

Scarlett dusted the straw from her dress, stood and pointed across the cattle bridge to a more northerly field as I shook my head and smiled.

'She's telling the truth.' Hazel said. 'My aunty told me the same thing.'

'*Both* aunties? I don't believe it.'

'My Gran is Scarlett's aunt,' Hazel replied, disappointed at my disbelief. 'They're sisters; they used to share a room together on Ivy Farm. They saw them out the window.'

'Which farm is this?'

'My farm.'

The ever enthusiastic Ishaq, was already making haste up the bank; too diminutive to see above the barley fields beyond.

'I know the farm,' Robert idly agreed, tying and untying another knot. 'I've seen it… at the top of the tree.'

'Ahh, indeed.' Ishaq said, stretching his neck.

Standing, hands on hips, he stared far into the distance, satisfied at this corroboration. Robert didn't care either way, resuming with his knot, still upside down.

'So what did they look like? How many of them were there?' I regulated the level of intrigue in my tone.

'They said they looked like ghosts… transparent, but then fuller.'

There was a quiet pause, as all pondered. And I was giving great consideration to the word "transparent," when Robert interrupted. 'Ishaq, can you bring a ghost-busting device so we can settle this once and for all?'

It was a joke. No such device existed. It made us laugh, though.

Ghostbusters, the movie, would hit our local cinema later this month and every kid I knew was going nuts for it. The adverts looked thrilling. There was no wonder we were readily identifying with spirits, and all things ghostly.

'I can do that! I can bring something!'

Ishaq was serious.

'You're kidding.' Robert said. 'I didn't mean it.'

'Ghosts come out at night,' I quickly, and smartly added, swift to nip this in the bud. 'And, there's no way I'm camping out here. Besides, most our parents say things happen during the day. They're lying. It's nonsense.'

'And we haven't seen anything.' Ishaq added.

'Exactly. Nothing to see.'

'I think we will. We just need to be patient,' Robert said. 'Remember, Scarlett claims she saw a boy.'

'I did.'

I scowled, looking squarely at Scarlett. 'Where again?'

Like a jack-in-the-box, bouncing back to her feet, and signalling the spot where we'd been playing for the larger part of the day. I didn't like this one bit.

'Okay, so mum and I were passing over the bridge when we saw a little boy bobbing up and down in the water. Right there.' Her finger remained steady, as she fixed her gaze. 'My mum asked him if he was okay... cos he was by himself. He kept bobbing up and down and didn't say a thing. Then he went under... and didn't come up.'

This had to be a lie.

Nobody said anything. We'd heard this at least half a dozen times. It had the same effect *every* time. Scared the hell out of me. Last year, we'd even asked Scarlett to get her mum to write a note of her account. *And she did.*

Both Scarlett, and her Mum immediately ran to the farm to fetch a stricken Mr Hislop, the farmer who owned this land, green welly racing to the scene, wading straight in and finding... nobody.

It was a bit too visceral; a bit *too* real. In August of last year, Ishaq had subsequently conducted an 'interview' with Mr Hislop about it all, while standing at his massive front door. His response had been, 'Them there ghosts... up to no good, lad. That's all I have to say.'

He was a measured man; quiet even. Definitely good-natured, but he hid it. He didn't elaborate, nor did he need to. His simple, honest answer chilled me to the bone because I was standing right next to Ishaq as he interviewed; a disbeliever. But, I saw the look on the farmer's face. I heard him with my own ears.

Despite not finding anything, Mr Hislop had - not only confirmed Scarlett's account - but cryptically built upon it with a reference to more.

Later that afternoon, now back at home, I reflected on the day.

Scarlett had promised to bring her mother's project book of newspaper clippings, and magazine articles - written over the years - about the river.

I rubbed Aftersun lotion into my arms and forehead, because I'd been told to, and then came downstairs, taking my place for tea. It was Alphabetti spaghetti with crispy pancakes tonight; slice apart, and roll a fork full in orange sauce. Absolutely perfect. Of course, I'd already asked mum to recount her tales of the beck once again, and she was happy to oblige... as always. Her own account, in equal parts, fascinated and alarmed me.

On the day in question, she'd been part of a larger group, sometime in the backyard of the greyish 1950s (a weird, unimaginable time period for me). They all gathered in the river at the same time, on a particularly hot day, by all accounts. Most were splashing and grabbing each other in youthful abandon, trying to dunk one another. My mum said she felt hungry, but she was enjoying herself too much for it to matter. There were other fruit trees around to pick at back then. She was so caught up in a fun occasion she wasn't paying attention to the increased numbers of older children beginning to hush each other. Eventually, she said, she followed suit, went quiet - not knowing why - and watched. Despite being one of the younger kids there that day, her memory of the event hadn't faded; recalling how several of the bigger boys stood bolt still in the water.

They were a little way under, and past the cattle bridge, further downstream… pointing. Her height, being a disadvantage, she couldn't see at what.

A few of the others waded towards the middle of the beck, to get a better view of what was catching everyone's eye. So she did too and saw it. Now, caught in the universal silence, she watched a small wooden boat floating against the current towards them all.

It kept a steady trajectory, not once deviating from the centre. At no point, did it remotely come near to being caught in the reeds, as if being steered. The closer it got, the faster it picked up speed.

'*Against the current!*' mum emphasised, her eyes widening as she searched my own at the dinner table. She said, a boy shouted, 'How's it moving? It's got no oars!'

And there was nobody inside, either.

Every child screamed and scrambled onto the bank, cutting and grazing themselves on stones and bricks jutting out from the side. Kids were sliding back in; everybody - out for themselves. When she finally made it to the top, all were running hell for leather away from the beck, towards the farm. Mum said that she'd glanced back and watched the boat disappear under the small cattle bridge right at the point where they were all playing… exactly where me and the gang play. It *didn't* come out the other side.

She took flight, screaming all the way home.

The very next evening, *every* parent in the village met in the small parish hall to discuss the event. Corroborating and convincing terror tales from their sons and daughters, necessitated it. Older kids were relied upon for a more

21

mature testimony. There, my mum heard grown adults recall their own similar experiences from years and years ago.

And, for the rest of that summer, parents took it in turns to supervise the kids by the beck. Regardless, the numbers of children dropped significantly within a few days, down to none.

Her account… without fail, scared me. Each and every single time. Importantly, a local news reporter came to the meeting that evening - having heard of a dramatic incident in the midst of the sleepy hills - and the story about the *'Ghost Boat'* made the local newspaper within a couple of days. The journalist, and a couple of colleagues, even traced the river up and down for a few miles on either side, before it joined the River Swale, but there wasn't a single boat of any description throughout the entire course. To compound matters, mum brought the news-clipping out for me to read, shortly before I went to bed. I never wanted to see that boat in our beck, ever. That evening, as I cocooned within a superhero duvet, I had second thoughts about visiting the river again. In fact, I hoped it would rain that evening so Scarlett *wouldn't* bring her mum's project book with its spooky articles. Before I kissed mum good night, I asked her why she continued going back.

She replied, 'I think the children just want to talk to us. We went back next year too, and the year after.'

'What children?'

'I don't know what makes me think they're children,' she wistfully replied, staring over my head in my dim-lit room. 'I thought they might be just like us. It *was* a very small boat.'

I got the impression she wasn't telling me everything; a nugget of key information, being concealed.

'What do you think they wanted to talk about?'

Mum shook her head.

'Maybe not even talk. Maybe they just wanted us around.'

A steady mix of fear and intrigue pumped in my head, and I remained quiet and alert, smitten by her every syllable.

She winked reassuringly. 'I don't know, honey… maybe you, Robert, Ishaq and the girls can find out what they want on behalf of us all.'

'What? No way. Why?'

'Well, some mysteries need to be solved, don't they?'

Kissing me again, mum instructed me to put sun-cream on my forehead tomorrow. As she left my bedroom, her hand resting on the door frame, I asked: 'Mum… how do you know they're even children… and not something else?'

She didn't reply; shaking her head at first, unsure.

'Enough ghost stories for tonight… you'll never sleep.'

She was absolutely right. With my heartbeat thudding in my head, I flipped my pillow to the cooler side, and yanked my sheets over my head. I didn't care how hot it got under here. And as soon as I pressed my head down, the rhythmic throbbing in my ears sounded like somebody running up the stairs. They were coming for me; they'd found me. I'd rather take another punch in the face at the bus-stop. As the hours passed, I regretted asking her.

In our house, eighteen steps led to the first floor landing, and a further four would reach my open door. With pulsing veins in each temple, I could not grasp hold of any rational, happy thoughts. None whatsoever. Each pulse was a footstep. Even when I counted well past forty - more than enough to see something enter and pounce on my bed - I reset and started again. *It* was *always* at the foot of the stairs, waiting. Again, and again, and forever again.

Creeping up.

I was awake for hours.

Terrified out of my mind.

~ ~ ~

The next day would be slightly cloudier, but just as warm.

At this point, shortly after eight in the morning, the air carried its customary early morning chill.

Instead of taking a left on to the field, I cycled to the end of the farm track and across the grass to a more easterly part of the river, secluded and set slightly back from where we usually gathered. It was the first time I'd been here, and I was wary of loose, enthusiastic sheep dogs prowling around. Was I even allowed in this part of the farm? The same river, just further down stream. Nothing stirred, nothing moved, and it was more a drop - not a staggered descent - into the beck below. To peer into the waters, I would need to climb off my bike. And with the grass here being particularly rugged and unkempt, a brash fool could be in danger of tumbling in, mistaking river reeds for solid ground.

But I had to look. I had to face the fear that kept me awake for hours.

So, I carefully, almost hesitantly, made my way forwards, past an old, dilapidated barn to my left. The beck was wider and a little faster here; the shadow of the dawn sun making it harder to see to the brown bottom. In fact, I couldn't. Thick, like gravy. A turgid, chocolaty syrup. Long stalks stuck out in clusters on both sides, and the river here - in larger parts - seemingly sucked the submerged stems into the uninviting dark. Centrally, snail-like trails gathered in bubbling pools, caught in scummy spiral. This wasn't remotely a pleasant part of the beck at all. All around, massive weeds - with pretty white flowers and thick, peppered trunks - grew out from the bank side, throwing themselves partly across the body of water. This was a dirtier, more abandoned area. Lots of rusted farming implements were now coated in straggly, yellow grass.

Dried, and left behind.

It felt as if I was standing by a different river, entirely.

In the distance, I spied our cattle bridge and studied the whole stretch, with great suspicion. Up and down, over and over, and all with great trepidation. Despite its name, I'd never actually seen any cows cross to the other side, and even though I'd heard some calling in the distance, apparently there weren't many left on Hislop's farm. I knew I'd be the first one of our gang here today; I made sure of it, but why? I wasn't sure. The sun glinted off my washed and polished handle bars. With the morning chill receding, I found it hard to savour the eerie silence.

Something... wasn't in keeping.

Outside the field of vision.

But with no obvious visible clues, I was content for my eyes to over-rule my brain.

A little further up the murky stretch, I noticed something shimmering in the morning light, with water ever cascading over and around it. Clearly, it was nothing, but it still made me uneasy. In my heart of hearts, I knew it was a rock - only a rock - and so I steadily moved along the long grass to inspect, and reassure. My mind tried to keep order, and a balanced perspective, but I couldn't help the odd glance over my shoulder... just in case. If *that* boat came swimming against the current, I'd be out of here like a blue-arse fly. And so it was - as anticipated - a big ol' rusted bucket; shining surface water sliding over and around its abandoned adversary.

I mused over boat and bucket for a good, long while.

Was this all a case of mistaken identity?

From further up, where we played, this might look like the hull of a capsized boat. But mum described wood, and this looked more metallic. However, the rust was key. As minutes passed, I found myself assessing the parish hall meeting. The journalists had even walked the length of the river searching for clues. They found *nothing*.

No evidence.

Surely, this wasn't real.

It was all utter rubbish, like the previous evening's fiendish "footstep" freak; all in my imagination.

Only voices in the distance dislodged me from my reverie. Staring up and squinting, I made out the floral attire of two girls heading over the cattle bridge. (So, this is what

25

time they got here.) Glancing down at my Casio watch, I could read 8.17.

Early birds.

They arrived from the opposite direction to me, Ishaq and Robert, and they *did* come from over the fields on the opposite side after all. At least one mystery had been solved this morning. Why they would get here so early was anyone's guess? Now… had Hazel brought any buns today? This hope alone, would curtail any horrible thoughts. I was grateful for company. I didn't want to be here by myself for too much longer.

~ ~ ~

Chocolate butterfly buns, in fact.

Over the course of the day, I was hoping for two or maybe three at a push: the ice-cream tub, brimming full with the things.

'If real butterflies were made of chocolate,' Scarlett said, 'would you catch and eat one?'

'No.' Hazel replied.

'Why not?'

'Because it's wrong.'

'I agree.' Scarlett slowly nodded.

I was glad I wasn't asked. It was still quite early - too early to listen to this tripe - but if one fluttered by, they'd definitely reconsider. Sitting on the bank now, flanked by both girls, I examined the giant book with black paper that was way too large for my lap. Robert and Ishaq had arrived, and were standing behind us. Four massive pages in, I found the article my mum described.

"Haunted river gives children a right old fright."

'This is the one my mum was part of.' I said.

'Which one's your mum?'

Tracing the names at the bottom - thirty, in fact, including parents - I singled her out on the bottom right. My Granny "W" stood directly behind her in the grainy, black and white still.

'Why are both your Gran and mum's surnames different to yours?' A little perturbed, Hazel continued studying the names at the bottom. 'You're not... adopted, are you?'

'No, that's her *maid* name... before she met my dad.'

'Maiden name.' Scarlett corrected.

'She married my dad and became an Austin.'

'Ahh, good.' A blushing Hazel was relieved.

'I read that article again last night,' - Scarlett was eager to take charge - 'and it was *really* scary.'

Together, we all stared down at the beck. Everything was quiet and sedate. Needless to say, I could visualise a boat steaming towards the horrified children.

'Are you sure you weren't just imagining that boy?' I asked. 'Like a hallucination or something... or maybe you saw the belly of a fish. That would look like quite like a head, wouldn't it?'

'I'm telling you straight, me and mum saw him bobbing up and down, right there. He had hair on his head; and the water came up to chest height.' She pointed at a subdued patch, directly in front of us.

'Right, let's sort this out once and for all.' Ishaq crouched, forcibly opened his satchel, and moved to the water's edge. Carrying a portable cassette recorder, he pushed it into tufts of dry grass, wedging it as firmly as he could. We all watched on in astonishment.

'Ish, what on earth are you doing?' Hazel asked.

'I'm going to record any voices we hear.'

'Voices?'

Ishaq had been true to his word; this, his rational attempt at ghost-busting. But, to me, it was quite absurd, despite his insistence it might pick up whispers and echoes that "untrained ears" were not "accustomed" to. Ignoring him, I continued flipping through the saggy pages instead. That's where clues lay as far as I was concerned, noting...

27

my finger-tips were quite moist, leaving marks on the black backing. A particular article from the nineteen forties had grabbed my attention, my eyes drawn to the accompanying photo and headline:

"Are these ghostly faces in the mysterious mist?"

A farmer and his four sons, standing next to the beck. Black and white. They looked rigid and austere, clearly unacquainted with a camera. The cattle bridge was visible in the background, so I surmised they were only forty or fifty feet due east of our location. The image troubled me. Stretching the entire width and length of the beck was a blanket of thick fog, contained within basin; never spilling over the sides. It billowed straight up, but not out, and at some height too; probably seven or eight feet. I read it went back miles and miles, right into the dales, and no expert could explain the source. The newspaper speculated everything, from Nazi bomb contamination, to the chemical constituents on the river bed. A chain reaction. All explanations were half-baked and unconvincing. What's more, the journalists were happy to perpetuate river myths; this was definitely the "slant" of the story.

Now, with my all my friends back by my side, we carefully examined the picture for clues, and it was damn creepy. Faces were everywhere. Although most… were subject to wild and fantastical interpretation; some seemed distinctly human.

I heard myself swallow, furtively glancing above the page as I carefully scanned the beck. I'd experienced nothing but joy here. Maybe what was once here… left, and I bloody hoped so? For comfort, I stared at Hazel's ice cream tub; still unopened. In the photo, the clusters at the bottom were the most convincing: spectral infants - to the right of welly-clad legs - staring directly up at the farmer and his sons. A frenzied mass of gaping mouths, imploring the able-bodied to notice.

'Nah, it's the camera,' Robert said. 'It's a problem with the reel.'

'Old too. Double exposure,' Ishaq said.

'I agree.' I said.

In the twilight, when I stared at my bedroom curtains, fear eventually formed faces in the patterns and folds. The more I looked, the more they appeared. Even though I *knew* I was doing it, my eyes would *still do it*. In later years, I came to learn of pareidolia. A small written segment at the bottom of the photo read, "New farm owners ask for all men, women and children to stay clear. The river has its seasons and must be respected. The owners also appeal for information concerning the whereabouts of a friend, a Mister Robert Worthington." I turned away, outright asking Hazel for a bun, desperate for a time-out.

Sorry, I wasn't going to entertain any of this happening in *our* beck.

From the moment you stepped into the cool waters, without worry of it getting too deep... to the tranquility and calm it bestowed on you, with only slight car noise in the distance... and then, the glorious cycle-ride home, alongside your mates, after a great day at the river - sated and the enchanted - the completeness of knowing you lived life to its fullest.

This was our beck.

And these ancient clippings - from a superstitious era - delineated in detail, a haunted, meandering tributary full of lost and desperate souls. *Nah, not having it!* Thankfully, a child's mind is a fickle place, and as soon as Hazel unsealed the tub, and at least a dozen chocolate cakes homed into view, I put everything out of mine.

The project book, full of the macabre, was placed to one side, and that's where it stayed the rest of the day.

Chapter 4

The second half of the June school holidays

By the Tuesday afternoon, word got round that kids were meeting at the beck again.

Our numbers doubled in a couple of hours. By Wednesday, five became fifteen. Warily, I kept clear of two lads who had pitched up from a neighbouring village. Both, unsavoury characters who flashed us the occasional menacing look, picking and choosing their prey, seeking weaknesses in the vulnerable. They were real Jekyll and Hyde types; I'd heard of them. But trouble didn't brew. There was no rubber-stamping of territory with the customary introductory fight. Again, this place seemed to have a transcendent effect on all, and soon, every child was being bathed in its inimitable glow. In fact, I'd received a strange reassurance from Robert, who whispered he'd heard they'd scrapped with each other at the weekend. With sanguine antibodies still coursing through their system - self-regulating their patchy friendship - all they did was watch us play in the shallows.

They were gone within an hour; quickly bored by the lack of action.

Later on it began to spit a little, and the slate heavens drizzled every child into a retreat away from the farm. It was the same on Thursday, but this time it chucked it down. And on Friday, more rain. However, by lunchtime on that day, the thick, bilious grey clouds were blowing over and the sun was generating more heat again. One of our final opportunities.

No cell phones existed, no calls needed. Intuition, and peek at the weather outside. After all, these were the good old days when you'd knock on your mates' door, and they'd shout to their parents, "Going out," and that's all that was needed. These exits were condoned far more often than not. Growing up in a village was good on that front; lots of implicit trust.

Me, Ishaq and Robert cycled to the river after sandwiches and crisps, early in the afternoon. Our minds were collectively tuned, happy for beneficial skies, and we wanted to take full advantage. We all laughed when we saw Hazel and Scarlett looking out over the cattle bridge at the water below. *Already here...* again. I was glad. Before cycling towards them, I asked Ishaq if he'd heard anything on his tape cassette player, skeptical of the concept of catching ghost voices. Ishaq replied he'd forgotten to wind the tape back. There was only twelve minutes' worth of recording, and all of it was interference. Wind.

'Wot cha looking at?' Robert called to the girls.

Covertly, we were creeping ever closer, and both girls jumped, startled. They looked at each other several times before Scarlett called, 'There're dozens of boats in the water!'

I ceased turning the pedals... my fingers hovering over the left brake lever. With blood rushing to my head, I directed my front wheel into a crusty groove - a previous tread mark - forged into the dried earth. There, I let it languish, formulating excuses, while my two compatriots kept their forward momentum.

Robert (*thankfully*) yelled the question desperately forming in my head. 'What do you mean, *boats?*'

But the girls didn't reply, instead staring down from their elevated position... clamouring and pointing. I could not handle seeing this. This was nightmare fuel. *Dozens of boats?* Scarlett continued waving us over with big sweeping gestures of "hurry". Nothing else. I made it another six feet and then bade my bike, like a weak pony, to halt. Scratching my ankle, I tried to disguise my turning tummy as an insect bite, not wanting to display cowardice, but feeling it entirely. Construing its way into my mind - a burden too heavy to bear - tens of wooden boats filling the entire basin, with no natural explanation for their presence.

Then, from my position on the side, I saw something just peeking out from under the bridge. Small, and white. And then another. A pair... sailing *with* the current. Shock surrendering itself to relief, I processed the sight; my head re-aligning fearful imagery - a cruel conjuring - with a clear reality.

A third vessel embarked on its voyage, pulling itself free from the smooth supporting stone. Reinvigorated, I cycled hard to catch up - the *only* reason I was able - because I now *knew* precisely what lay waiting. Paper boats. Like the ones my Gran would make me in her massive back garden, tearing apart women's home magazines while lounging on a striped deckchair, me, attentively waiting by her sandled feet. She'd make dozens for me to set afloat in a paddling pool.

Rip, fold, "There you go."

Those colourful pages rendered the most vibrant of yachts, with the gloss proving more water resistant than any pressed from newspaper. The red and blue ones were always the flag ships. I was smitten by these. In my imagination, they were outstanding; the seat of admiralty. Cook, Drake, and Colombus would plan their ocean quests together. (I discovered Colombus was Italian much later.)

Now at the river's edge, I leaned on my handlebars, and counted twenty or so. A little Armada anchored to the side, with one or two periodically shifting centrally. I cycled closer to a wide-eyed Scarlett.

'How on earth... did they get here?' Scarlett said.

'I dunno.' Hazel slowly shook her head. 'It's weird.'

I had the answer, however. I always had a bloody answer. 'You two came earlier... and put them here.'

I received a scornful, withering look, like when a young kid drops one of those bad words you shouldn't use.

'We certainly did not!' Scarlett asserted.

'Well, it was raining an hour ago. Someone must have.'

'Maybe they dried off,' Robert said.

'But it was chucking it down, and paper boats get soggy quickly,' I said. 'I know. My Gran makes me similar ones to these.'

'Well, maybe your Gran came here.' Scarlett spicily remarked.

I was grateful for Ishaq's timely intervention. 'There's only one way to solve this mystery.'

And with this, he marched down the bank, taking his tiny frame onto the small grassy ledge, positioning himself directly next to the beck. On his knees, Ishaq reached out and plucked the nearest, carefully unfolding it.

'It's definitely a newspaper,' he called to the four inquisitive bridge gazers. Delicately peeling it apart, holding it upside down, he squinted through his massive glasses. 'It's yesterday's edition.'

I wasn't sure how any of this analysis was helpful. Neither did a shrugging Robert. 'So what, Ish?'

'There's a rational explanation,' Ishaq dropped the mushy paper on the bank, pressing his spectacles closer to his nose. 'Ghosts couldn't make these, unless they have newsagent subscriptions and queue on a morning to collect.'

We all grunted, rather than laugh, but he wasn't done.

'There are large footprints here on the grass, next to me.'

He was now kneeling, examining.

'They look like a welly or a boot. They're big.'

'A man?' Hazel said.

'Probably. Logically.'

Ishaq had turned things around, but this was puzzling.

'Why would a bloke come down here... and bother making boats in the rain?' I called.

'Fishermen like to fish after a downpour,' Ishaq countered.

At first, this confused me; totally failing to grasp what he was implying. In fact, I thought he was being stupid.

'What's *that* got to do with paper boats?'

'He made them… while waiting for the fish to rise to the surface. Rain stirs food up.'

'Oh.'

'How come we've never seen anybody fishing here before?' Hazel replied, doubtfully.

'We've seen them further down. Last year. They got grumpy - remember? - and stormed off because we were making a right racket.'

'Oh… yeah.'

Our joint verbal epiphany came at *exactly* the same time.

Finally, my own common sense got its house in order. 'But a fisherman… wouldn't make paper boats; they'd scare the fish away, right?'

But my friends were having none of it. They all charged down to join the Nobel prize winner for detective work. All I could do was chunter. 'But, he'd *scare* the fish away if he made boats.'

It made no difference whatsoever.

Mystery solved.

The de facto, absentee fisherman did it.

Choosing water… that rarely reached a primary school kid's mid thigh… to fish.

~~~

Everybody had a tan of sorts, even Scarlett.

Rainfall from previous days had given everyone's skin a chance to heal. And that afternoon, ten browner legs waded through the beck.

In the birch tree above, and across the fields, birds chirped their merry songs of warmth and joy. Our hearts were welcomed by nature, and innocence embraced us with wholesomeness. We laughed at each other, splashed at each other, and then stopped and nattered about anything and everything — all tinged with the healthy adventure of a well-spent youth. A quarter of an hour was all it took for anything above our knees to dry. By now, our commotion had sent all the tiny boats further down stream… to disappear from memory. Some had made good distance, while others entangled themselves in the hollow reeds on one side. Pink-breasted finches rested on tall, white, flowery stems to our left, and sparrows darted over the remaining paper frigates directly to our right. One even mischievously flew straight down into the bow of the largest, staying a while, comfortably nestled in the helm. This was an unusual and exciting sight for us. We willed it to stay, careful not to scare it. We named him Captain Crackpot, and his new boat, the Endeavour.

Robert continued dangling upside down on the rope he made, secured by his stopper knots; his hair perilously close to the water. He was a strong lad; his family owning a haulage company at the end of the village, and the time would soon come when he would leave us and go and work the holidays, like his older brother. As friends went, after a rocky "ping-pong" of a start - he was one of the best. No airs and graces, just honest and upfront. He was as stoic as a lot of folk were around here, but he possessed a wry smile, and a dry sense of humour.

In the quiet moments between conversations, I continued to contemplate how the boats even got here. It was niggling me more than the others. We hadn't passed anybody on our bikes, and Hazel and Scarlett would have mentioned if they'd met anyone on the other side. There was no other route here unless the mysterious stranger walked from the west side of the river and under the unnavigable, sloping underpass.

Why bother?

Up until the bridge, this was all Mr Hislop's land... with no other public footpath around, as far as I could tell; nothing sign-posted, anyway.

This was a lull in the day; nobody talking now. All were lost in private, imaginary worlds, with the sun beating down on our heads, draining energy in a good way and encouraging half-formed thoughts. With my eyes shut fast, I turned and raised my face, pushing my hair back with a damp hand. Squinting, I enjoyed the dry heat on my nose and cheeks. If there was anything supernatural here, I was convinced it would never find us.

This was *such* a sanctuary.

There was extra hope brewing on this particular day; fish and chip Friday, for our family. No amount of chocolate buns could sate that. Moreover, Ishaq's parents had promised to take me and Robert to see a matinee of Ghostbusters on Saturday. There was a cubicle in the foyer of our local cinema - a hole in the wall - where you could buy the biggest bags of sweets you'd ever seen around here: a special place that no one ever witnessed unless you specifically entered. Secret, and special, just like our secluded brook.

Mum had promised me one pound coin to spend on a big bag of sweets. Those coins had come into circulation only the previous year, and holding one was as important as its monetary value. It was a *status* thing, and I could guarantee I'd be flashing it around in my palm.

All was really well in the world.

Head angled, I soaked myself in the sun and listened to inquisitive bees in flight.

'Can you hear that?' Robert broke the silence.

Nobody spoke, but everybody stopped and looked. Lazily turning, I let the sun's yellow and orange explosions, seared across my retina, slowly ebb and fade. Then I adjusted to the sight of my inverted friend, as he motionlessly studied the river; the tip of his nose and chin nearly touching the surface. He'd remained in this position for at least twenty minutes. I don't know how he did it.

'What?' Scarlett said.

'That.'

'What are you hearing?' Ishaq asked.

Swift, sudden movement. Robert... adeptly flipping himself upright, and then carefully lowering himself into the beck.

Crouching, left cheek below the water; done so in earnest.

'What is it?' Scarlett said.

'Shh!'

Robert concentrated, as Hazel shrugged at her friend, before he straightened his arched back and stared at us all. 'I'm not kidding; listen to the water.'

No one did anything. Instead, we appraised the concern on each other's faces. Robert was serious. The stocky young boy bent over again as we quizzically observed.

'Listen to the top of the water,' he said, this time with his left arm aloft to motion silence.

One by one we stooped, with me being the last.

Seconds passed...

'Oh yeah, *what is it?*' Hazel said.

'What?' I said.

Hovering, I tried to block out the sequence of surprised agreement from my friends. At first I heard nothing, just the gentle running water, centuries of the same drops recycled in the Dales miles behind.

And then...

'What the heck?'

'Voices,' Robert replied, still staring down.

I stooped once again, hoping to correct my senses, allay my fears, but there they were. Indistinct sounds. Quiet chatter. Very much a long wave radio station picking out distant foreign languages while you turned the tuning dial. As intently as possible, I listened to the incessant, fading whispers on the surface, ebbing and flowing as if carried by the tide.

Both Ishaq and Hazel kept standing upright, at least twice. Now it was my turn. The wave of casual, indiscernible murmuring grew louder, suddenly forming something distinct and alarming in my ears.

'*Enemy.*'

It was coolly delivered, crystal clear.

I stayed still only a moment longer before striding to the edge of the beck, churning over piles of water in my attempt to leave. Scarlett wasn't far behind.

'Hazel,' Scarlett called, waving her arm as if to gather. But her friend was rigid… staring incredulously at a gap between her bare legs. 'Hazel, come out,' Scarlett implored. 'Hazel, come on.'

I didn't say anything, but something was really, *really* off.

Without provocation, Scarlett swivelled my way, whispering, 'She's been having nightmares. She needs to come out. Her mum's worried.'

'Did you… hear?' I said.

'Yes.' She turned. *'Hazel!'*

At Scarlett's insistent and escalating calls, the girl stirred - her expression, a haze of confusion - and then she belted towards the bank - toppling - with Ishaq closely following. In shock, I watched him agitatedly shaking his head; a computer unable to process an illogical line of code.

Robert stayed put.

The side of his face now dipping deeper in the river, closer and closer to covering half. To my horror, he appeared to be mouthing something, or repeating something, his expression transfixed.

'*Robert, come out!*'

Scarlett started shouting alongside me, but he was entranced.

And then another voice… from above, this time.

'Hello kids.'

Behind us, on the bank. And all four shrieked, jumping by the side of the beck. I have never been *so* startled; my legs going to jelly as I tried staying upright. The girls continued bouncing backwards, and away. And at six feet tall, the man staring at the top, surveying us, *wasn't* Mr Hislop, the farmer. Grizzled. Virtually toothless, with only one solitary yellow-stained peg… jutting out in his upper gum. He stepped back, raising his hands, surrendering; sensing alarm.

'Only saying hello to you good folk, on this here, gorgeous day.'

We were encased below on the lower bank; like caged animals.

'Did you see my boats?' he gently enquired, astutely observing collective dismay. 'I tried fishing here this morning, but I had no luck, so I made some boats while I waited.'

It was then - and only then - I 'knew' precisely who this was; despite my whirling mind. Eminently recognisable in our locality, just not in this context. A few times I'd passed him with mum in the car, but only ever caught a fleeting look. On each occasion, he was walking. *Always* walking. This man was a tramp; a well-known one, in our area. Particularly in the summer months, he'd appear out of nowhere in our tiny village, and my mum would chat with him from time to time.

'I'm Ol' Bobby.' he said. 'Sorry for scaring you.'

His tone was calm, trying to reassure the frightened starlings at his feet. 'I know kids like to come here and play, so I left you some boats to look at.'

His whitish, greying hair slotted down either side of his ears, morphing into a yellowish tint further down. It was the same with the moustache - drooped over his top lip - curled and matted. He crouched, picked up a stone, and hurled it.

In Robert's direction.

Naturally, the fear recommenced. Under attack now, from a mad, homeless man… the four of us bundling to one side, bunching tightly together, before tumbling partly into some reeds.

'Boy, be careful.'

Robert sensed the stone plop inches from his face. And he slowly turned to stare; his reverie broken; the entire left side of his clothing, drenched. He quizzically pushed his palm over the sopping T-shirt and shorts - before reconnecting with the here and now - and staring up at his assailant.

'Boy, those Sirens will call and call. You've got to watch out for 'em.'

Robert was pretty fearless.

Even I have to admit this.

And I watched my friend as he analysed the man above for a couple of seconds, before nonchalantly saying, 'Who's this guy?'

Then Robert stared our way, a tumbled mass in the reeds.

'People call me Ol' Bobby. I go from place to place but I come back here in the summer; I like it here.'

'What do you want?'

'Well, nothing... really. Just thought I'd come and say hello.'

Ol' Bobby scratched the damp armpit of his off-white shirt, 'I go searching for work... live off the land... make hay while the sun shines... and then hibernate in the winter, like a bear.'

Robert paused only briefly, assessing the stranger, before resuming, 'You're that tramp guy?'

'Aye.'

'Why are you here?'

'Well, I go tramping here, there and nowhere... and I end up here.'

With Robert *eyeing* him up and down, the tramp continued, undeterred. 'I do a lot of walking, I guess. What about the rest of you kids?' he shifted his focus to our uneasy huddle, 'Sorry for lobbing that stone. I didn't mean to scare you. It's just this beck can be... well, let's just say... it captivates young and old minds alike.'

The dearth of teeth in his mouth, meant he struggled to pronounce larger words; instead, rasping out of his mouth as he rolled his tongue around them. He looked odd. He sounded odd. For once I was brave, *wanting* to engage, like I'd seen my mum do. He was giving both protection, and distraction from the murmuring currents beneath. Besides, he was skinny; surely physically incapable of fighting.

Increasingly, I was feeling less and less like Superman on a mountain of Kryptonite.

'I've seen my mum talking to you,' I said. 'She's chatted with you over our wall and given you eggs and potatoes. I think she gave you one of my dad's shirts; it was a checked one, in white and pink.'

'Still got it! Still wear it.' Another toothless grin. 'Ahh… yes, in the village, last year.' He pointed a spindly finger east. 'People are kind to me around here. I stay away from the towns. Please, do thank your mum for me again.'

Next to me, I sensed a shivering Hazel, and Scarlett clasping her friend around her wet shoulder. We were upright again, at least, and despite her subdued demeanour, Hazel managed to say, 'You come and potato pick for us in the summer.'

'Which farm is yours, love?'

'Ivy farm.'

'Ooh, I like it there. One of my favourites. Tell your father I said hello, and I'll be knocking on his door in August.'

'Sorry, the crops aren't looking so good.'

'Blighted, are they?'

The disquieted girl nodded, her mind elsewhere.

From out of nowhere, an adjusting Ishaq finally piped-up. 'Mister, is this place haunted?'

Placing his hands on his boney hips, the man surveyed the river course from east to west, 'Could well be, could well be.'

'How? Why?'

The tramp sighed, and rubbed a watery, hay-fevered right eye.

'Well, lad. You'd need to ask William 'bout that.'

This answer… startled me, and I nervously looked at my friends. Even in this baking heat, I was starting to shiver. The word "enemy" thrust itself in and out of my head; a sword of an unwelcome, intrusive thought. Over and over, spinning and dislodging reason. Precariously, I climbed to the top level of the bank, Ol' Bobby offering to help with an outstretched arm, but I purposefully angled my

41

flight at a diagonal, avoiding him. Scarlett and the gang followed… with a shaken Hazel struggling with most of the ascent.

'What nightmares?' I whispered to Scarlett.

She scowled back. Too close.

Robert made his way out, arriving at the river edge, effortlessly clambering out. I did… and didn't want to talk about what I'd just heard. It felt like something had defiled me deep within, in a similar way to entering a school toilet, only to find someone preferred using all the floor. My head was a clean place in terms of normal thoughts. *Until now.* The presence of the homeless man was a welcome distraction from the beguiling waters around us, especially when Hazel suddenly became very upset, pushing her forearm over her eyes to shield her tears.

'We're going to go now,' Scarlett asserted, taking her friend by the waist and gently guiding her towards the cattle bridge.

'Okay, bye,' I said.

'Bye.' Scarlett replied.

This turned out to be the final word I heard from them in many weeks.

The staccato farewell was all a group of kids could manage when a life-defining moment had presented its unwelcome self. With Robert pulling alongside us, I marched towards my bike. My friend was confused. 'Where are you going?'

'I need to get home… fish and chips.'

'What, at *half past four*?'

Ishaq was also itching to join me on his bike - a new white racer The tramp remained in place… and this made it awkward to even mention what had happened, but I decided I *didn't* want to discuss it. I needed time to internalise. Away from everyone. Time to get the hell away.

'I'll call you,' I said.

This was a lie: kids never used telephone lines… unless they were forced into thanking relatives for gifts.

Robert turned to Ishaq. 'Well, I'm gonna see you both tomorrow, anyway… for Ghostbusters, right?'

Ishaq sheepishly stared away. 'Yeah,' he replied, weakly.

'Okay, deal: see you both tomorrow at one-thirty, right?'

'Yeah, see you tomorrow, Rob,' I replied, wanting to finish this.

Ol' Bobby was listening all the while. We remained polite with him - saying our respectful goodbyes - and then Ishaq and I cycled home. I plucked up enough courage to talk to my logical friend as we approached the driveway to his large house; one of the most sizable and newest in the village. In of itself, this driveway was intimidating, but I needed to hear a bit of Ishaq 'logic' more than ever.

I *needed* to know I was wrong.

I waited for his reply.

But, he quietly and apologetically said, 'I don't want to talk about it.'

And that was it. He cycled up the immaculately kept tarmac, and I cycled away.

~ ~ ~

We didn't get to see Ghostbusters the following day. I watched it on VHS several years later. Around seven-thirty, that very evening, there came a knock on our front door. This was the formal door, unlike the side.

It was Mrs Khan, Ishaq's mother.

My mum was delighted to see her, always describing her as a "very gracious lady". She wanted a quiet word… in private. I'd barely touched my fish and chips, happy to skip them and leave the kitchen, where the conversation took place over a cup of tea.

And about half an hour later, mum came into the lounge.

Mrs Khan had left.

She took a spot on the sofa next to me. 'Mrs Khan asked… if it's okay… postponing seeing the movie for the time being. Maybe, for a couple of weeks?'

This was *beautiful* news.

Mum continued. 'Was everything okay at the beck today? You were awfully quiet when you got it in. I thought you'd fallen out with your friends and that's why you didn't touch your chips.'

I shifted uncomfortably. I remember *that* uncomfortable twist to this day. It wasn't quite as bad as the "What is sex talk", but it came pretty close. I didn't want to recall the word I'd heard… let alone discuss it.

'Mum, I think… I'll leave going down to the river for a while.'

'That's a good idea,' she opened her mouth as if to continue, and then changed tack, 'Is there anything you wanted to talk about, from today?'

I shook my head. 'No.'

She paused for a few moments, anticipating I might change my mind, but I wasn't going to.

'Okay, honey. But if you need to talk, let me know.'

'I will.'

'Ishaq's pretty shook up, by the way.'

It was obvious she was fishing. I nodded, saying nothing. She left to clear the plates, but as she made it to the living room door, I called after her, 'Mum, can I sleep in your room tonight?'

I could tell she was going to say no - I could see it in her eyes - but then she thought about it a little.

'I remember asking the same question once,' she smiled. 'You can help me put up that camp bed later. Does that sound okay? I'll tell your dad.'

'Thanks.'

I was *so* very grateful.

And felt a *whole* lot safer.

Chapter 5

The summer holidays - the first day back

Time has a way of cementing and compressing a claustrophobic brand of horror.

Drying it hard under a filament of tight skin. Immovable. Set within tiny bubble boundaries of thought. In fleeting moments, like harrowing déjà vu, they inexplicably appear. It's faint, concealed in the dullest tint, but it's *still* fear.

But even the details eventually wear thin, and you stop revisiting the event. And they *really do* wear thin… blurring as they do so.

We learn. We adapt; colouring over the difficult details in our conscious, consigning them to the subconscious. We're all expert artists in these matters, dousing thicker paint over the pain in a revealed pentimento. Coating it blander, until it's a more tolerable, safer impression. Uncertainty, wrapped in little comfort blankets of certainty.

The peg is square. The hole is still round. But we *believe* we have the correct peg.

That's *all* that matters.

~ ~ ~

We went to South Wales in the first week of the summer holiday, and it was fantastic. The sandy beach and the rocky crevices provided me with hours of fun and exploration.

I stayed away from the sea in the main.

Arcades, full of games I never knew existed, lit my eyes with eager anticipation. I *begged* to go in. The sound and smell of electricity, and those machines… and the salty sea breeze drifting in through the open archway into this cavern of delights. These *were* good times. And the fish and chip stands, blitzing my nostrils into constant surrender in sudden, powerful waves of salt and vinegar. Battered and chunky cod, with tomato sauce squeezed from a humongous red bottle, tasting every bit as good as they smelled.

I "compensated" for those I'd left going cold on the kitchen table.

To coin a phrase: I was in my element. Excitement was my constant companion. Danger didn't exist. I felt low on the long, long drive back… but even my sadness was tinged with the blessed happiness of forever memories.

Ishaq and Robert weren't around for the week after, either.

By this point, the year tipped into early August, and potato-picking season was upon us. My ears pricked when mum said she was "picking" for twenty pounds a day, at a certain… Cherry Tree Farm.

'I do hope they get a better yield this year,' she admitted. 'I'm not sure this land was made for spuds.'

I thought about Ol' Bobby. And, of course, I thought about Scarlett. I couldn't quite explain it… but I'd been thinking about her a lot. I'd inferred her farm was Cherry Tree ages ago.

Back in June, her fairer skin hadn't browned as well as mine, and certainly nowhere near as well as Ishaq's. Her curly, auburn hair, would swing from side to side as she bustled and fidgeted her way everywhere. Always alert, and ready to take action. She had cute freckles that laced her cheeks and a tiny button nose. Her smile was full of mischief - intentionally so - but above all, there was a warmth and genuineness behind that smile. I remember how she cried last year when she thought Robert had hurt the river by jumping in. Her connection with the beck was the most natural of the five of us. I'd never had a girlfriend lasting more than two days and I couldn't imagine having a 'full-on' one either. This was in danger of being a crush, but I'd never admit to it.

I was at the age where you didn't know what to do with a girlfriend, anyway.

Stand next to each other more and more frequently? Hold hands, talk about, and study flowers together? *But, what about Star Wars?* Most I knew liked creating dance-routines with their friends, and then performing in front of their folks.

There's no way I'd be doing that.

I had *no* idea; not a blinking clue. I knew more about the solar system than I did about girls.

When mum got back from the farm later, she was browner already, and tired... but content with her day's work.

'I have a message for you.' she said.

This caught me off-guard, immediately perking me up at the kitchen table where I'd been writing a story about the abominable snowman. This was a bit like a surprise parcel popping through your letterbox, addressed to you.

'What message?'

'It's from Scarlett. You know her, don't you?'

My heart kind of (can't explain it)... whizzed?

'Oh, yeah.'

'I was talking with her dad; he's a jovial chap, isn't he? She overhead, and came to the door and introduced herself. She's very smart. A pretty little thing.'

I didn't like the intonation she used on the last line, but nodded politely (trying to display indifference), waiting for the message.

'She wants to know when you're next going down to the beck.'

47

(I swallowed.)

Mum continued. 'She's going down there tomorrow with a girl from the next farm along. I think she's called Hazel. Said, from about eight?'

This shocked and excited me. It's quite possible I jolted, but I certainly didn't know where to look. Then my mum did something very cunning, although I didn't click-on at the time.

'You know… we could go down there together tomorrow,' she began. 'I'm picking again. You bring your bike. I'll leave you at the beck. I'm only three or four fields over from Mr Hislop's. We can make a picnic of it if you like… and you can meet me for lunch. About 12.30?'

A quandary had presented itself, alongside the ambivalence of fear-imbued elation. A chance to talk, to discuss what happened back in June, with a getaway car around the corner. Finally, get *it* off our chests. I desperately wanted to discuss my theories about the "Enemy". Two weeks into the holiday, and I was already listless from self-confinement. Robert came back from his holiday, yesterday, and Ishaq was flying back this evening. Scarlett was definitely going to be there in the morning.

In fact, she'd *asked* for me to be there too.

Mum would be close. Four fields away; like a safety harness. Stay till lunch, eat, and then ride home if things got too freaky.

'What do you think, sweetheart?'

'Erm…'

'It's meant to be gorgeous again, tomorrow. We can go as far as the farm, together… and meet there if you like. It sounds like she's raring to go.'

'Yes, alright.'

I swallowed hard with optimism and turmoil, scarcely believing what a single minute could present. Would I call in for Robert for back-up? Would I even be brave enough to be there by myself an entire day with *two whole girls?*

Later that night, I would dream Scarlett and I were on the ocean together in a small, wooden boat with a low hull almost parallel with the waves. We were like the owl and the pussycat, out to sea, on a beautiful pea-green boat.

Except, the sea gnashed at us.

Hands reached up, clawing us, grabbing our arms and slicing blood out of our skin with serrated nail tips. The arms gripped so tight, dragging us into a whirlpool throat of devouring waters. Faces in the waves opened their insatiable, writhing mouths, and sank decay-infested teeth into our soft flesh. Slowly eating and swallowing us in torturous agony; limb by open limb.

The fear I overcame the next morning, to even leave the house and cycle with my mother, was a pretty *landmark* moment in my life. I was coming to terms with the fact that ghosts were not exclusively a night-time thing.

~ ~ ~

Since our encounter, the rumour mill had spun pretty fast in the adjoining school half-term.

Two stories, carried around the village; both untrue.

The first, the river spoke to us in audible voices and sent us packing in terror.

Something tried drowning us.

By all accounts, a journalist from the local newspaper got wind of our saga and wanted to interview us, but nothing came of this. If anything, parents conferred with friends about the incident, and they, in turn, delivered a half-baked version to their own kids. Even though Ishaq was a bit of a chatterbox, I couldn't see him revealing anything to anyone; I certainly never heard him giving playground 'story-time' for that half term. For seven entire weeks, not a single word was uttered about the matter. An unwritten agreement between the three of us. Slightly weird.

49

Certainly for inquisitive kids. In fact, Ishaq - the logician - bordered on being solemn and restrained; less enthusiastic about even answering teachers' questions, as he once did. Robert, on the other hand: *had anything even happened?*

He was completely unaffected by the incident; no noticeable changes in behaviour.

It took less than a week before I started deflecting questions about the incident. I lost friends by not revealing anything; classed as *boring*. But then - despite our absence - the beck became a hotbed on an evening again; youths from neighbouring villages spicing things up, stirring up the young ones with hysterical nonsense. This seemed to work; with many leaving in tears. Fights had taken place. Bottles had been shattered over the cattle bridge. Waste had been discarded.

Mr Hislop wasn't happy.

He banned children until the summer holidays.

It seemed to do the trick; nulling the crazed zeal for an experience.

~ ~ ~

When mum and I approached the river at 7.45 am, I knew I wouldn't be entering the water this day. A deeply profound power overshadowed this place, and I felt the palpable unease. Meandering from hills in the west, to the sea in the east, but not before first joining the powerful and dangerous River Swale. There was an unearthly essence in these currents.

As we approached, I stared into the distance at a quarter mile stretch of reeds; the tension stretching out my chest from the inside. Why *couldn't* I be the only member of our party who'd heard something that day? I could easily cart that off to a sensible place, demontage the hell out of it in my head, and then smothering it with comforting reason. We took a left, and walked across the field, angling towards the cattle bridge.

In the distance, I spotted Scarlett and Hazel, standing someway back on the bank. This made my heart leap. I'd actually... missed them both, and thankfully, I didn't even have to walk as far as the farm.

'Are you going to be okay? Remember, I'm just across the fields.'

A few weeks prior, I'd eventually revealed to mum we'd heard voices, without explaining the specifics. (It was a confession for an extra night in her room.)

'Thanks, mum. I'll be fine.'

'Have fun.'

She winked, but I doubted *pure* fun could happen here again. Two generations of villagers were vicariously living their own experiences through us. They weren't averse to using us as Guinea-pigs either, clinging to the belief the river was both enchanted and wholly salubrious. As we were about to part ways, I recalled what Ol' Bobby said two months earlier.

'Mum, do you know any other William's around here?'

My mother blew out her cheeks, as if weighing up a whole bunch, while rubbing my head.

'Well, there's William Grobatard - the wealthy farmer over there; William Lowstock, the young lad who came with his dad in the air force, and went off with the merchant navy.'

'I remember him.'

'Bill Tinker - a bit of a handy-man round here; Bill Thorpe, the fish-and-chip van man. Yes, quite a few... William Wordsworth. Why?'

I nodded, surprised at the breadth and distribution in profession; a tad disappointed there were so many. Scarlett and Hazel were now waving, and close enough for me to ignore answering my mum's final enquiry. They looked happy to see me, too.

Time to play it cool.

Mum lifted a plastic bag out of her rucksack containing a pair of jeans, a shirt and a few packets of biscuits - for Ol' Bobby - should he appear again (as I'd also revealed). We'd also seen him in the village on several occasions. To my surprise, on a weekend drive, we passed him in our car, and it was a good four or five miles away from here. My parents pulled over and offered him a lift, but he was quite happy just to... keep on tramping. He refused money.

By all accounts he *hadn't* been potato-picking with the locals, yesterday.

'Hi.'

'Hi.'

'How have you been?'

My mother left us at this point, but not before beaming at Scarlett in particular. The three of us performed the customary pleasantries, helping thaw the ice. It didn't take long to melt. But, even in the presence of running water, nobody dared yet acknowledge the sinister stream metres from our bare legs. Scarlett must have possessed a disposition of steel, with everything she'd encountered here.

And... I could tell she was brewing; back for more.

Despite Hazel's kindness and affability, it was quickly obvious she was the subdued one of the pair; content with letting her friend take the lead. And it was clear that Scarlett would cut to the chase any moment; a blurting bomb ready to explode, but this time - for once - she used diplomacy to address the elephant in the room.

'Back in June... what do you think happened?'

'I heard a voice.'

'Me too. What did it say to you?' She turned to her pal, adding, 'Oh... Hazel's mum had a word with me, and she's not going to talk about any of this. And that's perfectly fine.'

This made things a little weird, especially when Scarlett took hold of Hazel's shoulder, reassuringly squeezing and rocking her, before darting her eyes straight back to me. Her hair, like a frenzy of red curls, swished back and forth.

She waited. 'Well?'

I sat down on the bank and dubiously peered at the beck. This was a place of other's wild stories and exaggerated memories. I should never have had my own tale to tell. But I did.

'Enemy,' I said, almost whispering, so the river couldn't hear.

'*Enemy?*'

I actually shushed Scarlett with glaring eyes. Scarlett got the message and ungraciously plonked herself down next to me.

'It said *enemy* to you?'

'Yeah…'

Hazel sat behind us, but between us, so she could listen in.

'What do you think it meant by enemy?'

'Didn't it say that to you?'

'No, it said… *play hide-and-seek with us.*'

I jolted. Couldn't hide it. The red head delivered this calmly, in her typical matter-of-fact way. But ice instantly chilled my veins. I looked at the beck, lowering my voice again. 'Hide… *and seek?*'

'And then it said,' she abruptly started, giving me no chance to process, nor stopping her mouth moving, 'You're *going* to find us.'

Hairs bounced upright on my neck. I couldn't accept this. She *had* to be lying. But the tongue was back in gear.

'Enemy? It said "enemy" to you?' Scarlett looked amazed. 'Maybe… it was telling you *who* their enemy is?'

'William.' Hazel said.

Scarlett was momentarily caught off guard, stunned by the link, instantly gushing, '*Yes, Hazel! Yes!*'

'No, I don't think it was.' I swallowed. 'I don't think it was specifically telling me who the enemy is. Well, maybe it was… I don't know.'

'Then what did it mean?'

I was still appalled by what Scarlett revealed, assuming we'd all heard the same. I shrugged, aware our excitable voices were being raised in front of the menacing brook.

'Why would it tell *you* that?' she said.

53

I shrugged again.

She wouldn't stop. 'So, what exactly… *is it in there*? I think they're ghost children.'

'You can't *know* that.'

'I saw the boy.' She pointed at herself. 'There are kids in there!'

'I don't know. There can't-' I scrabbled for common sense, reason, anything…

'It was warning you about *their* enemy.'

'Scarlett, I-I just don't know.'

Revelation overload.

Out of the corner of my eye, I glanced at Hazel, now staring off into the distance. She hadn't brought any buns; and maybe her mum was upset with us all for scaring her daughter.

'What did it say to Robert and Ishaq?' she said.

I assessed Scarlett's relentless, insistent exuberance, recalling how she exited the water just as sharply as me. However, unlike me, she'd fired this into a full-blown investigation with an air-tight, unshakable hypothesis. If you gave her a Rubik's cube, I swear she'd not stop revolving: she *could not* stop.

'They haven't talked about it.'

'But Ishaq's a ghost-buster.'

'Not any more. Definitely not.'

'What?'

'We never went to see the movie in the end. His mum cancelled. He was too scared.'

This news stopped her, but only for a millisecond.

'So, what about Robert? What happened to him in there? Me and Hazel think he was hypnotized.'

Truthfully, so did I. Ishaq hadn't been his typically bubbly self at school for weeks. Robert, however, had remained stolid.

'Did you know Robert's been coming here… by himself?' Scarlett said.

This truly *hammered* me.

'He's been doing what?'

'On a night, by himself.'

A high-energy bomb had dropped this time. No sirens. No warning. Unexpected. But, I felt somewhat betrayed.

'*Here?*' I said.

'When mum and I deliver eggs to the village we walk this way, and Robert's been here on an evening after school.'

'I didn't know that.'

I'd hung out with Robert and Ishaq a couple of times on our bikes, but there was never a hint of this secret attendance.

'Yeah, we saw him in the river - we deliver on Monday's - and he was either in the water, or building his tree house.'

I gazed up at the tall, sprawling birch; instantly astonished. And stood. How easy it is to miss things above your eye-line? There it was. The platform, transformed. Now indeed, a fully enclosed tree house, in receipt of a circle for an open window on the nearest of its six sides. Three ropes dangled down to the waters, secured to an additional flat platform, hovering two inches above the surface.

Why hadn't he mentioned this?

I felt put out.

A bizarre, conflicting emotion burned through me like a forest fire. I'd been deceived and yet… there was no way *in hell* I'd come back here if he asked. But somehow, it was the table-tennis debacle all over again - or at least, I was making it so. And yet, I was back here, only because Scarlett suggested it…

'What did he say?' I said.

'I said hello, and we talked over the cattle bridge, but he was always very busy. He seemed engrossed in building stuff. He's quite quiet, isn't he?'

He was, but not unduly.

Hazel slowly piped up, 'look. He's even built something coming out from the side.'

Intrigued, puzzled… I clambered to my feet, unsure of what she meant. And then I saw it, peeking out of the reeds to our left. A small wooden jetty - a miniature dock -

spreading out several feet. I was flabbergasted. He'd even added moorings for boats to attach themselves to.

My jaw sagged.

One was… already moored there.

~ ~ ~

Now sitting with my calves resting flat on the jetty, I tried picturing Robert carrying planks of wood on bike handle bars. Over and over. Backwards and forwards, evening after evening. This expertly crafted structure stuck a full five feet into the cool (presently), peaceful water. Created over the last seven or eight weeks.

Sturdy.

The underside and supports were the biggest job, and there was nothing shoddy about his handiwork. But why on this green earth, had he done this? I swallowed. Boats. Was he expecting boats? Peering up, I examined the tree house from a distance, and the window he'd cut in the shape of a porthole - not by any means a perfect circle - but close enough. Bundles of curly, auburn hair were wafting in and out of the gap as Scarlett periodically stuck out her face; updating us on the contents.

Robert had left boxes inside.

Within - information on rivers in the area.

Many were concerned with the source of the headwaters in the dales. There were also a few antiquated pamphlets on the local history of the area, and this place in particular. He was protecting this hoard - even securing a deadbolt to one box - but as yet, had not brought a padlock. His parent's haulage firm was coming in handy; odds and sods were at his disposal.

'We need to ask him what he heard.'

I whispered this to myself, still afraid to raise my voice.

Hazel stood on the opposite side of bank staring up at the tree, reluctant to climb inside and follow her friend. Who could blame her? I wondered what she'd heard that silenced both her tongue, and bluster. She looked permanently troubled by all of this; probably more so than me, and that was saying something. Her motherliness had all but disappeared, as had the buns. Then I considered Scarlett's message; infinitely more terrifying than my own.

Play hide-and-seek… and you will find us…

Wasn't happening.

Why was I even here, in fact?

I'd hunted for an experience; mesmerized by a quest to follow in the footsteps of the wise elders, and maybe have my own black-and-white photograph in the local newspaper, to pass on to my kids. Now I couldn't care less. It had revealed enough of its secret, and I didn't like it one bit. Be careful what you wish for. Something else glistened in the corner of my eye. Leaning forward a fraction on the jetty, I looked to my left.

A patch of bull rushes - in the centre of the beck - slightly west of where we played, was moving. Gentle breezes and docile currents moving over and through clumps of river grass would always do this. Nothing out of the ordinary. I rubbed my eyes and studied a little longer. Nothing stirred. So, I looked back at Hazel, once more considering her obvious deflation. But then, a few seconds later, there it was again…

Something, down there, pushing apart the thick reeds, and not only within the water. Things were getting tugged under. And, it was big.

I jumped to my feet and stepped back off the boards.

Above, Scarlett commenced blaring out like a lighthouse foghorn: 'You both need to come and see this!'

I processed her command while remaining vigilant. Minnows sailed by in abundance here, and frequently we'd try to catch them in Hazel's empty bun carton. Fish, larger than three or four inches, were rare. But, *that* bobbing boy was now an intrusive thought, belting at my heart. In a fight-or-flight scenario, I would be useless at both.

Please *don't be* the bobbing boy.

'Did either of you hear me?' Scarlett called.

'Scarl, come down.' Hazel weakly replied.

I called. 'Both of you, *come here!*' My turn to shout, and with more urgency than Scarlett.

A cluster of reeds was being jerked to one side - something significant - happening right here, yards away from me. I was on the verge of staring directly at the forbidden. Climbing backwards up the bank, I remained transfixed, watching the beck, not wanting to look, but unable to stop myself. Next came the splash and the bubbling wake.

What the hell is it?

Things turned much quieter, and for close to a minute, I squinted at the clear water flowing around the green sedge.

And then it came… slithering out from the centre. A slippery, shadowed mass of gross proportions, breaking the surface; disproportionate for a beck this size. *Far* in excess, too large.

But it wasn't the boy.

Thank goodness, it *wasn't* the boy. Hazel and Scarlett advanced towards me, tracing my eye line for clues to my concern.

'*Holy Cow! Look at that.*'

'What is it?'

'It's a fish. It's *flipping* gigantic.'

The girls stopped, one on either side of me; amazed. It was an incredible sight for any youngster.

'Oh… my…' Hazel gasped.

'It's massive!' Scarlett blurted.

Jaws had aired on terrestrial TV two years previously. There wasn't a single kid in my class I knew who hadn't seen it. That very evening, while kids wrestled with sleep, it rained. And at school the very next day, every single playground puddle became a pond of deadly significance. All three of our own jaws dropped. This fish *was a monster.* Our beck was clearly hiding its own secret behemoth; a prowling, devouring beast.

'What type of fish-' Hazel began…

'It's called a Pike,' Ol' Bobby replied.

This was the first time in my life I swore in front of girls. He was here again. We all ducked as if electrocuted; blindsided by stealth. Scarlett toppled over, as if avoiding a swinging axe.

'You kids… are the jumpiest kids… I've ever met.'

Once again, Ol' bobby felt obliged to step back. Arms held out in a peace-offering, attempting to calm; giving us space to breathe and compose. And once more, he continued with his reassuring chatter. 'He's called Basil. He's Basil the Pike. He's been in there for years, and he's getting bigger and bigger. They're predators, y'know, but they won't bother you. He likes hanging out in those bull rushes.'

The tramp toothlessly smiled at each of us in turn. From one to another; waiting for fear to subside.

'I thought about catching him the other day. Quite tasty fish if cooked right; bit boney though. I can never hook any small fish here because Basil gobbles them before they can move downstream. He's a crafty one, old Basil.'

Still coping with the aftershock, Scarlett rose, readjusting her shorts and top.

'Sorry for scaring you again,' Ol' Bobby said.

We all held a single flat palm to our chests.

He continued. 'He sometimes hangs out by that bramble bush over there, so I call him Basil Bush.'

Scarlett suddenly got the giggles, and this broke the ice. For me, having seen him around the village in the last few weeks certainly helped matters.

'Mind, he is the beck's guardian after all,' the tramp continued, still allowing us time to settle. 'I can't fry him until a successor appears.'

And, I suddenly felt sorry for the guy. Nevertheless, I had to steel myself; and be the first to show courage.

'Ol' Bobby, my mother sent me with a few things to give you.'

Moving in the direction of the bridge, I stooped under the bramble bush, retrieving the plastic bag. Only a few blackberries were fully ripened, the rest seemingly brown and decayed. Grabbing the donations, I quickly returned.

The tramp was pleasantly surprised by the jeans.

He feigned interest in the shirt, but his eyes royally widened with delight at the packets of biscuits. He opened, in my opinion, the tastiest packet, and offered. As Hazel hadn't brought any buns, I was the first to dive in, with dry and slightly dirtied fingers. Ol' Bobby then explained he was heading back to the underside of the dual carriageway. He needed a nap because he'd worked a couple of night shifts for some cash-in-hand. We were all intrigued by this brief window into his world… and, saddened.

'Are you okay sleeping in there?' Hazel gently asked.

We all stared in the direction of the dual carriageway… shocked by his admission.

He waved Hazel's concern away with a gummy grin. 'It's all fine. All fine. I like the angle of the slope. Car vibrations can be quite soothing, but the water drowns out most road noise, anyway. Quite peaceful, 'cept when there's honking.'

'Do you need any blankets?' Hazel persisted.

'Young lady, I have plenty for now, but I won't be afraid to ask, if needed. Thank you. You're all very kind, just like most folk around here.'

Then he saluted, and I got to see how thin his arms were through his light cotton sleeves.

'Take care, gang. I need to get some shut-eye before I do an afternoon's potato picking. Say thanks to your mum from me for the clothes. I'll try banging a pot as I approach next time.'

We all partly raised our hands to wave.

'Remember… if you respect him, Old Basil is harmless. Don't be afraid.'

Nimbly, he trundled away in the direction of the bridge. When he was at a distance, Hazel pointed up, 'He could sleep… in Robert's tree house, couldn't he?'

We liked this idea.

'Does he potato pick at yours?' I asked Scarlett.

Hazel interrupted, 'No, he's picking at ours this week. My dad says he's a hard worker. He takes half cash and half vege as payment. There's something wrong with our crop again this year, though.'

'Yeah, same with us,' Scarlett dolefully observed, before adding, 'I wonder when he became a tramp. I don't mean to be rude, but does he use toothpaste?'

'What? For *one* tooth?'

'So, how does he eat with no teeth?' Scarlett concernedly continued.

'Maybe his gums are hard.'

'I suppose. He was fine with those biscuits,' Scarlett stooped, as we all cautiously checked for signs of Basil. 'Now, can I show you all these?'

She bent to retrieve a sheet of paper she'd brought down from the tree house, before reaching into a pocket.

'He won a medal. Look at this.'

In her palm was a metal star with a blue ribbon dangling through her tiny fingers. My heart froze.

'Look, it says, winner. He must be really good at competitions, or sport.'

A pang of jealousy shot through me. I wanted to say, you're *looking* at the winner. Right there and then, I fought the urge to take what was rightfully mine. I could feel my neck turning red because my conscience was prickling, and had Scarlett not immediately placed it back in her pocket, I would have made an excuse to "examine" it. As she sank to her knees, and I could still see the blue and yellow ribbon peeking out of her shorts.

'Now, take a look at this.'

Somehow, and maybe because of her wrong conclusion, I felt robbed… again. Guilt and justification warred within me as she, thankfully, brought our minds to more pressing matters. The large sheet unfolded several times into a large ordnance survey map.

'Is this Robert's?' I asked, trying to stop the whirring in my head. 'Where would he get this?'

'I dunno. It must be. It was in one of his boxes, along with his medal.'

Gathering together in a huddle, we perused the old black and white map Scarlett was having difficulty unfolding. As usual when I looked at a map, with symbols and faint lines, I had no idea what I was actually looking at. However, on this occasion, a solitary, yellow felt-tip pen provided an immediate focal point. Tracing its way across the entire map, the line suddenly dropped away to the east.

'He's coloured in the entire river.'

There was no hiding the hint of suspicion in Scarlett's tone.

'And look,' she pointed to the bottom right, sending the map crumpling, 'he's drawn arrows right here.'

Taking the top left-hand corner myself, we extended it, as Hazel peered over our shoulders, adding: 'Look, there's my farm.'

To the right of the centre was our beck - stretching further in the west than the east - before joining the turbulent, fast-flowing, Swale. It flowed through Bedale and its source was set back towards Constable Burton and a place called Bellerby, north of Leyburn, which felt like miles away for me.

'Is this, how long... the river goes?' Hazel said.

In truth, we were all pretty blown away. For some reason, I thought the river started just past the underpass, although - if anything - it did seem deeper there when we tried exploring last year.

'What are those two wheel shapes behind the cattle bridge?' I asked.

Scarlett and Hazel looked at each other in surprise.

'Haven't you seen the pulleys?'

'The *what*?'

'On our side of the bridge,' Hazel said.

'No.'

They could see I didn't have a clue. Not a clue.

Scarlett dived in, 'There's two rusted iron wheels caught up in the grass near the barley field. They used to be attached to either side of the river.'

'For pulling things out of the beck, or closing something, dad told me,' Hazel said.

'Okay.'

I had no interest in pursuing more rust for today. Why someone would bother signalling them on this old large sheet was anyone's guess, really. They looked larger than anything on the landscape I could visibly see around me. Straight lines threw themselves out horizontally from each, heading east and west for what looked like several miles. It was if the cartographer had purposefully taken a ruler to draw up plans.

'Rob's added crosses and words,' Scarlett said, pointing back down at a different section.

Squinting, I examined the bottom right in more detail as Hazel declared, 'The map's got our surnames in brackets, look! Pickford's Wilmott's... Grobatard's farm's there too!'

'Err, William Grobatard and his smelly pigs,' Scarlett scowled.

'William?' I probed, recalling what both Ol' Bobby, and my mum mentioned.

'Thinks he's the king of the fields.'

I couldn't understand Scarlett's insinuation... my attention drawn to three unusual words Robert had scrawled at the bottom. Mis-spellings, perhaps?

Vasta,
Sunt Amissa,
Saevus.

'He's marked off areas further down the river - towards the Swale,' Scarlett turned slightly, staring east beyond the cattle bridge. 'But why? What's he looking for?'

Noticeably, Hazel backed away. Something plopped in the waters to our left. The briefest snapshot of mottled grey... and then shadow again. Basil was in excess of two feet.

Two feet.

Dropping the map slightly we all watched the menacing pike near bull rushes.

'Do small fish have large teeth?' Scarlett asked.

'I dunno, but this whole place is weird. Do you think its cursed?' I whispered.

'The beck?' Scarlett instantly replied, '*No!*'

Hazel, however, didn't say a thing.

'Hold on, *you* heard the river tell you to play *hide-and-seek.*'

'So?'

'And you don't find that creepy?'

'A little I guess.'

'I think this place is dangerous. It's not what our parents led us to believe. I don't think they understood enough about it.'

'And do *we* know any more?' There was a shift in Scarlett's demeanor, like she was spoiling for an argument.

'Say you played a game of hide-and-seek, Scarlett… with those voices… and you *find them.* Then what do you do?'

'I dunno.'

'Scream?'

'Well, maybe they're trying to communicate with us.'

'Who is?' I insisted.

She shifted on the spot; getting antsy. But, I wasn't backing down. It was Hazel who suddenly replied. 'Scarlett was right earlier. They're children.' She shook as she said it, 'They're here. They're *all here* in the river.'

The map started to droop.

'What… children, Hazel?' This was the first clear admission… even to Scarlett.

'I don't know.' Hazel seemed to be forcing out information through gritted teeth.

'How do you know they were children?'

'They talked to me.'

I first looked at Scarlett for clarification. This matter was *not* to be discussed, but Hazel had instigated this, and I royally knew Scarlett *did* want me to pursue. 'Hazel, if you want to… what did they say?'

Hazel looked inexplicably confused by this question like she really didn't know how to answer. Her face contorted like she was struggling to recall information she barely understood herself.

'I don't know,' she meekly volunteered. 'Some words... I could understand.' She started staring beyond the cattle bridge to where the river disappeared from view - due east. 'Most of them are down there,' she pointed. 'Towards the end.'

Once again, I was conflicted. Did I really need to hear any of this? *Most of them?*

'They talked to Robert more,' she abruptly added, 'I heard them talking to him more.'

And there it was; a gaping wound enlarging in my horrified mind. I studied the plethora of his hand-crafted beck-additions. Had Ol' Bobby not hurled the stone at him, he would have stayed in - hypnotized.

'Did you hear what they told Robert?' Scarlett said.

'I don't know,' she looked confused again, like this was an emotion that couldn't be expressed.

Then she just shook her head: 'I don't want to speak about it.'

Silence ensued.

In my mind, I tried in vain to link Basil the pike to the bobbing boy, and I could make a case for it. But the voices? I could not deny that single word I heard.

Before us, the river gently flowed like it had done for centuries, unconcerned with our agitation.

Day after day, tonnes and tonnes of water funneled down from the Dales, endlessly lashing the hapless rocks below, and cutting the earth in its never ending advance. Finally it would level off, weaning itself from the hills, settling... making its peace in the flatter valleys below. Here, carefree birds chatted with one another, running up and down the boughs of hanging trees, watching. Bees danced across the faces of dainty flower heads growing from the sides, and cattle contentedly lowed in the surrounding fields.

And all the while, so it seemed, the spirits of children lived in these waters.

Lost in a timeless place where few cared to stop and consider.

My prevailing thought was: If they ended up dead here... can we?

~ ~ ~

Mum and I ate lunch with her friends on a tartan rug.

A portable radio was sitting on an old, flaking tractor bonnet a few yards away, weaving between humorous commentary and the latest pop songs. Clouds provided a little shade, as did a grand white wall at the side of Cherry Tree farm.

Scarlett's mother had baked the workers scones. They were warm and buttery. Absolutely divine. Hazel was upstairs in her best friend's bedroom.

I checked my digital watch.

As a kid, I remember thinking my arm felt so much more sophisticated having one; like I was part cyborg, or something. The girls would both be down again in ten minutes.

Gossip, and candid conversations were being wrapped up as the end of lunch neared, and people were tired. Potato picking was quite demanding by all accounts, and when the farm hands weren't around, people were quietly commenting on the large proportion of rotten spuds they'd heaved from the ground.

'You're a bit quiet, love,' mum piped up, keen to change the topic, 'How was it, earlier?'

'Mum, what do you know about pikes?'

'What? The big fish! Have you seen one?'

Thankfully, a slightly older farm-labourer sitting close by heard my question in the midst of the tired lull.

'Gotta be careful with them pike. Territorial.'

Just like Ol' Bobby, he too was wearing a light cotton shirt. Tufts of white chest hair wafted out over the top.

'Can give you a nasty nip if you're not careful,' he said. 'They'll sit and wait in the rushes for their prey; uses surprise tactics; their teeth are like the tip of a hacksaw.'

'Could they take an arm off?'

I genuinely meant this, and he laughed, wiping beads of sweat from his furrowed forehead.

'You've been watching Jaws, haven' yer? No, maybe a finger nail. There's one in the beck o'er there.'

'I've seen it.'

'You've done well, lad. They hide.'

'How big do they grow?'

'Foot an-a-alf… maybe two, tops. The bigger the river, the bigger they get. More for them to eat.'

Old Basil seemed a lot larger, but I also knew water magnified things. To be fair, all I'd really seen was grey, slippery flesh, and a shadow.

'No good to eat though; flesh is too boney.' he said.

Satisfied, but still somewhat intrigued, I changed tack. 'Do you know anyone called William around here?'

This triggered… everyone in the vicinity; many looking up from the tartan rug in response to my enquiry. The labourer folded his arms, and cleared his throat, shifting uncomfortably.

'I'm sure we all know one or two Billy goat's out there.'

I was shrewd enough to recognise I was causing atmospheric ripples, and pursuing it might be unwise. I thought I'd heard my mum quietly shush me too. It was hard to know what to say next in fact. I just seemed to stick fast, unsure of where to go. Hie manner caught me off guard. Needless to say, the same labourer jumped to my rescue.

'Those pike though… are shaped like torpedoes. Once they fire at a target, Wham!' He made one hand into a massive fist and punched the hard, weathered palm of his other. 'Talk to that fish, lad. They're meant to be old and wise.'

Scarlett and Hazel appeared at the corner of the house.

Hazel seemed a lot more animated, laughing at some quiet remark her friend had made. I stood up in great relief, not sure if I had sufficiently untangled myself from the inadvertent mess.

'Can I say thank-you to your mum sometime?' I said, fingers awkwardly sliding into my pockets, 'F-for those delicious scones.'

Scarlett stared at me, a little taken aback. Her blue eyes didn't move an inch, 'Yeah, sure. Of course you can.'

Waving at mum (who was wryly smiling) we walked away, but not before I sheepishly nodded a goodbye at everybody on the rug.

It was here, I realised, that the glare from the sun against the large white farmhouse wall had been hurting my eyes.

Leisurely, we ambled down a dirt track bordering a barley field; a light breeze refreshing us in the heat of the afternoon. My shirt was damp and clung to my back, pleasantly cooling me. Hazel proceeded to explain the many uses of barley as I watched sections of thigh-high ripening crop, shimmering and serenely rippling in the distance. Parts stood tall, and in abundance, while others were flatter, struggling to grow. Hazel mentioned words like malt and fodder, and when I enquired about the latter, both girls laughed at me.

'I have no clue. Don't laugh at me. What's fodder?'

It made me realise how little I appreciated and understood the cycles and seasons; how simple seeds on the stalks could actually get me blindingly drunk in certain circumstances. And then, I imagined me and Scarlett on a farm together; not sure if we outright owned it or not, but we were *there*, somehow, by ourselves. Breaking me from my reverie, Hazel taught me about what other fields could be used for. The moment she mentioned pigs, my mind sparked to life, recalling Scarlett's earlier disdain.

'Hazel, this William Grobatard… what's he actually like?'

'He's rich, and he doesn't speak much to many other farmers.'

'Okay. I asked all the pickers if they knew anyone called William... and they all went quiet.'

Hazel snorted, 'Aye! I bet that went down well. He's keen on buying Mr Hislop's farm, and there's been some bother.'

'Really?' I stuttered, in dismay. 'Mr Hislop's?'

'And it'll be, bye-bye beck, and welcome snouts and trotters.' said Scarlett.

It took a few seconds for me to register snouts and trotters as a pig reference. This was awful news and the fact that I deemed it "awful" surprised even me. I was equally impressed with how quickly Hazel's accent became colloquial in an hour of being around her family, but more so, her willingness to discuss this matter freely. Less so, Scarlett... who was massively quiet for a change, stripping a stalk of its grain, and hanging slightly back with her head cocked.

'What will he do to the beck?' I said.

'Well, he's more your kind of "Get off my land" farmer, not like Mr Hislop, who will let us come back... even after those boys made a mess with that rubbish.'

'Do you think he's the same William Ol' Bobby mentioned?'

'Hope not.' was Scarlett's singular response from the rear.

'He doesn't go about things in the right way,' Hazel added.

'Do you think he'll get Mr Hislop's land?'

'Probably.'

Scarlett disagreed entirely with her mate, angrily discarding the grain onto the ground. '*No, not probably*. He gets everything he wants. Have you seen him on a night? He comes out and stands by the river at midnight. Bet he's plotting to take every farm too - *the weirdo*.'

'He does *what* at midnight?' This intrigued me.

'Apparently so,' Hazel concurred.

If we were to - *ask William* - I really couldn't see myself conducting a similar "ghost" interview with this William Grobatard fella in the same way Ishaq interviewed Mr Hislop. I could only hope the reference from Ol' Bobby was an entirely different William altogether.

The trees gave way to a hedgerow and I could hear the tinkle of water. An hour had passed, and we were back at the cattle bridge. Beyond that, several bike frames glistened under a shimmering sun; many of the larger, teen variety. The crescendo of noise ahead was neither pleasant, nor inviting. Yesterday's rain had departed, and bright afternoon rays were beckoning all, illuminating the memories of this treasure trove for every local child; not only us.

Our beck had been rediscovered.

~~~

Cheers and jubilant cries of excitement reverberated around the riverside.

Hurriedly we engaged in a conflab, agreeing to sit on the bank a good distance away from the crowds. Mercifully, the birch tree, and reaching Rob's handiwork, proved an unassailable challenge for most. I doubted Ishaq, Hazel and myself could climb it ourselves. Scarlett was light and wiry and could adeptly slide through the two trickiest branches to reach the entrance. To be fair, if you tumbled at this point, the water would break your fall. Thankfully, she'd already returned the ordinance map to one of Robert's boxes, but the fact he'd attached a deadbolt concerned me. Most kids, however, seemed to be obsessing over the small boat he had docked there. Try as they might, they couldn't untie his specialist knot securing it to the jetty.

We had lots to discuss, and sitting back would give us a chance to further speculate. It would also allow us to study, watch and analyse developments; seek out any subtle spookiness.

But this wouldn't be easy.

The two boys - Jekyll and Hyde - were back; significantly larger than the rest of the clan, and entirely displaced in this setting. Like bullying sentries they'd stationed themselves at the far side of the bridge; spoiling all fun and *spoiling* for a scrap. As we approached, we could see two kids, younger than ourselves, shimmying up one of Robert's dangling ropes.

'They won't be able to get inside from underneath,' Scarlett read our minds. 'He's carved out a hole for the rope to poke through; but you can't get in from below.'

The two girls were content to walk past Jekyll and Hyde; already leering, and whispering. Unfortunately, for me, I was the strangest magnet for trouble. It seemed I only had to *exist* in a certain time or place, or look a certain way, and doom would be my oncoming Juggernaut. Staring down the eastern section of our beck, I attempted to appear "unconcerned".

'*Oi! You!*' There it was, right on cue… less than five feet past the guards. 'You been enjoying your threesome?'

I had *no* idea what this meant, but it was clearly barked at *me* - the final person to cross - so I turned, nodded, and said, 'Yes!'

In hindsight, my delivery could be interpreted as arrogance… but I didn't know what arrogance meant, either. One of the boys laughed, a little taken aback at what he deemed "wit", but my interrogator was less impressed; contemptuously scowling.

A second. That's all it took. That's all it *ever* took.

He wanted a fight; my mouth had signed the contract. He was brewing. Pure and simple. I was providing tinder for his fire with my beating heart alone. The three of us kept walking, and not talking, knowing our train was about to be added to. The other boy shouted, 'Aren't you three the ghost-busters?'

In June, Robert said these two had scrapped with each other, but now an alliance of ill intent had been forged. In actual fact, the grapevine had revealed their names. One was Craig; the other was nicknamed, "Dove". Why *Dove* exactly, was anyone's guess - a bird with connotations for the purest form of peace - and here stood the antithesis. They were both two or three years older than me and I wouldn't stand a chance in a fight. Thankfully, there were a good dozen kids splashing and marauding in and around the beck and I could argue that I didn't hear them properly over the commotion.

'Well, those two are idiots.' Scarlett declared… a bit too loudly.

I heard Craig shout, 'What?'

My heart bounced. 'Scarlett, keep walking. *Don't say anything else.*'

'*What, are you joking? Why shouldn't I?*'

Lowering my voice, 'Because they're dangerous idiots.'

Neither Craig nor Dove followed as we positioned ourselves further away than intended, on a dry, yellowing segment of grass, bearing the brunt of a roasting August day.

'Hey, guys, wait up!'

Immediately, we turned, recognising the voice. Robert was cycling straight at us, heading away from the bank. His was a timely and welcome introduction: a wave of eternal relief flooding over me. I knew a group of four was a good-sized number in my experience. It curtailed the onset of scrapping for some reason, even with a boy/girl mix, and the comfort of a group would deter these adolescent joy-saboteurs.

At least for now, it would.

'Hey, you lot; what's happening?'

'Rob!' we all called back.

'I can see why you're not in the river,' he laughed.

No hiding it: I felt a pang of guilt over our foray into his den and the discovery of the map. I glanced at Scarlett who knew exactly what I was thinking. What's more, she'd placed my medal back under lock and keep. Needless to say, he looked happy; *really* happy to see us.

Hazel asked, 'How was your holiday?'

But this seemed to be the wrong question.

'Okay,' he replied, a flash of discomfort and sadness in his eyes.

'Where did you go?'

'I went to my Gran's in Newhaven.'

Robert glared in the direction of the beck; clearly assessing the usage of his jetty. He shook his head.

'They better be careful over there.'

'Why did you build that jetty?' Scarlett was straight in; no stopping her.

'It reminds me of Newhaven. It has a harbour. You can sail to other places from there.'

'Did you build that boat too; where did you get that?'

'We had an old one... knocking about in the yard.'

'Okay, so a harbour is where boats dock, yeah?' Scarlett kept pressing.

'Pretty much.'

'But you have ropes for another, so who's boat are you expecting?'

My pal peeled his eyes away from the kids hurtling off his platform and quizzically looked at us all in turn before responding.

'Just in case we have visitors.'

Nobody spoke.

We all knew.

He was open book through and through, the first memorable line on the first page, each and every time.

'We all heard them speak to us didn't we?' he volunteered. 'So, what did they say to each of you?'

The time had come. Scarlett went first, no hesitation. I went second. Hazel visibly crawled back into her mental cave; no desire to divulge. And Robert didn't need any prompting... when it came to his turn.

'Some words I didn't understand because they were speaking in a foreign language. They told me I would see them soon and I should prepare for them. They're at the end of the river,' he pointed back over his shoulder, 'and they come upstream when they hear children.'

Precisely what Hazel had said.

This made me feel sick, but a *sicker part* wanted to hear more. Those delicious sandwiches I'd eaten with mum on the tartan rug; instantly induced queasiness. Why had I only heard one word?

'Oh, and they're *really* afraid of a guy called William,' he added.

We all reeled.

I continued to wonder if this was all some mass hysteria; a sun-stroke hallucinogen. Over-active imaginations. Again, I wanted this explained by a pike, a rusty bucket, and a gentle breeze.

'William?' Scarlett blazed, her eyes narrowing, 'Why are they afraid of William?'

Robert hesitated, even jolting a little; surprised we didn't know.

'Because he murdered them.'

~ ~ ~

'What are we supposed to do?' I said.

'Solve this.' Scarlett gasped.

'Oh, c'mon. Please be serious.'

'We should call the police,' Hazel weakly added.

'I agree.'

'So, where are the bodies? The police need bodies.' Scarlett said.

I pointed. 'Rob said, they come from down the river. So, down there.'

'I don't think they want us to solve anything.' That was Robert.

His muscular forearms twitched as he lifted his handlebars up and down by the wrists.

'Rob… this William bloke,' I swallowed, hushing my voice, 'he… might still be around.'

'It's William Grobatard,' Scarlett declared like she'd only gone and discovered the Holy Grail.

I immediately protested. 'The photo from the news clipping is from the 1940s… *this* Grobatard farmer would have been a kid.'

'No,' Scarlett's brain whizzed into life, 'I reckon he was in his twenties.'

'Well, how is old is he now?'

'I dunno!' her arms shot out like, "How the hell should I know!"

'But,' I continued, 'the legend of this place goes back years. We've got clippings going back to the 1920s.'

'Rob,' Hazel's tone was soft, concerned. 'Please… be careful… in all of this… *please.*'

Hazel was a kind soul; this kindness now in evidence. I once heard her mention she wanted to be a mid-wife when she was older. I thought this was crazy; all that blood and screaming. Now, her gentle eyes were boring into Robert's in a quietly knowing way.

'What does that mean exactly?' Scarlett said, clocking the inference.

She sensed this too, looking to me in exasperation, flinging her palms in the air… not liking "not knowing" every single detail of every single thing, in the history of forever.

To me, it was obvious. 'Rob,' I began. 'Are you sure you want to *meet* them?'

He flinched.

'Mate,' I continued, scrabbling for the right words. 'I don't think I would, if they were even real.'

'When I listened… they seemed fine.'

'We all agree,' I stared at the others, waiting for confirmation. 'It looked like you'd been hypnotized.'

'No, I hadn't.'

'In the water.'

'No, I wasn't.' he snorted.

'Yes, you were,' Hazel said.

75

Robert shrugged.

So I turned to Scarlett for support. 'Let's start being honest. There's no way, you'd *want to* play hide-and-seek… and actually *find them*, right?'

'But, I have already… when I saw that boy bobbing up and down.'

Not what I wanted to hear.

Mercifully, Hazel was on hand. 'I would never want to see them in a month of Sundays!'

'There you go; a voice of reason,' I exclaimed, clapping my hands. 'You two are *nutters*… and me and Hazel are the only normal ones.'

Somehow, this did the trick. Inadvertently, as usual. Maybe, it was the absurdity of this entire conversation, or maybe, it was the raucous kids in the rear having so much daft fun; blissfully unaware of our darkly, contrasting conversation. One by one, we started to laugh.

There was a *need* to let go.

Besides, Craig and Dove were constantly staring our way; still, suitably surly in disposition. But now their narrowing eyes, weren't aimed at me, as anticipated. They were assessing Rob. Quietly muttering stuff.

'I wonder what Ishaq heard,' Scarlett wondered out loud.

'Whatever it was, scared him. I asked him on the bike-ride home. Didn't say.'

'And we never got to see Ghostbusters,' Rob added.

Out of the corner of my eye, I saw Craig and Dove mobilizing bikes, preparing to cycle towards us.

'Okay, we've got trouble,' I said.

All of us slightly fanned out. Five feet away, they braked; Dove's bike particularly squeaky. Craig was quite tall and skinny. He had red hair, but it was a different shade to Scarlett's. Dove had a square head, thick eyebrows - meeting in the middle - and a podgy frame. In these parts, we'd say stout, or big-boned. Dove called out something about ghosts in a sarcastic manner, but it was Craig who took the lead.

'Is your name Robert Tipperton?'

'Yes.'

'Have you an older brother called, Mike?'

'Yes.'

Astonished, I couldn't believe I wasn't the one being pulverised with leading questions.

'And does your dad own the haulage place?'

'Yes.'

Robert was so matter of fact, unafraid. Heck, he was potentially fine with meeting up with the departed.

Craig flashed a noxious smile, 'Right, good to know.'

Nothing else was mentioned. Instead, he glanced at Dove who immediately raised an informed mono-brow, staring back. This exchange clearly confirmed their whispered discussion by the cattle bridge. Mounting their bikes, they swung them one-eighty and left.

Left the beck entirely.

I knew from experience… with *implied* questions like these - charged with surreptitious malice - there's planning, and scheming afoot. It meant something more troubling: the inquisitors are in receipt of information that amounts to a consequence - a consequence; days, weeks, or months from now - requires 'a follow-up'. They want you to know, in the scantest possible detail, *they know.*

Out of earshot, Scarlett proclaimed, 'What the hell was that about?'

Rob was as hard as nails. His brother would be as hard as nails - and a sure-fire deterrent if both boys wanted to fight him. But, this wasn't what was going on here. And if life provides you a clear *line in the sand* moment, for me, it was right there. I saw something shift in Rob's expression, as he watched them cycle away, his hands still grasping the handlebars rolling his fingers around them in a circular motion. It was only as he briefly showed his side profile, that I caught a glimmer of some inordinate, burdensome pain.

Gossip was beginning to circulate in our tiny village, and we weren't party to any of it.

In that moment, Robert knew. Quite what - I didn't. Not at this stage anyway, none of us could.

When I look back on these days, I had no idea his life was about to be sent spiralling.

And the depth of his fall... would haunt us all, as much as this river ever did.

Chapter 6

Somewhere in the middle of the summer holidays

Our county experienced changeable weather at the start of August.

On occasions, it drove many folk - young and old alike - to hide indoors. Manual workers and shoppers would risk the raindrops, ever hoping the suffocating clouds would lift, and part. Daylight was readily and frequently choked, and the sun allowed only the briefest of visits from solitary confinement.

All this changed in the second week.

Things settled down nicely and, once more, heat blazed a trail over Yorkshire's big, blue skies. By mid-afternoon, huge clouds would amass in the east and west, and the accompanying thunderstorms were both monumental, and majestic. In these situations, every kid knew the dangers of being near water and sheltering under trees, so the beck effectively closed early for business each day.

And you certainly *did not* climb electricity pylons! Man, you *knew* about those. Children received vivid and dire warnings about charred children dropping like zapped flies from the huge metal frames. Even looking in the direction of one of these steely sentinels evoked strenuous terror. Those imposing regiments, lining themselves up on the landscape, straddling the fields in the most imposing of gaits. If you so much as happened to be in a bath when lightning announced its arrival - albeit, several miles away -

you no longer feared the shark; electricity would *fry you* in the tub, instead.

That countdown. Count the silent spaces. Divide by seven.

I'd fling myself out of the bath on to a thick, furry rug, absolutely sopping… but safe, staring back to see if the Matey bubble bath bottle was fizzing and sparking.

Close call.

Ishaq had returned from Pakistan.

However, I hadn't seen him since term ended, and I missed him. I wondered what contraptions he'd set his mind to, what books on 'logic' he was reading through those massive glasses, and whether his courage would restore itself anytime soon. I doubted he'd ever return to the river again. Sure, he wouldn't reveal the words he'd heard, but he did mention that his parents had banned him from going because they, like him, believed in Jinn. Mischievous, evil spirits.

And, this William fella?

Well… I'd discovered something terrible in the days away from my friends; now itching to talk to Scarlett about it, in particular. (I was itching to see her, anyway.)

William Grobatard, the ageing farmer - shrouded in mystery - and, seemingly, reviled by many, was named after his father: William Grobatard senior. His father, and his *father's* father… were also named William. I was *bloody* good. All *my* detective work. This would impress the gang.

My Gran imparted me this information one sedate and sunny afternoon while we were eating a picnic on a tartan rug in her back garden. She was making me more beautiful boats, and she let me select the most colourful pages from a used glossy magazine. I learned it was a widely established tradition, in these rural parts, for the son to be named after the father, but the first my kiddie-head had ever heard of it. She then revealed - over a tasty crab paste sandwich - about one of my relatives living to a ripe old age, and how I came from 'good' stock.

'Do you know we have a coat-of-arms?' she said.

'Who does?'

'We do. Our family does. My side.'

'What, like one of those shield-things?'

'Shield things,' she laughed. 'It's called a crest.'

I was then informed I had strong farming genes in my body, and she was raised on a nearby farm, sold when she was young. It appeared that - for males anyway - it wasn't simply a case of generations and generations inheriting the same Christian name; it had been practiced for centuries (which I found weird). This news bowled me over. To possess a family crest, meant historical lineage. This also amazed me. *That* was like what *knights* had on their shields. My imagination was ablaze. It far eclipsed the boring truth that early June wasn't technically summer.

Later that evening, after dinner and jelly trifle, Granny W went over to her mahogany cabinet drawer, and brought out a tiny, metal badge. It was yellow and blue; in the shape of a shield. The pin at the back was particularly thick and sharp. I was always exceedingly wary of anything small and pointy; adult supervision was necessary.

'There you go, young Billy,' she said, placing it in my palm. 'Our crest.'

I stared at the object, and although I wanted it to be larger, I was delighted to see a knight's helmet, and three sharp looking forks - like tridents - in the centre.

On a Tuesday evening in the third week, the telephone rang in our hallway. At half-past six, it was bound to be someone in the village (or an aunt or uncle), but you always avidly listened for clues to the person's identity. On this occasion, Mum spoke very politely to whoever it was, asking sensible questions while listening intently, and even altering her own voice a smidgen. Eventually, the living room door swung wide open.

I was reading an old comic I owned, but had somehow misplaced. An unexpected, joyous discovery. I bought it at a jumble sale, and accidentally pushed it to the bottom, with those I'd already devoured. Mum leaned through with the cream phone chord, stretched a foot into the lounge - a sight I'd never encountered before.

'It's Ishaq… for you.'

Surprised and excited, I bounced off the sofa, taking the receiver.

'Hello.'

'Listen, I can't talk long,' his voice became low, 'I need to meet you down the river tomorrow.'

'How come?'

'It's about my tape recording.'

Bizarrely, my first thought was Sunday afternoon's Pop charts. 'The top forty?'

He didn't speak for a moment, quietly processing my response. 'The top forty what?'

'Music.'

'No, no, I mean the recording I made down by the river… in June. I've listened back to it.'

'You said it was blank, right?'

'Yeah, I thought all I got was static, but it's not. There are voices in different languages, and I've deciphered some - *in Latin*.'

'Voices?'

'In Latin.'

'The… ancient language?'

'Yes. I've translated some, but the others… I don't know. I think there's two languages.'

'Okay,' I started, intrigued. 'What time do you want to meet?'

Ishaq sounded back to his old self, but his tone was purposefully hushed. So, I covered the mouthpiece slightly, whispering. 'Are you okay, y'know, going back?'

'Yes, I interviewed lots of my relatives about Jinn in Karachi. All fine.'

I jumped on this. 'Okay, we can meet.'

'Well, in theory, my parents won't let me go to the beck, so I'm telling them I'm coming over to play with you.'

'Gotcha.'

'So I'll come over, but then we'll go down, right?'
'Okay.'
'What time?'
'Half-nine?'
'Cool. Okay, see you tomorrow.'
'Okay, Ish. Bye.'
'Bye.'

Ishaq sounded super refined and polite, even on the phone; also notably galvanized and focussed. He was back in the saddle. A rational perspective had been missing, even if things were edging towards the paranormal. Apart from Scarlett, none of us were big talkers. Ishaq wouldn't *stop talking* when he was on one. This could be very interesting.

Latin.

I remembered the phrases I saw on Robert's map: Vasta; Sunt Amissa; Saevus.

There was a big chance that tomorrow I'd learn what they mean.

~ ~ ~

The first startling component of the day involved Ishaq's attire.

Dressed top to tail in huge plastic armour; his face peeking out of a helmet two sizes too big. I laughed out loud as I opened the door to greet him, especially when the face grill kept slipping shut. As did my mum, who stared long and hard, suppressing her own mirth. Immediately, I wanted to do the same, join him in the mantle of Knighthood, but he wanted to get off. As it transpired, it was actually wrong of me to assume, this was a disguise to fool his parents into allowing him to play. Obviously, he was greeted with the same guffaws from the rest of our river gang.

He countered the "Why are you dressed up like a knight?" with a trivial retort: 'I'll tell you later.'

Questions were asked about Ishaq's unwillingness to step anywhere near to this place… and his subsequent change of heart.

'My parents now think this river is cursed and forbade me to attend.'

A brief conversation on the meaning of "forbade" ensued.

Ishaq revealed a little book he'd procured from the library; on *translations*. Then he produced his "bullet-proof… proof" as he termed it and hit play on the cassette already secured within the recorder. And together, we watched his wide-eyed bewilderment as Moonlight Shadow, by Mike Oldfield, blasted out of the speaker.

'I thought… you didn't record the charts,' I said.

'My sister!'

Behind the massive helmet, Ishaq looked agitated, almost dispirited. His moment was being scuppered. Obviously, a sibling was secretly commandeering his device for her own interests.

'No… keep it playing; I *love* this song,' Hazel said.

'This is from last summer,' Scarlett shouted, already up and jigging along the bank, her curly hair bouncing in joyful abandon. Ishaq's visor slipped down as he hastily leaned forward, trying to halt the Pop. Now blinded by plastic, he fruitlessly pawed the grass for his machine, missing by several inches, and I started to laugh.

Really laugh.

It looked ridiculous.

Personalities, perceptions, and agendas - all scattered, yet immediately colliding - to change the course of the moment. A supernatural backdrop - instantly kicked to the wind - in favour of a wholesome humanity. There was a real, normal world… still here by this river. And as Ishaq threw his helmet off in frustration and disgust, I kept an eye on Scarlett, wildly throwing her head back and forth, mimicking a guitar solo.

(Is that how you play the guitar?)

Even after Ishaq pulled off a plastic gauntlet, clicked stop, and began fast-forwarding, we were all hooping with giddy, red-faced delight.

'668, 668,' he kept muttering, watching the counter spin at the top. 'Right, you lot; let's get serious.'

Scarlett returned, flopping herself down in a pretty floral dress, as Ishaq continued his disconsolate mumbling.

'She's banned. She's *absolutely* banned from my room.'

By ten o'clock, we all crowded around the portable cassette player again, calmer, and listening intently. Distinguishing any clear speech or phrases was extremely difficult. In June, Ishaq had nestled this directly next to the beck, and in the twelve minutes of viable material, all we heard was splashing, and laughter.

'There!' he said, pointing. 'Did you hear it?'

He was insistent.

'Hear… *what?*' Robert said.

Deciphering lyrics in the nation's pop songs was hard enough for any kid (let alone, meanings); many, well outside my lexicon.

"Egg-o chee-bum fray-tus mouse," he ardently replied.

Even Scarlett frowned at his spurious evidence. 'That was me. Ishaq!'

'No, it wasn't.'

'Yes, it was,' Hazel disagreed. 'It's Scarl. She's saying, "Stop being cheeky."'

'No, *she's not!*' He rewound back. 'Listen again.'

But, that's how the one line sounded on Ishaq's recording, even with the volume ramped to the max.

'Egg-o? You and your mum deliver eggs… maybe they want some eggs?' Rob said.

'And some cheese?' Hazel agreed.

'Okay, listen to *this*…' An irritated Ishaq whirred the tape forward, this time whispering, '777, 777.'

Even from this point, the sounds were indistinct, and distant. Seventy-five percent belonged to either Scarlett or Ishaq himself; the rest of us consigned to a quarter of the discourse, but it was all still… barely audible, until.

"Egg-o Famay."

'There, there!' Ishaq sat bolt upright, feeling vindicated.

This was closer, more distinct, more disturbing. Ishaq played it again. It *wasn't* one of us.

'There's that egg-o word again?' Ishaq teased, knowing full well what was coming.

Nobody disagreed.

'Yeah… I heard that.' Hazel said.

'Me too.' Scarlett looked astonished. 'What does it mean?'

'It's Latin,' Ishaq replied.

'Latin? People haven't spoken that in centuries!'

'Exactly.'

'Play it again,' Scarlett said.

And he did. It sounded like it was spoken inches from the microphone, isolated from our frivolities further upstream.

'Now, listen to this one coming up. Look, it comes up at ninety-eight.'

Ishaq pointed to three small numbered dials above the cassette slowly whirring round next to each other.

"Helpe… helpe… fyr… fyr…"

Not only did nobody speak this time; the silence was palpable. A foreign child was screeching in the background, and despite the grainy quality of the tape and interference, these were obviously desperate cries; none matching our own.

Help. Help. Fire. Fire.

'That's in English,' Hazel said.

'Kind of,' Ishaq replied, puffing out his chest plate, 'I finally figured it out last night; keep listening…'

On the recording, Rob was telling us all about Juggernauts, and I recalled the June conversation. Interspersed between his pauses, "For late Mec, For late mec!"

Ishaq placed his tape cassette recorder on the ground but kept it playing. My eyes took to my surroundings, slowly, turning three-sixty, assessing the environment: fields of wheat and barley; fallow fields; barns made out of a mix of stone and corrugated iron - the distantly humming dual carriageway - and the rest of Mr Hislop's sprawling farm. Carefully, I searched for clues as to why there *would even be* cries of "fire".

What fire?

I looked at the river; *plenty* of water to put any fire out. Ishaq was retrieving a rolled sheet - like a scroll - slotted in his plastic armoured thigh. He unfolded it and set it on a parched piece of grass, dotted with daisies. It looked like algebra, but it wasn't.

'When I was in the river, I heard the voices telling me… to protect them. I would be their guard and protector.'

This was a stunning admission. I now understood perfectly why he'd chosen his clunky attire, but it was absolutely nothing compared to his paper full of crude translations.

'There's a child, or children here,' he pointed to the top left, 'who must have been taught to speak Latin.'

'And these who sound German and Italian,' he pointed all along the bottom this time, 'I think they speak a medieval language, which was called Olde English. I got two books from the library before I went to Pakistan. It took me ages to figure out what some of them meant.'

I was flabbergasted.

He pointed to a phrase which I didn't recognise. 'Ego famay means, "I starve". This is one of the Latin voices.' His tiny fingers traced their way back to the bottom. 'Forlaete mec is in Olde English! It means, "Leave me alone".'

Between us, a pin could have dropped…

'The voices also told me *who* I needed to protect them from,' he finished.

It was absolutely red hot out here on the farm; my whole body, now rippling with goosebumps.

'They spoke to me in Latin too, and said Defendat nos William.'

'Defend William,' Scarlett deduced, nearly toppling over.

'No, defend us *from* William.'

I swallowed.

'That's right,' Ishaq continued, 'There were other phrases, but that's the one I remember because Ol' Bobby told us to, "ask William", seconds later.'

Now I understood in completeness… why Ishaq was so silent as we cycled home together back in June.

'Good grief,' Robert replied.

'Has anyone else got the shivers?' Hazel asked.

We all nodded.

Scarlett gasped. 'This means… he's alive and well… and out there, *somewhere*.'

At this precise moment, another voice took over from the rest, and even though the recording was quiet, this was an insistent voice,

"*Dabis carnes vestras,*" it spoke over and over.

Ghosts, *and* a real murderer.

Paranoid, I stared behind me. That *Ripper* bloke from around here had been imprisoned not three years ago. Not possessing all the details, I worried about even crossing the road in front of our house when he was around. He'd appear out of nowhere - like Spring-heeled Jack - and *rip* you to pieces. That's *how* murder happened in my mind; you got shredded into bloodied chunks. Then someone found the remains, and somehow figured it was you.

I jumped at the popping sound directly by my ear; a seal being broken, a lid being released.

'Does anyone want a butterfly bun? I think I do.'

Hazel shakily held out the container and my eyes momentarily over-ruled my lack of appetite. It would be rude to say no; grateful her mum had resumed her baking.

'And that last voice,' Ishaq concluded, 'is also someone starving. I think they're fighting for whatever food there is.'

The ice-cream container wobbled out of Hazel's hands on hearing this, contents suddenly spilling over the grass. Half a dozen buns rolled down the slope, plopping into the beck.

'This is why I'm wearing this costume,' Ishaq pointed to himself, 'if this William guy shows up, he has a fight on his hands.'

I rued the depleted cake, but embraced Ishaq's absurdity. He wasn't particularly savvy at reading a room socially, but he could be unintentionally hilarious. However, he *was* deadly serious this time.

'If we see William - and no disrespect, Scarlett - if he comes from *that* period; then we need to intimidate him.'

Scarlett frowned. 'From *that* period?'

'That's nuts,' Robert said, peering at his belt, with the holstered, plastic sword. 'What are you going to do? Whack him with *that*?'

'Rob's right,' I said. 'We need the police.'

'Ishaq, has a point,' Hazel said. 'What if he's not a real human - but a ghost, and he's already in there... with them?'

She was also a voice of reason, but I didn't want to hear her talk like this. The cassette reached the end of the reel, and clicked itself off, and I instantly recalled in the World War two photo we studied - the one with the misty river - all those indistinct faces peering up, looked confused.

'What if it's... Ol' Bobby?' Scarlett volunteered.

We all went quiet.

'No, that's not right,' I said, disappointed in her.

And Robert backed me up. 'Nah, he wouldn't be called Ol' *Bobby* then would he?'

Everybody agreed, but Robert wasn't done, pressing his palm to his chest. 'My own Gran... calls me *Bobby*.'

'What?'

He searched the eyes of his stunned audience.

'Robert. Bobby.'

Momentarily, a sea of perplexed faces stared at him.

'You lot call me Rob, but Bobby's a nickname for Robert.'

'Ohhh...'

'I didn't know that, at all!' Hazel said.

'So, when we're older, we'll call *you* Ol' Bobby,' Scarlett guffawed, swinging her arms into the air.

Rob smiled a tiny bit more. 'yeah, when I'm a bit older.'

'Awww, why not now? We'll call you it now.'

It was a light interlude; much needed nevertheless. You could rib Robert plentifully, as he never took it seriously. However, the gravity of what we'd heard soon called us back to the cassette. *Defendat nos William.* At this point, I steeled myself... for the inevitable... the question that should have been asked *long* before now.

For some reason, it never came.

I waited some more, and thought about jumping on board the great *reveal* train, alongside Rob. But, mine was a higher stake. Because something in that voice I heard back in June, made me hold back. It wasn't just telling me the word, "Enemy."

It called me *it*.

I knew this beyond any shadow of a doubt.

Maybe this was the key to my half-hearted engagement in every part of this matter. I could still step away, putting it all down to zealous intrigue. The beck told my friends significant things... but it accused me with a single word. Those things in there *knew* who I was. So, I needed to close this down.

I turned to Ishaq, hoping common sense would prevail. 'Ish, if you meet William, and he appeared to you like a Jinn, or a real murderer - who kills children - would you really protect these ghosts from him?'

He'd left his helmet off - and there was no hiding - and I watched his neck convulse in the hardest swallow.

'I dunno,' he eventually replied.

I knew in that second, he was as half-hearted as me.

Scarlett looked me square in the face. 'You sound like you don't want to find out what's really happening. This William could be dangerous?'

'Precisely.' I stared at everyone. 'Exactly! Our parents always tell us, don't play with fire unless you want to get burned.'

Hazel grounded the bun tub. Planting her hands firmly on her hips, she cocked her head, staring at Robert; immovably fixing him with her gaze. 'Tell them what else they told you,' she suddenly said.

Rob's eyes widened.

'I heard they were saying to you,' she continued. '*Tell them* what else they said.'

Even Scarlett looked shocked at the accusatory pitch. Robert instantly turned away.

'If they don't decide to come up the river... then what's going to happen, Robert?'

'They *will*, Hazel, they *will*.'

And there it was, from out of absolutely nowhere. Hidden tension laced with cryptic meaning. A stand-off between the pair, and three stunned passengers watching on. She chastised this response with a dismissive shake of her head. 'They asked *you*... to go down the river to meet them. That's why you brought that boat, isn't it?'

Robert didn't speak.

Hazel wasn't done.

'And there's more, isn't there, Rob?'

'I won't do it, Hazel... I promise.'

Scarlett, Ishaq, and I, listened on in slack-jawed shock. '*D-do* what?' Scarlett said.

'They want him to *join* them.'

In every store, and on every door - at around 5.30 - that little white and black placard, dangling on two pieces of string, was flicked over by the owner. Without fail. On the dot. Closed, was closed. And I'd attempted shutting shop on this entire matter, by highlighting Ishaq's unwillingness to tackle a real perpetrator. I'd done this for the welfare of our group.

However, *technically*, the customer could still walk in off the street unless you locked it.

This is what Hazel was doing.

With a deadbolt.

'And they want you... to bring *us* with you... don't they?'

Robert's denial was instant, but we'd already taken a winding punch; the remaining three of us, now aghast.

'Take us where?' Scarlett implored.

'To the end of the river,' Hazel said.

'What d-do you mean?' Ishaq's voice wobbled.

'Join them how?' Scarlett angrily demanded.

Rob didn't respond.

I waited for Hazel to jump in with another rebuttal, but she'd quit. No wonder her mum was concerned. No wonder she'd been having nightmares. Since her sullen, fraught steps away from the beck, back in June - gently guided by Scarlett's hand - hers, had been the most gruelling burden.

Apologetically, Robert met our eyes, one by one. 'I wasn't going to do it, I promise. There's no way.'

He pointed to his jetty.

'Look, that's why I built this, so they could dock, if they came. I don't even know if they will... if they're even real. My boat can only fit two people - maybe three at a push.'

'There's space for two boats!' Scarlett was losing her cool. 'Yours... and *theirs.*'

I stared over at his dock. She was right. What the hell was going on? Instantly, the words of Ol' Bobby, rang in my ears; those he told us when we first met? "Boy, those Sirens will *call and call.*"

Every kid knew their Minotaurs and Medusas in Greek mythology; the more gruesome the beast, the more memorable. They certainly knew that Sirens dashed you against the rocks to drown you. This was getting out of hand. I silently thanked the heavens for Hazel's intervention.

Our journey was over.

I didn't want my frightened mugshot appearing in the local newspaper as another component of this sorry saga.

'If that's the case, Rob,' Scarlett positively exploded now, 'Why have *you* got a map of X's in your tree house?'

Something flashed across my mate's face - like he'd been betrayed by this trespass - but he reasserted his dignity almost instantly.

'That's where I think they might be, that's all,' Robert said. 'I think that's where they come from because that's where William threw their bodies.'

I got up, preparing to leave. *Enough.*
'What!' Ishaq shouted.
'You're bloody joking!' Scarlett shouted.
To be fair, Robert was never given a full crack at explaining what they'd said, but had it not been for Hazel, I doubt he would.
'They told me that they were burned, or hacked-up or drown, and thrown in, further down the river.'
'I'm sorry,' I started, knowing I was no longer the odd one out, 'I don't think I ever want to come to this place again… *ever*. Our parents should never have let us come. They should have warned us… not *invited* us.'
I looked to the others for visual confirmation. It was definitely simmering behind their eyes. In fact, Ishaq leapt to his feet, tearing off his remaining armour.
'That phrase, you idiots think means egg and cheese,' he scowled, clawing away his chest plate, 'Ego cibum fratus meue? Remember that one? The one you *all* laughed at?' We waited, listening to his frenzied panting. 'That's a Latin one. I translated it last night.' He tossed everything on the grass, whilst angrily eyeballing Robert.
'It means I ate my brother.'

He pulled off his final gauntlet, pointing at the accused.
'If *you* think you're going to sail me down this river and feed me to them - *like some ghost-snack* - think again!'
He then shouted something quite forcibly in Arabic, before finishing with, 'you *got that*… mate!'

~~~

'I wasn't going to do it, was I?'

93

Kids typically forgave one another, especially when they held common ground.

This was far harder.

Ishaq continued fuming until it became little forced; surprised by, and most definitely keen to retain, this new found emotion. He stomped around the grass for ages. Within five minutes, Robert became quite down and sullen.

He was being ignored, so he quietly crept to the half-eaten bramble bush, sticking a solitary thorn into the skin on his forefinger, letting a blob of blood form at the tip.

'All I've got is this river,' I heard him say. 'I'm going to Newhaven… see Gran.'

Scarlett and Hazel were still giving him the cold-shoulder. Ishaq was some way in the distance, venting. Only I caught the unusual streak of pain flashing across Rob's face; a hopeless moment of burgeoning acceptance. What did he mean by that?

His secret had been revealed; forced out in the open. What about mine?

My next action was designed to deflect attention away from Rob, to try and ease the tension. It was also my 'Get out of Jail' card; my final exit from this situation. The shop hadn't just shut; it was going out of business - permanently. I stood, waving for all to stand.

'Hey everybody, I need to tell you something.'

I called louder for Ishaq and waited. My friends gathered, arms folded; Scarlett, contemptuously glaring Robert's way. I cleared my throat, girding myself. Selfishly, I knew, mine was a lesser admission - a bullet to Rob's bomb - but it needed to come out now.

'So, this William fella.' I swallowed. 'It's me.'

Absolutely nobody processed this. All stood there, befuddled by this statement, so I clarified. 'I'm William. I'm the enemy!'

'Eh?' Ishaq said.

'Yes, yes I am… by the time I started Nursery, everyone called me Billy - parents, relatives, teachers - that's always how my name appears on the register, but my Christian name… is William.'

I looked to the dour haulier's son, who suddenly got it. 'Like Robert becomes Bobby,' I confirmed.

Everybody else just stared.

Hazel finally said, '*But, you're Billy Austin!*'

'You know I have an Irish cousin, Liam O'Connell?' I replied. 'He was born William O'Connell.'

'Sorry!' Scarlett said, rubbing her face. 'Liam and Billy, are short for *William?*'

'Sometimes.'

It was beginning to sink in quickly, so I dived right in. 'Ol' Bobby said these voices were like Sirens. We learned about them in school, right? They lull you in with lies.' I turned, staring at the river. 'They were definitely calling me the enemy. One hundred per cent, me.'

Then I turned to Rob. 'Clearly, I haven't been chucking any dead children down there.' Followed by Ishaq, 'And they can't possibly expect *you* to protect them?'

This instantly stopped the steam whistling out both his ears.

I wasn't done.

Scarlett's turn.

'Say you play a game of hide-and-seek with ghosts… and find them; then what do you do? Tag them, and say: "You're it." Well, you can't… they're ghosts.'

As the red-head glowered, Ishaq said; 'This is very logical.'

'Thank-you, Ishaq.'

I pointed at the cassette recorder. 'They're speaking Latin. If they haven't eaten, they haven't eaten in *centuries.*'

Then, I jabbed my hand at the chocolate butterfly-buns that spilled into the beck earlier, soggily bobbing along in the centre. 'What about those? Hazel's actually given them food, and they haven't taken any… not even the minnows have.'

Mine was a watertight case.

'Billy's got a point.' Hazel nodded, before correcting. 'Sorry, William's got a point.'

'Remember, Ol' Bobby had to chuck that rock to break the spell over Rob, because he was in there longer than us.' Four young minds pondered, as I concluded. 'I think he's right. I think they're Sirens.'

All the while, I purposefully withheld what Gran said about generations of families naming son after father. I didn't want Scarlett banging on her "William Grobatard" drum any longer, so I quickly made haste, keen to wrap matters up.

'My folks think this place is enchanted, and I think it is too - in a bad way.'

Every face now displayed a range of expressions, from the morose to the crestfallen. Stupidity, and wild imaginations had been resolutely tackled.

'I'm done with this place,' I concluded. 'And if you lot have any sense; you will be, too.'

Ishaq and Hazel agreed. Rob remained stolid, and impassive. Scarlett abruptly said, '*You* should apologise.'

'What!'

This caught me off-guard in its completeness.

'You need to apologise.' she repeated.

'To who?'

'To the beck.'

Talk about the countenance of the supremely puzzled; a gamut of curious looks immediately funnelled Scarlett's way.

'Sorry,' I said. 'For what?'

'It thinks you're William. It thinks you're the murderer.'

'So?'

'If they're actually Sirens, or it's other confused stuff; you should come clean and tell it. That way, this can end. We need to break the spell.'

'I'm not apologising for something I didn't do.'

'No, I'm not saying you should *feel* sorry; I'm saying you need to,' her voice dropped several octaves, down to a whisper, 'tell it… you are.'

Hazel gasped. 'It thinks you're its *real* enemy. Scarl's right; it's confused.'

I threw out my hands in despair. I wasn't expecting any of this. And I should have realised, in those scant few seconds, a forming pattern characterizing the rest of my adult life, namely, *inane dialogue* with women.

'If you do it,' Scarlett said. 'You'll be my hero.'

This was the other thought pattern I'd eventually wrestle…

In despair, I shrugged, staring at the jetty.

If I did this, I wouldn't mean it of course, but it might drop the final curtain on this pathetic charade. And besides… I started towards Robert's dock, showing the others I was both the brains and the courage… I had a girl to impress.

~ ~ ~

I was buying time, deliberately angling my face, so I couldn't be seen. All my verbal bravado, crumbling.

I knew this was *all* real.

My movements were brittle; someone pouring cement down my throat, now slithering into, and drying my legs hard. The truth was, in the village, I'd frequently pull out of the easiest ramps, when trying stunts. All twice as high for the other kids enthusiastically hurtling towards them. I'd blame my sagging handlebars. And when it came to climbing the birch just over there… breaking an arm sounded a deadly serious thing for any kid. If something got broken, it was permanently broken: and you were too.

Even cuts and grazes gave me second thoughts.

But there were girls here, and pressure.

The onus was on providing tangible proof of heroism, so I tried making it appear I wasn't creeping over the wooden slats. However, there was no disguising how precariously I was seated, with folded legs away from the edge, warily watching the beck like I was on shark watch. Thankfully, the shallow water by my feet was sedate. It innocently tickled the reeds on the fringes as it continued its ancient, soothing lullaby. Three Painted Ladies fluttered across to a patch of pretty wild, white flowers on the opposite bank.

'I don't know if you can hear me,' my voice began to shake.

Please don't respond… and please don't send the boy to the surface.

Everything remained still, quiet. I searched the waters - no more than a foot deep - down to the sandy bottom; senses firing. And I listened, but not too hard. Everything was tranquil, like it should be, with only the dual carriageway in the distance supplying any obtrusive noise. With an expectant audience behind me, I steadily grew accustomed to how stupid this all was. Feeling rather more cavalier, I leaned closer, a little more confident I wouldn't be dragged under by water spirits, but more importantly, that it wouldn't address me personally.

'I'm sorry. I'm not the William you think I am. I am *not… your* enemy.'

The calmness and truth of nature, and the balance restored. A sanguine river; a thoughtlessly beautiful feature on a gorgeous landscape, we could all begin to trust and appreciate once more.

'My name's Billy. I respect you. We… respect you, and wish you peace, but we don't want to hear from you any more.'

I turned to the others for good measure; willing spectators of a young boy's valor.

'I think it's… done.' Hazel said, a smile forming.

I nodded, imperiously.

We waited for several seconds. Nothing.

If there was anything really here, it *had* departed.

Then, in the gap between Robert's boat, and his makeshift wooden dock, a bottle plopped to the surface.

Chapter 7

Revelations

In bed later that evening, I considered the contents of that bottle, and the note in particular.

The paper inside was old, and rolled up, reading:

We will see you on the 29th of August.

If you don't see us first.

Robert.

It was more an ultimatum than an invitation; find us, or we'll find you.

As far as messages go, it was casually written, but the effect it had was astonishing. In a day of mind-blowing realisations, this was huge, and deeply terrifying. At first, Robert was suspected of planting the misshapen, corked bottle, because his name was on the note, but he denied all involvement… and did so strenuously.

'Look at the glass. It's been wrapped up in reeds for bloody ages! *Look how old it is!*'

No denying it. And Robert didn't do 'mad'. His outburst shifted all our focus, sadly, back on to Ol' Bobby again. But we knew this was a stretch as well. The parchment was old and the fountain pen ink, faded. Surely this was a long-lost message for others, but our childish minds all too easily leapt the gap of sanity.

However, it could well be for us, timed to perfection, and I regretted opening my mouth to the river. My good work was ruined, and Scarlett's 'hide-and-seek' belief system, reinvigorated. Not only reinvigorated; *bolstered*.

'We might find them first!' she shouted.

'We don't want to,' I reminded her. 'I've just spent ten minutes getting it to leave us alone.'

'It answered you,' she gasped. 'It heard *you* and answered you.' (The hero stuff had clearly flown far from her mind.)

The truth was, two weeks from now - if not sooner - we'd be finding out.

Thankfully, at first, Ishaq shared my skepticism, attempting to rein Scarlett in. 'Logically, this message was written long before we even existed.'

'Well, brains, explain the coincidence.' she replied.

Further problems developed when Ishaq was shown the *Latin* words in Robert's map. Using his little library book, he hastily discovered: Vasta meant waste. Sunta Amissa, many were lost, and Saevus meant cruel or cruelty.

Needless to say, I had no choice - *I'd really tried* - and was now scheming to be away on the 29th. I was growing tired of increasing revelations and decreasing control. *Especially* when Scarlett suggested a *night watch*. I really fancied her on one hand, but on the other…

Ghosts definitely *came out* at night!

That was blindingly obvious, even to unbelievers, but if the daytime was anything to go by, it would be far, far scarier after dark. The note, for me, sounded threatening too. Even if somebody had innocently popped it into the water centuries ago, how could they hope for it to reach the intended person? Had it travelled down stream and lodged itself in the reeds; wrapped in a sinewy, creeping nest? Maybe Robert's excavation work - creating the jetty - had loosened its yellow, straggling bonds. Thoughts in my head bounced over and over: whoever it was intended for didn't receive it.

If it was an important message, they'd *surely* deliver it on horseback - assuming it came from that era.

And, of course, ghosts don't have fingers and can't write, but if they can speak and send boats upstream, then they could easily dislodge an old Victorian note - just for us - at exactly the right moment.

In bed, I thought about the note's age, its curly handwriting, and the beautifully rendered words. It *looked* over a hundred years old. Disturbingly, the more I considered origins… the more I silently agreed with Scarlett. This was very coincidental: The name, the stated date, the tone. And I didn't like it one bit.

I was tired, though.

Days in the sun wore you out. The sun bronzed your skin and being outdoors revitalized your well-being; you felt you'd had a 'full' day by the time you reached the front door to your house. The instant you stepped over the threshold, the energy dissipated. As I drifted off to sleep, I thought about Ol' Bobby. Surely, in all his summer visits here, he had seen things he could tell us.

He warned Rob.

I would suggest a visit to the crew in the morning, if he was around. Laying there, I tried forming an excuse for my absence on the 29th but it became less important than my tired bones and an oncoming voyage in to the valley of sleep.

~ ~ ~

Dew covered every inch, of every blade.

If you crouched low, you could feel the cool morning air on the ground.

The sun was charging its furnaces a little slower than we were accustomed, our socks and shoes growing soggier, as we walked the countless acres. In the distance, we could hear the earthy chugging of tractors rambling to fields to toil another day. And Mr Hislop had clearly mowed his lawns the previous evening, as the refreshing smell of the newly cut-grass pinged our nostrils.

We entered the barn yard, and I particularly liked this section of the journey - and always would - but the end was now tinged with trepidation. It was like going downstairs on Christmas morning, to find your parents bound and gagged, and, more importantly, no presents. The last vestige of intrigue, rapidly evaporating, along with the moisture beneath our feet. Passing a giant sycamore, I watched as the damp leaves glistened, all gently swaying; playing games with the friendly breezes.

Ishaq had ditched his armour - armed instead with lies - all delivered first-class to his parents. Should anybody ask, the party line was that the village kids were involved in a massive game of tag; a real activity that worked surprisingly well year-after-year, *if* you owned a bike. However, Ishaq was fretting because Scarlett was gathering provisional dates for our sleep-over. He'd never be allowed to come. And I was being out-right duplicitous in my fake-bravery, agreeing with many of her proposals... while plotting excuses.. and *definitely* planning a stay-over at Granny W's on the 29th.

'I will ask Mr Hislop if it's okay for us all,' Scarlett suggested. 'I have two tents. We can have a boys' tent and a girls'.'

My nod was enthusiastic, and believable.

We trod a worn furrow towards the beck, and then straight past it, all of us watching the river as we marched forwards. Our destination was the underpass.

And Ol' Bobby.

'Do you think he's even awake yet?' Robert asked.

Listening to the cars flying by on the approaching dual carriageway, and the increasingly pungent smell of exhaust fumes; I wondered how he *actually got any* sleep. The reeds grew taller in this section of river; tightly packed in dense clusters. In their midst, patches of white flowers grew - pretty enough with their dainty umbrella heads - but giving off a distinctly musty aroma. It was as if soot and smoke held all the good scents hostage. The dank grey was being illuminated by the eastern sun - no shadows until the afternoon - and yet, this felt every bit a forbidden place. As we got closer, I glanced at Ishaq, recalling his tumble down the slope, his shoulders, already visibly sagging. But our remit would be brief, and simple: ask Ol' Bobby about his experiences. Although nobody was saying it, we all felt sorry for the homeless man under the bridge. He didn't seem to mind living like this, but to me, it was horrific.

From our viewpoint, this elevated part of road - travelling north and south - was an endlessly long rectangle with an *inverted* triangle cut into the middle; an invisible bridge to the motorists above. The ground rose sharply as we approached; morning light shimmering across the entire stretch of concrete. And at the end, inside the underpass, in the part not caught in the sun... was a shadowy bundle of clothes.

All of us stopped.

Uncertain.

'W-what do we do?' Hazel whispered.

Ol' Bobby could well be inside this bundle, but in the form that's pale, clammy, and has a fixed stare. Right on cue, Ishaq asked: 'What if he's dead? We haven't seen him in days?'

And he was correct.

'Hazel, has he been potato-picking at yours recently?' I asked.

Hazel shook her head; concern sweeping her face. 'No, he only did that *one* afternoon.'

Overhead, a passing truck blasted its horn at a perceived road misdemeanour. Most of us jumped - frightened out of skins - Robert barely flinching, of course. And nothing stirred in the bundle, either.

'Maybe he's left his clothes, and he's not in there,' Scarlett said.

'Who's going to look?' I asked.

(Cleverly negating my willingness.)

'Fat chance I'm doing it,' Ishaq declared, with vigorous head-shakes.

I knew nobody would ask Hazel... and that left Scarlett and Robert to stare at each other.

'I'll do it.' Robert agreed, immediately hoisting himself onto the slope - which must have been at about a thirty-degree angle.

He crouched as he tried to balance on the unusual contour but didn't move, carefully watching ahead. The river echoed more here, and the lack of sunlight did nothing to dispel the air of the mysterious and the unhallowed. Robert suddenly unleashed a sharp whistle into the chamber, the shrill sound bouncing off the dark walls. This caught us by surprise, but it was a good idea. And then, the nimble boy whistled more, elevating the pitch over the din of cars.

'Ol' Bobby... are you... there?'

Robert expertly scrambled ten yards further in and turned to look over at us. 'Guys, I don't think he's here. Come on in.'

I couldn't believe it when Scarlett followed. In an instant I thought part of her wanted to be closer to Robert - and I felt a strange pang - so I immediately darted after her, leaving Ishaq and Hazel on the bank. Of course, I was less adept and far less agile - struggling to maintain grip, in my foolish vanity - the soles of my trainers (or maybe piss-weak legs) fighting to cope with the gradient. Robert whistled and then called out again. At this distance, the outline in the bundle of clothes looked increasingly human.

And I knew - beyond any doubt - we were about to discover a body.

The realisation.

I stopped moving. My heart froze: he really *is* dead and has been for *days*. Without warning, the intrepid haulier's son launched towards the mass of tatty fabric, setting himself mere feet away. Scarlett and I caught up, and I examined my filthy hands before peering closely. The noise above was horrendous. Next to the messy array of clothing was a wooden box, containing many shiny trinkets; a collection of gold, silver, and brass antiques.

'Ol' Bobby,' Robert called again, and then paused, 'Are you... okay?'

Suddenly, the swaddling clothes jerked to a life, and a bewildered, pale face appeared. Blinking, staring at us. The light wasn't great, but his eyes looked yellow, and his face, gaunt. I hoped this was caused by the strange ambiance cast on the underside of the bridge, and we hadn't triggered his Zombie alter-ego. Life had cut the harshest grooves into his weathered, startled face.

'K-kids,' he croaked, immediately coughing. Ol' Bobby fixed his eyes on Robert in particular. Pulling back a pink cover, he painfully sat up. Cars and trucks continued their rumble overhead as he wiped phlegm from his mouth.

'Oh, *you slept in…* you silly, silly man,' he said to himself.

This soliloquy echoed around the underpass, interspersed with violent hacking. He didn't look well.

'Are you okay?' Scarlett called over Robert's shoulders.

'Ahh… I'm a little under the weather, actually. A cold.'

He wiped his brow with the sleeve on his forearm. 'Just a little fever. What can I do for you pleasant lot? This is a nice surprise.'

Scarlett, of course, immediately took the lead. 'Is it okay if we ask you a few questions? Sorry for waking you.'

'S-sure,' Ol' Bobby nodded, still adjusting to the real world; a little taken aback. 'Here, let me come over there to your side. Mind that you don't tumble. I've rolled down this slope many a time during the night. The water's *bracing*.'

I made a royal hash of trying to navigate my way back out. Ol' Bobby simply slid down to the bottom, carefully tracing a narrow ledge, and beating all but Rob back to the bank. In the morning rays, he appeared only marginally better, his skin looking sallow. He plonked himself down on the bank and smiled a weaker, toothless grin.

'So,' he coughed. 'What would you like to know?'

~ ~ ~

'Ol' Bobby,' Scarlett started, 'You've been coming here for years; what do you know about the ghosts here?'

He replied, 'How old are you all? Nine, ten?'

We looked from one to another innocently stating our ages, the eldest - with more pride. Ol' Bobby nodded, quietly assessing how to engage.

'Do you know what a guardian is?'

This was unexpected, nobody saying anything for several seconds, until Ishaq said, 'Yes, they're protectors.'

'Well, I'm one.'

He appeared feverish, and strands of matted white hair stuck to his forehead, as he spoke. The tramp continued, 'I guard the river... and I guard people *from* the river.'

'What exactly does that mean?' Ishaq said.

'It means, year after year, different kids come here... and I try to protect them.'

'From the *what*?' Hazel said.

'From the river. Well, I try.'

Then he changed tack. 'I actually don't have a clue how old I am, that's why I get the nickname Ol' Bobby. It feels like I've been here forever. Probably have.'

Then, he stared us all down - demanding complete and undivided attention - waiting for us to fully register the true weight of this, before continuing. 'The clothing's a lot comfier these days, and I remember seeing tooth brushes for the first time... but it was way too late for my toothypegs. I once used river reeds to floss. Break them to expose the green stem inside. Very handy.'

This time, he fixed on Scarlett. 'You see, I was a kid - like you - over a century ago.'

Kids *are* easily impressionable.

But they're not stupid.

I was one such case; honed in the rational and pragmatic. I wasn't dopey. His implications were outlandish, preposterously so. Even though I was a child, his was the classic *wind-up*, and I wasn't gullible. The staple Birthday, or Christmas gift you got around here was the Guinness Book of World records... and the oldest living man looked *nothing* like Ol' Bobby. Wind-up merchant, or the fever was making him delirious, or both! I was once sent home from school with the same thing. The raging fever made me dream that the entire solar system was somehow crammed into my tiny bedroom. I was squeezed against my wall by Jupiter. Vicious virus. Claustrophobic nightmare.

However, we all remained respectfully quiet, listening to his nonsense, while flashing each other startled glances.

'All folk around here know about the boat that sailed upstream,' he continued, undeterred. 'This year I thought: if I make loads of little boats - you'd see the link - and it'd scare you away, but it didn't for some reason.'

He wiped his forehead with his dirty sleeve.

'Even Basil didn't put you off. Perhaps it's his name - not particularly frightening - or perhaps it's because he's diffident. Anyways, the river's been calling to me for several evenings now.' He pointed a gangly arm back the way he came. 'I was listening, under the bridge, when you all jumped in... and heard them. Their songs are dangerous. You all need to be extremely careful.'

He sighed, rubbing his stubbly chin.

'My father warned me about this place, but I was young and reckless, always smoking and drinking in these same fields.' He paused, deliberating... cautiously choosing his next words. 'Drunkenly fell in the river one night, didn't I? That's when it began for me. Heard the voices myself. Never aged much after.'

This was disorientating.

Confusion etched its way over five impressionable faces. What *on earth* was he saying? I felt I was living in one of my own mystery stories. Were we seeing Ol' Bobby's true colours? A bright collage of barking madness?

'Well,' he continued, blowing out his cheeks, 'I got bladdered on some strong barley wine, or summat, but I heard their voices when I was thrashing around. I was too drunk to pick myself up, so I just lay there. It's never deep unless it floods. To this day, I remember the gist of what they were saying.'

'What?' Scarlett's voice faltered.

'*This Siren* - or whatever it is - told me my Grandfather would pass later that day… and he did. I hadn't even sobered by the time I learned the news.'

Five of us stood in deathly silence; motionless. We knew what *pass* meant.

Scarlett said, 'The *river* told you this?'

'Aye, and then, I never seemed to age. I saw people around me grow old, but I didn't. They'd die; their children would grow… and they'd die, too.'

Ishaq started scowling - and I was with him, one hundred per cent - darting dismissive glances our way; he wasn't buying this one bit.

'My Grandfather owned this land,' Ol' Bobby continued. 'Came down to my father, who passed it on to my cousins, not to me… but I hung around.' Then he became wistful. 'Met a beautiful lady; Annabel was her name, Ahh, my Annie - a really kind farm lass. I didn't have any birth records, but I still looked like I was in my twenties. She thought I was nineteen or twenty, like her. We were happy for a few years. Small pox took her. Caught it in Gloucester.'

He sighed some more, shaking his head at the memory. 'Anyway, about ten years after the war, folk started noticing and called me Peter Pan, after that book that'd just come out. It was a joke around here… until it wasn't.'

Ol' Bobby stopped and waited.

'So, you're *over* one hundred years old?' Ishaq stated incredulously; close to a condescending tone.

If this was a lie, it was the most immaculately crafted lie I'd ever seen. Ol' Bobby caught Ishaq winking at us, so he reached into his pocket and extracted a golden pocket watch, throwing it his way. 'Here, lad. Flick the lid and read the inscription.'

A startled Ishaq stared down; his mind, whirring.

'Read it,' Ol' Bobby gently repeated. 'To your friends… so they can hear.'

"To Robert - Ol' Bobby - in recognition of your tireless services to the estate."

'Now carefully close the lid and flip it over.'

'It says…' An increasingly troubled look brewed over Ishaq. 'It says 1926.'

'Yes, my cousin gave me a fourteen carat gold watch. We talked a lot together about my future around here. I left this area in the mid twenties - too many memories of Annabel, and I guess,' the tramp took a deep breath, composing the next line. 'I was distancing myself from the river - and I didn't return until the mid fifties. Mr Hislop senior came and found me and asked me to return. The river was causing some serious bother.'

Ishaq frowned as he passed the pocket watch back.

And Ol' Bobby changed tack again, almost nonchalantly side-stepping the weight of his previous admission.

'The river was enticing children back. Even when Hislop senior banned kids from coming; they'd find another stretch to play in. Grobatard let them play on his land further down, but the waters were deeper and more dangerous there, so I encouraged Mr Hislop to lift the ban, which he did, on my return. Then, I started scaring kids.'

'*Scaring* kids?'

This was declared in unison.

'Yeah. Scaring them off.'

'What?' Scarlett said. 'Like… deliberately?'

'Well, I could back then: fewer movies around, and that stuff. Mention a headless horseman, or stamp a few devil hoof prints in circles in wet morning grass where kids played, and they'd scarper. Even fishermen would avoid the beck for miles and miles on either side. Folk were more religious and scared easier.'

'So, what's… in here, exactly?' Scarlett insisted, growing impatient; a hint of frustration in her tone. She was getting jittery.

'Have you heard of the harrying of the North?'

We all shook our heads.

'Pity,' he said, disappointedly. 'This region's forgotten genocide. It's not really taught as much. So, you haven't figured who William is?'

Every one of our jaws sagged in expectancy. I sparked out of my intermittent reverie at this name.

'It's William Grobatard.' Ishaq declared.

Scarlett chipped in, annoyed at Ishaq stealing her thunder. 'And he wants to get his filthy mitts on this land. He'd ban every kid from coming.'

'Well, that wealthy farmer… may have played his part,' Ol' Bobby said, staring east along the river.

'He's got his oars in everything,' Hazel added. 'Nobody likes him. Falls out with every farmer, but makes lots of money. Waits for them to struggle, and then offers peanuts for their land.'

Ol' Bobby acknowledged their passionate discourse.

'Well, young lady, be that as it may; Grobatard's only a lieutenant. I'm talking about his Commander-in-Chief. Unless he's a thousand year's old… you've got the wrong fella.'

It was one thing to hear him claim an age above a century, but a millennium? My eyes met with Ishaq's in ardently shared disbelief. I wondered if exhaust fumes were making him hallucinate, or something else? And at that moment, Ol' Bobby stopped, sensing the cynicism.

For several moments, he stood there, making a crown shape over his frail head, until Hazel became the first to take the prompt.

'What are you doing?'

'I'm showing you.'

'Showing us what?'

'Their murderer.'

'I don-'

'The children in this river weren't dumped here by a farmer. They were all slaughtered by a King.'

~ ~ ~

William was a Duke, in Normandy, as well as a nation's conqueror.

As kids, none of us had heard of such butchery, neither in the north, nor on the earth. All directly beneath our feet, on the land where we stood; his soldiers unleashing the most savage and unimaginable cruelty.

Scorched earth. *No one* escaped.

Of course, the people William targeted weren't rebelling; they were lowly peasants trying to live. Caught up in the politics of megalomaniacs; always the way, it seems. The troops used the old Roman road for ease of access, suddenly appearing during the freezing winter months, when earth stood hard as iron. This didn't deter them: burning crops to lifeless cinders - field by field - and torching every barn full of provisions, carts, homes, and all manner of livestock, until absolutely nothing existed. Nothing left for the people; nothing at all. Land too ruined for anything to grow, *for decades*. Those who weren't hung, raped, or put-through with sword, starved to death.

Ol' Bobby didn't hold back.

Hazel turned white and sat on the grass.

As my own stomach started to turn, I reminded myself: we did come *here* for answers.

Later, in adulthood, I learned two particular things from the Domesday book about the harrying, *or harrowing* of the North. Seventeen years on from the genocide, not a single household remained in any of the villages around here. And for each record, an attached word, scrawled in Latin.

Vasta. *Waste.*

Just two miles up the road from here is Brennigston. Ask any local around here how you get there, and they'll look at you funny, and with a thick dialect, say. "Where?"

Post-scorching, Brennigston was renamed, Burneston.

William.

That *great* king.

Three of the five of us were seated at this point. Every word Ol' Bobby spoke checked out with the voices Ishaq had translated. Famine, fire, starvation… *fear*. I'd heard of cannibalism already. And imagined the few desperate, surviving infants - stricken out of their minds - and famished beyond repair, resorting to eating the remains of their family; brothers, sisters. On this warm, August morning, with the eastern sun reflecting off light stone on the busy road above, I felt defiled for the second time in two months.

This could not have happened here, not here.

Strangely, the bramble bush always looked desolate; half-dead at best. The few cows we heard were always in distant fields. The grass had its share of yellow patches. Then, Ol' Bobby, somehow, went up a gear.

'William's knight's drowned kids in this river - that's what the voices tell me, anyway - and their bodies floated down with the current.'

I looked at Robert in shock. He was staring straight ahead.

'How can you…' Hazel's voice quivered 'possibly know that?'

'They told me… on a number of occasions. Mainly when I first fell in, but on an evening I'll hear them when my head touches stone. It's like a hypnotic breeze sweeping over me, and I'm ready to plunge straight in and rescue a child, *who isn't even there*. But, there's something off.' This was abruptly stated. 'This place harbours dark secrets. I get why there are kids here speaking in Olde English, because that was the language of the time…'

'So, it's definitely Olde English, then?' Ishaq said.

'You've heard it being spoken?'

'Yes, but I wasn't exactly sure.'

'Well, there's something else here.'

He eyed the waters with suspicion. 'Latin is the language of the educated. Rare in those days, yet I'm hearing it on occasions. Unless there was some religious order teaching kids around here, but I don't think there was.'

'So, what about Grobatard, then?' Scarlett said.

'I'd say… be wary of him.'

Scarlett flashed a vindicated look *at me*.

'And of course this all troubles me greatly,' Ol' Bobby continued, 'Sometimes, I think they're not even kids at all - just blended memories - that the Sirens enjoy singing to me; fooling me. I thought I was maybe protecting the young spirits in there, from them… but the longer I go, the less certain I am.'

My blood ran cold. No feeling prior had ever presented itself in my young body, like someone stepping over your grave. 'So… what *is* in there?' I asked.

Ol' Bobby shook his head.

'I don't know, but I don't trust it. Maybe *they're* the souls of trapped children. There's real pain. I feel it. I know this much.'

'I don't believe you're as old as you say you are,' Ishaq suddenly blurted, 'It isn't logical. None of this…' he started to stutter. 'It doesn't make-'

'I know, I know.'

With sadness in his eyes, the tramp accepted this - almost as if this *wasn't* the first time - while Hazel stared disapprovingly at Ishaq, but I got him: I felt overwhelmed too.

'I get that. Hard to believe, isn't it? You've visited me for answers, and you're the first generation to do so.' Ol' Bobby sighed. 'All I'll say is, I remember seeing my first ever motor car. It was a Vulcan. It astonished me. I was so proud of that invention. The Worthingtons bought one.' he turned, addressing the beck, 'The only other thing I know, is whatever's in there has me trapped… in this painful life, and won't let me go… not yet.'

A troubling dilemma was presenting itself to Ol' Bobby, and he pondered it intently; as if he could not reach a solution.

'Kids,' he spoke again, swallowing hard, '*If* I am a good man, you'll heed my advice and stay *well away* from this river, and its tricks. Your parents made this an enchanting place in their memories and encouraged you to come.'

Then his face shifted, and he angrily commanded, '*Don't!*'

Then he balled at us.

'Do not… come here!'

And we all jumped.

In that moment, what saved him from *forever* being the terrifying troll under the bridge - for now, and any subsequent visit - was his sudden coughing fit. It was distracting enough to make him appear less hostile than his directive.

And it allowed me to think.

For a man over one hundred - who looked closer to fifty - he was hardly displaying invincibility. Despite his impassioned conviction, he was clearly very unwell and equally deluded. I wondered if this was common among the isolated who spent so much time on the roads, wandering the wilderness, year after year. His illness was affecting his mental state. The pocket watch could have been addressed to one of *countless* Robert's of that era. And that box of shiny junk he kept with him under the bridge - who was to say he hadn't gathered, or stolen it, along with the watch? Despite his hacking up phlegm, I didn't care for any of his anger.

'I think we should leave.' I said.

Out of the blue, I was beginning to dislike and distrust this man. Robert didn't hesitate, either. He already picked himself up, more than ready to depart. Scarlett looked flabbergasted, as if I'd presented the worst possible suggestion.

'Kids, I do hope I haven't upset you; I didn't mean to,' he wiped his brow, 'just promise me one thing because I know you'll want to come back, whatever happens…' He coughed one last violent cough. 'Do not - under any circumstances - sail to the end of the river, past Grobatard's farm, where it gets deeper.'

Our quintet briefly assessed another mysterious (but for me, empty) statement, before Ishaq finally asked: 'Because it meets the Swale?'

'That too.' The exhausted man replied. 'But this is where the Sirens sing louder. That's where I believe these things are.'

A line had been crossed; the borders of believability pushed to breaking. The wandering man could see it too. Regret flashed over his face. Sirens? No sea anywhere near here. If he got too weird, he'd be hearing police sirens. I wouldn't hesitate. No Greek sailors. Plenty of mythology. No facts.

'I believe you Ol' Bobby,' Hazel said.

'Thank you, young lady,' he gushed, warmth flooding his haggard face.

Despite my personal aversion, I was torn. My mum treated him with respect, as did most in the village. She almost looked out for him.

'Are we leaving?' Robert said.

He clearly didn't feel the same pang of remorse I was experiencing, and he turned and walked a few steps back, eager to separate himself from the tramp.

'Young man, please be careful. Please stay away.'

The haulier's son, swivelled and scowled at him once, and kept on walking.

Ol' Bobby lowered his voice, 'The river really spoke to him. He's been coming back without you, hasn't he? Making that jetty. Extending that dock. You've all got to look out for him.'

'Why?' Scarlett enquired.

'The boy's hiding crosses.'

None of us knew what this meant, but he was already explaining, 'It latched to him like a leech.'

'Ol' Bobby, do you like buns?' Hazel suddenly, and inexplicably said.

This instantly grabbed my attention.

'Of course.'

'How about butterfly buns?'

Then came the joyous sound of an ice cream carton being clicked open. My attention stolen, I got caught between watching Robert trundling further away, and the chance to munch. But then she gave the tramp the entire ice-cream container, and my heart sank.

'What, all for me… thank you for your kindness, young lady; you're going to be kind to a lot of people in your life, of that I'm sure.'

There was a chance he would offer…

But instead, he wiped his brow and sighed: 'Would you mind if I save them for later, when I feel a little more awake?'

Hazel gently nodded. Some low-lying part of my stomach growled its sugary betrayal.

'We'll come and see you again soon, Ol' Bobby,' I partly lied.

The homeless man tipped an imaginary hat our way, as we turned to leave. Robert was nearly out of sight, having collected his bike, disappearing around the corner of the barn. As expected, no one spoke for the first few dozen yards as we left; pondering silently in the gorgeous, morning sunshine; our unusual thoughts not matching with the natural world around us. Speckled thrushes skipped along the grassy expanse at our feet and somewhere in the distance, a cuckoo called in the branches.

So, William Grobatard was trying to buy this place.

This created ambivalence within.

Part of me hoped he'd command trucks to fill the whole river course with fast-setting concrete. I'd also overheard murmurings the dual carriageway was being extended into motorway. Maybe this would close this section of beck indefinitely. Every scenario I entertained was a conscious avoidance scheme, designed to *not accept* and self-preserve.

I stared at the green grass, imagining countless bodies beneath.

Ishaq spoke first, 'Oh, c'mon… he wasn't telling the truth.'

A pause and then, Hazel 'Well, I believe him.'

'Me as well,' Scarlett concurred.

The Guinness book of world record's popped into my head again.

'The oldest man in the world is Japanese, and he's like, one hundred and fifteen or sixteen or something.'

Ishaq was grateful for my backing, but clearly annoyed, he hadn't come up with this.

'That's correct,' he replied.

'But he fell into the river and it stopped him growing older,' Hazel countered.

'So, why does he look like he's about to die?' I stated; a little too unsympathetically.

This didn't go down well.

'He isn't *dying!*' Scarlett angrily retorted, 'He's just under the weather. That's not a nice thing to say, Billy.'

'Yeah, he's just got a bad cold or something.' Hazel was less aggressive.

I couldn't or maybe didn't want to think of response. Needless to say, I couldn't believe they were buying his crap about inflated age. Somehow, Scarlett was retaining some form of building anger, and aiming it at me. 'Everything we've seen in this river is unusual, Billy. We've felt its power. Those ghosts may have possibly lived here centuries; why couldn't they make a human live a long time too?'

'Because… it's *impossible.*'

'You're jealous because it spoke more to us than it did you.'

'No, I'm not.'

'It couldn't be *bothered* speaking to you; *that's why.*'

Something hurtful bobbed up and down in my heart. Scarlett had fired a nasty accusation… and I didn't like it one bit.

'That's not true.'

'And it called you their enemy; saw *right through you.*'

'No, I'm not,' I answered, now irked. I'd done heroic things.

'That's why you don't want to come here,' she persisted. 'because they don't like *you* - and you're too afraid.'

We were approaching the end of the field about to enter the farmyard - Ishaq and Hazel - quietly listening in.

'I'm not afraid.'

'You were the *first* to leap out of the river.'

117

'That's *bullshit.*'

I barked this, surprising them all.

Scarlett was really flushing; I'd never seen her like this. Ishaq and Hazel looked shocked.

'You try to block everything!' she shouted back. 'You're deliberately *stopping us* finding the truth.'

Scarlett's conclusion to my retort was both savage and timely. I felt like I should explode, but instead - felt exposed by truth. We had reached the corner of the barn, and the long dirt track, leading to the village.

I was about to respond angrily with some loud nonsense when Hazel shushed us all. Louder noises echoed from around the corner.

My legs were wobbling all the way down from the inside of my thighs. I was learning I wasn't a fan of direct confrontation. It was affecting my body similarly to the moments before getting punched.

But… apparently there was a situation more pressing than my perceived victimisation. As we all walked onto the track, the tension reset. We were about to stumble on something requiring our *immediate* attention.

~ ~ ~

Further up the worn and weathered track, was Robert.

A pack of kids, on bike and on foot, were gathering around him like menacing vultures; agitated, scurrying around their stricken victim. Body language was set to impose, and with great hostility. On viewing the mob of thirteen or fourteen, Ishaq immediately mis-read. 'We've got to stop them going to the river - how do we do that?'

'They're not going there,' I said.

'It's Dove and Chris.' Hazel said.

Robert was engaged in a heated exchange.

My mind plotted an alternative exit - down to the beck, and then take a right. East. This would take us closer to the end of the river. Reality versus myth; and my adrenalin was already deciding. This was a dead end.

'We need to help him,' Scarlett hissed - straight at me - *directly* at me.

Ishaq wiped his brow, 'If my parents find out… I've been coming down here.'

'We can't just leave him.'

But we could. We really could. If we'd hung around longer with Ol' Bobby, we wouldn't even be witnessing this. Robert had *chosen* to walk away.

'We need to help him,' Hazel implored.

Voices were being raised; accusations flying.

The throng were about three hundred yards from our position and I knew the only time little kids hopped around older kids - like scampering sparrows - were when fights were imminent; *every time*. A rumour would start that there was going to be a scrap, and everyone would gravitate to the location.

'Billy, he's your mate; *do something!*' Scarlett was delivering more undesirable truths; crushing every ounce of my puny spirit. 'Why did they ask him if *he was* Robert *Tipperton*, the other day?'

There was a hidden reason for this fracas; a sinister slant to Craig's question.

I traced back my friend's reputation at school; quiet, respectful. Not massively academic, but studious and hard-working. He wouldn't have started anything, but he'd help others where injustice was served. *He'd* help *me*. No doubt, a proper beat-down would be painful, but, more importantly, in a contained location like this village, you'd become a target *forever* from that point on. It didn't matter how many piled in; losing was for losers, and losers got bullied more.

'Come on,' I said.

This was far worse than the voices in the haunted beck: *far, far,* worse; a direct physical threat as opposed to an indirect, implied one. Maybe the courage I'd shown at the river was helping me here, or I was trying to prove Scarlett

119

wrong about her *cowardly* inference. Perhaps, I was doing this to impress her. Or, maybe I was showing genuine integrity and loyalty to a friend. Truly I planned only to walk forwards. *That was all.*

I learned in later years, sometimes courage comes in the showing up, even if you don't feel courageous. With legs quivering beneath me, I silently cursed my decision-making; not quite believing I was moving forwards. A few of the smaller kids noticed our approach and started pointing. They may as well be shouting, "More prey, more prey." Like sycophants and lick-spittles, alerting their superior vultures to the fresh "soon-to-be-dying".

Serious threats were being made. I could see Craig towering over Robert; viciously berating him, calling him a thief.

A thief?

Ishaq lagged the furthest, and at a noticeable distance, but Scarlett was right up by my side.

'No, *they're not!*' Robert fired back.

As Craig shifted forward, Robert closed the distance. Face-to-face. It was about to start; no question.

'Stealing bricks from other properties, piles of wood, not paying debts. Tipperton Thieves who live in a tip.'

'No we don't!'

Eyeball-to-eyeball.

'You're taking all that stolen timber and using it for your tree house, *aren't you?*'

Craig was impassioned, jabbing fingers at the farm.

'What's happening?' Scarlett whispered, as we closed the last one hundred yards.

She sensed it too.

The 'reason' behind this.

This was no, *Oi You, punch!* There was a bizarre legitimacy to Craig's words.

'You're *all* a bunch of criminals,' he argued. 'Breaking into trucks parked in laybys, waiting till the driver's asleep and looting the containers.'

Craig was probably two and half years older than Rob. A teen growth spurt worked in his favour, but I couldn't imagine Rob being defeated by anyone - he'd *never* lose a fight. Strangely, none of the gang now cared for our presence as we slowly came to a halt. Ishaq was lagging a long way back. And my mind was now shrieking at me: walk past, walk on. I watched Dove with his fat arms resting on his handle-bars briefly glance at us, and then away. He clenched a rolled newspaper between his podgy fingers.

And I finally realised... these weren't threats.

These were allegations.

I turned to Scarlett and whispered back, 'I don't know... what's happening.'

And she at least nodded. At least we were here - standing for Rob - but verbally defending him seemed an impossibility. There was far too much clamour. The situation was steaming beyond remedy. I didn't know what the hell was going on.

'Your brother's going down for a long time, son,' Craig said.

Then I noticed another smaller boy holding the same rolled newspaper. And another... already pointing something out to a small girl. Scarlett angled to see as Dove barged into the argument: 'Your whole family's being arrested for dodgy stuff. Burglary, violence...'

His stubby finger pointed at a news column in the regional newspaper; a big paper in these parts. *Arrested?* Rob wore a valiant, stoic face, but he was *also* concealing. I could see this, too.

'Those are lies!' I shouted.

It was a powerful moment, and for a split-second I part turned, expecting to see Franz Reichelt leaping from the Eiffel Tower in his brown jump-suit. A voice from elsewhere. Brave, intrepid and *profoundly* foolishly. Entering the fray, like a moron. And then Rob did something I'd never expected of him in a position like this - not in my wildest dreams. My loyal, courageous, 'rock-hard' friend...

Turned... and walked.

'Where do you think you're going?' Craig barked.

Rob swivelled around, wearing an expression of utter revilement and gave him the 'V's' with both hands. The fight was on. Craig ran after him, as the cacophonous throng of wildlings hit their cycle pedals in hard pursuit. Dove missed his own, ramming his flabby leg straight into the track. You'd laugh at the bully in other circumstances; but not these.

He wanted to swing his arms.

With the entire track being filled with bikes, I moved onto the furrowed soil to our right, trying to circumnavigate the cluster. Traversing dry, lumpy soil was tricky. I caught sight of Craig grabbing Rob's shoulder, yanking him round. And it was on. The two punch rule was out of the question. Craig was older - possessing universal backing from his audience - and Rob was, somehow, the 'deserving' enemy. This alone stunned me. Craig threw a punch that grazed the left temple; the nimble boy riding the strike, before launching his own fist straight back, partially connecting with arm and upper chest. This startled Craig, clearly not expecting retaliation in any form from someone younger. So he just started *swinging* wild, over-hands. They always looked fast and impressive.

This was real fight-punching... except it really wasn't.

A left hand connected with Rob's right cheek jerking him to his left, and making the most impressive *thumping* sound I'd ever heard. I'd be done there, in truth. And you could see this spurred Craig on, but Rob didn't back down, despite the pain. He stepped forward and started throwing a load himself. And his punches were faster, truer. He caught Craig flush in the face with a right, and smack in the chin with a left. The wiry red-head staggered at the weight of the impact, his legs buckling at the knees.

It looked weird, like in the cartoons.

Rob stepped forward to finish him off; poised, and in control. But then, a kid clattered into him full-force with his bike. It hurt the kid too; who threw his bike down and hobbled away... but it hurt Rob more. Gasping, winded. Rob doubled-over and tried pushing his hand down his shin, while protecting his body from further assault.

'*Do something!*' Scarlett implored me.

And suddenly I felt it, like I'd never felt it before. My mate was about to get beat and kicked with each and every implement lying strewn on this farm-track. Kids were grabbing sticks, branches - their own bikes - their own hands… newspapers even. I couldn't stand it. I could *not* stand *for it*. So, I grabbed the largest stone I could find - clod with dried earth from the bottom of a furrow - and lobbed it at the crowd as hard as I could.

Some kid *really* screamed.

It hit at head-height, somewhere in the midst of the crowd. Dove was off his bike gathering Rob in a bear-hug and swinging him into a prickly hedge. I managed to scramble off the soil, tipping forward and nearly losing balance, before hurtling towards the front, just as Dove was driving his hefty leg into the prostrate Rob. To my amazement, my pal sprang to his feet, and despite hairline cuts to his face and blood streaming from his right knee, he was fighting back with all his might.

As was I.

You see, the thing is… Dove was the *very* same boy "sanctioned" to give me that solitary punch by the bus-stop. The same boy *invited* to the village to punch me. *No way* I'd forgotten. And I wanted to clout this fat tub of lard as hard as I possibly could.

Rob from the front and me from the back. I made a fist… and banged Dove around the back of his left ear. Hurt *like hell*. Dove staggered, clutching, trying to steer his bulbous frame away, now losing to those younger. Inches from victory, I felt totally empowered, fighting side-by-side with my best pal. But then my feet were taken out from under me - literally so - and my head was repeatedly stamped upon. There were many trainers of different sizes, conditions and colours, and despite the brutal battering I was receiving, I noted many *untied* shoelaces.

It was extremely painful.

Independently, far away from prying eyes - and the village's real BMX stunt men - I once tried hopping the gap between pavement and road on my bike. Construction

123

workers had dug up the surface, leaving behind a long, foot-deep, clay-like chasm. The new kerb would be fitted in the gap the next day. It was an opportunity. I failed the jump. The pain I felt, as I lay sprawled in the road, was *indescribable* for twenty seconds.

But not as bad as this.

My ear was damp and soggy, and the whole side of my head throbbed with an exquisite burn. I'd been released from the melee, but left with stabbing pains rifling through my right ankle. I could smell strong cow pat or horse manure; and blades of grass tickled my nose. An odd sensation to experience - to be tickled - while lying utterly pulverised. Then, while prostrate, someone threw a large stone into my back, just under my shoulder-blade.

I'm guessing it was the boy who I'd hit with a stone earlier.

At this point, I thought Death was paying me a visit, plunging his white hot poker into my spine. I could survive the rest, but not this. The blow sucked the air from my lungs, and in my breathlessness, I recall - in panic - thinking: young kids *can't* actually kill other young kids, right; only adults can?

Maybe it was a higher level of consciousness, I don't know, but I could sense the crowd moving away from me. Was Rob still fighting further down the track? I could hear a commotion.

But then it shifted all rather quickly. There was this *big* booming voice.

In my present state, it was impossible to discern words, but it seemed to be a game-changer, whatever he was bellowing. I heard the unmistakable click of gears shifting, and bike chains re-aligning. I hoped Rob was sensibly legging it. Why didn't we bring bikes today?

'Billy, are you - are you okay?'

I expected a hail of trainers, but instead I got soft hands and feminine tones.

'He's bleeding bad out of his ear.'

'We need an ambulance.'

'Is he unconscious?'

'Quick, call Mr. Hislop over.'

My eyes were closed, but for protective reasons; deliberately playing dead.

'He's awake! He's okay, he's alive.'

'Billy, are you alright?'

'What happened?' I croaked, genuinely dazed.

'Craig and another boy kicked you off your feet and started kicking you in the face.'

'And then someone threw a rock in your back.' Ishaq said.

'Where's… R-Rob?'

'He managed to get onto the soil where the kids couldn't follow on their bikes. Then Mr Hislop appeared and chased them all away.'

I raised my left hand to my ear, smeared in a startling amount of blood. When you're a kid, a *lot* of blood is a very serious thing. If you're alive after an attack, then you think you'll stay alive.

'What the hell were you lot up to?'

There was the voice, *bellowing* again. Then I heard Scarlett calmly talking back, explaining.

Seconds later.

'Son, are you alright?' and 'He's taken a beating. Bloody thugs!'

I attempted sitting upright, massively embarrassed that I'd been fighting on *his* land. If he kicked me off right now, I would find it difficult to get anywhere fast. But that was the last of his intentions. Instead, he grabbed me around the shoulders and hoisted me to my feet, as I groaned in pain. Mr Hislop replied with typical Yorkshire stoicism: 'He'll be right. They breed em strong around 'ere.'

And,

'Where d'ya live, lad?'

Ishaq kindly responded on my behalf.

'Reet, that's too far. Yer better come inside for a bit, till yer get yer wits about yer again.'

Then those big arms grabbed me and lifted me to somewhere between chest and shoulder level, and he marched me back in the direction of the beck. Mr Hislop's overalls smelled of hay and his hands of something much more ancient and musty. His palms were bleeding rock hard. He could easily toss sheep with those huge cleavers. By our side, Ishaq, Scarlett and Hazel continued peppering him with details, that he neither seemed to care for, nor respond to. I was hoping he'd recognise us - the loyal cohort of good guys; faithful to his beck - which I think he did. Surely, he remembered Ishaq's interview, and Scarlett and her mother enquiring with him about their own experience.

'Put yer hand on yer ear to stop tawd bleeding,' was the only thing he said.

That, and the occasional, "Aye" to the others.

He never broke a sweat, nor did I sag even slightly in his arms for a full four hundred yards. He manfully opened his farm-house door with his gargantuan free hand and led us into a dismal-looking kitchen. Kicking a solid oak chair out from under a table with his foot, he placed me down.

Silently, he left us, and walked across to the opposite side to switch on a kettle.

'How are you feeling?' Hazel whispered.

'B-bit sh-shook up.'

And I was shaking, as I replied.

'You had Dove on the run. You got him, good.' Scarlett observed.

It was a nice thing to say, but heroes are left in a fit state. I could feel an underlying embarrassment brewing. But, at least our argument had clearly been forgotten. Heroism surely didn't feel like this, though.

'There was too many of them, but did you see how I was warding them off by thrashing that branch?'

Ishaq was having his say, but nobody responded to his inflated claims. Despite the powerful aches all over my body, I was thinking about Rob's family and the accusations... *within* the *numerous* rolled newspapers.

As if she was reading my mind, Scarlett quipped: 'Do you think... what they said... is true?'

And this was why I felt so *shockingly* awful.

126

'Rob wouldn't steal any wood to build his jetty, would he?' Hazel said.

This prompted a silent segment of consideration, that lasted all of three seconds, resulting in them rigorously shaking their heads.

'Unless, he didn't know it was stolen,' Ishaq said.

'Good point. There's *no way* he would, otherwise.' Scarlett agreed.

Again, everyone fell quiet. What if he was an unwitting victim, somehow duped into partaking in a crime; what then? I hoped this was true. Then I recalled what he said about Newhaven and sailing back to his Gran's. In my injured state, it nagged me that his extended stay may not have been a holiday after all; more circumstantial necessity. I'd seen the pain flush across his face when he described sailing back to meet her there.

The river was all he had.

But those thoughts were temporary, as my own incendiary pain didn't cease. In fact, I was on the verge of tears. What on this earth *had I just gone and done*? I may have supported a potential criminal. Certainly in the eyes of these kids, he *was*. I knew bullying, but this wasn't even remotely close to the standard.

Craig was genuinely having a go.

Moreover, I had no idea how to explain the cuts, wounds and limping to my family. This was an all round 'dire' situation to be in.

And then there was the river.

Temporarily blotted from my mind, but back.

It was still there - with all its ghoulies - overseen by a fella, apparently, well over a century old. I was increasingly certain that enchanted meant cursed, and the waters had the power to influence everything associated with it; even causing fights.

And of course, I was completely correct about this.

Chapter 8

The Road is Long

There was an expression banded around these parts when I was a kid.

"Being in deep shit."

I very much was.
Deeper and deeper I sank, as the days passed.

Ishaq had already left us, wisely deciding to walk home and formulate an excuse that didn't place him at this location. As we stood in the functional farm kitchen, me just about upright, Mr Hislop appeared with a damp cloth and started wiping my wounds with Dettol. He didn't ask, he didn't forewarn, he just went straight ahead and did it. The sting, the pain. Oh, *my* goodness! I cried, nearly screeched, and cemented my loser's status in my mind.

'Aye, he'll live,' was all he said.

Scarlett and Hazel accompanied me on the journey back home in Mr Hislop's dusty, dirty car. It smelled of damp, and the upholstery was fading. His was a practical car; wellies and gloves thrust everywhere. His explanation to my horrified mother (eyes bulging, mouth gaping) - as I was part carried to the front door - simply entailed: 'Ello, Mrs Austin. Your lad's been in a scrap, but I gather it wasn't his fault. He might need a check-up, though.'

The girls gently, and very convincingly, explained everything to my mum, and then trundled off home.

Mum whisked me straight off to the Friarage hospital.

There was swelling, a lot of cuts, and bruising - particularly on my back. Bleeding from the ear came from the lobe, and the drum itself was intact. I was having a bit of difficulty hearing out of it, though. The nurses praised Mr Hislop for his prompt action - burning half my face off with antiseptic - and I flinched when they produced more wipes. After more unholy stinging, they were soft and kind as they bandaged my head, arm and, partly sprained ankle. I genuinely looked like an ancient Mummy, but more importantly, I resembled the wounded warrior. I hated taking my trousers off, even though I was wearing Superman briefs (which I deemed wholly inappropriate, considering my condition). There was no lasting damage, and I didn't need a tetanus booster.

Mum could have done with an injection.

She was *hell-bent* on driving to the police station straight after, but she was savvy enough - with the help of the matron - to allow herself a cool-down, especially when I repeated the events, and reminded her of who I was defending.

'It was Robert you helped, yes?'

'Yeah. Rob Tipperton.'

My mum exhaled a deep breath, staring directly ahead. We were in the car now, heading over Morton bridge, which crossed the river Swale. I briefly studied it out the window, while her hands grasped tightly to the steering wheel. She didn't say a thing for a few seconds.

'He was being accused… of stealing,' I said.

Not another word from her… not until we finally pulled up outside the house.

'I'm going to call your dad.'

This scared me. Needless to say, he came straight home from work.

In the years to come, I encountered *another* phrase that perfectly summarised the events of that afternoon. *Frontier Justice*. My dad was livid. He wanted to go straight round to Craig and Dove's dads' and give them a proper "bunch of

129

fives" (because he never liked him anyway). But this was the point things got *markedly* worse for me. The problem: I defended the wrong kid in the whole entire universe.

When dad learned this, he didn't know what do with his anger. His mate's down the pub wouldn't support him when they heard who I fought alongside. His rage turned to outright embarrassment.

On returning from the pub later that evening, he and mum had a *huge* row. The whole of the village would have heard it. It woke me up - and despite reduced hearing capacity in my left ear - I caught the gist. News spread fast. I was physically wounded, but my soul was bruised, too. My heart felt continually low, like it was constantly slipping down in my chest. The emotions I was experiencing were new… and *extremely* unpleasant.

I'd disappointed people.

Worse, I'd disappointed my dad.

I thought mine was the correct, moral course of action. In the next few days, it turns out I was wrong. His friends down the pub voiced their displeasure at my defence of public enemy number one (or where ever Robert stood in the Tipperton pecking order). It leads to - what we call in these parts - *bother*. This was a small village; and his mates were fathers of the kids haranguing Rob on the track, and one of them was the kid I hit with a rock. Despite me coming worse-off in the exchange, it was honours even in the eyes of the locals; no need for the police.

But the pot still simmered, and eventually boiled over, when dad got into a fight outside the pub. *He won,* but his was a Pyrrhic victory. Subsequent evenings were then spent meeting folk to sort grievances, but the scrap aversely affected his reputation. The following morning, after his dust-up, he gave me the bollocking of a lifetime. It took me years to come up with a single word that encapsulated how I felt about Rob in the days that followed: dissonance.

He was my best pal, and we'd swung fists at the enemy, like comrades on the front line. But, he was *also* the enemy.

I continued to feel so low, and confused. My little mind struggled to process conflicting emotions, eventually settling on betrayal.

Didn't anybody else feel sorry for Rob?

I was grounded for the rest of the month, but I didn't want to leave the house, anyway. This was my hovel of rightful shame. Moreover, scabs stretched across the entire left side of my face, and my ankle left me with a distinctive hobble. Although my hearing was restored, my back throbbed for ages afterwards, and sleeping was difficult; although my insomnia was a more mental thing. But, I was no dummy either. Stepping out the front door made me a target for every kid, regardless of age or gender. Even though the bandage eventually came off my head, I wanted to retain it as a physical deterrent. Thoughts of the beck continued to stir extreme revulsion for what it caused. I loathed it like food you ate and instantly puked back up; a sustained and nauseous association.

Perhaps the only shred of comfort concerned the bottle's note, and August the 29th. With this date rapidly approaching, it was of absolutely *no* concern to me.

We will see you… if you don't see us first.

No, you won't.

Good riddance.

In the next few days, Mum exchanged various calls with Scarlett and Hazel's parents in the evenings that followed. They were supportive conversations; and they understood. But she didn't potato-pick for the rest of the season, her reason being there was a reduced demand for pickers, anyway. She also received another visit from the lovely Mrs Khan who explained that although she'd grounded her son for *lying through his teeth* (Apparently, he'd only lasted thirty minutes before confessing.), she'd love for us to meet together for a play-date soon.

I studied two newspaper reports concerning the Tippertons. Not good. Shocking, in fact. I could scarcely believe what I was reading: breaking into farms, stealing tonnes of expensive equipment, ransacking truck containers. Folk being targetted, intimidated, and purposefully attacked by their guard dogs.

The list went on.

A smidgen of kindness hoped that Rob was in Newhaven with his Gran, but the larger part of me wanted him to serve a prison sentence along with his family.

Dad eventually calmed, and my play-ban was lifted; not that I cared. And one evening, around the dinner table, he even asked me about the fight. I recall how small my voice sounded - my reluctance and shame to speak - and told him I'd launched in to fend off the mob (now, excluding any mention of Rob). I was terrified I'd be told-off again.

'What, you just... went against them all?'

'Yeah,' I could hear the crisp brokenness in each word, like there was gravel in my mouth.

'Did anyone help?'

'No.'

'How many kids?'

'About fourteen.'

'Older than you?'

'Half and half.'

I really didn't want to discuss this any more. My eyes fixed on anything in the kitchen, other than my folks. Paranoia was leading me to believe this was a preordained trap; a prelude to another sanction (one I deserved).

'You punched that fat "Dove" kid?'

'Yeah.'

'What did he do?'

'He tried... running. He was hitting... people.'

'Tried?'

'He's not very agile.'

My father paused for a moment and laughed. 'Not agile,' he repeated, tittering. Mum was listening intently, and something - I don't know what - lifted in my heart. *He laughed.*

'Then someone kicked your legs out from under you. Was it that Craig lad?'

'Yeah, Scarlett and Hazel saw him. I didn't see him.'

I rolled my spaghetti onto my fork. Mum had been keeping a careful eye on me at the meal table, encouraging me to eat every two minutes, for the last few nights.

'Then a few of them stamped on your head.'

These re-collections, in of themselves, were truly horrible, but I couldn't back out of this discussion. He paused again, and I heard mum clear her throat. In hindsight, I didn't realise how rehearsed this conversation really was.

'Well, Billy,' he said. 'What you did was very brave; you stood up for a friend when most wouldn't. That takes real guts.'

To this day…

These are some of the most empowering words I have ever heard spoken.

My dad 'respected' my motivation; nothing else mattered. I wanted to go out *right now*, and fight the *whole* damn village. My heart continued to sparkle and blaze back to life that evening.

One week from this day, however; cowardice would return… to forever haunt me.

~ ~ ~

Locals always knocked on your side door, for a cuppa and a natter.

The front door was formal.

It was the tail end of the holiday's penultimate week when somebody used the knocker. Quite startling, in fact. Only older people with weaker wrists, or strangers, ever used this. This audible transaction alerted a family to more a 'business' engagement with the person standing outside.

I was upstairs writing a story upstairs, a whole eight pages in, with no sign of an ending. My teachers wouldn't make me read this one out because I'd surpassed the four-page threshold. I didn't think holiday stories could be submitted as it stood. When the iron door knocker went, mum answered, and I listened upstairs with my bedroom door ajar.

A male voice.

It made me nervous.

I'd heard rumours that parents were unhappy with my actions earlier on this month, and there was every chance one might call round to vent their frustration. I knew I'd be able to tell by mother's pitch what kind of person this was.

She sounded delighted… and *compassionate* at the same time.

'Come on in for a cuppa. I insist.'

The man at the door protested, but quickly relented, because my mother was a seasoned pro at forcible hospitality. Climbing to my feet, I moved to the edge of my room and listened a little more intently. For someone to be invited - in through the front - must mean they're special. The man had a low voice and did a lot of talking, none of which I could discern. My mum was also notably quiet, especially after her initial enthusiasm. After a few minutes, she started contributing, and I could sense the concern in her voice. I thought about Robert. Don't know why; he just sprung to mind.

A conversation I'd had with an older cousin earlier in the week had entirely changed my perspective; eye-opening. The gist was… Robert hadn't known *anything* about his family's activities. More recent news identified his older brother, Mike, as the main culprit. Robert's mother had subsequently tried protecting him from the incoming shrapnel by sending him down to his Grandmother's on the south coast. Somehow, the sense of betrayal still lingered, because he hadn't been in touch to thank me for my valiance, nor the scars I wore on his behalf. Lots of cupboards were being opened downstairs and I could hear the man protest. Then mum came upstairs and went into her room.

She bustled back out a few moments later, stating, 'He never wears these, anyway.'

And then my juvenile brain finally caught up.

Ol' Bobby was downstairs.

But not for much longer.

I heard mum thank him for the fish!

After a few more pleasantries, they said their goodbyes and the door closed. Standing close to my own, I waited. Had he come over to deliver fish as a thank-you, or did he need company? This was odd, unexpected. I royally flinched when mum called my name from the bottom of the stairs, knowing I'd be eavesdropping. Peering round the corner, I saw her holding a large fish in both hands. Good grief! Had he gone and caught Old Basil?

'Is that a… pike?' I said.

'No. They're not good fish to eat. That was Ol' Bobby at the door.'

'Ahh, right?'

'Come into the kitchen, love.'

I felt a strong sense of intrigue.

'Is he feeling better?' I said.

'No, I noticed that… he doesn't look well at all. I tried convincing him to go to the doctors.'

'Oh.'

'Come and sit at the table; I want to ask you something.'

Quietly and a little apprehensively, I descended the eighteen night-terror steps, entered the kitchen, and took the chair nearest the net curtain. My mother was very matter of fact; there was no window dressing questions in Yorkshire.

'He told me Robert's being going to the beck by himself.'

'What, since the-' I paused, still a little ashamed to use the word, 'since the fight?'

'You do know you're no longer grounded, Billy.'

135

And suddenly I didn't like where this was going.

'Yeah.'

'Well, your actions were *definitely* the right thing… because Robert wasn't to blame for this in any way, shape or form. He's only young! It seems like his older brother is the criminal.'

I nodded.

'You're a kind lad, Billy, and Ol' Bobby is concerned that Rob's there all by himself… with no friends.'

Immediately, I recalled the tramp telling the four of us to look out for Rob; a thought I'd somehow supplanted with the furore. The river was having a profound effect on him. It was difficult, nigh on impossible, to believe he was returning! The threat of getting beaten again; the accusations of the stolen wood… and no support from his closest crew. What on earth was he thinking?

'Billy, Ol' Bobby is very concerned about him. He's building a dock or something and he'll work from dawn to dusk. He thinks Rob's in a difficult place, and he's tried talking to him, but he won't listen.'

'Mum, I defended him and he hasn't been in touch.'

'He's probably embarrassed about his family and thinks everybody hates him.'

'But, I stood up for him.'

'Even so. The news had only just come out. He might *feel* ashamed and guilty because he *knows* his family is, so he'll feel he's somehow to blame, too.'

Wham. I nodded. I'd had a taster.

Mum continued. 'Apparently the Tipperton's had their phone line disconnected, and so he couldn't call even if he wanted.'

That made sense.

'Billy, I'm going to ask you a massive favour.'

Uh oh. '*Mum.*'

'Will you go down the river and check on him?'

Every inch of my soul protested at this; my voice box, the first to sound out rampant objections.

'The river's cursed. It's not enchanted; *it's cursed*. It's not a place for building memories… it's deadly and its affecting Rob, and all of us. *I won't go.*'

'I understand,' she said, but she wasn't done. 'Look, I know you've been through a lot these last few weeks, and,' she leaned in closer to whisper, 'I'm *very, very* proud of you, son. It was *my* son against the masses, and you rightly defended your mate.'

She rubbed her hands together and smiled. She was poised… *strangely* poised.

'So, me and your dad were talking, and we both agreed; we'd like to buy you the BMX you always wanted; the one with blue with yellow wheels.'

My mouth dropped.

My heart leapt.

Holy shit; did she *just* say that? 'You're kidding.'

'No, you deserve it. We thought about surprising you later with a trip in to Bedale, so, if you could do for me this one incy, wincy…' she squeezed her forefinger and thumb tightly together, squinting. 'Teeny-tiny, *ickle* favour.'

She left it hanging.

Talk about excitement; I was on the verge of becoming a BMX bandit! The glorious, vindicated knight - about to be granted a pedigree steed - not that crappy, bent pony in the garage. Needless to say, dreams and bribery cluttered neuronal pathways, vanquishing each and every ghost. It wasn't *that bad* down there, surely?

'Can I have it tonight, please?'

Mum smiled. 'Well, that is our plan.'

I remained stunned. 'You're joking.'

'Your dad's getting back at four, which leaves us an hour or so.'

I could ride and see Rob, and then Scarlett. No more pseudo stunt bike with bent handle bars.

'Okay, can I see him after the weekend?'

Mum thought about this.

'How about we buy you it later, and you go down the beck and show it off to him tomorrow?'

This was soon - and I must admit - I did feel a transitory resistance; an internal tugging, but it was fleeting.

'Deal.' I said.

This was a very, very good outcome. Presents usually came at Christmas. My mind was absolutely reeling; I was deliriously happy. The beck could *get lost!* In fact, it could admire me riding alongside it on a shiny new bike. And If the spectres were spying, they could embrace how modernity was kicking their medieval arses.

Immediately, mum added icing to cake - completely out of the blue - to make this a near perfect day. 'Shall I call Scarlett's mum and ask if she wants to meet you there?'

Jackpot.

I tried to play it cool; appear almost nonchalant.

'I suppose,' I said, shrugging my shoulders.

Mum smiled and winked.

Why was she was winking?

It really didn't matter that I'd been suckered into this.

All that *actually* mattered now was avoiding as much dust and dirt as I cycled the farm lane. My BMX Burner looked immaculate, and I'd do my best to keep it this way.

I refrained from invoking the super-power capacity of the bike; stunts could wait. For now, it was the prize for all to behold; golden rays to moisten jealous eyes, as they glinted along a polished frame, and wheels spinning like yellow suns.

Everything was rosy.

Except, I thought I'd seen a group of boys at the end of the village, near the pub and local shop. That was no problem, though; I merely turned down the next available right and headed to the track the back way. Hopefully, they hadn't clocked me - but even if they did - my BMX was bigger and faster. Honestly, I felt like a King, parading himself after battle. I wanted people in their front gardens to stop, stare and comment. In my mind was the burgeoning acceptance I *had* done the honorable thing in defending Rob. If the rest of the village was coming around to my actions, then all the better.

Scarlett would love this.

Looking over the sturdy and widely parted handlebars - encased in soft, yellow padding - I carefully inspected the route ahead; particularly the long, grassy tuft in the middle of the track. It was essential that tyre grips were not clogged in mud and everything remained brand, spanking new. Taking a left at the barn, I suddenly felt a little anxious. It was hardly a full-blown experience (my Burner, bestowing shield-like positivity). I moved across the grass to the side of the beck and cycled along. Over two weeks had passed since I was last here. Scabs had become scars - war wounds - and I wore the white lines around my left cheek with pride.

As important as it was to show off my bike, Rob needed to see these marks.

In the distance, I caught sight of the cattle bridge and Scarlett standing on top, looking over the far-side. My eyes edged over to the grey, turgid waters beneath. Nothing there. No ghosts peering up with desolate, hollow expressions. They hated me anyway.

My heart was beginning to hammer as I approached her, and Hazel also came into view. The moment was here. King Billy, riding on his imperious stallion and they'd all...

But my breath was instantly taken away.

Expelled from my lungs

Our quiet area of the beck presented itself before me. *What beck?* There were wooden structures everywhere. An extended jetty, tyres galore, ropes in abundance... a new wooden outpost. The tree house now stretched out across the river, running parallel to the bridge. And there were two boats - one larger than the other. Both were docked and fastened to new posts. Just about all the wood had been varnished. And Robert was sitting in the largest, sanding a pole. Hazel was standing on a wide plinth, talking to him from above.

I managed to bring my front wheel to a halt, squelching it in a fresh cow pat.

Scarlett looked over at me, and didn't speak. She shrugged her shoulders and exasperatedly flung out her palms, signalling her own bewilderment. The sight was *astonishing*. Robert stared up at me for the briefest moment before staring back at the small mast he was rubbing. A small sail was fastened to it, drooping and slightly unfurling in a light morning breeze.

He wasn't even looking, when he commented, 'Nice wheels.'

It felt weird. This wasn't how *any of this* was supposed to happen; not even slightly. Surveying the scene some more, I noticed he'd even erected a flag with some unusual symbols; like an ancient coat of arms. I waited, for more praise… an acknowledgment of arrival; affording him some more time to appreciate my presence, and importance, but none came.

Was that it?

Was that all he could say?

I'd had my arse soundly kicked for this guy, and he could only manage two words. Not even, "How are you?" But the truth was, I was mesmerized by what I beheld. I was hurting though, and couldn't resist sharply calling something that was more of a challenge than a question: 'Does Mr. Hislop know you've been building this?'

He ignored me.

My knuckles turned white on the handle bars as I used my right foot to carefully shoe the wet cow pat away.

'Did you hear me?' I sternly repeated.

Again, he ignored me.

I sensed spittle on my lips as anger began building. I was about to turn and ride home when Scarlett walked forward and placed her hand on my shoulder. 'Hey, Billy. Good to see you; how are you doing?'

This was a warm, *magical* smile.

Her curly red hair flowed down over her shoulders until she angled a finger, preening part of it to one side, delicately placing it behind a cute, Elven ear. Her eyes caught the light like sapphires and her freckles had slightly darkened in the sun, giving her an earthy, wholesome beauty. She'd completely forgotten our bickering just prior to the big fight and… left her hand firmly planted on my shoulder. It felt like a golden touch, channeling warmth through my chest.

'I'm fine.' I was melting.

She moved around to my left side, checking my face, paying… painstakingly precise attention to my scars. She looked wounded for me, as she softly touched several, tracing the lines.

'Does it hurt?'

'No.' I told the truth.

'I like your haircut.'

She'd noticed that too; a quick trip to the barbers after the cycle purchase. I'd forgotten it had even happened.

'Your mum rang last night and said you had a new bike. Is it a BMX Burner?'

She'd even identified the make!

Then she beamed enthusiastically. 'I really like it.'

This was all rather compensating. Of course, I was far too young to recognise being hit on. On an evening, admittedly, while lying in bed, I'd imagine scenarios of being with her. It wasn't love - not at all - but for some strange reason, I was a knight and she was the damsel; a damn intelligent one. Throughout the sequence, the knight never shed his armour, nor the damsel - her flowing garments. Real-life holding hands and kissing were *way* off the agenda in this screen-play; social suicide, for lads.

But, right now, in this moment, the urge…

What Scarlett did next, soothed my entire soul with a sudden, rich abundance. Leaning in to my ear she whispered, 'Ignore him. He's not saying anything much to us, either. We think he's losing his marbles.'

This statement alarmed me… but the mode of delivery, was exciting. I initiated further closeness.

'What do you mean?'

Scarlett didn't pull away as she explained his single sentence communications, and rare eye-contact. The moment he looked up at me on my bike - she said - was his most significant response.

She finished with, 'He's been working on this like a mad-man. When mum and I drop eggs, we've tried talking to him, but he's... elsewhere in his head.'

Turning my head a fraction, so my lips were slightly closer, I replied: 'What do you think we can do?'

'I don't know. He doesn't even want any butterfly buns!'

'Oh, he's definitely lost it.'

Scarlett laughed, and it's perfectly feasible, that right there, I subconsciously licked my lips for two good reasons. Scarlett withdrew enough, and feeling quite empowered by her, I turned and called to Robert: 'We may have lost that fight, but neither of us were wimps.'

Robert slowed his vertical sanding motion.

'You're rock hard, mate,' I said. 'If it was just Craig... you would have knocked him clean out.'

Unexpectedly, Rob started rubbing the wood faster, and I wondered if I'd said the wrong thing. The trauma I experienced that morning wouldn't compare to his - and that was quite something. Who knows if the gang caught up with him further down the track? But he appeared *less* wounded. In a moment of insight, I changed my approach. And in that instance, for once, I think I got it partly right.

'No one here blames you, Rob. No one here thinks you did *anything* bad.'

He twitched, or he flinched; one of the two. For a few more seconds, he continued focussing on his project. As far as I could see, there weren't any outward signs of a beating. There was no doubt in my mind that he would heal faster than me, regardless.

Then he abruptly spoke. 'Mr Hislop said I may as well do what I like here... because he's selling this land soon, anyway.'

My advisor, Scarlett, leaned in again. 'He's banned those bloody bullies from coming back.'

I nodded, a trickle of remorse coating my conscience as I processed Rob's words. This land *was* being sold. I was a bit lost as to what to say next.

'Sorry.'

He suddenly said it.

A stand-alone word, while still turning away, and staring at the river in a hopelessly lost and dejected way. This profound action only served to further buckle my voice box. Words wouldn't form in my head from this point on.

Thankfully, they could in Hazel's.

'Please don't feel bad, Rob; we're here for you. It's not your fault; it's your brother's. My mother said that some folks around here are narrow minded… and like to gossip because there's nowt better to do, but *everyone knows* you had no part in it. Not a sausage.'

Lost and forlorn, Robert gazed on, like an empty plastic bottle trapped at the bottom of a waterfall while the crushing torrent crashes over it. He muttered something like, 'Everybody hates *my* family.'

No one responded.

I didn't like what happened next. I never forgot it because of how macabre and detached it seemed. He started to smile, but it wasn't pleasant. He nodded too, but it wasn't aimed at any of us. His lips moved, and he spoke something directly to the beck. 'Uton we gamolian geowine.'

'See,' Scarlett confirmed. 'He's got a screw loose.'

I shivered, unable to accept this; not one bit. Carefully lowering my bike and stepping off, I marched down the bank and onto the jetty. I could see now why this river - this damned, cursed body of flowing filth - thought I was the enemy, and if it didn't know it already, I was about to stamp upon it my status. I ignored Hazel's gentle enquiry about my welfare as I bustled past her. And I began *repeatedly* pounding my foot on the floorboards to get my friend's attention, smacking it down with as much force as I could muster. This, unequivocally broke his stupor; his head snapping around to me; a devilish fire in his eye balls.

'Stop that!'

'Stop what? This?' I jumped and slammed both feet down again.

He stood.

He faced me.

'What?' I said, hammering at the sturdy boards with all my might. 'Is me stamping on your wood, making you angry?'

'Knobhead.' he snarled.

'Yeah, I'm a knobhead for defending you.' I slammed my leg down again. 'See this?' I pounded it as hard as I possibly could. 'That's *how hard* they stamped on my head!'

Immediately I ceased my assault and turned my cheek towards him. 'Can you see these?' I stabbed my finger into the side of my face. But he was already staring; giving me his undivided attention.

So lost.

'I… I didn't ask you to do that.' he said.

'What? Was I just going to stand there and let them beat you?'

He didn't reply; plagued with unrelenting anguish.

'That's what real mates do, don't they?' I shouted.

'I thought you'd never want to speak to me again,' came the faintest of anemic responses, 'I thought when you found out why… you'd regret it.'

'You didn't do anything wrong.'

'Sorry.'

He looked one breath away from vanishing altogether. Such was his pitiful posture, clearly losing weight, too; half the boy, he was a from a fortnight earlier.

'Have you been bringing food with you when you come here?' I said.

At this he paused, like he was considering lying, but in the end he shook his head; close to tears. And I just felt completely sorry for him. Turning to Hazel, I asked her if she could crack open her buns. I didn't want one. She reached into a new satchel and took out the ice-cream container.

'Here, eat as many as you want now, and take the rest home.'

144

Rob quietly thanked her as he pathetically grasped hold of the container.

'Ol' Bobby's been cooking me fish,' he said, before taking his first mouthful. 'Every day, he brings me some. I don't talk to him... so he leaves it in a newspaper - like fish and chips.'

Hazel turned and stared in the direction of the underpass. Now he was distracted, nourishing himself, I asked the smouldering question as I surveyed his handy work. 'Rob, w*hy* have you been building this?'

'I didn't... didn't really have... an awful lot else to do... or anywhere... to go...'

His voice tailed off.

As much as I loathed to admit anything remotely good could come from these waters, in a twisted and malevolent way, they were giving Robert Tipperton his only hope. This was terribly saddening. With weeks having passed, I once again hoped that whatever was in there had either departed, or wasn't there in the first place, and that the haulier's son was simply driving forward with a practical hobby. However, I'd just heard him mouth something sounding Olde English; clearly bound and tied to this location. Equally worrying were all these new materials, evidently sourced from the Tipperton's own yard. This could be a problem.

'It's really impressive,' I nodded, genuinely meaning it.

'Thanks.'

'Why have you two boats?'

'Oh, I made one.'

'You made it!'

'I know what you're thinking,' Rob quietly anticipated. 'And its *not* to sail you all to the end.'

'Where then?'

'I dunno - Newhaven, or somewhere.'

'Where exactly is that?'

'Far down south.'

'Can you get there by rivers?'

'It's on the River Ouse.'

'Won't that be dangerous?'

Rob shifted uncomfortably. 'Depends.'

This segment of questioning had not escaped the girls' attention, and they both piled in.

'How far away is it?'

There was no intention on my behalf to rat-out my friend but the boat he was sanding - had oars and it even had a sail.

'Rob, you can't seriously be thinking of sailing to the south coast along rivers - the Swale alone is dangerous.'

Little did I know back then, that you couldn't even *reach* Newhaven via any network of rivers up here. The currents would drag you through the Humber estuary and out into the freezing North Sea.

'I haven't decided,' he replied.

'Good. Well don't. Because its nuts.' Scarlett said.

'I'm only building something that reminds me of Granny's home, where she lives, y'know.'

We waited, and he obliged us with further explanations.

'It's nice down there. The sea air. The seagulls. It's got a nice harbour full of boats. My Gran and I would sit on a bench eating chips and watching the fishing trawlers come in and out. It was sunny… and peaceful.'

Memories flooded back to my time in South Wales, and I could smell his Newhaven salted chips as he spoke.

'I had no troubles there,' he continued. 'I knew before I left that bad things were happening to my family but nobody told me what. My Gran told me Mike was in a load of trouble, and I should be prepared. I didn't know how bad it was. I had no idea about the newspapers until Craig showed me. I ran away for a couple of nights. I don't want to be here anymore.'

I swallowed.

'Can't your mum drive you back down to your Gran's or something?'

This was a very astute observation from Hazel.

'No - the police have impounded the car and the trucks, because… Mike's been using them. Some might not even be legally ours.'

146

Three of us quizzically looked to one another, correctly surmising what impounded meant.

'We're under surveillance. We've been asked not to travel far while they continue their investigation; two of our employees are under suspicion for helping my brother.'

'That's awful!' exclaimed Hazel.

'Yeah, I don't want to be trapped at home with them. We get threatening phone calls, and letters. The yard feels like a dirty place, and this wood,' he waved at the whole of his construction, 'is what's left over from when dad dismantled a giant shed on our property, and bits of it are what Mr Hislop gave me, too.'

I hung my head, quietly ashamed of judging him.

'Rob, please don't think about sailing to Newhaven. Promise us.' Scarlett wasn't admonishing; more projecting her sustained concern.

'Well, I don't know how else to get down there.'

'A bus, or even a train from Northallerton,' Scarlett answered.

'I have no money.'

A strange aching enveloped my heart; I didn't want to lose a friend to… well, anywhere else, even if it made complete sense he found sanctuary from the hail of abuse. Needless to say, our tiny minds were hopelessly ill-equipped to suggest any other way out for Rob. This country seemed massive. My car journey to Wales went on forever. There's no way Rob would make it to the South Coast.

'I've extended the tree house so I can escape and sleep here on a night. My mum and dad know I'm doing this and they don't mind because they know I can look after myself. I've got sleeping bags in there and everything. You're all welcome to stay over one night. Scarlett, I know you said you'd be up for it.'

For a split second I actually entertained she'd display common sense, and dismiss it out right.

But of course, 'Oh, yes! That's… a *great* idea.' She did a little bounce on the spot. 'What about tonight?' she added.

I felt conflicted. Rob was all alone, and I was experiencing, hitherto unknown, levels of pity and sympathy. On the other-hand, 'While you have been here, have there been any other incidents?'

'What, like… hassle?'

'No, I mean, the ghosts.'

'No.'

'Are you sure?'

'Nothing. It's been really quiet. I think Ol' Bobby's scared them off. He still doesn't look well by the way.'

'I heard.'

'Hazel, are you up for staying?' Scarlett said.

'Not really. How many people can even fit in that… bridge thing?'

I looked up, studying the impressive structure that appeared more like a covered gantry. Hazel was rightly panicked at the prospect of sleeping directly above the river.

'Five, of course. It's a shame Ishaq's not here. How is he?'

We all shook our heads. Nobody knew.

'That's quite alright,' Scarlett affirmed her mate, 'Me, Billy and Rob will test it, and we'll let you know.'

And there it was: the clincher; the decision-maker. I sensed I was winning the battle for Scarlett. My mother would approve both of this, and my attention to Rob. My heart was now hammering at the thought of an overnighter, and I wasn't about to relinquish this visible charade of courage.

'What time shall we come?' I said.

Robert's shoulders perked; visibly grateful for physical company, and encouragement to his plans. 'Say six?'

'I'll go and ask my mum and dad; I know they'll be fine.'

'Mine too,' Scarlett agreed.

'Have you got anything here to cover my new BMX?' I deliberately drew attention to my forgotten "King-Machine."

'Yeah, I have sheets.'

'Cool.'

'Right, when I go back for lunch I'll ask.'

'Billy,' Scarlett suddenly interrupted, dancing straight up to me, pushing her face closer to my own. 'Can I have a go on your Burner please?'

I felt inexplicably conflicted. Would anyone ask for *your* pile of presents under the Christmas tree? But, her sapphire-eyed hypnosis far outmatched my defenses.

'Go on, then.' I replied, with a lump in my throat.

'Can I have a go after?' Rob said.

'And then me?' said Hazel.

In shock, I nodded. Allow one; allow all… or give away true motives.

As I let go of the handlebars, it felt an awful lot like allowing someone to use *your* fork, to eat their food with.

~ ~ ~

The rest of the morning, Rob had us sanding things, and discussions revolved around sleeping arrangements.

At lunch, I cycled home. Things were starting to feel a lot better. As I pulled up to our front door, to my surprise, Ishaq and his mother were standing directly outside.

'Ah, here he is,' Mum buoyantly proclaimed.

'Hello, Billy,' Mrs Khan beamed. 'That's a lovely bike you've got there.'

'Hello, mate,' Ishaq chirped - pleased to see me - but more instantly smitten by my wheels.

'Mum, can I have one?' he said.

Mrs Khan laughed, and it was slightly forced. I noted she didn't answer either, letting the note ring out. (No way she'd let her son do stunts.) As Ishaq waited for a reply, mum stepped in, saving the day.

'Mrs Khan wondered if you'd like to go over to theirs, for a sleepover later?'

'Ahh,' - very much an awkward moment - 'I'd love to, but I've come to ask you about one tonight with Robert, Scarlett, and maybe, Hazel.'

Ishaq looked doubly crestfallen, so I swiftly added, 'Ishaq's more than welcome to join us.' And then - in a rare second of genius - shrewdly followed with, 'We're camping by the river, and Mr Hislop and Ol' Bobby said they'd watch out for us all.'

'Oh,' Mrs Khan proclaimed, a little taken aback.

Even my mum was impressed.

Seizing the opportunity with both hands I flattered Ishaq in front of his mother: 'Ishaq always keeps us level-headed and rational by the river; we've missed him… and I know Rob hasn't got many friends… and everyone now knows he played no part in his families… their…'

My speech appeared to be powerfully persuasive - drenched in youthful exuberance - and sufficiently challenging to break Mrs Khan formula for her son's schedule.

'Oh,' she said again, trying to give herself time to think.

Thankfully, my mother jumped in with, 'That's quite a nice idea, isn't it, Mrs Khan? It's meant to be a lovely evening; there'll be stars out tonight. Did you say, Mr Hislop would be looking out for you all?'

My mother was sharp and insightful.

'Yes, and he's banned those ruffians too,' I added, 'because of their truly appalling behaviour. Mr Hislop trusts us because we're *always* responsible.'

I'd never used "ruffian" in a sentence before, but considering Mrs Khan's stature, it was a wholly appropriate choice. Moreover, Ishaq was pretty quick to the starting line: 'Oh, mum, that would be nice. I can take my telescope and show them all Andromeda.'

Overwhelmed, Mrs Khan instantly queried the river: 'What… you all want to go camping at the place… that scared you so much?'

'Ahh, Arubiyyah,' Mum addressed her by name, 'We'd always camp out there as kids. Back in the day, we'd always scare each other with ghost stories and all that nonsense around the campfire. It's a beautiful location. Not a safer place around.'

'And those other boys are completely banned?'

'Yes, they can't come anywhere near.' I said.

'If they do, they'll be *trespassing*, mum.' Ishaq added.

Mrs Khan looked at her son, weighing up her own personal concern against his lack of positive social interaction.

He whispered, *'Please*, mum.'

'Oh, right, okay,' Mrs Khan acknowledged. 'And you said the farmer would look out for you, didn't you, Billy?'

'Yes, definitely.'

Mum interjected again - clearly an expert at reading the room. 'Dennis Hislop. Stout fella. Upstanding member of the community if ever there was one; he's one of the school governors.'

'Oh, really… that's very good,' Mrs Khan cooed, warming, 'I know who you mean; he's a soft-spoken man, isn't he?'

'He's been helping young Robert Tipperton in his current family situation too,' mum added for good measure.

It was kind of true to be fair.

Mrs Khan liked this. 'That's nice to hear; that *poor* boy!'

She turned to Ishaq, 'Well, don't be getting nightmares again, that's all I'll say on the matter.' And then to mum, 'They grow up so fast; and we've been encouraging Ishaq to become more independent.'

Ishaq looked like he'd just scored the winning goal at the World cup.

'What time will you be camping?' Mrs Khan said.

'Meeting at six.'

'Are you okay with this time, Ishaq?'

She was giving her son one more chance to reconsider.

His response made me inwardly chuckle, 'I'm bringing armour.'

Bingo.

As they walked away together, back up to the top of the village, I heard Ishaq ask his mum for a BMX again.

'Absolutely not.'

Then my mum made me peanut butter sandwiches inside, and I thanked her for her involvement. She gave me a wry smile.

151

'Worked like a charm, didn't it?'

At ten-past-six, me and Ishaq cycled past the spot where I'd battled the yobbish hyenas; our jubilant conversation calming a fraction as we remembered. My friend clunked and clicked as he tried riding his racer in his plastic armour.

He looked ridiculous.

I looked cool.

He confessed that an uncle - high up in the police - had revealed to his parents that the youngest Tipperton boy was periodically running away from home, and screamed when they tried taking him back. This had melted their hearts. The Khan's were fair people. Along with this, Ishaq had gathered a wealth of new information. No stone unturned as it happened: the harrying of the north; Olde English; ghosts; and people who had mysteriously appeared and disappeared. He chatted ten-to-the-dozen and gave his conclusions for each. It was mostly... very interesting; he'd be an effective public speaker one day. Then, he deciphered the entire recording he'd taken by the river.

'They're describing the horrific smell of their cattle being burned... and then weeks later, they're forced to eat their dead siblings.'

'That's sick. Why did he do it?'

'The people of the North weren't obedient, so he crushed them.'

'Even the kids?'

'Yeah.'

'But, kids don't rebel, do they? They can't do anything like that.'

This utterly disturbed me.

'It was his way, or the highway.'

'But, why the animals?'

'Killed the lot, so they'd all starve to death. Burned all these fields we see, which still don't grow crops well. In the Domesday book, it said most places around here were uninhabitable twenty years on. William ordered the harrying in the winter, so there was no hope of survival.'

I thought about this some more. Why was William always painted as an important figure in lessons, when his soldiers were maniacs?

'So, how did *they* all come to be in the river?' I knew the answer, but was morbidly curious for Ishaq's confirmation.

'There's a phrase I hear, over and over again; it's quite faint. I'm sure it means "drowned". But the Latin voices, I don't have a clue how they fit in.'

'Did they not learn it in the Abbeys?'

'No, they came later.'

'Really?'

'Yes. The closest around here - and they're not that close - were built long after the harrying.'

'What about Jervaulx abbey?'

'Established after 1145. 8 miles away. Tricky to get to on foot from here.'

I arched my head towards him. 'So, what do you reckon?'

'Dunno. They keep calling for mercy…' Ishaq dropped his head. 'Whoever they're screaming at doesn't listen: "Obsecro ut miserere mei" is what they say: *please have mercy on me.*'

This chilled me.

'I wonder why they don't go through to the afterlife.'

'I think they're all trapped.'

Ol' Bobby himself had warned us there was *something else* lingering in there.

Passing the first barn, we turned onto the grass. The treads on my yellow tyres were beginning to stain green, and I'd already given up cleaning them. In a short while, we approached the others at our rendezvous point. I was both nervous and excited… and super pleased to see Hazel had changed her mind and joined us. It was my first time camping, and I wouldn't have to worry about a cool evening - it was already a sweltering day. Ishaq's appearance was a welcome surprise to them all, and they spent a few moments fussing over him as he puffed his armour-clad chest out.

'Guess what?'

Scarlett bounced towards us.

'Hazel and I have brought a *massive* feast… and later on, we're going to have a big game of hide-and-seek.'

'What, *here?*' I was appalled. 'Scarlett, *remember what they told you?*'

She leaned in again, 'Not by the river, yer greyt nana. We'll use those barns over there.' Scarlett couldn't help herself; when she was excited, she was excited.

'Won't Mr Hislop mind? He doesn't even know we're staying here tonight.'

'What!' Ishaq said.

I ignored him. 'What about the animals? We'll disturb them.'

'There are only a few cows and sheep left. My dad said he's sold nearly all his beast.' She tapped a rucksack she was holding. 'I've brought five torches; one each.'

My mind wrestled with this - it wasn't the greatest of ideas - but at least it wasn't by the river.

'What if Mr Hislop sees us?' I said.

'He'll be asleep by ten.'

'Ten! How do you know?'

Her eyes twinkled with mischief.

'He's a farmer! My dad's a farmer, and Hazel's. Early to bed, early to rise, and all that stuff.'

~ ~ ~

The August heat *really* took hold of Robert's bridge extension.

Mr Hislop was undoubtedly aware of his constructions. (I'd overheard the words 'Hislop', 'farm' and 'sale' in our kitchen), and the farmer clearly thought to heck with it; the lad can do as he pleases. Part of me was glad if he sold it. But looking at the effort Rob had ploughed in, I wondered

154

what *he'd* do next. His gantry was like a passageway with a small square chamber at the end. Half of the original tree house had been dismantled to connect this together. There was enough space for two people to climb in and shuffle along. The wood was warm, and we all lasted fifteen minutes in our sleeping bags before roasting like sausage rolls.

The supplied feast we ate inside was fantastic.

Truly scrumptious.

All the while, however, I was acutely aware we were only ten feet above the water and my thoughts periodically drifted back to Ol' Bobby and the singing Sirens. Nobody was saying anything about the voices; no one admitting to their paranoia, nor unease. I kept reminding myself I doing a good duty; primarily here for Robert. But I could all but guarantee most of us were hearing faint songs on the delicate breeze. Extremely faint, barely audible, but definitely, *definitely* there.

Hazel was aware; continually shifting uncomfortably on the spot.

Robert, on the other hand, was the happiest I'd seen him in a while. Very chatty. Ishaq was talking non-stop and loving his own ideas far too much to pay any attention. He refused to take off his plastic armour and pseudo-chain mail. He wanted to appear brave, and ready for action - to atone for his lack of involvement in the scrap. Scarlett - as always - consumed the lion's share of the conversation, along with Ishaq.

It was getting stuffier and stuffier. The thought of breaking away from the beck, and this lofty cabin, and playing hide-and-seek outside was steadily becoming *appealing*. From this precarious perch (and despite the masterful supports Rob had planted into the river) I felt like I was flying a hang-glider over a simmering volcano. I was feeling anxious.

It wasn't long before the equally reticent Hazel was begging for the game to begin.

At around half past ten, we trundled along the bank in the direction of the farmhouse.

Cool air was beginning to descend, and stars pricked the heavens above. It was a truly beautiful evening. Ishaq hadn't brought his telescope - banned from bringing an expensive piece of kit - so he had brought a pair of high-powered binoculars instead. There was something inherently forbidden about our traipse along the grass towards the farm at this time of evening. The beck was to our right, and in places I could swear it was bubbling. I passed it off as something to do with currents. On cue, the upstairs light in the farm went off.

'Told you so,' Scarlett said.

'I wonder what farmer's dream about?' Robert randomly enquired.

'Meat.'

'*Meat?*'

Ishaq's statement bamboozled us all.

'Why meat?' Hazel asked, unable to suppress her smile.

'Well,' Ishaq started - surprised agreement wasn't forthcoming - 'they're surrounded by cows, pigs, chickens and sheep - so it makes sense.'

'Oh my goodness.' Scarlett shook her head. 'Me and Hazel are farm lasses and *we don't dream of meat*! What on *earth* do you dream about?'

'Well, not earth.'

'What then?'

'Space.'

'So are *you* surrounded by space?'

Ishaq thought about it a split second, before throwing his armoured gloves out to the starry night. '*Yes! I am right now!*'

Maybe it was Scarlett's slack-jawed amazement in that moment; or her first ever stunning defeat to illogical logic. Maybe it was Ishaq's ludicrous attire, or his suddenly presented get-out-of-jail card. Whichever... we fell, and rolled around the grass laughing, for a good minute. Then we purposefully shushed each other, but in a joking manner, wiping our eyes of tears, while staring in the direction of the barns all the while. Such a good memory. It was decades before an evening came where I could belly-laugh like this again.

'Are the batteries in these torches old?' I finally said, calming a little.

'Brand new. Long-life,' Hazel replied.

We were approaching the periphery of the barn buildings; it becoming quickly apparent there was a distinct lack of lowing cattle, and whinnying horses. No clucking chickens, nor bleating sheep either. Nearly all had been removed from the farm. This star-spun evening was solemnly quiet too, like a weaned child in the deepest depths of peaceful sleep. I thought of the millions surrendering their thoughts to the night as they slumbered, their cares gently drifting into the sparkly blanket above. Only the distant noise of solitary drivers - making final journeys home - slightly encroached on this tranquility.

The barn area was dark and eerie, though.

I looked at the shadowy structures, flinching when an over-zealous, Scarlett boomed: 'We need to decide on teams.'

'Shh.'

'And only use the torches, if you need them,' she added.

'What if Mr Hislop comes out?' Hazel said.

'Leg it.' Scarlett replied.

I didn't mind who I was paired with… so long as I was paired; the odd number was going to be awkward. Of course, I wasn't going to brazenly admit this.

'I think it's only fair we do a two and a three, and then swap around half way through,' Hazel suggested.

Problem solved.

For the first round, it was me, Rob and Hazel hiding, and Scarlett and Ishaq finding.

The night sky was providing us a good dose of guiding light, and we managed to ascend a ladder to a mezzanine floor in the largest wooden barn, hiding behind some hay bales. Gaps in the vertical slats meant we could peer out and see both Scarlett and Ishaq quietly creeping around. We nearly made ourselves bad with laughter as we peeked, tracing the oddity of their search pattern from our lofty position. The two most naturally confident members of our gang, were quite the strangest match up.

Scarlett pranced on her tip-toes like some pale, silent vampire, while the robust knight bundled along beside her with his visor down - constantly tripping over every tuft of grass - fully illuminated by the moon. Both Hazel and I found it nearly impossible to conceal our laughter, and I watched her tear-up with joy, wiping her eyes and cheeks; we just could not stay quiet. As they both entered the barn, all three of us heard the muffled but serious voice of Ishaq declare: 'Shh, I will now employ logic to find them.'

And that was it; all three of us splitting our sides, surrendering our position.

Climbing down the ladder, we discussed the irony that humour *beat* logic in selling us out, and we spent several minutes describing their bizarre search technique back to them. This cracked them up too, and Scarlett needed to go and pee. That first round was such a laugh; I've never forgotten it. The teams seemed to work, so we decided on keeping them from that point forwards.

Our turn to seek. And they were both excellent at hiding. One hundred percent. At one point, the three of us agreed we'd split up - but in roughly the same area - searching parts of the farm yard in quadrants. Hazel eventually found them both with a flash of the torch, under the wheels of a large tractor. It had taken a good ten minutes to discover them. More rounds ensued. It was the best fun. And fun unanimously beat fear into distant non-existence. So, with our confidence brimming, we agreed our team would hide separately, but in a similar area.

This worked too.

It was getting closer to midnight when I clicked the side of my digital wrist watch, lighting up the screen. This was maybe the seventh or eighth round we'd played. All three of us were hiding behind three separate rectangular wooden supports, set far back in one of the outbuildings. Obscured by their thick frames, we could look at each other - four or five metres apart - and whisper when we heard Scarlett and Ishaq approaching. This was a large building, open at the front, containing tractors, carts and all kinds of discarded paraphernalia. We were confident these would be distracting and checked first by the opposition, when they entered.

Although very dark in here, our eyes were now adjusting. Flurries of moonlight lit up the dry earth outside the barn, while the shadows within concealed us. This allowed us a chance to fleetingly glance around, before ducking back behind the columns. Ishaq and Scarlett had economised their search - splitting up themselves - and my armour-clad pal was now measuring the time it was taking to find us. They'd already gained eight and half minutes on us, that we had to claw back somehow. It didn't help that we couldn't stop laughing, and I suspected this was precisely what Robert needed right now. He was enjoying himself - and even in this moment - enthusiastically whispering at Hazel who was hiding behind the central support.

After a couple of minutes, we heard distant voices and shushed each other, before breaking into more (barely suppressed) chuckling. We waited. Everything was quiet again. This was a sure sign they'd split up. And, for once, the three of us managed to maintain both decorum and silence. I listened with all my might for a sign of shuffling either side of this outbuilding. Nothing. Maybe two minutes had passed, possibly less. Then, somebody started tapping on the corrugated exterior panel to my left, on the outside. I flashed a look in the direction of my friends who were sure to have heard it too. Heavily camouflaged by darkness, I raised my forefinger to my mouth, hoping they could see my warning.

I whispered, 'They're here.'

The tapping moved along the side panel. Slowly, purposefully, until it reached the very end, and then stopped. This was a ruse. Disconcerting. A clever ploy, undoubtedly employed by Ishaq to elicit more uncontrollable laughter; a give-away to our whereabouts that he'd instantly home in on. The sight of him jumping out at the front in his over-sized armour would be too much to take. But something about it, was making the hairs on my neck stand. I gritted my teeth and clung tightly to the support; concentrating on my composure. Whichever of the pair it was, they were about to make themselves visible in the large open space. The tapping had finished right at the end, and they were literally inches away.

I waited.

Nothing.

A few more seconds passed, and still no one. (Did they turn left at the end instead?) More seconds deteriorated in the blackness. This was a sharply shrewd move on their behalf; one of the few locations that hadn't been hidden in, and a natural, next point of investigation. Still, nothing stirred. Then the tapping began again. And, in the darkness, I flinched. It was back at exactly the same position it started, directly to my left. Somebody was moving along the old iron wall periodically prodding it every half a metre or so. Louder, this time. The systematic tap, increasing in volume the further it travelled, now pounding and shaking the sides.

Once again it reached the end and stopped.

And no one appeared.

I considered the foolishness of the tactic; the level of noise *bound* to wake Mr Hislop. Game over. Beck over. What *were they thinking?* With my heart thudding in my head, and I swivelled to catch the remotest sight of Hazel and Robert, unable to see either. It felt crazy because I knew they were there - *right there* - no more than ten or twelve feet away, but my rational mind was saturating with fear.

Am I... alone in here?

I wanted to break cover, and I was about to, suddenly overwhelmed and trapped in the dark, when Ishaq and Scarlett appeared. Swallowing hard with relief, I shuffled back behind my column. Clever... so, *so* clever. My fears released, I smiled in the inky black. Ishaq was looking at his wrist - between the gauntlet - checking the time.

'We have four minutes and thirteen seconds to find them.'

'Was it coming from this one, or the next one along?' Scarlett asked.

'I'm not sure.'

'You go check the next one, Ish,' Scarlett patted him on his grey shoulder pad.

'Sure.'

Ishaq shuffled along awkwardly, pushing down his visor. How and why he was maintaining this costume was beyond me. Normally, the simplest sight of Ishaq would cause one of us to break rank, and guffaw - but, not this time - knowing full well we were thinking exactly the same thing at the same time. Scarlett lit her torch, as Ishaq disappeared from view. She shone it at the front of the outbuilding lighting up rusted tillers and cultivators that hadn't been used in decades. Then she motioned to the side - where I was hiding - the beam catching a long plank of wood - set on a diagonal. Slowly she investigated this implement as the rays drew closer and closer to my pillar. I watched as she brought her torch within two feet of my position, now focussing upon an exceedingly worn rope, set high above the dirty ground. It was attached through a hole and knotted at the top; cobwebs covering its entirety. Scarlett clearly caught sight of these and immediately pulled the torch back along.

'Huh. A see-saw.' she said.

And she was right; that's what I thought it was, too. There was a fulcrum in the middle of the plank, for tipping up and down. Beneath this, two rollers enabled the whole contraption to be moved from place to place. Scarlett illuminated her way diagonally down - to the bottom end - close to the spot where I last heard the knocking. There she intensified the light on the most bizarre of attachments. An old wooden chair - fixed to the end.

I heard her mutter. 'Weird. How does that even work?'

An unusual attempt to alter a popular playground ride; to its detriment. Pretty useless in fact; no wonder it had been left here in the barn to rot.

161

'Come out, come out… where ever you are…' Scarlett said, adding, 'I'm not coming into that creepy *flipping* building.'

The torch light resumed its surveillance, first brightly registering the vanguard supports at the front of the shed as she let it ascend up to the ceiling, checking for other lofts and mezzanine floors. Scarlett's presence was a welcome sight indeed, and I studied her in the dark. Certainly the most serious I'd ever seen her, as she carefully and slowly inspected the fringes and corners of this huge space.

'Not coming in with those…' she paused, deliberately. '*Enormous spiders* in there.'

She waited a couple of seconds for a response.

'Enormous!' she repeated. 'Absolutely enormous.'

Shining the torch further back, the beam hit the stone wall behind us, and for the first time I could make out the silhouettes of my two friends. I was reassured (even though, rationally, I knew they were *always* here). The light then shone against my post and my heart beat faster. Still standing outside the barn, she moved it away, towards the column where Robert was hiding before moving to Hazel's in the centre. And straight passed that one, too. Onto mine again, illuminating either side, and I looked down, checking if I'd left my foot exposed.

I hadn't, and the beam moved away.

The realisation suddenly hit; we were on the verge of remaining *undiscovered*. We were about to win. Four minutes, and thirteen seconds had been seriously depleted, and I fought the urge to check my own watch. Then, out-of-the blue, Scarlett declared, 'We *heard* you in there.' she paused, before adding, 'Or was it in the next *onnneeee* along?'

The light continued to sway within our hide-out, but she wasn't coming in.

'*Bang, bang, bang,*' she said, before clicking out her torch light. 'We heard you…'

In the black, I puzzled over this. It made no sense. She continued staring inside without the beam for assistance. Something was off.

'Must have come from the next one.' I heard her say; the barn an echo-chamber.

I peered out from around the post and watched her - now staring in the direction Ishaq had headed - placing the torch back in her pocket; visibly shivering in the warm night. Scarlett shouldn't have been releasing a stream of cold breath from her mouth, not in these temperatures. I watched the tiny cloud steadily rising into the sky. And here, the other visual discrepancy firmly gripped tight; the thing I'd blocked out the second they appeared. Such was my relief, I'd instantly reconciled the anomaly. Now, I could not.

Scarlett and Ishaq had appeared from the right side, opposite the noise.

The tapping was to my left.

Above, the silvery moon glow cast its white-wash sheen over clumps of earth and sporadic patches of grass, where she now stood - like an angel - a frown etching her face. Akin to a nursery game of musical statues, Scarlett froze. One elbow jutting out, hand still clasped on her pocket, like she'd forgotten the purpose of what she was rummaging for. Facing the barn, her head thrown at ninety degrees, staring away from us. She didn't budge an inch. Only her eyes were blinking, rapidly blinking. This lasted several seconds. Her jaw then suddenly sagged, as she mouthed something, like: 'Wha-'

With the same intensity in her furrowed brow, she continued focussing on something, out-of-sight; her eyes now wider, in shocked disbelief. My mind reeled. Was this the final cunning ruse to flush us out; fear causing us to cave? Where was she looking? At the river? No noisy Ishaq, either. No clattering around in his plastic. I could feel myself shifting behind my column, wishing Hazel would capitulate first, surrendering our whereabouts.

But, then Scarlett was gone.

Utterly transfixed, she edged slowly and deliberately out of view. Time froze, time moved fast. Was someone going

163

to speak, and comment? In a frenzied whisper, Hazel finally did.

'Billy, was that *you* banging on the side?'

'No.'

Seconds of silence ensued before she spoke again, 'But, they both came in from the right side.'

'I know.'

Her words hung in the darkness as a savage chill started coating my spine.

'C'mon, mate. That had to be you.' Rob sounded annoyed, behind her.

'*It wasn't.*'

'Stop messing. They couldn't have got round that quickly,' he insisted, almost hissing, 'There's only two of them.'

A third player.

Making the sides even.

I slowly edged away from the side panel, Hazel shuffling into view on my right, and striding towards the front of the barn. 'Let's get out of here.'

Rob and I appeared at the same time, him, resolutely glaring. 'You nearly gave us away, mate. Did you want us to lose?'

'It… *wasn't*… me…'

'*Billy.*'

'Hazel, I promise you. It wasn't me. I wouldn't sca-'

My tone was panicking Hazel, now standing at the open front… except it wasn't. She was *alerting* me - staring out past the last farm buildings on the fringes - and back down the slope towards the beck. We joined her, and from our loftier position, the slight descent of the track enabled a view of everything. Everything, including Ishaq. Standing in the river. Scarlett, stood behind him on the bank. Motionless, staring into deeper waters, cascading around the mail of his armour-clad waist.

I stopped dead.

The further the river went, the more dangerous. Closer to the Swale. We *knew* never to go more than thirty feet east of the cattle bridge, but here we were, right back at the far end of Hislop's farm. And here was the smallest member of our contingent... trying to grab something in the river.

'Wh-what is h-he?' Hazel said, voice shaking.

Rob looked appalled.

And we could see Scarlett muttering something above him; her words indistinguishable. Out of all us, Ishaq would be the last to lose his mind... but he was trying to pull something out from below the surface - his chest submerging, losing his footing - pushing it down, as if to gain traction, and then yanking it up with all his strength. Tiny arms, and legs. Strong currents. On the verge of being swept away.

The three of us bolted.

Headlong desperation... past the remaining outbuildings, many just crumbling red brick and completely roofless.

'*Scarlett!*' Hazel shouted.

She didn't hear, concerning herself with rigid communications. We closed in, skipping past more rusted, weed-ridden farming implements, now being swallowed by grass and ground, laying haphazardly everywhere. And then, to our right, the cow appeared. From nowhere. On the stony track... between us and our friends. Every inch of it ablaze, orange flames licking its brown fur.

My heart clamoured to exit my throat... as we all fell back, cowering.

It hollered in agony; the most deathly of blood-curdling screams, lurching unsteadily, fire rising and crackling; immersed in a wall of bluish, orange. Hands grabbed at my jacket, as we clung to each other. I couldn't fathom this; *couldn't comprehend this*.

Then, the cow bolted along the bank behind Scarlett, writhing in agony, twisting in every direction; it's seared, empty eye sockets, incapable of setting a horrific flight path. Hazel whimpered, pushing her face into my chest. I was speechless. The cow launched itself along the remainder of the bank until its blazing torch of a torso was out of sight - its final cries piercing the dead of night.

'*What's happening?*' Rob gasped.

My mind scrambled for reason.

Beyond, on the bank, Scarlett remained stationary… staring down, into the water. She hadn't even noticed; her concentration undiminished, hypnotically watching Ishaq's strange, repetitive actions.

'What's going on?' I croaked back.

'Scarlett.' Hazel called, through dry vocal chords.

As we shakily stepped closer, I cleared my throat, attempting to snap her out. 'Scarlett!'

I was barely any louder, hugging Hazel just as tight as she was me. Rob's eyes were wide; lost in the vault of unspeakable sights, as I reached Scarlett first… gently touching her shoulder, trying to decipher her speech. I wanted our first ever *proper, meaningful* touch to be warm and wholesome, not icy; not this.

'Scarl-' I said.

Then Ishaq appeared.

On our left.

Springing out from between two crumbling outbuildings. 'Gotcha!'

He punched the sky with both his plastic gauntlets, checking his watch, and whooping. 'Seven seconds! Seven seconds! *We win!*'

The terror I felt in that moment, to this day, remains… unrivalled. I stared at Ishaq; the Ishaq… on land. Hazel twisted her head out from my chest her eyes shot-through with terror. This *was* Ishaq. Standing here, right here.

But he wasn't.

Ishaq was in the river.

The boy next to us immediately stopped talking, pulling his visor up. 'What's up with you lot?'

And we all twisted back towards the beck, and the curly redhead - now turned - staring at us all. Her colourless expression. Her vacant morbidity. The listless terror sealed in her eyes.

'Steorfan. Sweltan. Ãdrincan.'

Over and over, she repeated these words. In an accent not her own. A voice *not* her own. And behind, the knight viciously bobbing up and down in the river, wasn't pulling anything out of the river. He was pushing something in. A child. Deeper. Under. Over and over again.

'Steorfan. Sweltan. Ãdrincan.'

His armour was different to Ishaq's, obscured by the night. I thought I was so brave when I jumped in to defend Rob. I think I'd do it again. Pathways of physical bravery were a definite possibility. Not this. I couldn't *move* to help Scarlett. (Learning in later years, she'd mouthed: dying, drowning, burning.)

'*Sccarlettt!!*' Hazel screamed.

The knight pulled himself upright from the river to look intently at us. His chain mail covered his entire torso and arms, down to the waist. Blood dripped down his hands, splattering the water.

He said, 'You found me.'

From behind I could see Scarlett start to shake; her whole body convulsing.

Then, lights illuminated the back of my head, and the earth started to shake. So much screaming. And now… the sound of a giant bear, creeping behind us, awoken from hibernation… because they existed back then, in *that* time. Charging closer, clearing its wind-pipe, expanding its hollow stomach, in a steady predatory rhythm; two massive eyes honing in on its prey. A door clattered above us. Mechanical. Man-made. The stomach stopped growling, and brakes screeched.

'What the bloody 'ell?' And louder. 'What the *bloody 'ell*… are *you lot* doing here?'

The large man is wearing overalls… and he's irate, leaning out from above on an angle. The tractor engine chugs. Two headlamps blaze. No bear.

Clambering to our feet I remembered piling towards the bewildered farmer. Our salvation.

'What the *hell* is happening!'

He turned off the ignition, dimming the lights slightly.

'In the river,' somebody wailed, pointing. '*In the river!*'

Mr Hislop paused, rubbing his eyes. Not too long before this, he'd been fast asleep.

'Well, yer all keep comin' down t'bloody water's don't yer? Haven' yer learned a bloody thing?'

Scarlett joined us, silently shaking; drained of blood, and robbed of soul. I looked over her shoulder, in massive trepidation - actually blinking, expecting - but the beck was silent in the moonlight.

No murderer in the shallow waters. Nobody at all.

'Right, I've just about had enough of this.'

'One of your cows,' Hazel cried, stuttering, 'It's... it's *on fire.*'

The stocky man jolted, rubbing his stubbly chin, pondering her.

'No, Lovey. No, it isn't.'

Hazel pointed back to the river, tears stinging her eyes. 'It's shrieking. It's in... *pain.*'

Mr Hislop sighed, drumming the glass panel at the top of the door with his thick fingers, studying her. Everything was deathly quiet now. Nothing stirred. Occasionally, somewhere far back up the farm, cattle lowed, and in the twinkle of the silvery night, the farmer scanned the river ahead of him, blowing out his cheeks. 'Cow's on fire, eh?'

'Y-yes,' Hazel sobbed.

'Can yer hear them beast in the distance? Next farm along. No cows here.'

He said nothing else, expertly hoisting himself off the tractor and standing with his hands on his overalled hips taking in the ambiance of the night, giving us terrified children time to settle. Many of us were breathing heavily, and he analysed each of us in turn, but it was hard to tell if this was in pity. A strong smell of manure emanated from the large front tyre. I never liked this smell, but it reassured me earth was *real again.*

He never broke his gaze.

Then he said. 'None of it wer real... but when I was your age, I thought it wor.'

His broad, balanced tone was giving us a focal point; calming. The stocky farmer turned his attention to Scarlett.

'Now, lass. If yer got sense, yer don't ever speak to them again. *Got that?*'

Scarlett nodded.

'Some bad uns in there. They'll come visit yer at night... if yer not careful.'

My extremely pale friend swallowed hard. The Farmer's expression was immutable. Yorkshire stoicism. He'd rinse Las Vegas with a disposition like this. He took a final look around, especially at the crumbling bricks on the two oldest outhouses.

'I don't want anymore midnight shenanigans. Yer know this farm's been sold. I'll be gone in days.'

'What? Definitely, *definitely?*' Hazel looked crushed.

As did Rob. '*What?*'

Mr Hislop stooped into us all. 'I need me sleep. Pack up, and go home.'

To be fair to him, his kindness extended even further that grim evening. Still registering our unease, he let us hitch a ride in the cart on the back of his tractor towards the tree house and the jetty. As we hastily gathered our belongings (and me my new bike) we were grateful for his watchful eye. He stood on the bank, at well over six feet, a hulking mass of a stocky man. This welly-wearing warrior wasn't in the least bit perturbed by spirits in the beck, but he was mightily impressed by Rob's handy-work.

'I never did. T'awd architect, aren't yer lad?'

Then we confessed everything. Staying in the tree-house. The overnighter. Hide-and-seek. Lying to parents... and we *begged* him for the use of his tiled, kitchen floor. He shook his head. 'You went an' told yer folks, I *gave* you permission?'

But ten minutes later - either his good nature, or some other thought-process - saw us all safely back in his cooling kitchen. He generously stoked the embers of the fire, adding a few more sticks, and a couple more logs.

169

'When it's out, it's out. Don't be pestering me for more.'

We huddled close, laying out sleeping bags, and thanking him incessantly.

'Right you are. Now calm the sens.'

He turned and walked upstairs.

Nobody (and I mean no one in our party) talked at all about what we'd seen after he departed. Surely, like me, we all stared at the lingering flames for only the briefest moments. Instead of the reassuring crackle and homeliness a hearth would normally create, one by one, *all* shuffled their sleeping bags over in the opposite direction. Facing the door. Mr Hislop had a sturdy one. I'd seen him lock it. I prayed it was strong enough to keep *everything* on the other side.

As we finally drifted off, I thought I heard Scarlett weeping.

Years later, I learned it was Rob.

Chapter 9

The Removal

On Tuesday 28th August, I was suffering with a severe bout of the doldrums because I knew this time next week, I'd be back in school. But at least school was a safe, contained environment with structure, *daylight*, and only a half an hour playtime.

I hadn't seen my mates since the mad morning scramble away from the farm kitchen. That was last week. The death knell had sounded. None of us would return. No need for my escape plan on the 29th. So, all I'd really done was practise stunts on a cul-de-sac around from the corner of our house. It was full of bungalows where mostly retired people lived.

Great bike. Wrong audience.

The phone rang early that morning.

'Oh, oh, right? How sad? End of an era. I'll give Mrs Khan a call. Thank you.'

The receiver clicked back in its holder, and then a new number was dialled. I listened intently in the lounge to mum's side of exchanges.

'Yes. It's exchanged.'

'Private sale.'

'Last day's tomorrow.'

'Don't know what that lad of Tipperton's going to do.'

'Yeah, apparently, he's still been going.'

I spread my comic out over my lap. He's been going... *where*? Surely, *surely* not! Mum knew I'd been undisputedly spooked by something significant, but I hadn't cracked. No reveal. No point. I didn't want to remember an iota of the event. *They might follow me home.*

Then I heard her say over the receiver, 'Mrs Wilmott says there's a big crowd of kids gathering, seeing Mr Hislop off. Her Scarlett and that young lass of Pickford's, are already there.'

There was a brief pause, before she piped up again. 'Oh, you've sent Ishaq down with a thank-you card. That's nice.'

I leapt off the chair and shouted 'Going out' as I passed her in the hallway. Daytime and big crowds put ghosts off, right?

As I rode down the final stretch of farm track, my sadness was compounded by the sight of two large removal lorries. It was over. And it felt strange, and positively detached, like it was a lie; and this was a film set, with actors pretending something was happening, when it wasn't. Although in reality, we hardly knew Mr Hislop, he'd massively impacted our lives both directly and indirectly. Whether the rumours were true (about a pressured sale), he didn't seem unduly bothered on the fleeting occasions I'd seen him. From tomorrow, two hundred plus acres transferred from one farmer to another, and there was chatter around the village of guard dogs and electric fences. A grimacing Scarlett had already made it clear Grobatard hated people and *despised* trespassers. He was an introverted, unusual man who kept himself to himself. I wondered where he acquired such wealth, power, and conceit.

The yellow wheels on my BMX still bore great treads, but they were caked in dry earth.

Drawing closer to the barn yard, I saw the massive mob of kids on their bikes ahead. Undoubtedly, Mr Hislop's exit had drawn nostalgic juveniles with half-hearted claims to 'good times'. My heart started to race, but this time I quickly became aware of its effects. I wasn't scared; I was justified. Part of me - I confess - felt a little thrilled. No one dare lay a finger on me; not when I was riding a BMX. I eye-balled as many children as I could, who stopped and stared; even the newbies *knew* who I was. Particularly, I didn't break my gaze from either Craig or Dove. Craig smirked. Dove didn't. They had a nerve being here.

I found myself whistling, and purposefully slowing down, spinning my handlebars three-sixty several times before doing a couple of bunny hops. Dove was too fat to even do a wheelie; my actions speaking louder than his nerves. Some of the smaller, unsuspecting kids started talking excitedly about this skill.

Job done.

Whistling *The Great Escape* (without knowing its title), I veered left at the first barn onto the grass. That felt good. *They* had *no idea* what real fear was. As soon as they were out of sight the *real* dread crept in.

Scarlett, Hazel, Rob and Ishaq were all sitting by the bank as I approached the cattle bridge.

'Morning.'

They raised an acknowledgment, but immediately resumed an intense discussion.

'He's totally lost it.'

'I'm telling you, he's at death's door.'

'Kept saying, *I'm sorry, I'm so sorry*, over and over.'

'But he wasn't even looking at us.'

'I think we should tell someone.'

Placing my forearms on the soft yellow padding of my handlebars, I leaned forward and listened. Scarlett took the courtesy of filling me in.

'Ol' Bobby,' she said, pointing her forefinger at the side of her head and twirling it. 'Totally lost it. Gone completely gaga.'

Ishaq jumped in. 'I got here early with a card. Rob was here. And Ol' Bobby was pacing back and forth along the bank like a mad man. It was like he was talking to us... but not.'

'Probably talking to the river,' Robert calmly added.

My eyes shifted westward towards the underpass.

'Is he in there?'

'We think so,' Hazel said.

The other's fiercely nodded.

'Do you think he's only just found out this land's sold? I heard mum say on the phone it was a private sale.'

It was like watching collective brainpower being simultaneously charged.

'That must be it.' Scarlett said. 'He knows he can't come back here. Grobatard uses guard dogs.'

I finished. 'Ol' Bobby loves *this* part of the river. It's been so special to him.'

Leaning forward a little, I savoured the moment of being the astute genius, whilst considering the credibility of my own observations. I kind of guessed at this, but the others had embraced this as fact. Regardless, I was both sorry and shocked at this news, but I was probably right. He could freely come here for years, and years without a care in the world. Maybe the rumours about Grobatard were true; maybe this was all about to end.

Centreing my attention on Robert, I asked: 'What if wants to take this all down?'

'I'll ask him. Beg him if I have to. I'll work his land for free in exchange.'

'Really?'

We were all stunned. Robert shrugged. I looked at the beck. His boat now had a mast and a sail. If William Grobatard did only the briefest recce around his new land, there was a small chance he might be so incredibly impressed that he would keep the port and tree house intact. If he had kids or grandkids himself, you would want to do that, right? I immediately shared these thoughts with the gang.

'Billy might be right,' Scarlett excitedly agreed. 'Introduce yourself, show him this, and ask him if he wants any carpentry jobs… for free.'

Robert slowly nodded with a slight sparkle in his eyes.

'We can give you lots of vege to live one,' Hazel said. 'And, I'm learning to bake.'

Scarlett nodded. 'Just remember to be polite. Tell him you how much you love this river and farming.'

'And I can learn to trap fish.' Robert even *looked* optimistic.

Despite this refreshing outlook, my mind drew straight back to Ol' Bobby. I felt uneasy: why was he marching around profusely apologising? If anything, *he* was about to be turfed off the land. On the overpass, in the distance, many cars and lorries continued to drive by. I thought about the tramp lying directly beneath them, resting on the angled slope. He loved this spot; he should always have it. When lunch time drew closer, I would ride home and ask mum for some spare clothes and food. In the afternoon, we could all go and see him and check on his state. If he really wasn't well, then we would tell our parents.

'Guys… I have an idea.'

I interrupted again and shared these new thoughts. I was on a roll, and once more they were met with enthusiastic approval. Man, I was on fire.

As I cycled home for lunch, I noticed the same group of kids on the track. Craig, Dove… the kid I'd clobbered with a stone.

I could have sworn I'd heard Craig say, 'Nearly there.'

Back at the house, I ate two chicken paste sandwiches and told mum about Ol' Bobby. She looked deeply concerned.

'Will you go and check on him this afternoon, and give him these scones?' she said, crouching at our biscuit cupboard.

'I will.'

'If he's unwell, we may need to take him to the hospital later.'

'What do you think might be wrong with him?'

Mum shrugged.

Shortly after lunch, I cycled back down the track. Same group of kids, still here. The removal trucks had departed,

175

but there was a smart silver Jaguar parked next to Mr Hislop's Landrover. It was then that I considered something that hadn't occurred prior. If this was William Grobatard's posh car - and contracts had been exchanged - could he immediately set up residence? Officially, we'd become trespassers. But... tomorrow was our final day, *not* today, and I'd darn well make it count. The most harassing thought of all, however, was the continued presence of Craig and Dove's parasitic gang of on-lookers. Mr Hislop didn't mean that much to them; I'd keep a wary eye. Just as I was about to turn left, onto the stretch of grass, I noticed Craig was no longer in the midst of the throng. His bike was on the ground, and he was at the entrance to the farm house peering in and out through the door, occasionally stepping on the huge, worn flagstone and placing both hands on the wooden frame to get a better look.

Watching, observing.

He would then move to an open shed next to the house and stare in there. His head moved slowly from side to side as he assessed the interior, smiling as he headed back to the farmhouse door. Bringing my BMX to a halt, I let my eyes bore into the back of his head. If he turned around and saw me, I would *stare* him out.

How dare he? While backs were turned, and business took place indoors, *he* was the opportunist thief, with the nerve of accusing Rob. I'd heard he was a rogue himself; his name mentioned with all manner of petty thievery, in and around this area. Incensed, I quickly turned to face him directly; my bike - a primed stallion - ready to charge and smash shin and ankle. But, within seconds, he jolted straight up right - and scampered away - grabbing his own bike and moving twenty or so yards back to the edge of the property.

What a tosser.

Then three men exited the front door. Mr Hislop was one of them. The second was an estate agent that my parents knew from the local town.

The third man, I didn't know at all.

He was smaller than the others; in receipt of silvery hair and strong cheek bones. His posture was unusual, and he flashed fleeting glances everywhere like he was shiftily sizing a bank job. Neither did he smile; not once. And Mr Hislop didn't say a word as they parted; just got into his Landrover… and slowly drove away. Then, I was left to contemplate, would I ever see him again, and a sudden sadness seeped through me. And in my heart of hearts, I knew this was our last ever full day together here by the beck.

If this was William Grobatard - he didn't look a pleasant man? Certainly not a people-pleaser, nor a friend of kids. It didn't appear he liked anyone. All those wise suggestions… and reasons for optimism I'd shared with every one - particularly Rob - wouldn't stand a chance. I knew this now.

How could I break this to him? Should I even?

Utterly dejected, I swung my bike back around and cycled to meet the others, slowing to a halt a little way back, so I could process it some more. I'd literally just seen the estate agent speaking to him, with no register of his presence. I was done with the beck, but if Robert was denied access to this place - his life blood - I didn't know how he'd cope.

So, I made an additional plan for after I'd seen Ol' Bobby this afternoon: later - just as we about to leave - I'd be exceptionally brave, and go and knock on Mr Grobatard's door myself, and ask, beg, or plead with him on Rob's behalf. Do anything. As I approached my friends for the second time that day, my heart felt, really, really heavy.

Hazel noticed it first. 'Hey Billy, you okay?'

'I guess.'

'Were Dove and Craig still there?'

'Yeah.'

'Any grief?'

'No, I'm not bothered, anyway.'

My attention was drawn to the beck. Mist was just starting to form on the surface. I pointed.

'How long has it been doing that?'

'About half an hour,' Ishaq answered.

Ish had brought a packed lunch and had stayed with Robert. Behind, light wisps were beginning to spiral across the entire breadth. This was very different to morning condensation on a baking hot day. In patches, it was thicker, and richly voluminous.

'Do you think the river knows what's happening?' Hazel said.

'Well, we've never seen *that* before.'

Scarlett's statement was accompanied by an uncomfortable shuffle backwards, away from the beck. She'd handled things pretty well, but even her unbridled enthusiasm had been curbed by the murderous knight. My mind hurtled back to Hazel's observation. Did *it* know? Did it care that it would have no kids to hypnotise once we'd gone? The mist was building slowly, very slowly.

'I think it does.' Robert affirmed.

'Logically, I'm not sure it can. It's not sentient.' Ishaq surmised.

'I don't think there's anything logical here at all, Ishaq,' I said.

Then I remembered. I reached down to the small plastic bag wrapped around the frame of my BMX and felt the rugged contours of scones through the surface.

'Listen, I'm going to give these to Ol' Bobby. Who's coming?'

'I'll come,' Scarlett said.

Others agreed, and I was pleased they were seeing past his inane rant from earlier, and cared enough to check on his welfare. But then - from out of nowhere - everybody looked startled, heads darting to their left. I turned in the direction of the alarmed expressions, sensing approaching people. And a group was indeed gathering behind us, at the end of the cattle bridge. Many children, slightly younger than us, and quite a few, at least two or three years older. At the helm; Craig and Dove.

I was the closest, but I didn't noticeably falter. From our position next to the jetty, to be blindsided in this manner, meant they must have walked directly next to the beck. And, as the troop of youths suddenly fanned out - like a flower unfurling its petals - the half-moon configuration they adopted seemed entirely purposeful, preordained.

None in my party, spoke.

Something deep in my gut lurched; a persuasive unease. This was a planned, patterned formation; premeditated and rehearsed. Some of the younger children were trying hard to suppress smirks and laughter. *Under orders.*

'What's on earth do *you* lot want?' Scarlett said.

Her tone was the prefect blend of condescension and disdain.

'Just… seeing what you're all up to,' Craig replied, fixing her with an imperious stare. 'Free country.'

I wasn't physically afraid of these two, not anymore: I'd given the bullies food for thought. But, this *was* seriously off. Craig turned his attention to Robert, viciously rolling his tongue along his top lip. 'Wow, look at what you made.'

Robert glared back menacingly. If it wasn't for the numbers game, he would have soundly kicked Craig's arse earlier this month.

'Look, he's been building a whole harbour,' Dove said.

'Shipping? A new line of business for the Tipperton's,' Craig mocked, 'After prison.'

'What are you talking about, mate? They ain't coming out.' Dove said. 'All this wood would have rotted by then.'

'Well, pirates were thieves, too. Control all the rivers. Maybe that's their post-prison plan.'

Then I noticed it. The little boy closest to me. Something in his left hand; dangling behind his back. The lower portion of Rob's face angled as his angry thoughts simmered. He remained deathly still on the bank; deflecting disparaging remarks.

'I guess today's removal day for you, son,' Craig said.

'Yeah, where are your family legging it to?' Dove said.

Suddenly, I was confused. The others too. It was etched all over their faces. Rob contemptuously shook his head at Craig.

'No, seriously, son,' Craig cleared his throat. 'Where are you moving to?'

179

He signalled over his shoulder. 'My dad said the removal firm is shifting the last of Mr Hislop's crap; and then they're heading up your haulage place to take everything, and lock it up.'

Before resuming his cocky position, I saw something behind Craig's back.

'So what?' Robert said.

'Well, you might get back at tea-time and you're suddenly a trespasser in your own home. And you'll have nowhere to live.'

'Stop talking rubbish,' Scarlett angrily lambasted.

'Well, it's true,' Craig calmly replied, 'With his home gone, he's a trespasser... just like you all are.'

And then, the kids started sniggering. A cue had been given. Forced laughter from brainless, cowardly conformists; themselves, too immature and afraid to know any better.

Rob snorted, 'If we're trespassing, then, so are you... *idiot.*'

Craig's smile was wide. He cleared his throat and slightly inflated his chest. 'I'm afraid... I'm going to have to... ask you all to leave now.'

Satisfied contempt wrapped his every word in a scornful sneer. We all scoffed, releasing half-breaths of disdain from our nostrils. Craig didn't blink. He didn't budge one bit. Addressing us once more, in a demeaning tone, he nodded at us. 'I'm afraid to say... today is your *removal* day.'

He reached down behind him and produced a hammer, gripping the handle in his right hand, while choking the wooden neck in his left. Then, the rest of the kids did the same. Smaller versions: Ball-Pein; Claw; Mallet. A lot were rusting, only a few - close to being new. Some of the older boys and girls had slightly larger versions. Dove produced an axe.

'Have you lost your marbles?' I shouted.

I edged my BMX back a fraction.

'You're no longer allowed on this land,' Craig said.

'*Nor are you, then!*' Scarlett was on her feet, shouting at him angrily.

Had Craig lost it? What was he thinking?

'Well, I did ask them nicely, didn't I, mate?' He looked at Dove for fake approval.

'You did, mate,' Dove nodded. 'You couldn't have been politer.'

'What are you going to do with those hammers?' Hazel sounded terrified as she rose to her feet. She immediately turned her attention to Rob, who had sprung up like a rabid cat.

He knew.

Ishaq was absolutely incensed. He ran up the bank right next to me, and eye-balled the two biggest lads.

'If you come any closer, we'll tell Mr Hislop.'

'Paki-boy - as from midday, today - Mr Hislop no longer owns this land.'

Ishaq was undeterred. 'That doesn't matter. In that case, I'll report you to William Grobatard… and say you're vandalising *his* property.'

Craig looked momentarily puzzled.

Ishaq continued bouncing up and down on his haunches. Craig stepped back, letting his hammer list at his side. That was smart from Ishaq.

Except…

Craig then turned to Dove, who was killing himself with laughter.

'Dove… what if Mr Grobatard finds out… wh-what do I do?'

Dove laughed harder, his fat tummy rippling, and Craig immediately walked down the slope, making the river bank his stage. He threw his hands out, launching into a performance; a vicious soliloquy.

"Mr Grobatard, Mr Grobatard, Mr Grobatard… some *nasty* boys are breaking up… all of Robert Tipperton's wooden constructions, right here on *your property*." He purposefully mimicked Ishaq, before deepening his voice, alternating the exchange.

"*What*, right here on *my* land?"

181

"That's correct, Mr Grobatard. Mr Grobatard… right here on *your* property, down by the river."

"Wait… isn't one of them that Robert Tipperton; the boy whose family are *all* criminals."

"No. No. Not exactly, Mr Grobatard. He's actually a really nice boy."

"A really nice boy, you say? But, isn't this the same Robert Tipperton who attacked… *my son?*"

"No sir, Mr Grobatard, sir. Robert Tipperton would never do *anything* like that, not to your son."

"Yes, he would. He attacked my son… on this very piece of land when Mr Hislop owned it."

"Sir. Mr Grobatard, sir. I think you are mistaken."

"No, I'm definitely not mistaken."

"Sir. Who is your son, Mr Grobatard, sir, sir?"

"My son? Why, my son's name is Craig… *Craig Grobatard.*"

Finishing majestically, he stood there imperiously, letting it all sink in for the astonished spectators. I couldn't believe it. Hideous. The reality of what this…

'Oh, shit,' I whispered.

$\sim\sim\sim$

'Now, get off *my* land.'

Robert turned ashen. Hit by a thousand poison-tipped darts, straight to his heart. The back wheel of my bike slipped backwards down the bank, sending me sprawling. All sense of time and coordination, gone from me. From floor level, I watched as Robert buried his head in his hands; silent tears spilling over his fingers. Between the gaps, the pain of a dying soul tore across his face; the muscles contorting in lines, unspeakable.

'Look, please. I'll do anything.' He wept. 'I'll pay you. *Anything.* Please…'

182

My friend crumpled to his knees. And he pleaded.

I caught sight of Scarlett: my crestfallen princess; red curls limply hanging as she bowed her head, as if she was surveying the many decaying carcasses of lost hope. Her own tears were the size of snow drops, cascading down her nose onto the grass.

I thought about fighting back. But Dove had an axe, this time.

Even if these tools would never actually be used on us; they served as a massive psychological symbol: the room had turned black forever... and this would be far too painful to ever, *ever* remember.

'Get off my land, you cry-baby,' he turned to the throng, 'C'mon let's trash it all.'

Craig purposefully moved down the bank, as Robert leapt up and stepped back on his jetty, spreading his arms out, begging them to stop. Kids flocked down. Buzzards on a kill. Two stayed at the top, unsure about their actions; kids with a conscience. But, the rest were ready to follow orders: *smash, smash, smash!* As Craig stepped onto the wooden planks, Robert lost it. He flipped. His right hander sent Craig straight down into some reed slush to the left of the jetty; his hammer making a slurping sound as mud devoured it. Craig struggled to coordinate, clearly concussed. Robert then punched another boy, perhaps older than him, with his left fist, sending him down... and completely knocked out. He kind of just... dropped. In a blind rage, my friend then simultaneously grabbed a younger boy and an older girl around their necks - with each separate arm - and *yanked* them both back towards the river. The smaller boy tumbled into the beck with a scream. The girl looked in shock as she came to rest, knees first, on the jetty. She grimaced, her right arm touching her neck; afraid to move it.

Then Robert came face-to-face with Dove... who looked completely unsure as to what action he should take. Screeching in undiluted rage, Rob grabbed the axe and tussled the larger boy. And Dove wore the perfect expression of someone who'd decided, climbing into a tiger enclosure wasn't that smart. Alarmed at Rob's strength and desire, he lost grip after only a few solitary seconds, and then turned and half cowered - half slouched away, covering his face.

Now, Rob had the axe; the most powerful weapon on show. Like a Viking King, consumed with blood lust, he hollered at all in defiance. His scream was epic. For a moment, the tables had turned, and I *honestly* thought he was going to win. But, then I worried he might actually *kill* someone; his focus switching to Craig below him, clamouring to clamber out from the reeds.

Incensed and distracted, the claw hammer that struck Rob's temple from behind, brought everything to an end. He immediately dropped, to me, in slow-motion. This was an older boy - maybe a year older than us - who had just seen Rob grab his younger brother and sister in a headlock. This kid was wicked pissed. Equally enraged. Pounding Rob's ribs with no remorse, he ordered everyone to pile in. Most used feet. Some fists. Violence at an unprecedented level.

Right there, on the jetty.

Some shouted insults at Rob and his family, as if this was somehow excusable. It was a relief that his dock couldn't house this many kids, and some tipped into the beck themselves as they tried to muscle in on the action. Those who did get to use their tools concentrated on pounding legs, or arms, and thankfully, not with any great conviction. The new lion - the *usurper* - switched to booting Rob in the back of his head before stamping on his hands. And my mate was conscious; *conscious* throughout every blow.

He tried to right himself - one last stand - but he was too bloody and damaged. Had he not been so winded by the stomach strikes, he might have made it back upright. Arching over onto his back, in agony, I saw blood streaming from his mouth through his broken teeth.

Then, suddenly, everybody scarpered.

~ ~ ~

Rob was left sprawled across his jetty.

I hadn't done anything; my bike, my prize, rested on top of me, unmoved. I would use the frame as protection from the hammers. The mist was rising faster now, pushing above head height and beginning to envelop every child close to the river. Our beck wasn't deep, but kids who had tumbled in were resurfacing in a dense, unusual cloud; startled by this inexplicable blindness. The confused children scrambled to the river's edge; alarm being urgently expressed by those on the bank, as flailing hands grabbed at weeds for leverage, unaccustomed to the specific entry and exit points. Water was violently churning, and distressed cries rose an octave as the panic mounted, as thickening spirals wrapped themselves around the desperate foes like pythons.

The suddenness, the strangeness.

This was something 'other' and every child here *knew it*. Ascending to a great height now, and obscuring most of the water, the tree house was being encased in white vapor. Rob was just about conscious in its midst, singular limbs moving slowly and painfully. Craig righted himself in a clump of brown sedge, his head jolting back and forth as he struggled to comprehend the situation. Wide-eyed, he hastened to join the others.

Seeing Rob, he halted.

He wasn't done.

Even from my position, I recognised his nefarious intent; his hell-bent *need* for revenge. He was every bit an unsocialised fiend. Twice now, he'd been humbled by a boy - two or three years his junior - and his enemy was at his disposal, only a few feet away. Although his hammer had sunk straight down to the bottom, the wooden handle poked above the surface. He immediately grabbed it. Now I knew why he'd been loitering by the farm house and shed earlier. He'd deliberately waited until both Mr Hislop and his own father had left to seize this moment, and he wouldn't let it pass.

A villain through and through; rotten to the core.

Most of the others were legging it; younger kids, in floods of tears, inconsolably shrieking there were ghosts in the water.

'*Billy!*' Scarlett screamed. '*Help him!*'

Craig waded towards Rob with his weapon clasped in both hands. Surely, he wouldn't... '*Make sure he can't get off. I'm going to give this village some early justice.*'

Indecisive and frightened, the kid he was bellowing his command to, was Dove. He stared at the billowing cloud in dismay; his podgy arms and legs, trembling.

'*You idiot! I said grab his legs.*'

One shaky step was all it took for Dove to lose balance and land on his stomach. Raising his face, he glanced once at Craig before resuming his dreaded vigil. Shoving my Burner to one side, I tried standing, but my legs were jelly. I'd stepped in before - flung myself in - true heroism. I studied the dismay woven in Scarlett's face, also in Hazel's and Ishaq. It was me, or never. But here I was rationalising my unwillingness: Rob's almost gone; he has nothing left; we'll never see this place again; the hammer's too big...

Courage deserted me, unable to move an inch towards my wounded friend.

'You useless fat twat!' Craig shouted. 'Hold him!'

Rob opened his eyes, groaning, and tried pushing himself onto his side, as Craig raised the hammer. Momentarily, he considered his action, his knuckles whitening as he gripped the wooden shaft. Rob's entire face was exposed, and his left arm sloped out to one side. The jetty was now a sacrificial alter for a crazed fool. Craig smashed it hard into Rob's hand.

He screamed.

Agony.

Again, Craig stopped. Shouting at the prostrate boy - justifying his assault - he berated him and his family. Somehow, it seemed forced, like even Craig himself knew he'd crossed the sacred line. Turning, to Dove, he screamed: 'Fetch the axe.'

He didn't want to be alone in doing this; desiring joint responsibility for this disgrace. Dove blubbered on the side and shook his head. 'Voices, voices.' he whispered, over and over.

'Throw me… *the damn axe!*'

Dove tossed it.

Angrily, Craig attacked the vertical supports, decimating one, causing the jetty to list. He'd willingly send the hapless boy into the water, knowing he wouldn't get out; drowning of his own accord. Twisted exoneration. Then, he turned his attention to the largest of the two moored boats, striking the mast and splitting it. Smiling inanely, the force of the third hit cracked the hull, sending it careening into him. Craig was pushed back further upstream, as Rob howled in anguish, holding his wrist, writhing on the sloping floorboards.

I cried at my weakness. *Please…* just move.

Craig set himself again, his new position even closer to the tip of Rob's handiwork, and Rob himself. 'Let's finish this,' he said, puffing his chest out for the biggest blow he could muster. And, then… he screamed. The axe fell. It raised, and then instantly tumbled out of his hands like he'd been electrocuted. A shadow in the water attached itself to his right thigh, clamping his flesh through his corduroy trousers. And his assailant coaxed the stricken young Grobatard into a tortuously painful dance.

'*What is it? Help meeeee!*'

Something brown and mottled let go, but then immediately lurched forward again, dragging him with great intent. Losing his footing, Craig fell deeper. He wailed as he submerged this time, as if screaming had become a pointless pursuit.

No one would help him.

Then, he managed to reset in the shallows and with life-threatening resolve, grabbed at his aggressor. He gripped tail in one hand, and throat in the other, but lifting aloft did not abate the pike's fury; undulating, sinking a slicing bite deeper into Craig's fingers. Shaking it, only saw his hands slip over the slimy surface, and jostling continued as Craig resorted to bear-hugging the fish in order to prize its mouth.

Basil was smaller than expected; his shadow had deceived me.

Nowhere near the three-foot monster I anticipated.

Size, however, was of no concern to Basil.

In the darker recesses of the beck, week after week, he would have watched us play - at any point - reminding us not to stray too close, but he never did. Maybe he liked us being in the beck near him; our playful banter pattering over joyful currents his way. Or maybe he enjoyed watching Rob through the gaps in his sedge, respectfully tending the river while gently crafting. For a territorial fish, he wasn't unduly bothered by us. But, Craig had royally pissed him off. Even now - completely removed from water - Basil was more than a handful, his sharp, serrated teeth tearing lines of blood. Craig death-hugged the fish - interspersed with growling - like he was squeezing the tube of its last dregs of stubborn toothpaste. He heaved with all his might, part concealed in the spiralling mist.

None of us noticed the boy standing next to him.

Not even Craig. Smaller, greyer... hairless head. His skin was pallid, bloodless, and water slid down his bare chest and arms straight into the beck. He'd simply appeared in the mist, positioned immediately to Craig's left, facing his unwanted guest. Body of an infant. Head of a baby. A viscous torrent of water spilled from his mouth, coating his lips with mucus. Craig turned and stared. The drowned apparition... stared back. Then it wiped the dribbling sputum away with the back of its palm and spoke. 'Put that fish down.'

Craig shrieked. Basil plopped.

I swear, in that moment, Craig farted, and resoundingly shit his corduroys. He didn't even run out of the beck, instead launching himself face first into the reeds nearest the bank. Scrambling, frenzied scrambling. Grabbing the stalk of some overhanging white flowers he pulled himself out, immediately clutching his hand; howling in agony. In front of him, Dove blubbered, terrified at the sight - rendered rigid - as the bobbing boy now fixed on him.

'Come here. I haven't seen a whale in ages.'

Sure, I'd pissed myself in the past… who hasn't? But I didn't know you could stream it *that far* in a straight line *from* out of trouser fabric. I could have sworn Dove was discreetly pouring from a watering-can, nestled by his side. Then, with one wet leg, he fled, like he'd been hit by high voltage.

Craig clambered out of the bank and screeched forwards, pursuing his comrade. I smelled his shit as he ran past. The boy sank back down.

Instantly.

Gone.

Tiny ripples pushed out from a central point. In seconds, they too vanished. And the four of us stayed seated or standing on the bank, astonished, scared, and scarred. Rob's pain was so immense he could only groan; too much effort to howl. Basil broke the surface a couple of times as he slithered back upstream to his sanctuary.

Above, the sun shone golden - a glowing alien in the sky - belonging to another time, space and world, in its entirety.

Chapter 10

Resolution

Rob was in terrible shape.

His hand was swollen, pigmenting in a large patch of darkened red, especially near the thumb pad. Was carrying him a mistake? Hazel was on one side. I was under his other injured shoulder. We hoisted and dragged our friend towards Cherry Tree farm.

Scarlett - by far the most nimble of our crew - had run ahead to call her parents and phone the police. Rob didn't speak, but he squealed and writhed, and winced continuously. Every single step. Alive was alive. Dead people *looked* dead. You stayed alive if you were conscious. But, I wasn't sure anymore. I knew harvesting season hadn't ended, so I silently invoked a group of potato pickers to come to our assistance. Ishaq had scuttled to the front, and then to the rear to support our lumbering movement. Taking Rob by the chest was a mistake, so he'd settled for taking hold of Rob from behind and keeping him steady.

Clumps of barley grew tall to our right, while the rest of the field remained flat. We were out of sight and out of mind, and we were positively *out of our own minds*. I was tiring. Hazel was exhausted. Thankfully, a blue tractor homed into view on the track ahead. It chugged towards us at what I knew was its fastest speed. Smoke blow out of its vertical exhaust as the British Leyland made ground. Either Scarlett was lightning fast at getting to the farm, or she'd managed a chance encounter further up. The door opened before it ground to a halt.

'Hazel!'

'Uncle Mick.' She burst into tears, ready to drop Rob.

Mick Wilmott - Scarlett's father - a tall, thin, and ruddy man, in navy overalls, a hue darker than his tractor.

'He's really hurt,' Hazel pleaded.

'Right lad.' Mick rushed forwards. 'What happened?'

'He was beaten up badly,' Ishaq added, almost apologetically.

'Where does it hurt, lad?'

But Rob was hardly conscious, and the farmer fell silent; recognising the gravity of his injuries.

Ishaq blathered. 'His right ankle, his chest, his face - and he's broken his wrist and hand - you can't go near his left side. You won't be able to fireman's lift.'

Mr Wilmott quickly assessed.

Gracefully, he took over Hazel's position, and swiftly lifted him horizontally. 'Hazel. There's a blanket in the cab. Run, and lay it in the trailer. You two, get in the back and hold him steady.'

We bounced up and down in the trailer, on the rugged track back, using our bodies to cushion Rob, careful not to fall over and onto him in our zeal. He had cuts to his face, but it was difficult to see how badly hurt he was beneath his clothing. His hand was a mess; it looked crushed and slightly deformed.

~ ~ ~

At Cherry Tree farm, an ambulance had already been called, as had the police.

Based in Bedale, they arrived faster.

And they were very good. It was my first encounter with the law and the two men oozed authority. Mrs Wilmott had preempted them over the phone that, "Tipperton's lad's been badly assaulted. *The young un.*"

Of course, Rob was on their radar, and had been for several weeks. They asked us questions, but focused on Rob's wellbeing. He drifted in and out of consciousness, groaning the second he came to.

The point I accepted he'd live was when the ambulance arrived. That vehicle brought life, and hope, just like my BMX, brought prestige. Just having one here, was it all it took. Rob would be repaired. The exiting medics possessed natural healing abilities with words and fingers alone; their uniforms were a sign of this. More importantly, they got Rob talking, fussing over him in all the right ways; compassion, professionalism.

In all of this, the saddest part was the failed attempts to contact his parents. Mrs Wilmott didn't want Rob to be alone, so she volunteered herself and Scarlett to accompany him to the Friarage while the Police attempted a visit to the Tippertons. They would drive Rob's parents down (because of the impounding) and bring the Wilmott's back - a straight swap. Needless to say, matters were ripped from our hands in a hasty sequence of events.

We managed to say goodbye to Rob while he was stretchered into the back of the ambulance, but he didn't really acknowledge any of us. More statements were taken, as the police bore grave faces of concern. They asked us to get ourselves home as soon as we could.

And so, after an hour of frenetic trauma, me and Ishaq wearily walked the lonely walk back towards the cattle bridge to retrieve our bikes. Mine, thankfully, was still there. Rob's white bike looked lost and forlorn. I wasn't going to take it back up to his haulage place - no way - so I placed it upright just behind the withered bramble bush, so it was resting partly against the bridge. It was out of sight of anyone looking from the farm's direction. I didn't consider taking it to Cherry Tree farm either; I just wanted to get home. I was dejected and terrified on every quarter of my soul. The mist-covered river. The Grobatard's new farmland. We would have to travel back through the barn yard, but it wasn't the thought of encountering the gang that stopped us. It was a tonne of barking, and we'd *never* heard that here before.

Newly installed guard dogs.

We'd be ripped to shreds, so Ishaq and I agreed to a ridiculous plan; circumnavigate the beck along the north side. This harboured danger in of itself, but the risk was high, rather than severe. We would have to trespass on unknown farms and hoist our bikes over fences and hedges to get anywhere near the B-road that approached our village. We were also being taken closer to the lion's den; the parts where the children were apparently murdered and where it deepened on its approach to the Swale.

The first half of our journey was fine, and there was even a gate connecting several fields. Then, I smelled it and my heart stopped. Remembering Rob's map, and Scarlett's comment about stinking pigs, I realised - with more absolute horror - that we were approaching (or possibly already in) one of Grobatard's other farms. Thankfully, we were on the periphery, at the very edge and - as we'd neither bumped into a farm-hand, nor seen a tractor - we both should go for it. We calculated it wouldn't be too far from here now, and we were right. Hugging close to the river, our diminutive stature was a decisive advantage. We passed some blotches of blighted crop, making a beeline to a small, forested outcrop, always warily watching the clouded beck to our side. The trees within grew at diagonals, and the whole cluster was in the shape of a rectangle perhaps a hundred feet long, and sixty feet in breadth. It was surrounded by a black, but fading metal fence that reached chest height.

The enclosure looked dark, menacing, and neglected. Unvisited. Grateful for the camouflage, we moved towards the fence next to it (the welcoming sight of an open expanse of grass on the other side). Ishaq stopped, studying the small copse.

'Look.'

Turning, I followed the angle of his gaze, staring directly into the middle of the trees.

'It's like a... I dunno... What is it?'

Joining him, I peered inside the dank canopy. Moss-coloured rectangular stones lay flat on the ground, perpendicular to one another in a half-moon crescent pushing their way around the central trees - the bark of which - looked emaciated. Those stones lying furthest away looked newer than those closest. All were inscribed, although the older ones were worn. There was an equal portion of large and small stones. Some had split, and all had a pattern in the top right corner.

'Look, they all have a crest,' Ishaq pointed out.

'Oh yeah. We've got one of those.'

'What do you mean?'

'Our family has one.'

'Really?' Ishaq was slightly interested, but in a subdued way.

'Yeah.'

'They belong to important families.'

This made me feel sick. I thought about Craig belonging to an 'important' family while flashing back to Rob's injuries, and him sagging in my arms. Directly above each stone, hanging from the branches, were baskets. All had carefully arranged flowers in the exact same two colours: red and yellow. And further ahead, through the trees, I could see another entrance gate. On either side, was a shield which was also red and yellow. It appeared as if there were two lions - one atop the other - etched into each plate.

This was Grobatard land, and this was a place of importance to them.

'Creepy place,' Ishaq added.

'We need to hurry.'

We pressed on, over the fence; the gateway to final escape. When I saw the Garth to our left - the old people's care home - I knew salvation was in sight. I saw the main bridge leading into our village and felt an astonishing sense of relief. The only potential issue to contend with, here in this final field, were horses, and there were four of them grazing in the distance; spotting us very quickly. I quickly discovered that Ishaq - like me - had a love/hate relationship with them. In fact, we waited in the corner for about ten minutes hoping they would look away, which in due course, they did - out of boredom.

The grass at the far end of the field sloped up towards the bridge, and we'd have to push our bikes up the incline to reach it. The horses couldn't be bothered with our mad dash either, resuming their puzzled staring all the way to our journey's end. I averted my eyes from the river, which was wider and deeper here; noticing that there was hardly any mist at all on this part. Reaching the perimeter, we helped each other with our bikes, lifting them over the fence.

And, we'd made it. The relief, however, was transitory; the shame of the day walloping me, as I realised I was close to *home*. I felt broken, like I'd plundered every conceivable shipwreck at great depths of disgrace, stealing precious rings from boney fingers. I had transgressed every single moral duty today. I'd either bypassed, or ignored every rule of courage; and now I was consumed with sickening self-condemnation.

We both cycled back in silence.

I knew Ishaq would be feeling the same.

My house was first, and I said goodbye to him and he nodded and sped off quickly. Home and trouble. Wow, I weaved this sick tapestry together with perfection these days. I waited on my bike and stared at our brown front door, frantically preparing a convincing opening line.

~ ~ ~

'You better come into the kitchen. There's been trouble down the beck again.'

This is what mum told dad when he got home from work. He despairingly shook his head. 'Not again.' He didn't say anything else, just solemnly took the nearest chair, and sat down.

Mum gave the perfect summary, and I chipped in frequently. The big revelation was Craig's identity *after* describing what he'd physically done to Robert.

Dad was appalled. 'Hammers?'

Then came, police involvement… *and* the possibility they'd be coming around ours for further statements. This stopped dad from driving straight round to Grobatard's new farm. *Pointless anyway*, as we were about to find out. And, my father was fuming, but not at me, flashing a look of pure vindication my way, proudly puffing out his chest.

'No matter. I bet my son gave them a *bloody good hiding!*'

I wilted.

Of course, dad being dad, his concern was about the other kids at the scene and seeing their fathers down the pub later. Rifts had healed a little between him and the majority, but this was sure to open old wounds. However, a neighbour called round fifteen minutes later wanting a word. It turns out that the *two kids* who had stayed on the bank, refusing to get involved in the melee, had cycled straight home and told their parents, who in turn had *also* called the police.

These parents had even driven to the scene themselves, but the incident was all over by this point. They found when they knocked on Mr Hislop's old door - no one was around - Mr Grobatard, clearly back in residence at another one of his farms; probably none-the-wiser as to what had transpired. I wondered if these parents had seen the mist. They'd definitely seen hammers and axes strewn across the grass.

An hour later, two more neighbours called. One of them had a son at the scene, and she was extremely apologetic. 'I've banned him from going out the rest of this year as a punishment. I'm terribly upset by his actions.'

For my parents, this acted as much needed barometer concerning the mood of the village. Back in June, it had taken a couple of weeks for my defence of Rob to be viewed as, quite possibly, justified. This was by no means universal. The lady informed us there was a police car currently outside Mr Monkton's house - and I knew his son had stamped Rob repeatedly on his jetty. Despite all of this - and probably as a distraction - the two neighbours were *far* keener to broach another topic.

Voices.

Their kids heard them in the mist, sending them packing. Many were inconsolable, and more police had been called. The immediate (and extensive) chitter-chatter from door-to-door was about an event of the same magnitude (or even eclipsing) the 'boat' incident they themselves experienced. Not many had moved away from the village since. They were keen to hear my take on this (but not so much the horrific assault on Robert). It's safe to say, I had the floor for all four pairs of ears, including my skeptical father. He wasn't born around here and assumed it was rural, hill-billy nonsense. It felt strange - and I mean utterly bizarre - to be amongst believers who would hang on every word. Although I never heard any myself that afternoon, I summarised some (and only some) of our experiences.

'Well, we did see that boat with no one sailing it against the current, didn't we, Trish?'

'Aye. We did.'

This met with approving murmurs, apart from my dad, who slowly, mockingly, shook his head. (He was itching to get down the pub.) I explained that Craig would have bite marks from a pike on his thigh, bloodied fingers, and a cut lip. I also purposefully mentioned Dove in all of this. I had no idea where he came from and was almost fishing for information myself.

'He's the lad of Normanton's. Farmers from past Bedale way,' one said.

'Oh, I don't like them,' said the other.

197

'Yeah, he punched me in the face the year before last, too.' I said.

'Wa-ah?' my dad proclaimed. 'You didn't mention that.'

Then my mum said something that stunned me a little. 'Where was Ol' Bobby? Was he around at all?'

My mind reeled.

It flashed back to the morning, and the mad, almost inconsolable man walking backwards and forwards, apologising to the others. Then I thought about the scones in the plastic bag I was meant to give him. Where were they? Had the bag fallen off my bike in the frenzy? The intention to go and visit, and events aborting that mission. *Surely,* the commotion would have brought him out from the underpass anyway, or the mist, at least.

'No,' I truthfully replied, 'The others saw him in the morning.'

These neighbours eventually left.

The phone rang all evening, and conversations were genial. I listened at my bedroom door for any other new tidbits, but got none. Kids were terrified by what had taken place though. One call was clearly from Mrs Khan because my mother's voice changed accordingly, but as usual she was very articulate, calm and informative. Above everything else, I was waiting for a big knock at the door from the police - seeking further statements - or giving updates on Rob, but that didn't happen. They must have been ridiculously busy.

Looking out of the bathroom window, I saw the sky was overcast.

Our bathroom faced in the direction of the farm, but there were far too many roofs in the way to see. Today, was the last day we'd probably ever see the beck, and I felt numb. It was certainly an enchanting place; but enchanting no longer meant *good* in my eyes. Far more troubling to me was the cattle bridge - the shortcut to Scarlett and Hazel's - the only route I knew. How on earth would we reach each other? Our friendships were forged *there*. I was too young to cycle main roads. In the quiet and lonely solitude away from the people that mattered most to me, I considered how this had all ended. Terribly. Flashbacks to Rob being savagely beaten. My inaction. The police, the ambulance. Mine and Ishaq's crazy journey back home.

Most of all, I thought about the boy in the river.

Now, alone in my room, a wretched fear beset me. He looked both dead and alive. Goosebumps pricked my arms as I remembered; finally seeing *what* was *in* the river: me, Scarlett, Ishaq, Hazel… and now Craig and Dove. The grey, bloated and blotchy skin and the spew coming out of its mouth. The vicious words it slew both bullies with. It wanted to take kids; nothing but vile intent behind those cruel, narrow eyes. This ghost boy didn't seem trapped, nor distressed in the least, and he spoke perfect English, not medieval.

It was half-past nine - way past my bedtime. The clock hands turned for another hour, as my thoughts turned more and more petrifying. As mum and dad came up to bed, shortly before eleven (no pub trip for dad tonight), I peeked out of my room and asked them if I could stay with them.

This time they said no.

My bedroom light remained on the entire evening.

I sat in my bed with my legs drawn up, anxiously staring around the room. Eventually, I pulled my desk against the door and shoved as many heavy books (and even cuddly toys) against it as I could. This boy *must not* enter my room. I fell asleep in a seated position. There was no way I'd risk the pillow and hear my pulsing head pounding out imaginary footsteps coming up the stairs.

~ ~ ~

The knock on the door.

'Are you coming down for breakfast?'

I spluttered something back in the direction of the voice, caught halfway between sleep and awake. It was 10 O'clock.

Sunlight peeked through the bottom of my thick curtains, illuminating the more vivid red and yellow twirls on my carpet. I just stared and stared at the soft shards, bringing their peace and vitality through every pigment of fabric. So, it appears I made it. I survived the night. Mum tried opening the door. 'You slept well, sleepy head.' It immediately hit my blockade. 'What's this?'

I was sprawled out to one side, where I must have finally drifted off and pitched. 'Hang on a tick,' I said, leaping off the bed, and dragging my desk. She peered through the gap, puzzled... but, only for a few seconds. 'Oh, I see what you did,' she said.

'I was a bit...'

'No need to explain.' Mum smiled. 'Come on down when you're ready.'

At breakfast, I listened to her car engine turn over and over in the garage as I spooned Rice Crispies into my mouth. My coordination had deserted me, and I was constantly wiping milk from my chin. It looked like another lovely day out there, and the steady - but not unpleasant - grate of a manual grass-cutter drifted in through the open window. People were already out in their gardens, making the most of it. Mum looked disappointed when she re-entered.

'Either I've flooded the engine with the ruddy choke, or it's knackered.'

And then,

'Right, I'm just slipping out to see if Billy Tinker's in.'

Billy Tinker (not his real surname) was the local handy man; jack of all trades; master of none. My mind was still blurry, barely registering the conversation. Somehow, I had a sense of relief that this was finally over. My hopeful imagination conjured a mending Rob - more bandaged than me - and a complete end to anything supernatural happening in my life ever again. The beck would be sealed and closed for visitors, forever. Then, I thought long and hard about an alternative bike-route to Scarlett's; I wasn't familiar with where the main entrance was to her farm: possibly, somewhere on the Bedale road?

For fifteen minutes, Billy tried all manner of fixes under the bonnet. Nothing worked. Eventually, the battery died from all attempts at resuscitation. The stand-in-joke in the village was that the Austin family only ever drove Austin cars. Normally very reliable too, but not on this occasion.

Mum thanked her friend and returned to the kitchen. She took the chair near me and had a little think.

'Sorry, honey. I won't be able to take you to Granny's until later; not until your dad gets home.'

'Granny's?'

'Yeah. Later.'

'Huh.'

'We arranged for today, remember? You requested… a few weeks back.'

My tea was cold, but still quite sugary at the bottom. I flashed her a puzzled look.

'It's the 29th, silly *Billy*,' she laughed. 'You asked for a stay over with Granny W.'

My heart flipped. The message in the bottle! *We will see you on the 29th of August. If you don't see us first. Robert.*

Like mum's flooded car engine, far more relief gushed through every inch of me. It was genuinely over. No one could go there! Now fully awake, I began to rationalise the note's contents, realising *we'd already seen them* - the latter part, fulfilled - by a collision of circumstance. I swigged down the best part of my tea and felt disappointed that I wasn't seeing Granny now until much later. It was Wednesday, so I would be staying there until at least Saturday - a great end to the summer holiday - miles away from rivers and fear.

The rest of my day was comic reading and story-writing. My abilities to incorporate emotions and drama into the plot were in great supply. I clock-watched, waiting for dad to get home so mum could swap cars. By about five, I knew it wouldn't be long, and Granny W had already told my mother I could have tea with her rather than here at home. And this meant being lavished with abundance. A couple of neighbours had called round with gossipy updates - nothing new - so I wasn't surprised when the door was knocked on again.

Except it was the front door, and it was loud and insistent.

I was in the lounge, and mum was in the back garden, so being closer, I answered. A Police Officer. A different one to yesterday, wearing an intensely grave expression.

'Hello, are you Billy Austin?'

'Yes.'

'Is your mum around, Billy?'

'She's in the back.'

Mum had heard, and was already arriving, extricating her gardening gloves, and wiping her hands with a cloth.

'Hello, is everything okay?' she said.

'Hello, I'm PC Travis. Well, not exactly, no. We're trying to find the whereabouts of Robert Tipperton, and we wondered if you can help?'

This was aimed directly at me.

'He's in hospital,' I said.

'Yes,' mum interjected, taking over. 'He was rushed there, yesterday. Your boys were dealing with it.'

'He certainly went there… but he was collected and taken home this morning.'

'What?' Mum was rarely confused, but she was right now. 'What do you mean, taken home?'

'Monitored overnight, discharged first thing… but he's gone missing again.'

'That… can't… possibly be.'

His words were far beyond what a child can process; my insides plummeting. Missing meant, *vanished*. Gone for good. Cloistered in unknown, invisible spaces.

The Police Officer continued, 'Billy, do you have any idea where he could be?'

It was like being asked a question in the classroom - on the spot - that you didn't know the answer to. Except I did.

'The beck…'

'How could he be sent home?' Mum jumped in ahead of me. 'He was severely injured, right?'

The Policeman addressed her first, 'He had a sprained wrist, and two fractured fingers, but he got off lucky. Lad has a strong constitution. Bandaged, and sent home.' He stooped a little, addressing me next. 'Billy. We already checked around the jetty, and his tree-house. He wasn't there. Barns, and outbuildings too. I have a couple of officers there now.'

I had no idea.

Mum still had questions.

'*Who* brought him home?'

'His mother.'

'What?'

'Tuesday evenings are pretty quiet down the Friarage, so the doctors X-rayed him and patched him up pretty quickly. His mother borrowed a car and collected him this morning, but he ran away around two-ish.' He turned back to me. 'His mum said he has a white bike, but he'd left it there yesterday; is that correct?'

'Yes,' I said. 'I put it behind the bramble bush.'

The Police Officer stroked his chin. 'So, he didn't come back and take it. We saw it.'

'Haven't they put his arm in a sling?' Mum said.

The policeman nodded. 'Yes, so he's got one good arm, and a lot of determination. His mother couldn't stop him from leaving.'

'Billy,' mum turned to me, in shock. 'Sweetheart… is there anywhere else he could have gone?'

At this, the Officer added, 'We've checked Cherry Tree and Ivy farm, and he's not hiding there either. We hoped he'd maybe come round and see you.'

I shook my head. I knew Mrs Khan would be *straight on to* the police if he'd gone round there.

'He seemed pretty determined to get to where he was going.' The policeman repeated.

Those *exact* words.

What happened next… felt like a balloon rapidly inflating in my head… followed by someone skewering out my heart. My knees buckled, and both adults saw it. The Police officer's eyes blinked, recognising arcane revelation.

'What is it?'

'The boat! Was the boat still there?'

'Yes. It was… capsized. Part submerged.'

'No, no. The other boat… the small one.'

The man thought very quickly. 'Where was it?'

'On the other side of the jetty.'

The Officer shook his head. 'There were *two* boats?'

A form of realisation dawned on his face, and he reached into his pocket, 'There was a loose rope floating in the river. Here, he'd sellotaped this to that broken jetty. Does this mean anything?'

The officer quickly unfolded the scrap of paper. "Uton we gamolian, geowine - Let's grow old together, old friend."

'He's sailing down the river,' I blurted.

His expression froze. 'In a boat? How big is it?'

'Small.'

His Adam's apple shifted in his throat.

Mum chimed in again, 'Didn't you check down the river, anyway?'

'We did. But the mist…'

'What mist?' she said.

'You can't see far in at all. It's so thick. We've never seen anything like it.'

'The mist's still there?' I said.

The Officer stepped back off the front step and pointed to the end of the village. I leaned out and stared. From our house's position, you couldn't quite see the river, but this didn't remotely matter. There before me - stretching from east to west - visible in the gaps between the village fringe houses, and the main road, was a tall, dense bank of white.

'Billy,' his voice startled me. 'Which friend does he mean?'

Another police car suddenly appeared, quickly parking on the road outside our house, and an officer hastily exited, waving over to his colleague. 'Excuse me for one second.' PC Travis said, immediately striding over to meet him.

This appeared to be extremely urgent. They met each other partly inside our driveway, only yards away. Mum stepped out to listen, the new Officer only partly concealing his mouth, and tilting his head.

'We found a body.'

Mum gasped. I heard it too.

And my whole world crumbled.

Mum's posture altered on the step below, wilting like a pretty garden flower. Every child growing up in those days was afraid of sharks, Adder bites, pylons, weirs, reservoirs and plastic bags over your head. On hearing this news, I felt a huge whooshing-down, like the whole earth had dropped away. I was falling off a pylon... while getting electrocuted, straight into the garden below, instantly expanding, into slow-death quicksand.

'The boy?'

'No, an old man.'

The officer tried hushing himself, but we could still hear. 'We think it's that tramp in the area - the one they call Ol' Bobby.'

'Whereabouts?'

'In the underpass, the one further back beneath the carriageway. We think he drowned. Looks like he's been dead a day.'

PC Travis grimly nodded, 'I know who you mean.' He sighed, 'But still no sign of the boy?'

'Not yet.'

'He's possibly on the river... in a boat.'

'What?'

'That loose rope we saw was tied to it.'

'In the river? I couldn't see how... he could. Not in these conditions... or any.'

'Was there a boat near the body?'

This time his colleague shook his head, 'No, it's upstream and the reeds are denser.'

PC Travis turned slightly back to me.

Mum gently touched my arm. 'Billy, I think you better go into the lounge for a bit.'

She then rubbed it and gently pushed.

A large collection of neighbours were materialising from out of nowhere. Many, either walking dogs or inspecting their front lawns. Several police cars had visited our village in the last twenty-four hours. Their presence was a magnet of significance for somewhere so insignificant on a world map. One woman who I recognised - living two doors down from us - was returning from the shop at the top of the village. It seemed a legitimate errand, and she appeared genuinely perplexed. She leaned over the wall, but mum was already striding across the garden to meet her.

'Everything alright, Tara?'

'No, the boy of Tipperton's gone missing.'

'I thought… he was in the Friarage?'

'No, he's come back and run away again.'

'Right. Shall we go look?'

'Totally agree.' Mum called to the policemen. 'We'll get a group and go down the river.'

'Thanks, Mrs Austin,' PC Travis acknowledged. 'Take it steady down there. It's dicey.'

The number of adults who suddenly appeared to help was unbelievable. I waited on the step for guidance. Mum turned to me. 'Billy, get some squash from the fridge, and go and sit in the back.'

'I can help.'

'You heard the officer; it's dangerous down there. Go and do that, honey.'

I reluctantly departed, heading straight through the lounge, and out our French windows. Ol' Bobby… was dead. Drowned. My mind somersaulted. Not once did it land correctly. The westerly sun was hitting our back garden now. It lit a sprawling, lilac coloured Aster, and I went and sat on the lawn directly in front of it, watching dozens of harmless, yellow and black bodied Hoverflies zipping between its petals. Each year, they'd fascinate me - forever hanging in the sky - rarely moving closer to the flower itself.

Darting to different aerial positions and resuming their same pointless cycle of observation.

Were they scared?

Afraid to enter?

Rob wasn't. He was desperate.

He'd got closer… He'd gone all the way in.

I stayed there, mesmerised, for the better part of ten minutes. Then, I couldn't stand it any longer, and ran to the garage for my BMX.

~ ~ ~

No police cars.

No locals.

They were prioritising the north of the village for the search, using the farm track to reach the beck.

Instead, I aimed straight for the bridge me and Ishaq used to escape. All I needed was to round a corner, and I'd see it directly ahead. My pedals were barely spinning when the shouting commenced; drastic, beseeching - and very close. So I flew out of the blocks, charging my bike at breakneck speed, knowing I'd never heard cries like these here before. The final house jutted out like a church buttress, and I was past it no time. And then countryside opened before me, and I was looking down at the mist-laden river, just like in the black-and-white photo.

I slowed on the decline, tracing the source of the shrieks.

Two girls on two bikes - braving many main roads - now leaning over the bridge connecting our village to the next, hollering and pointing with all their might. Dislocated, and far-removed from home - and I knew - the only reason they'd ever be remotely close to here, was for me.

'Scarlett!' I shouted.

She turned. '*Billy! Quickly.*'

There was a flurry of hand signals; frenetic gesturing and insistent body movements. All imploring me to come - beckoning me - like life depended upon it; because it did.

'*Billy, he's in the river!*'

'He won't listen!' Hazel panted. 'He's got a caste on his arm. It's him.'

No denying. Indelible proof. I stood upright and powered my bike down the road towards them. I could do with an adult in the vicinity, but none were around.

I arrived, just as Scarlett said. 'He's gone under the bridge!'

'What?'

'He's not listening to us,' Hazel blurted. 'We saw him as we crossed the bridge and stopped.'

Only the road crossing the bridge was clear of mist, now simmering either side of the walls.

Scarlett added, 'He keeps muttering the river will protect him.'

I looked down. It was difficult to make anything out; spiralling gaps only fleetingly appearing. No one there.

'Are you sure?'

But the girls were already pulling their bikes to the opposite side. *They were sure.* I joined them, peering over the side.

Fields all around us were being spared the strange, coiling fog - as from east to west - it clung to the entire river basin, ascending to about twenty feet at its highest point. I was terrified the bobbing boy might suddenly clamber up from the supports beneath the bridge, and wrap his tongue around my neck.

But, Rob... I had to help my friend. I had to atone.

Then I saw him; the bow of his boat emerging from the shadows. A single oar in a single working hand, dragging at water, slightly ahead of the massive vaporous entourage. I thought he'd be seated, but instead he was leaning on his tummy, propelling the boat forward by any means he could. Scarlett and Hazel were already shouting and calling.

On this side of the river, there was a fence that led to a steep drop off. It always felt like no-man's-land here; a definite cut-off point, with no public footpath. Private farm land. If we had to, we could and would hoist ourselves over and down. A solitary car came around the bend, purposefully slowing as it reached the river; its inhabitants gawping at the astonishing bank of cloud. Hazel, bless her, flagged it down, frantically explaining there was a boy in the river. The two old ladies within, avidly listened, eager to help.

I called over, 'The police are over at Hislop's farm, searching. We've found *him*. *Please* tell them to come.'

The ladies nodded and drove off.

Propping my Burner against the bridge, I called out alongside Scarlett. Enormous white flowers and trees pushed out from the bank, combining with the mist, to allow only partial, fragmented views, but there were parts where he became clearly visible.

'*Rob, Rob, Robbbbbbb!*'

Then I realised. He wasn't just ignoring us; he was entranced. Beyond him, the river continued its relatively straight furrow.

'We need to get down.' I instructed Scarlett.

She nodded. Rob was approaching a smaller bridge - a walk way of sorts - that I'd never ever noticed before, neither in our car, or on my bike.

'I'll stay here and tell people.' Hazel said.

'Good plan.'

Then she looked shocked. 'Can you hear that?'

I was desperate to reach my friend, and we were running out of time. I knew the Swale wasn't far from here. Briefly, I stopped, listening to a humming - a bleak and distant chant - I couldn't quite discern. Calling...

'Billy, they're singing to him.'

She was ashen.

Scarlett and I launched back up the road, leaping over the fence, both of us... *immediately* tumbling and rolling down the severe grassy drop. I slid stomach first, cocking my head at the bottom, seeing a cluster of dark trees arching

209

across the river in the distance. The beck weaved directly through this shadowed canopy, before bearing slightly left. From this point on, our options ended. We had to reach the small wooden bridge and call; the fog, too perilous - the waters, *too deep* - to hope for a grasp and a grab.

Scarlett was faster. I didn't think a girl could be, but she was. Panting behind her, I reached the small path across the river, and we shrieked and beseeched Rob who was passing underneath. It was a precarious rope bridge with a flimsy handrail and wobbly planks to step over. I hated them. Scarlett, of course, moved straight to the middle, me standing a little way back on purpose - one false step forward or back - and you were falling over ten feet into the river. The billowing, spiralling cloud was... thicker behind Rob. As if, accompanying him, and drawing ever closer to us.

We roared at him over and over again. Screams I'll never forget. Lung-busting desperation.

He laid out across his boat towards the front, with his hand clasping the centre of the paddle. This was the most comfortable position his broken body would allow. His arm hypnotically reached out and occasionally guided, but the current was stronger here, carrying him along faster and faster. We kept shouting with no response, so I tried tracing the route ahead. And I didn't know what I was suddenly witnessing...

The deeper beck did indeed veer to the left. But there was something else; some kind of gravel, a clump of reeds, or maybe even rocks. In the fog, it was hard to distinguish, but when it briefly shifted I saw it; a sandbar of sorts, jutting into the river. And within this space, under the canopy of overhanging trees, a hundred yards ahead, stood several small children.

Not moving.

Watching.

They looked tiny, malnourished, dressed in brown. Loose tunics, some reaching their knees; others, their ankles. Waiting.

The mist moved over the small bridge and I grabbed at Scarlett to support her, stopping her from toppling. Covering us in its entirety, I could no longer see my arm and prayed I still had hold. It was impenetrable, and I witnessed small lights sparking in its midst. The voices were loud here, and they shouted, shrieked and sang in something close to frenzied ecstasy: 'Welcome, welcome, welcome.'

Then there was nothing.

Nothing at all.

Chapter 11

Final Thoughts

The previous Christmas, I had a wicked fever dream.

I don't know how my young mind conjured blood, bodies, and dead nurses on operating tables. But it did. Somehow, I'd left my bed and was standing at the top of the stairs on the landing. That's where my parents found me. Gently, and with great reassurances, they guided me away from the dangerous steps, back to the security of my bed. I remember it took me ages to snap back to reality, and accept the here and now. *This* particular nightmare wasn't real.

They found Scarlett and I in a hysterical state.

I didn't think the people gently talking to us were even real. Familiar faces were off. Different. Uncanny valley, we say these days. We weren't exactly screaming, but apparently we were shouting and declaring things that made no sense.

The parents - both Austin's and Wilmott's - had a job on their hands calming us in front of crowds of gathering searchers. We were still in the field, but further back from the river; the mist now virtually evaporated, the waters becoming increasingly visible. Those not surrounding us, were helping the police comb the river. Mrs Tipperton was there.

She was screaming.

The days, weeks, months, and years that followed were patchy and traumatic.

I recall the police attempting many open questions to the three of us at the scene, but it was nigh on impossible. The beck was now clear and calm. No boat, no boy. We were hysterical, and driven away to hospital. And as the days and weeks passed, the questions took a turn - becoming slightly more leading - as if we'd helped plan his disappearance. Looking back, that's what I now believe.

Our teachers gave an assembly, asking the pupils to be mindful around me. But one day - a few months later - a kid in the playground asserted that we'd all conspired with Ol' Bobby to have Robert kidnapped and murdered. It was far too inventive a claim for it to come from him. He'd heard it elsewhere - from his parents - or from hearsay. He wasn't *that* imaginative: I'd heard his stories read out loud at the front of class… and they were shit. His words hurt, though. Year six was sheer hell, though. However, to be fair, I did make similar leaps in my own mind, linking Ol' Bobby's death with Rob's disappearance. But Ol' Bobby had apparently died about twenty-four hours before. He'd rolled into the water and drowned while Rob was still in hospital. He may even have fallen unconscious and slid down while the fighting took place at the beck.

So, the days became weeks, and the weeks became endless months. All the while, hope was being pierced with an invisible needle; the more that good news *didn't come*, the faster it deflated.

The hunt for Rob was extensive, both formally and informally, in the weeks that followed. A group of fishermen - less than a mile away hadn't seen him - but they had probably left a fraction before a boat could reach them. They'd fished mere yards away from where the mist ended, where the beck joined the Swale.

Despite tracing the beck back to its origin, and the Swale to the Ure, and the Ouse through York, nothing was ever found. Ramblers, and other conscientious folk, immediately set up sentry points on many bridges overlooking its course. Many tributaries and dykes were also checked; all to no avail. The area where we last spotted him was Grobatard's land, and they weren't entirely helpful with

213

the search. This bred suspicion their way, which I didn't mind. And, of course, supernatural explanations were readily dismissed in favour of the practical and rational.

No boat, no body.

Eventually, the police questioned whether there was even a second boat, apart from the sunken one they found by Rob's jetty. Thankfully, several kids who were cautioned for assaulting Rob did testify there was.

I never saw Scarlett and Hazel after this. Not once.

The trauma was too great for them both, and they didn't attend the same Secondary as me, anyway. I'd heard conflicting reports: that they were either being home-schooled, or were spending extended periods in the Dales to recover. And although Ishaq and I remained friends in year six, he pulled away from me towards the end. Besides, we were both spending days, and sometimes - for me - the odd week off school. I didn't want to go outside. The days were too bright, exposing every recess of the hidden darkness I held. Ishaq's parents had money, and so he started year seven in a Private school, somewhere near Richmond. They moved close by shortly after.

The remaining Tipperton's did jail time, and were strongly suspected of being complicit in everything. Rob's mother was the last to see him - apart from us - and she became an endless source of speculation. She'd *accidentally* left the sling for his arm by the shed. His brother, Michael - soon to be charged - had hastily tucked Rob's farewell note on the jetty - making it purposefully weird, and vague. Rob apparently knew too much, and could reveal more about their nefarious activities, so he had to be 'got rid of'. Of course, there wasn't a shred of evidence pertaining to this.

Our personal testimony, and more importantly, *our personal experience,* was tossed to one side and rejected. Hence, *we* were rejected. I was bullied at secondary school for what happened and was treated like a pariah. In my later teen years, I sank into myself, and rarely socialised. The sun became my enemy, and the shadows, more obliging. I wanted to be forgotten. My wilderness years were long, and fraught with poor decision-making.

Thankfully, I still had an imagination. Eventually, I learned to mask and disguise the negative thoughts, the depression, and accepted the purity of a flawed perception... that life held any hope. My imagination was a buffer - a rescuer - pulling me from the most remote, and deserted and unreachable of dark highways.

It was strong enough to do this.

It was the *only* thing.

PART II

Chapter 1

The Glam and the Glitter

I walked across the marble patio to the veranda and leaned against the smooth Grenadil fence.

Goodness knows how much it cost.

Down below, the expansive garden was immaculately manicured, visionary designers and landscapers pouring their soul into crafting its resplendence. A detailed aesthetic - nuanced, pleasing to the eye - and made to be marvelled, especially from this vantage.

On this balmy evening it felt good to push myself away and escape the crowds, especially the air-conditioned Grand room with its predominantly shallow conversations. Shrill voices and meaningless chatter drained me more these days. I was less tolerant. I also didn't smoke much, but at this moment, sequestered on the balcony, I opened the packet of Kreteks I'd brought back from a trip to Sulawesi.

It was a good view to smoke too.

I lit, and inhaled deeply, watching the cloves within crackling and sparkling red. Why these were banned in the US? No clue. Occasions like these had their own rules. I was a law-keeper and cloves barely constituted a misdemeanour in light of other prevalent substances. But I had to be careful with addiction.

From my lofty position, I stared at the aqua-marine swimming pool, illuminated from below with subtle lights. I listened to the rhythmic torrents of water gushing out of the mouths of a Poseidon and Amphitrite statue; forever locking horns in a perpetual war of words, spewing their watery bile.

I quite enjoyed life now.

Placing my hand in my blazer pocket, I pulled out the tiny, blue and yellow badge, flicking it between forefinger and thumb. A gift from my Granny W - this little shield went with me everywhere - a beautiful reminder of a dear old woman whose paper boats were as colourful as the love she freely gave.

I'd like to think of these as memories from simpler times...

The gratitude and thankfulness group I attended, when I was in town, had helped me put perspective into things, especially when life was so rocket-paced. Sure, this aspect - right here, right now; partying with the elite and the wannabees - was pure razzmatazz and show business, but at least I knew the hosts well, and had friends in attendance.

It felt strange here.

Los Angeles.

I regularly traced my life journey... and considered how I even got here. Frequently I felt a charlatan, faking my work and fooling millions; the inadvertent leader of a Sect, adept in the art of charming duplicity. But parties like these, thickly layered with fickle people, served to reinforce I wasn't actually that bad.

It was a useful comparison.

For some reason, most of the people here liked me, and as polite as I always was, I could only take so much before withdrawing. I did social in spurts. A sizable majority only *ever* talk about themselves anyway, and I needed to be patient. Face-to-face, I'd take to analysing priorities and motivations, and quite inexplicably, they would become interesting again. In some ways, it was quite the divine and perplexing paradox, that the truly rich and famous were much easier to converse with.

I eyed a spiral staircase leading down to the gardens; I had options if need be (bound to be shadows under this balcony) should I require an escape room.

This was Simone Chapdelaine's spectacular mansion in Beverley Hills.

Acclaimed director, social activist and motivational supremo. A big fan of mine, and a genuine friend. Born in Brittany, raised in Louisiana.

I'd given him the nickname, 'the Prospector' because my novels had made him nine figure sums, and more importantly, they'd set his path to world-wide acclaim. It was a symbiotic partnership - insightful director, and the author - with him coveting, and then converting my novels into movies that rarely missed the mark. All those screen-plays we'd poured over… had been hard, hard work, but so worth it. Simone coated my work with his own ethereal hue, helping me visualise the unimaginable; always adding, never taking.

Suffice to say, we'd well and truly hit the serendipitous jackpot together. And together we now surfed the crests of glam and glitz along with the many A-listers we'd got to know through casting. That was years ago. Established. I mentioned his name a lot in my thankfulness group, to approving - closed eyed murmurs - from those within the closed meditative circle. Most importantly, I got to help the people he knew, particularly his daughters, in a time of crisis; the passing of his beloved wife. I was one of the few who saw past his magnetic public persona, and almost rhapsodic facade. He was a walking hollow shell, balancing a tightrope; desperate to shake the leash to this world. All this, for the better part of two years now. My glowing cloves were gravy in comparison with what he now took, and probably this evening.

In about ten minutes, he would definitely come looking for me. I inhaled some more night air and stared across the trees at the lights of downtown LA. Sipping a dry champagne, I studied the stairwell, preparing to disembark to the wonderful turquoise pool below.

'Excuse me, are you William P. Austin?'

A little startled, I turned and looked at the slim, tall brunette in a tight red dress.

'Yes.'

'Your books are *so* amazing,' she gushed, thrusting palms down by her waist like she was marshalling a standing start.

'Thank-you. That's kind.'

She counted her finger-tips. 'Her Bravest Song', 'Grace in Star-Spun Places', 'A Fountain of Falsehood', 'A Hat Full of Phantoms,' and 'The Nearly and Mostly Shackled'... and I love them. I mean *genuinely* love them.'

'Thanks.'

Her hands nervously shot down by her sides again, and everything above the shoulders remained fixed, unmoving. She was genuinely overwhelmed, bordering on the bashful. I admired her courage - not that it was needed.

'Thank-you. I'm genuinely glad you enjoyed them. Which did you like the most?'

'Oh, it's close,' she finally pouted a little, rubbing her left shoulder in a slow, self-comforting arch.

'Her Bravest Song shades it for me, but Star-Spun, probably... on other days. Phantoms is great... but scary and intense... and I also really like, The Eighteenth Loneliest Chapter, but it makes me cry.'

I smiled warmly because I could. She was a looker.

I hadn't noticed her earlier in the evening, mingling around Simone's entourage; not like me at all.

She said, 'Can I ask what inspires you because... they're all so different?'

She rested an elegant, toned arm against the Blackwood railing, threw back her hair, cocked her head to one side, and gazed directly into my eyes.

To my shame, I'd lost my Yorkshire tones years ago, and I purposefully ramped up the Queen's English, with a dash of smooth ASMR. I'd fielded this question for years and had crafted intelligent (sometimes witty) responses. It was audience dependent: the interview version, the mysterious version, and also, the charming, ulterior version.

For moments like these.

'Do you want the press version - at two minutes - or the ten minute one for the genuine enquirers?'

'I love your accent,' she said. 'Take as long as you want. Give me the long one.'

That made me smile. I wish I could.

She couldn't help herself. Within minutes, fingers tentatively reached over, occasionally grazing my lower arm; soft butterfly strokes down. I tactically ignored it, not disclosing I fully understood her subconscious posturing was speaking volumes. It didn't help I was on some recent top ten eligible bachelor's list. To me, this was utter garbage - I couldn't have cared one iota - but if people see it in a magazine, and it's glossy, and involves a swanky suit...

Photographed doing Simone a favour, collecting his Aston Martin, and wearing a pair of sunglasses, tipping one hundred thousand dollars. I would never have touched them had I known. Saw them lying in a glove compartment, and thought, "They'll do for a sunny Californian day".

Regardless - the mystery of me was too much for some - even though the mystery was a social construct, wrapped in neophilia (or possibly something sapiosexual at my age). An erroneously imagined life with someone special who could paint *their* perfection.

Prenuptial fodder.

But in all of this, I felt a responsibility too, not to abuse my status. Strange thing, really. It seemed to kick in - most times. Simone smirked at me on many occasions, especially at the end of elite social gatherings, and would astutely remark: 'Austin, you're like the star footballer dribbling past every defender, rounding the keeper... and then deliberately kicking out for a goal kick. Complete sitter.'

'I want to see I've still got it.'

'You have… *so, stick it in the net!*'

Sometimes I did.

I studied the woman some more, estimating she was 5"7, her heels taking her a shade under six. She was currently a couple of inches taller than me, in her clothes. The dress was tight, rising high up her thigh, and her arms and legs were immaculately toned. Two hours in the gym per day; running, and lots of light-weight repetitions: absolutely no swimming, though.

I gave her an honest answer and described, truthfully, unusual moments of inspiration. Then, I offered her a Kretek while explaining that I didn't really smoke except for special occasions. She didn't appear willing until I added they were banned in America. She favourably commented on my maroon suit (one I'd actually searched for and chosen myself), and disclosed that she thought it made me look poised and racey. Of course, she was super imposing a self-description, as our colours were closely matched, like we were in a his-and-hers photoshoot. She was drinking flavoured Gin which she offered. (It tasted more like a liquor.) At one point she glared at two older women who were edging my way, stepping even closer. Mine. I nearly laughed out loud at this.

For the next five minutes, I charmed her, and studied her; searching for intelligence. It was definitely, definitely there; but she certainly wasn't the 'girl next door' I'd stupidly imagined myself finding. She told me her name was Kenzie, which I thought was pretty. At the eight-minute mark, she unconsciously and swiftly swept her hands straight over her breasts a second time. She wasn't adjusting her bra and had no idea she'd done it. I'd become familiar with this 'touch me here' body language.

It was game on, if I wanted.

And she didn't talk about herself once, not until I asked her to.

Kenzie was here with her sister - who was apparently quite famous - and she was a sports and life coach for kids. She was hitting full-flow about her work, when Simone

223

appeared behind me, wrapping his arms around my shoulders from behind. Kenzie gushed a coy smile - recognising the host.

'Hello kind sir and kind dear. Are we both enjoying this exquisite evening?'

There was a Gatsby flamboyance to his intro; his eyes twinkling as they deftly approved Kenzie's 'red dress' before instantly diverting away, and then briefly moving round so they could meet my own: *silently showing approval.*

'Wearing good football boots?' he said.

'Pardon.' Kenzie replied.

'Ignore him. That's... for me.'

He pulled his arms away from my neck and started stroking his own Grenadil barrier, in a subtle, non too obvious manner, exercising restraint on behalf of his friend.

'It's lovely, Mr Chapdelaine. All your gatherings are.'

'Good... good,' he acknowledged with a smile, but I could tell he was waiting for something deeper, so I took over.

'This is Kenzie. She works with kids, likes my books and appreciates the imperceptible tones in your movies.'

'Ahh,' he sparkled into life and raised his spectacles over his speckled fringe. This is what he wanted.

Kenzie *had not* mentioned his movies, but I smiled at her as if... she would have done. There was no chance for further engagement because a group of Simone's friends - including the two older ladies - gathered around.

Nervously, my eyes sought out the spiral stair-case down to the garden and pool. I had an escape, if I needed it. Kenzie was now having to make do with joint conversations, her bluster fading a little, but I noted this tended to happen at parties when extroverts competed.

The next ten minutes were back to pleasantries, which I tried to steer in unusual directions, but warmly and respectfully. I could feel myself becoming mischievous as this tiny group was palpably into *self-promotion*, and I had to remain punctilious, because Americans didn't always understand my dry disapproval of superficiality. It was obvious Simone had coaxed his unwanted hangers-on my way for his own personal satisfaction, knowing *full well* I didn't enjoy it. (I watched him, leaning against his railing, silently laughing at me, as I silently despaired.) With me being the quintessential English man, and - "apparently" - *his* main writer, I was the perfect foil.

We double-teamed with style and panache for a good couple of minutes, telling them what they wanted to hear about our careers. Eventually, one of Simone's house managers or butlers (I was never sure what they were called in America) declared that cocktails were ready in the Grand room. This did the trick, and most people left the veranda, except Kenzie. Simone sneakily facilitated our extended conversation by gently shooing everyone in the direction of alcohol. I was prepared for *how he would tell me* about his "altruistic act" later, or maybe in the morning.

Kenzie used small talk to re-connect with where we left off, and she was doing well. I asked her about life-coaching kids and it was fast becoming a conversation of substance.

It was going well, better than expected.

But then she was suddenly scowling again, and right royally this time; the most unequivocal *go away bitch* face I'd seen in a while, and it caught me completely by surprise, such was its magnitude.

I turned and saw it was aimed at the tall woman approaching us across the balcony… who didn't stop her advance, not one bit; not even remotely undaunted by dirty looks.

'Hello there.'

She thrust her hand out at Kenzie - who had no choice - but to submissively slip her own smaller hand in. I was quite surprised to see the woman approach me with such formality at this, a social event. It was Friday evening - her evening off - but I knew, based on past experience, she could make these occasions a busman's holiday.

She was loved by the Chapdelaine's too, and quite rightly so.

'Sorry to disturb you, Bill. Can I have a word… in private?' she held my gaze, lowering her tone.

Uh oh, I thought.

'Sure.'

I gave my apologies to Kenzie (that was probably *that* for this evening) and wished her well with her coaching, and the both of us moved to the far end of the balcony.

'What's happening?' I smiled, laughing at the strangeness, 'Enjoying your... *night off?*'

'Emails,' she replied.

'Oh Shizz... *really?*'

She nodded. 'Don't worry, you're not being sued.'

I give her the benefit of the doubt; she'd only do this if important.

'An unusual one, Bill. I wouldn't have disturbed you otherwise; she's pretty.'

'And this definitely can't wait till Monday?'

'No.'

This was my personal assistant - Verity Schulenburg - who, for some reason, I nicknamed Shizz-bang, or Shizz-banger. I don't know how I got there with that, but she did remind me of Molotov cocktail. It was to do with her height and demeanour. She was six-foot-one, and tonight, wearing flat-sole, yellow, baseball shoes. Her dark hair was short, and packed into small curls, making her a little Medusa-rish, and her wide, blood-red rimmed spectacles, were purposefully OTT.

She gave me *that* look. The "I know what's best for you" look.

'You're going to want to read these.'

I swigged back my flute of champagne and let her continue.

'You know that thing that happened when you were younger?'

She waited for me to process... while my eyes immediately searched for a waiter with a tray.

'Go on,' I said.

'It was probably only a matter of time, really.'

'I didn't think it was.'

'Well, they found bones.'

I could feel the shock pummel me, and I sighed. And then I impatiently clicked my fingers in the direction of waiters.

'Here,' she said, reaching into her yellow handbag, retrieving an ornate hipflask. 'Just swig this.'

'Thanks.' I did. 'Whereabouts?'

'In the river you told me about.'

Nearly forty years had passed. It was another world, in another life. On a beautiful, balmy evening, where thoughts and priorities embraced the ostentatious to the extent you allowed them, a single magpie had just landed.

Verity continued, 'One email from a parent who discovered you used to live around there, and her boy was recently, apparently, attacked and nearly kidnapped by... something.'

She flicked through her phone; blue, pointy nails tapping against the screen.

'And the bones?'

'Yeah, a kid's bones, by all accounts.'

'Go on.' I sighed.

'You received an email - well written too - from the Conservative councillor in the area.'

'You're bloody joking.' I could feel my eyes widen. A waiter crossed the threshold towards me with a tray. 'Why?'

'Concerned for the community, and he... also mentions the boy who was grabbed by,' she raised her hand and did the inverted comma sign, 'the "something!".'

The waiter poured more champagne, and I kept listening.

'There's more... you know where this is heading.'

I sighed again, 'Go on.'

'Someone updated your early years on that site.'

'Shit.'

'Clearly, the locals knew it was you. You've done well deflecting it this long. Journalists are sending requests for a statement; things are hotting up, Billy.'

I shook my head. 'Anything else on the bones?'

'Found at the spot where you say that kid disappeared.'

My mouth sagged, and I stared at my feet. Years had vanished into the ether, and the mystery was over. Right here, on a veranda, after a sun-drenched Californian day. I took a lengthy swig, annoyed at the bubbles.

'Need a minute?' she said.

'No.'

'Billy, I know you told me about all this… but the supernatural element…' she took back the hip flask. 'Thoughts?'

'Too soon, Shizz.' The flute went back to my lips, and I took a long, slow gulp.

'Well, hopefully, now they found bones it finishes everything. And you can move on.' Shizz pulled her big glasses over her head. 'Sorry for breaking it this way. How do you feel?'

'Feels… weird.'

She acknowledged, nodding down to me. She never used her height to impose. 'I've been reading a bit about it again since these emails came in,' she said, her blue eyes conveying concern. 'That was quite a big deal back then in your area, wasn't it? They couldn't legally name you.'

I assumed by this, she'd fully read the journalist's email, so I nodded. 'It *swept* the nation, but it was only ever a missing boy enquiry… from what I recall, anyway. We were pretty young.'

Verity was more than my PA.

She was my confidante, adviser, inventor, and a slick manager of every component of my affairs. She was the best spin-doctor and spokesperson you could wish for. She liked to be kept in the loop too, so she could be prepared for all eventualities.

'This is really big… Billy. It might just kick off, big time! I honestly think something's simmering here. You might be fine with it, across the pond… to an extent.'

I rubbed my eyes, and expelled more audible displeasure. 'I'm going back there next week for a wedding, aren't I? Bloody perfect timing.'

Shizz nodded. 'They're going to be searching your novels now for clues about this boy, and your mental state.

Your recovery, if any? Are you psychologically sound? Extra pizza orders for conspiracists to fuel their armchair brilliance.'

I snorted.

'And of course,' she slowly tapped the edge of her phone (tapping for my complete attention), 'whether you had anything to do with it... now they have bones. You know the drill.'

'British tabloids.' I murmured, feeling suddenly distant.

'Exactly.'

I stroked my chin and closed my eyes as my PA outlined more and more scenarios; a kind of choose your own shit adventure.

'The boy also emailed you.' she said.

'Pardon.'

'Yeah, I'm giving you a chance to acclimatise. How am I doing?'

'Which boy?'

'The one who was attacked. he loves your Young Sinbad series... and has asked for help in understanding what happened to him. It's a lovely email.'

'Bloody hell.'

'Said something tried to claw him into the river... in front of his mum.' Shizz left that hanging, on purpose, studying me for a response. 'I can arrange him a free copy of A Hat Full of Phantoms.'

'Okay, I'll reply direct.'

'No. For goodness' sake, don't do that. Not yet. That might go into the wrong hands.'

I nodded; she was absolutely correct. My mind was at sea.

'Billy,' she thoughtfully began, 'Did you ever receive counselling for any of that... trauma...?'

My hideous teen years briefly tried battling out of my subconscious. I stiffened, fighting for composure.

'Yeah, I did.' I lied.

'Good.'

'Well, informally.'

She looked at me quizzically.

229

'The books, Shizz.' I took a huge swig. 'They were my counselling.'

Verity shook her head.

'If *those books* are a snapshot to your soul - Mr Austin - then we're totally and utterly screwed.'

~ ~ ~

Nearly always a Dreamliner.

Whenever available, for long haul.

Exclusively private. Opulence incarnate. A guilty pleasure. My trusted inner circle of employees got business class as standard, and for this journey, I was being accompanied by Verity. This had never been my intention, but circumstances had conspired, making this a necessity. I'd offered to upgrade her to first, which she took without a moment's hesitation.

Eight years had elapsed since Verity's recommended employment, and it took three of those to fine-tune our frequencies. Then, it was plain-sailing in honesty. I made sure I paid her the best rates around because good people were hard to find. She'd impressed me with some sudden etymology in her interview. The root word of her first name was, "Truth", and she was impassioned in explaining its personal significance. This, her brave attire, harmonious vibe, and the recommendations, saw her win the race from pole-position.

She co-owned an apartment in Los Feliz with her girlfriend, Cassie Starr, the guitarist in the popular local band, *Woes Almanac,* who had so far hit the Heatseekers chart and grazed the Billboard top two hundred. With a little cajoling, Simone was using one of their songs as the title track on his latest adaptation. It would be good exposure for Cassie's band, and the tune was in keeping with my writing themes. She was currently touring and then finishing some filming for her Internet show, "Crazy Ghosts". The *Woes Almanac* crew were doing all kinds of paranormal investigations from State-to-State, and the combination of gigging, writing and vlogging was gruelling. Verity was concerned for her wellbeing. The solution: Cassie would be flying out to join Verity by the weekend… visiting the Yorkshire Dales for some "fresh air", as they constantly repeated, as if the phrase was cemented in my DNA (which it was).

Business for Verity, and then a well-earned break.

Wedding for me, and a rocket ship home.

A huge storm was already gathering, threatening to sweep the North Atlantic: *William. P. Austin and the Vanishing Boat Boy.* Pseudo psycho-analysts were studying prior interviews for signs of trauma and "finding" the signs. View counts were rising to five digits. And, as Shizz correctly prognosticated: a fraction believed I *may* have been complicit; lines from my novels readily being quoted aplenty - revealing my true motives.

Of course, you doubt yourself.

Was my trauma about Rob in my books? Was I to *blame* for his death? I felt it was a *strong* yes for both.

Recognising the need to avoid a potential public relations disaster, Shizz-bang insisted she accompany before her holiday. 'It will help me with the jet lag, and that will seriously help Cass out, too. At least one of us won't be knackered and we can get into the groove.'

Weirdly, my book sales had spiked - by at least twenty per cent - with The Eighteenth Loneliest Chapter seeing particular increases; it being my latest. Not that I needed more sales; I was doing just fine - but it made me wonder if people were buying out of sympathy, curiosity, or blatant morbidity. More concerning was the emerging theory I'd subtly populated my Young Sinbad series with clues to Rob's disappearance, purposefully hiding them in children's books so adults wouldn't see. Clever pieces of prose. Allegory. In one, I'd made a reference to kelp-farming in

Sulawesi and *covertly alluded* to its potential for countering climate change.

This had somehow been morphed into Kelpie-farming. I was actively encouraging kids to *summon* Kelpie - Scottish water-dwelling spirits - that would entice, drag and devour kids in rivers and lakes. My novels were secret blueprints; providing ingredients for concocting supernatural napalm. The leaps some folk made were extraordinary.

After our arrival in London, we waited around in a private corner of the Platinum Plus lounge before catching a chartered flight to Teesside, successfully navigating our secret escape. Shizz even changed her bright red glasses to a more mundane pair, to keep with the more chameleon approach to cloak and dagger. The Bombardier Lear jet touched down shortly after ten, and more importantly, after dark. I loved this area. Thankfully, the press weren't quite so keen. An airport nestled between Middlesbrough and Darlington was like a trek into no-man's-land for more southerly-based journalists. At this stage, it was difficult to unpick what the story actually was. Headlines wouldn't comfortably form.

The private barn conversion I'd hired was booked under the name: Rolly Bridgeson.

Not my idea.

There was no meaning behind the name whatsoever, and I made sure I hired a nondescript car for our twenty-five mile journey to our accommodation - set in the middle of nowhere. Shizz was staying with me the evening, before heading over to her own lodge within reachable distance - close enough for any code reds. She shook her head as she checked emails and news on the journey there. 'So, you know how people like tracking flights?' was the beginning of her grim assessment. 'You were spotted at LAX. They know you're London bound.'

'Hopefully, the trail ends there. Promotional stuff.'

Shizz nodded, adding, 'You've had two seven figure offers for your autobiography.'

'No way.'

She kept scrolling, and declaring news like a parent reading out a bad school report - with unmitigated disapproval.

'Requests galore for statements, TV and radio interviews.'

'No to all.'

Eventually, we reached our lodgings, and I stepped out on the gravelly driveway, bags in both hands. This location was purposefully close, but not too close to the action. My shoes crunched along the stones, spilling them everywhere. It was hard not to make any noise, but the single light in the farm kitchen opposite showed no signs of disturbance. Our arrival time was deliberate. Shizz quietly collected the keys, and I heard the brief, hushed 'night hour' conversation between her and the proprietor - a woman in her late sixties.

The sky was starry.

I missed these skies.

On request, the host had lit the fire, now crackling with pleasant invitation - not that it was really needed - it was quite a warm August evening for the North. Shizz and I sat on a huge rug in the lounge/diner with its wooden floors and high ceilings and crooked beams. Two glasses and two bottles of Malbec (one of my favourite reds) rested on a tray on a mahogany coffee table. We helped ourselves and our discussion turned to the style and age of the Persian rug. It was quite simply humongous and must have cost a bob or two. I was paying a premium rate for this place, especially at short notice. There was a huge courtyard outside with a giant wall separating us from the main road. The archway we drove through was set a good distance back along the wall, so privacy was secured. I went and showered and changed into my slacks. My colour coordination was terrible; violet T-shirt, violet joggers. When I arrived back in the open plan lounge - considerable to say the least - Shizz was examining some bulky looking pictures on the walls. She'd swapped her glasses back to the imposing red ones.

'Have you seen these?' she observed, with a healthy mix of humour and curiosity.

'What?'

'These animals.'

Moving over, I studied the source of her intrigue. Nothing seemed out of sorts to me; just frames of small mammal skeletons: voles; rabbits; hedgehogs; foxes and squirrels.

'You were born in Montana!' I said.

'What's that supposed to mean?'

'You've never seen a moose's head on a wall?'

'Of course.'

'Goodbye seething metropolis. Hello rural life.'

'I get it. I just don't see the point. They're tiny. Have you seen that weird stuffed creature by the door?'

I had, and this made me laugh. I hadn't thought twice about it, in honesty.

'You mean… this county's cultural emblem?'

'*That* thing! Okay, okay…' she scowled disbelievingly (scowling more on noticing my violet attire). 'Bill, it's been a long, long day, and I'm too tired for your dry British wit. *County emblem?*'

'No, I'm being serious.'

The stuffed ferret was stationed at the entrance, attached to a branch, and sitting on a small table near a coat rack, *poised and ready for action.*

'You know, we did get free pyjamas on the flight?' she said, holding her gaze on my wardrobe.

'Okay?'

'Did you pour the entire bottle down yourself?'

Touché.

'Verity… it's been a long day… and I'm too tired for your dry British wit.' I fake smiled. 'Oh, and it's called a ferret.'

She snorted, smiling.

I pointed to my bedroom. 'Guess I'll go and get changed… and fetch a fresh bottle, shall I?'

'Do hurry, old sport.'

Half an hour later, while opening the second bottle, Shizz asked, 'How do you feel being back here?'

I stroked the rug. There was a wholesome smell in this place. It felt warm and homely.

'Swapped bodies with the me in a parallel universe.'

'So, a little detached?'

'You could say,' I studied the timber ceiling. 'I was born here, but it's like... my roots were pulled up many years ago.'

She sipped some more wine, studying me. 'You know, if you tell it like you did as a kid, they'll think you're mad.'

'I can't avoid it, can I?'

'Yes, you can!' she blurted. 'Sorry, I don't mean to be blunt, but these are your friend's bones. Deflect, deflect, deflect until... the identity's confirmed.'

'And how long will that take?'

'We know people who can speed that up, Bill.'

She was right. I thought long and hard about it. We'd learned through careful study of local news they were discovered, more or less, where I'd last spotted Rob. In truth, I never wanted them found because it brought my sanity into question.

Verity advised, '*Everyone* will forgive the testimony of a nine-year-old. You need to take the line of not understanding what you saw. The reports talk about the mist; he got lost in it, and drowned.'

Her directness hit me hard.

'Shizz, they searched for weeks. When the search was formally called off, groups of locals still combed that stretch, and for decades after - searching and searching - and then suddenly and magically, they find bones, *right* where I said *he vanished!*'

'So what? They found bones?' she shrugged.

'Do you believe me?'

She sighed. 'Don't ask me that?'

'So, no.'

'My job is to plan the exit route. The rest doesn't matter.'

I stared into the fire, and with a long, sorrowful exhale, raised my glass back to my mouth. 'I hope you're playing devil's advocate; it matters to me.'

'Bill, don't be affronted. I have similar conversations with Cassie about this stuff *all the time.*'

There was a flash of compassion behind her blue eyes, peering out from behind the thick, red rims. Verity would get the low-down on Crazy Ghosts on a weekly basis.

'I'm sure you do, Shizz, but in a twisted way, had these things never have happened, I wouldn't be here. All *this* wouldn't be here.'

My response was impassioned, nearly spilling the wine now sloshing in the glass. 'I saw him vanish right before my eyes, and couldn't stop it. The cruel years that followed.' I shook my head. 'I was butchered by my peers. A total freak. I became a recluse, Shizz. I hid far, far away for many, many years. I had *no* choice except turn real pain into real books. *This* empire.'

'And I get that.'

I necked the glass, reaching for the bottle. 'My entire career, and raison d'être, is not based on one *false* memory. If I change my story, I betray myself and I become an outright liar.'

'Then, we've got problems,' she grabbed my hand as it wrapped the glass, squeezing my fingers tightly. 'None of this has to be false, Bill. If it's real to you, then none of this is imaginary.'

'It was real to that mother whose son was nearly taken.'

'But, there are other explanations for that.' she threw out her hands. 'Ghosts I may possibly entertain, but there's no way there's some child snatching demon in that river.'

'Hang on… *you* live in *LA*!'

This confused the hell out of her. 'And?'

'Los Angeles. City of Angels. Where there are angels, there are always demons.'

Shizz looked exasperated. 'Sometimes, I think you're so immersed in your writing, myth and fact get mixed.'

'C'mon, you've had your own experiences. Explain those. There's some good, honest people around here,

Shizz. Even a Conservative councillor is firing out distress signals, for goodness' sake.'

'Right, we can't agree. I'm going for a smoke, and then I'm off to bed.' she swiftly drained her wine.

'My apologies, Shizz.'

'No, I love you. I get it. I do. I just can't anticipate how this will ride.'

'It's getting late, isn't it?'

'Yep.'

She placed her glass down on the coffee table. 'Before I go, tell me about the other kids. Your other friends from back then. I take it you didn't keep in touch.'

'No. All my age... all messed up. Scarlett Wilmott, Hazel Pickford, Ishaq Khan. Great friends, really. The event separated us. Scarlett was there with me, right whe-'

Shizz shoved out her palm, immediately stopping me speaking. 'Say that name again.'

'Scarlett?'

She picked up her phone from the coffee table. 'No, the other one.'

'Hazel, Ishaq?'

'Yes, Ishaq.'

'Ishaq Khan?'

Her blue nails grazed the screen again. She scrolled up and down and then resorted to tapping into the search bar. The lighting in the lounge of the barn had been kept purposefully low, the fire remaining the brightest source of light. It was a conscious attempt to stay hidden even though it was a solitary abode, and a reasonable distance from the farm house.

The phone screen was now the second strongest source of light as she held it up to my face, 'Look!'

'... I haven't got my glasses...'

Withdrawing, she increased the size and held it back up. 'Billy, you've just had your first slice of luck.'

I squinted and read the bottom of what was clearly an email.

I. Khan

'Ishaq's… sent me an email!'

'*Conservative councillor* Ishaq has, yes.'

'No. *What!*'

'I did forward you all these. What did I say about reading your bleeding emails, Bill?'

'There's no way.'

I took hold and read the increased font.

I'd heard he'd gone to Oxford or Cambridge, scarcely believing he'd come back?

The long and short of each desperate line was that the local community were beseeching him to act decisively on recent events. He was asking me for "extra" details about the day Rob vanished. Of course, a young Ishaq wasn't there on August 29th 1984, to witness what we saw, but he had an association by proxy - by being part of our original group. The locals all knew it. The media had obviously dug around him too.

'You have a patsy, Bill,' Shizz noted.

'No, no I don't.'

I kind of grimaced at the cold-hearted assessment.

'Deflect, deflect, deflect,' she reminded me.

It sounded like Ishaq was receiving sustained grief from locals demanding an electric fence be built on either side of the river, running the entire course - *for miles*. For all intents and purposes, and certainly to the national tabloids, these primitive demands were bordering on farcical. Trumpesque. But, Ishaq understood the fear of his constituents and the gravity of Robert Tipperton's disappearance - wounds that were deep-seated and personal to his community. He was juggling many plates and running out of options. The local MP was now involved, demanding he 'get a grip' on the matter. Reading between the lines, he sounded overwrought.

"William, to me, you'll always be my good friend, Billy Austin. Please contact me."

I clicked a link which brought me to a snazzy website. Panache and professionalism were clearly the order of the day, and Mr I. Khan was keen to present style and substance in equal measure.

I studied the constituent news section.

It was troubling to say the least; the latest entry was delicately composed. It was worded to recognise a pressing issue, without fully admitting to it. Action was required, and the discussion would be rational, and the approach to the solution, pragmatic. Despite being smartly written, it was lengthy and replete with inference, letting the imagination run riot. It indirectly acknowledged the thing it desperately wanted to avoid: the elephant in the room.

'Shizz.'

'Not good reading, is it? It says more, by not saying.'

'Written to the many by a logical, rational man…' I let that one linger. 'Shizz, I need you to do me a favour tomorrow evening.'

'Go… on…' her voice carried a healthy dose of trepidation.

'I need you to attend your first ever council meeting. It's open to the locals, and the press.'

She didn't speak for several seconds.

'And that is *what exactly?*'

'Where the locals have a massive discussion, and Ishaq chairs it.'

'Geez, Billy. You mean like an *open forum?*'

'I do.'

'You can't be serious.'

'I know, I know… but you won't stick out like a sore thumb, I promise. The press will be there; you'll just look like a journalist.'

She stared at me. 'Go easy on the compliments.'

Continuing her disparaging glare, she ignored the glass, purposefully bringing the wine bottle straight to her lips. Not once did she break her gaze. 'You expect me to drive in England. How far is it?'

'Three miles.'

This was closer than she expected me to say, and was inadvertently offering her acceptance. 'Around here?'

'Close by. Leeming village. Just up the road. Good intel. Forewarned is forearmed.'

She let out a growl of despair, letting me hear her displeasure. It was risky, but smart, and she knew it.

'I am not opening my mouth to anyone; not a soul. Not even to anyone who tries saying hello.'

I nodded; her accent may arouse suspicion. This was Yorkshire. A lot of folk *would* greet her.

Reaching into her bag, she extricated her mundane black glasses.

'I literally can't *believe* you're asking me to *dress down*... but seeing as you're clearly the expert... where's the store you import all your frumpy clothes?'

Chapter 2

The Rough and the Rugged

Another email arrived the following morning.

At this point, Verity suggested she forgo the lodge I'd paid for, and stay put in the barn-conversion until Cassie arrived.

I agreed.

'This is going to get quite rough.'

Her assessment was fair. Especially as this was another message from Ishaq, and this time he sounded frantic. The venue had been changed to Bedale town hall to accommodate a larger capacity, and by all accounts, large press vans with satellite dishes were beginning to amass near the library along the cobble-stone parking areas across from Saint Gregory's.

He'd asked if I could join him in the hall via a live link from LA to discuss what happened as kids.

Shizz presented my options.

'Ignore it. I'll write a generic and polite "decline". What's with the WIFI around here by the way?'

She paused, and went silent.

I waited. 'And?'

'And what?'

'My other options.'

'That *is* your option.'

'What if I just tell the truth?'

'Ishaq's offering you some free Japanese knotweed. If you want to keep the structure of your house intact and sustain a credible career, then, *that's* your option.'

'Fair point.'

I'd be a fool to ignore Shizz's wise advice.

'I doubt that link will work for a start,' she continued. 'More importantly, I have it on authority your mate publicly denounced his own experiences as a flight of fantasy, in the name of political ambition.'

'He did... *what?*'

'Well, at first, but he's back-tracking a little. Said it was his, and others', overactive imagination. From what I've read, it went down like a lead-balloon with the locals. They're livid. So, if you join him *live*, he's not only presenting you the knotweed; he's using you to foot the bill.'

Shizz was right, I had no context. It could be the lion's den.

She continued. 'There are photos appearing online of the boy I mentioned - and others - with giant scratch marks on their arms and backs. Your friend is going to be eaten alive if major news-station's are covering it. Billy, more things will be uncovered between now and this evening alone. We can't anticipate the questions they'll ask.'

The feeling in the pit of my stomach was intensely uncomfortable. I should have cancelled the wedding. I was a duck running itself to a seated position.

'Remember, in all of this,' she advised. 'You were the *last* person to see him alive. We've all watched the shows about child murderers. Secret, psycho kids hiding in plain sight. One got away... wrote a few books... became a superstar. Hidden behind the Hollywood High-rise. And now, they found his first victim.'

Shizz was absolutely right. I would be taking a huge gamble. If these bones were Rob's, which they undoubtedly were, the validity of my testimony would be tested, and that was only the start.

I nodded and retrieved my mask from my pocket.

'I'm coming with you tonight. Get the lay of the land. I'll sit in the car.'

'I think it's a bad call.'

'I need to see how big this is getting for myself. Besides, the Wi-Fi here means I'm *totally* left in the dark.'

'Billy, I don't think you're getting this… *it's huge already.* I haven't even mentioned the thirty-seven statement requests you received overnight.'

She nodded until I gave visual cues I understood.

This did the trick. I acknowledged this, while feeling bad for Ishaq. I really couldn't handle the trauma from my past being in full view. Jet-lag, drink and stress had given me a near sleepless night. I kept thinking about Rob vanishing before me; *how could they find bones?*

'Okay, okay. I have a better idea,' Shizz suddenly declared; constructively, but bossily. 'The reception here's awful. Your account's plenty big enough. How about I call for another hire car with blacked-out windows? We'll drive there together. You stay inside, and I'll go in and stream the meeting straight to you.'

It was a super smart plan. I loved it.

'Shizz, before you make that call and email Ishaq, drive into town now, and give me a true indication of the scale of this, please.'

She looked nervous and twirled a sharp blue nail through a single, short curl.

'*Billy*, please don't ask me to drive in this country. I don't understand it.'

'All you have to do is keep to the left-hand side.'

She pulled her glasses up, rubbing her eyes.

'I look awful.'

'Good. The slipping out for a loaf and a pint of milk look is perfect.'

'When I drive in, how on earth do I turn around and come back?'

I coughed at this, trying to suppress my laugh.

'You drive through Bedale to the new roundabout, and use it to turn back.'

'Oh, not one of those…' she moaned. 'Why do you crazy people use those stupid things?'

'And just be aware: our rest-stops are called lay-bys, and they don't have billboards next to them advertising strip-joints.'

'Are there good clothes shops in this town?'

'I don't know.'

She shook her head. 'You know I'm going to resign next week.'

~ ~ ~

The press were gathering in force.

Verity saw residents getting stopped and interviewed near the north end of town.

'It's a very pretty, isn't it? It oozes history; all those lovely old cobbles.'

She was relieved to be back here, and safe. No one had beeped her, but apparently her parking was shoddy. Shizz had by no means escaped conversations; talking to a helpful assistant in the clothes store, instead resorting to mimicking my accent. (The recount had me in stitches.) "I was channelling Ross from Friends."

The laughter helped peel back the deeply ingrained difficulty I was facing, realising I had nothing but fondness for the area. It reminded me of a simpler, more wholesome pace of life - a juxtaposition to the life I was leading; and one I could never have. I loved how Shizz was cooing about her short visit, too.

'I didn't see the library you mentioned, but to be honest, I didn't really know what I was looking for. If it's that building that juts out at the far end, it's a museum. That's where all the vans are gathering... and they're everywhere!'

'Bedale... *has a museum?*'

'Yeah. There was a banner saying museum.'

'In Bedale?' I huffed at her observation in disbelief.

Shizz assertively pulled back her black-rimmed spectacles, glowering at me. 'Well, let's go and pay it a visit right now. Don't forget to wear your Gucci suit and Armani sunglasses.'

'Okay, okay.'

'You need to listen to me.' She jabbed her finger back at the door to the hire car outside. 'Seriously, Bill. You made me drive a road on the left-hand side. I navigated a sodding roundabout that I managed to circle… at least eight times. and I wasn't even wearing lipstick… What else can I do for you today, honey? What else?'

'Ohh, sassy.' I held up an apologetic hand to calm her. 'You did good. I mean it. I do appreciate it. I really do.'

We bantered and bickered like this often.

'I made you coffee.' I added in reconciliation.

'I want food, too. You've made me hangry.'

'I cooked you an omelette.'

'Thank goodness you have your uses,' she said.

We grabbed a mug each and sat outside on green, steel garden chairs. It was private here; a quaint and secluded sun trap. The farmhouse was clearly visible two hundred yards ahead, but the large wall encasing the property sealed out the world, providing us with exclusivity and deadened road noise.

'You British like your pubs,' she added, sipping her Americano, 'I love their names; I passed two, and both were called the Green Dragon.'

'Ahh, of course… you saw one in Bedale, and passed the other in Exelby. Many a good memory in them both.'

'There's a load in Bedale.'

'They named one of them after me, but it's closed down now.'

'Did they?'

'King Billy.'

'Really?'

'No.'

'Look… please, *just shut up*.' She shovelled in the final delicious spoonfuls. 'Tasty omelette, stick to cooking.'

The only available, reasonably priced and reasonably mundane 'dark tint' hatchback, was at a Depo near Bradford.

Quite rightly, the manager couldn't understand why we wouldn't choose his Audi RS straight from the forecourt a mere five miles away. (Too eye-catching.) I listened as Verity Schulenburg increased my offer - in increments of fifty - to secure a standard hatchback that would be delivered from sixty miles away. The dark tint was still a little see-through by all accounts. A deal was agreed very quickly; the vendor, reluctant to accept too much in terms of payment - and it would arrive between one and two in the afternoon.

In the meantime, I scoured the news for updates - with intermittent Internet.

This led to panic.

This was becoming *major* news.

One item of particular note, was the imminent coroner's report on the bones. Shizz informed me of the find at Simone's party, but they'd been with forensics for a number of weeks; the police withholding their discovery. We were only three or so miles from the beck at this location, and I repeatedly wrestled with this announcement.

It was about Rob, my friend.

And it was about me.

In many ways, the bare bones of my soul were being unearthed along with his. My novels, my studies - birthed, and marinaded - in survivor guilt. Words were my self-therapy. I purposefully organised myself to write and keep writing. If I took my foot off the gas, only briefly, I'd get restless... and tunnel my prior nadirs, sinking in more unchartered depths of disgrace, guided by the murky gutters in my mind. All wrought with addiction, the next one sure to finish me. His disappearance had become my fame... and I felt like worthless shit because of it.

When the announcement came, I'd probably retire.

This was bad.

If I thought about the moment he vanished from view, I felt a rush of sustained remorse. To know this remorse was currently being rationalised by the scientific community - the matter on the verge of being resolved - made my reason d'etre a fallacy. I didn't want these bones to be my friend's for many reasons... but mainly now, selfishly, because they'd rip the fabric of self-faith beyond repair.

I was screwed.

Shizz and I agreed to set off a full hour before the meeting commenced; this being essential. The hall was plenty big enough to accommodate a sizable gathering, but it was clear from the clamour it would be inundated. With reluctance, I parked the car at the south end, and coaxed my PA to walk the entire length of the high street in her new 'frumpy' attire. In the end, she'd opted for a long, plain cream coat and bonnet - making her *stylishly* plain.

After five minutes, she texted me to say "problems" were "imminent" and "obvious".

"What already?"

Five minutes later, more arrived.

Her height had been "an advantage" and she'd managed to take a seat right at the back; people assuming she was someone of importance... and that the library was "still here" so I shouldn't worry.

I replied: 'Thank goodness for the small things.'

Then another: the lady next to her was so friendly, she'd had to speak back.

I sent a smiley face.

The windows on the hatchback were tinted to only fifty per cent, and this was giving me heart palpitations. Folks would stare in - mostly just looking at their own reflection - but a car with every window tinted was a little at odds with the others parked around me.

Verity started live-streaming shortly after seven. I was surprised at how grand the room looked. She told her gregarious neighbour it was for *her* American audience...

who were taking an interest. She briefly fired me a three second clip of her hair bonnet and tapped her black glasses (while pulling a glum face), before pointing the camera towards the front.

I watched Ishaq take a seat behind a table, with two others, either side of him.

Closing in on forty years later, there he was.

He had grown in proportion with his small stature and was probably around 5 foot 6. He sported a groomed, speckled beard, and the same jet black hair. As Shizz zoomed in on him, I recognised his features; just like his dad's, all those years ago. He looked tired; a man forced into an impossible corner. Tributaries pushed out from the side of his eyes. Even his movements appeared slow and defeated, as he pulled the chair under him.

Shizz intuitively circumnavigated the ballroom with her phone, to give me a sense of scale; all seats were taken. People stretched down the sides, two or three abreast. I considered fire-safety for a moment, but many of the huge Georgian style windows and doors were already open along the west wing. There were many cameras - absolutely everywhere. Boom Mics galore.

It was similar to one of Simone Chapdelaine sets, particularly his earlier regency period movies. The room was lavishly painted in a rich, vibrant yellow, leading up to an exquisitely designed vestibule. My PA purposefully kept the phone aloft for me to marvel at the beautifully ornate curves and decorated trims. Characters from Greek mythology, rendered in white plaster, and interspersed with calming teal. This location had been carefully selected for an anticipated media event.

In this setting, and with all this tech, no wonder Ishaq appeared apprehensive.

His colleagues were introduced to the audience, and to be fair, he sounded very clear and assured. He then introduced the evening, thanking a whole gamut of different people, before undertaking a brief synopsis of why they were gathered. His prepared speech was controlled, measured, and precise. Attempted humour fell flat, but he persevered. Ishaq, once again, appealed for a pragmatic approach, and a reasonable discussion, frequently acknowledging the people sitting on either side of him. He then gave the floor to the locals.

Smartly, Shizz had remembered to click on the microphone, and although it was picking up lots of shuffling, murmuring, and the grating of chairs… it was also picking up their questions.

These were no nonsense - right from the outset.

'Are these bones Robert Tipperton's?'

The directness alone made Verity's camera hand wobble, as did Ishaq's voice. 'We're currently not in a position to clarify this. It's important the right protocols are followed. As soon as have an update, we'll tell you.'

Disgruntled murmurings from the floor. The man who asked the question followed up, 'We hear you already know, and you're deliberately withholding…'

A woman close by immediately followed suit. 'Is there a scientific explanation for what's happening?'

'In what regard?' Ishaq said.

'Could these burns be caused by Giant hogweed, or hemlock?'

Someone else asked, 'Can they make people hallucinate?'

This was new. Unexpected.

From the back, Shizz's panoramic footage enabled me a fifty-fifty view of locals nodding, and others, furiously shaking their disapproval. I knew hemlock finished-off Socrates back in the day, but *Giant Hogweed*? On cue, a question that provided context.

'Is the river being checked, and how are we supposed to know the difference between cow parsley, hogweed, and hemlock?'

More agreed this time.

Shizz whispered, 'Bill… I don't have a clue.'

I messaged, 'They're wild plants. Neither do I.'

249

Ishaq tried answering. 'Yes, let me reassure you. We've hired experts to check the length and breadth of the river for signs.'

'Signs?' - A man interrupted - 'It's *definitely* there... has been for years.'

The lady next to him held up an indistinguishable image on her phone. 'There's purple speckled stems everywhere. It's growing out of the ruddy beck.'

Before Councillor Khan could respond, the clamour reached fever-pitch; the couple triggering urgent enquiries.

'Is this a danger to dogs?'

'*Why* was the playground built so close to the river?'

'Is this why livestock's perishing?'

'What does the "Member of Parliament for Richmondshire and Hambleton District" believe is going on, and what does he intend to do about it?'

Ishaq was losing control.

'Okay, okay...' He flapped his hands defensively, pleading for calm.

'Give the man a chance,' someone shouted.

And as the crowd momentarily settled, an incisive question was asked about me. It was sudden, coming from the wings - just outside the open Georgian doors - timed to perfection by a journalist. It was the last thing to be heard, further reducing the noise; putting Ishaq on the spot.

'William P. Austin was a friend of yours when you were young. Is he aware of the situation and has he told you anything about it?'

Even the chair shuffling abated, everyone turning to face the front.

I listened to Ishaq cough once, clearly wanting to go back a step, but the die was cast. He was actually allowing a little space for more interruptions.

None came.

'I have tried contacting William... and as yet have had no response. I'm sure he will, in due course.'

A follow-up. 'Do you stay in touch with Mr Austin?'

He answered professionally. 'I'm afraid I do not.'

'Why not?'

'I think… time, and circumstances separated us, as they do with people, sometimes.'

He shifted uncomfortably.

'Do you have any comment to make on William's statement from August 30th 1984 - similar to your own - where you both cited supernatural occurrences at the river?'

'I cannot comment on the day Robert Tipperton disappeared because I wasn't there, nor can I comment on behalf of Billy Austin.'

This generated a lot of dissatisfaction.

'Councillor Khan, do you yourself subscribe to a supernatural or scientific explanation for these burns and scratches people are experiencing?'

'Scientific.'

He was too blunt in his delivery - almost, dismissive - inciting a frosty reaction. A lady in her early forties stood bolt upright on hearing this. Wearing an elegant white trouser suit, she unfurled the glossy cylinder in her hands, swivelling the A2 sheet round for the indignant crowd to see. Instantly, several other parents stood.

This was preset, planned for effect.

Eight or nine unrolled their own enlarged photos of child and animal injuries, to gasps.

They aimed them at the cameras.

Shizz zoomed in on a couple.

'Oh shit,' I whispered.

Lights immediately began flashing in abundance; the press sensing a pivotal moment. I tried to figure out the image before me, as Shizz calmly rotated the phone, homing-in on the first lady holding a picture of her son.

It was beyond disturbing, difficult to process.

Similar to claw marks, in batches of three, travelling up the spine between each scapula, and rising well into the hairline. They covered his arms, burying their sharp, bloodied points deep in his shoulder blades.

He'd been grabbed by something.

251

He'd tried tugging away.

And it had clung tight, slicing his skin asunder.

'Are you… getting this?' Verity whispered.

I managed a yes.

Either the kid had escaped a bear mauling, or he'd vigorously and repeatedly rubbed his back against barbed wire.

Out of sight, a woman wailed. 'They put my Missy down…'

As camera crews turned, I waited for Shizz to point.

But she didn't… her voice dropping a sullen octave. 'I'm… just… I'm sorry, I just can't Billy…'

The phone briefly went to thigh-level, streaming the back of a chair, only reluctantly raising after several seconds. In the car, my fingers turned the air-conditioning up a notch. This was visceral. Robert's bones, or not; there was *something* still in there.

It was tough for Ishaq, but it got a whole lot tougher when an audience member became emotional, launching into an impassioned soapbox rant.

Verity suddenly whispered to me, 'Billy… I'll show you some of the others…'

More photos appeared, albeit smaller - and less well prepared for the occasion. My personal assistant focussed in on several savaged creatures: badgers, pigs…

I stared out of the tinted window and listened to Missy's owner sobbing out her broken heart - ignoring protocol - and explaining to others about the invisible force that dragged her dog under. I could hear both her, and the woman shouting at Ishaq.

The next voice was Verity's.

'Billy… I had no clue how bad this was for you.' There was a pause, interspersed by the backdrop of anger. 'This river is messed up.'

It was.

But was it ever *this bad?* Sure, Rob vanished… and that was terrible, but this was different, and quickly escalating.

Temporarily, the trouser-suit lady's thunder was stolen by rage and weeping, but she remained composed, patiently waiting. Sensing the most salient figure, the cameras zeroed back to her, and she took her cue.

'I had social services contact me about this. In no way, shape, or form would I *ever* harm my son. We are a respectable family. He had forty-two stitches, and will not leave our room on an evening.' She paused, taking a huge inhale of breath. 'I saw him get yanked back... *by nothing...* and I want to know what you're going to do about this matter?'

Ishaq acted quickly.

'Thank you for your question, Mrs Levett. Is it okay if I pass you on to Professor Lindsay who holds a PHD in many disciplines, including Traumatology, which is the study of wounds?'

His response appalled me, and I watched his associate with short hair and glasses begin explaining what she thought was happening. She held up photos herself - a size smaller - to illustrate patients who had accidentally brushed against dangerous river-dwelling plants. The emphasis was on *Giant hogweed* in particular, the resulting lines - certainly red - but far more blistered, and less defined. The presentation might have held water, had not its delivery not been demeaning.

I knew this wouldn't be accepted, and it wasn't; one farmer brazenly remarking: 'Plants don't grab yer unless they're Triffids. I've worked this land for fifty years, and I haven't seen a single bloody Triffid yet. But... *I am* seeing my dogs returning from t'water's edge with huge gashes in their sides. It's costing me a fortune. Maybe Mr Khan's expert should bring her cossie and come down for a little swim.'

The ballroom erupted at the expert's perceived condescension. More cameras flashed. Things were rapidly boiling over.

This was now headline material.

I pulled up my phone and accessed my bank account, while listening in. I requested a BACs transfer and then resumed the show.

Ishaq tried pulling it back.

'I represent many good people here, and it is truly an honour to work with such a tight-knit community.'

He paused; caught between a rock and a hard place. For the sake of career progression, he couldn't admit to anything damaging to his political aspirations. He knew - in his heart of hearts - what happened to him, and no amount of window dressing would fool these honest folk.

I stared at my phone, wondering how on earth he'd do this.

'Something very real - and you have all read my testimonies - happened to me by that river when I was younger,' he courageously began, 'and to this day... I find comfort thinking there's a logical explanation behind it.'

He visibly swallowed, very quickly re-engaging.

'Seeing the photograph Mrs Levett bravely showed, reminds me very much of experiences I have tried to forget. I don't want this to be real any more than you all. Especially for your son, George, Mrs Levett... and for all the others.'

'What he's moving on to say,' a strong voice cut across from the back, 'is that we naturally need to exhaust every avenue in search of a robust explanation.'

Everybody turned.

As did Shizz, pointing her camera at the older man.

I immediately recognised him from the many sycophantic photos on Ishaq's councillor page - of them both together - his surrogate father. This was the local MP. *His* boss. Undoubtedly, assessing his performance from the rear, and not at all pleased with developments. He continued in an imperious voice. 'We used to believe bad smells caused illness before discovering bacterial microbes. We will launch an immediate and full investigation into the river to analyse what could be causing all of this. Rest assured.'

Ishaq looked crestfallen; he'd neither fully addressed his anxious constituents, nor pleased his condescending superior. His lot was a flickering neon exit sign.

So, that's why I walked in.

From the back.

Past the cameras, straight down the centre.

Jeans, black T-shirt, pointy brown shoes.

I even managed to make it half-way mark before the Journos clocked on. Their chatter went into overdrive; It was all rather frenzied.

People turned and gawped.

I even received a smattering of applause.

I kept my Ray-Bans on. Not to look cool. I just hated the flash of a thousand cameras.

Everybody on the table looked confused as I approached - not knowing who I was - with the exception of Ishaq, who bore a face of utter astonishment.

Of course, my entrance at the rear was subtle... even managing a detour to the lady with the cream coat and bonnet... placing her favourite red spectacles neatly on her lap.

She looked down in surprise, and then up.

I tapped her shoulder once and then continued walking. I was strapped inside the rocket and Houston was counting.

Caught in perfect unison between the numbers: three, two, one... I heard this American speaking to me... from Mission control.

'Oh... you... *dickhead*...'

Chapter 3

Shock and Reveal

How would I assess my performance?

Frank and honest, I suppose.

I hoped this was how it was received. I guess the standout moment was being overwhelmed to the point of sobbing. It was a sudden - hardly unexpected - question. Maybe it was the journalist's pitch, or intonation; possibly the perceived empathy.

"How would you feel if the discovered bones do belong to your old friend, Robert Tipperton?'

Regardless, I paused a fraction too long before answering. That was precisely the problem. A sequestered second for me to view a shadowy corner plot in my mind, where Rob's neglected tomb lay. Maybe, just fleetingly, I became aware of all the cameras, and some old local faces. I just about pushed out, 'Relieved... I'd be relieved...' Then it seized me like a convulsion, and a minute later, I managed to staccato-blurt my way through an emotional explanation - but then made the mistake of glancing at Verity - raising her red glasses to wipe her eyes.

I went again.

Somebody kindly placed a glass of water in front of me. A random hand reassuringly patted my shoulder. And somehow I stuck it out for the rest of the session, diverting attention away from Ishaq; this tactic, wholly working. I acknowledged Mrs Levett and the emails she'd sent me about her son, and her questions. Political predation between the MP and his councillor was replaced by a celebrity breakdown - all live - for the wide-eyed concern of the compassionate, and lustful delight of vicarious vultures.

Perfect.

Blessedly, the MP became my inadvertent compére; rapidly revising his penchant for limelight. He "stamped" his mark over proceedings by bringing everything a close an hour later; re-iterating an 'investigative' regime, and better communication to resolve the matter. This was met with disgruntled and disapproving murmurings and classic rural contempt. Juxtaposing himself against me in this way also served to reinforce any loose ends in my erratic display.

'Out you go,' and, 'Off to bed' were the directives issued by ushers to the astounded reporters - as the lights suddenly went down and fire doors were flung. Concluded. No messing around; this was full-frontal Yorkshire at its finest. And in the ensuing melee of scraping chairs, Ishaq uttered his first words to me in nearly four decades.

'I couldn't ask for more… in terms of what you just did there.'

'I'll need to watch it back. I don't have a clue what I said.'

'It changed everything.'

'Well, you were being swamped, and needed a dredge.'

'Billy, give me your number. I need to explain some other things.'

Other things?

Now wasn't the time for a tidbit as to what *that* meant, so we exchanged, shook hands, and tried speaking briefly… but a commotion towards the back ended these pleasantries. I had no choice but to intervene.

'She's my personal assistant; she's with me!' The enthusiastic attendant was all but grappling Shizz. '*It's okay, it's okay.*'

As he relinquished his hold, she vigorously brushed herself down, making sure he could blatantly see her expelling his contamination, and then she model-walked my way. 'Your kin-folk don't mess around, do they?'

Then, she just paused a moment in front of me, eye-to-eye… before grabbing me, and holding on tight, whispering, 'Talk about a Hail Mary pass.'

'Hopefully, caught.'

'Still in the air.'

She squeezed harder. 'It went surprisingly well… but you'll get a barrage of questions outside; they're waiting.'

It was inevitable, and I'd anticipated. 'Shizz, pull a map up on your phone and bring the car around the back to the Wynd. I'll stay put till you arrive.'

'Is that a wine bar?'

'Pardon?'

'Wined.'

'No, no, but it is a homophone.'

'What?'

'As in winding-you up. It's a road. W-y-n-d. Park, and wait for me by the Methodist church. Red building.'

I pointed in the rough direction.

'Oh, Billy. Not more driving, Billy… *please.*'

'You got this.'

She huffed more displeasure but on seeing the usher move back towards her, took the keys, and left out the open west wing, surprising her pursuer, who had a raft of chairs to navigate.

It was quite dark outside, and I made it clear to the Press, I could afford fifteen more minutes, knowing I was essentially agreeing to double. Questions centred on my unexpected entrance, current abode, and my real purpose for being here. When I answered that these were all personal reasons - (and I meant the wedding)- I sensed this was construed as some secretly covert operation. Invariably, one or two questions carried the pre-requisite darker tones, although subtly disguised.

"In hindsight, do you feel you could have prevented Rob's disappearance in any way?"

I stayed polite and deflected.

Cameras flashed and clicked.

'I think you'll agree that everything I said and did in there… was from the heart. I didn't expect these things to happen; I only learned of the discovery at the same time as you. I have nothing to hide, not even tears and anguish. For me to display it all like that - in front of you all - suggests how destroyed I am.'

Quite a few journalists nodded.

'There's a lot I need to deal with. It hasn't been easy. Don't look at my success as a highlight reel. I unravelled in a dark room years ago.'

I made some reasonable joke about not eating all day, and a journalist offered me half his roast beef and horseradish sandwich.

'Roast beef… and *horse-radish?*' I said, salivating. 'Haven't had one of those in years.'

He nodded.

'Where from?' I said.

'The Co-op.'

'On the high street?'

His colleague pointed, 'I can whip round the corner, and fetch you one.'

I nearly said yes (and they all knew it), smiling instead. 'Ahh, now that's smart. Gives you a bit of extra time, doesn't it?'

'Need to find, kill, and roast the cow.'

It took the edge off things, because I was a wreck.

I grabbed his sandwich, thanked him, and shoved half of it in my mouth, giving me a chance to ponder something else: I'd seen neither Scarlett of Hazel in there. Deep down, I wondered if they'd show up to support Ishaq… that they'd got wind of this meeting. Their absence surprised me, but maybe they didn't live around here any more.

Rapidly tiring now, and well passed the forty-minute mark, I said some hasty goodbyes and departed around the back of the hall, down a narrow road I hadn't used since I was a teen. Of course, some followed, and I kind of bantered, rather than answered - keeping it light-hearted and genial.

I was experienced in this.

I had a brain-wave and texted Shizz to jump into the passenger seat ready for when we met, and keep the engine running… praying she'd parked at the correct church.

She had.

The camera's flashed at Shizz as I got in.

She wound down the window, and clarified: 'Personal assistant, Personal assistant, et cetera, et cetera.' Then she took to some shameless promotion. 'Make sure you check out the brilliant music of *Woes Almanac* and *the Crazy Ghosts show* on the web. It's scary, and it's brilliant. Cassie Starr, *I love you!*'

It did the trick.

Giving me a chance to swing the car one-eighty. The press were neither expecting a getaway car, nor the three-point turn. Some tried calling their colleagues to make haste to the front of Bedale Hall, and come round to the Wynd. They assumed I'd drive up the high-street.

They were wrong.

Roads forked continuously here, allowing me to sell numerous red herrings before purposefully aiming for Masham, hoping a convoluted country road would shake-off my hangers-on.

It worked surprisingly well.

On an exceedingly dark road, all remained blank and bare in the rear-view mirror.

Until the two-mile mark.

Then, a motorbike appeared behind us, nearly a mile back - a solitary headlamp, increasing in size - as it steadily approached the rear of the car. Leaving the brake, lifting my foot off the throttle, I let the car slow a fraction… attempting to become the last weary night-traveller on their journey home.

If it overtook, we were off the hook; its initial speed, suggesting it would.

But it didn't.

'Damn it.'

'Company?'

Shizz took a breather from her verbal summary, checking the side-mirror.

'Looks like one of those zippy scooters,' I said.

'Only one?'

'Yeah.'

'But you're still driving… away from the barn, right?'

'Just about.'

'Can we shake them?'

'Dunno. I'll head into Masham. We'll wait there for a bit.'

Before reaching the small town, I pulled onto Limekiln lane; a small track heading down to the River Ure. As we passed a couple of farm entrances, I searched for a bumpy track - one too dicey for scooter navigation - but it never materialised. Reaching the bottom, I joined a main road again, and continued over a bridge, aiming for quaint town, trying to buy us some breathing space.

'So, which one will you take him to?'

'Who?'

'The journalist behind.'

I sensed a sarcastic remark was imminent. 'Go on. Where?'

She pointed to a sign. 'Which brewery? Black Sheep, or Theakston's?'

'Which do you suggest?'

'It's you… so Black Sheep.'

'Do they brew trouble, too?'

Taking the hire car further up the steep bank, I saw another sign I recognised. 'Actually, Shizz, the property you and Cass are renting is around here. I thought if I took him there, that would throw them off my scent.'

'I hope you're joking. Don't you dare.'

Her eyes bored into me, and I purposefully didn't meet her gaze, chuckling away. Instead, I slowly rolled the car to the left, into the picturesque centre.

The evening was warm and pleasant.

Above, a panorama of stars twinkled in the night sky, and the subtlest of glows from ambient street lighting cast a warm and sleepy mystique over the old market square.

'I'll have me a bit of this,' Shizz observed.

Smooth and worn steps led to a small cylinder of stone in the middle, centuries of moonlight shimmering over its rugged surface. I drove past it, and around the back.

'This is gorgeous,' my side-kick commented.

At this time of night, the place was deserted; resting in the sweetest of slumbers after the hustle and bustle of a busy day. The surrounding ancient houses themselves emanated their own blanket of sleepy shadows; the inhabitants within, cosily tucked-up in the warmest patterned quilts. It had the air of the tranquillity, a cubbyhole to sequester in beautiful solitude.

'Keep it nice and polite, Mr Austin,' Shizz reminded me. 'Don't undo your good work.'

I parked, bringing the window down and taking a big breath, waiting for the paparazzi to pull right alongside. The bike stayed back, around fifty feet away, on the opposite side of the memorial. Shizz read my mind, as we exchanged puzzled looks.

'A fan?'

'Maybe.'

I turned my face to look out the open window, as the rider stared down and then swivelled the handlebars sharply right, preparing to depart.

'Solitary fans sometimes do this, don't they?' Shizz noted.

'Yeah, I don't think it's a journo.'

'Look at their neck. No camera.'

'Ahh, yes.'

'Bill, I think they're leaving.'

The person let their scooter amble, aiming for the outer edge of the car park towards the front of the King's Head Hotel before stopping once more. They tuned their head ninety, studying us through their visor.

Their posture suggested an unwillingness to engage.

'Female. Not press at all,' Shizz said.

And she was correct. I silently nodded. Their body language denoted someone contemplative… but unsure, possibly even respectful.

'Someone you know, perhaps, Bill?'

This struck me.

My mind erupted.

'Oh, shit.'

She could be right. They looked slender in their fitted leather biking gear. A solitary white stripe descended the arm of the jacket. Periodically, they stared away, aware that we were watching. It was clear they didn't want to be intrusive, but…

They wrapped both rider gloves around the grips - intent on leaving - pulling out onto the tiny adjoining road that circumnavigated the market place, slowly heading away from the enclosed plaza.

But the brake was suddenly applied, and their head notably sagged.

And as the single red light blazed in the distance, they steadied their feet on the ground, still facing away. I opened the car door, and stepped out, hoping they would look over their shoulder again, as I waved, and called.

'*What the hell… is wrong with you, tonight?*'

Verity wasn't pleased, but they turned. A quick glance over the shoulder, and then a right turn back into the lonely market square again. My heart was savagely beating. I reached the square steps next to the memorial and stood waiting.

The scooter approached.

And stopped.

Calculating matters, I knew the physique was promising. As she gracefully disembarked, I noted she was wearing tight-fitting, black jeans. Hesitantly, she stayed stationary by the bike, with her right hand remaining on the handlebar.

I estimated she was 5 foot 7 now, kind of where I would have placed her in my memory.

Confidence hadn't posed an issue for me in many years, but this evening-hour was now pouring pure heavenly silver over us both, and I realised that the starry universe had, once again, had arranged another rendezvous with my past.

We both stepped forward at exactly the same time.

'Can I help?'

I kept it polite, unassumingly so.

I heard a muffled "Hi" and an apology for *following* as she lifted her helmet.

Immediately, bundles of curly auburn hair cascaded down each side of her face, hanging like rubies across her freckled cheeks. The same light blue eyes... twinkling with mischief and wisdom.

But, it wasn't Scarlett.

'Hi, I'm... I'm Serin...' she nervously began. 'You once knew my mother.'

~ ~ ~

For centuries, people took their seat at this very spot.

Midday, and midnight.

Sober, lucid. Rat-arsed, honest.

Worn and brow-beaten. Happy and hopeful.

A spot for the end of a hard day's work, or because age necessitated.

The plethora of thoughts; the deepest pitch of black, or the most vivid of natural white, depending on person, mood or circumstance - all converging to a single point, nestled in the grassy hills, on the cusp of the glorious Dales. This consummate crown of a worn, chiselled seat.

This cold, smooth... *thinkers* chair.

Reaching into the pocket of my jacket, I pulled out the maroon packet of Kreteks, lit one... looked up, and slowly exhaled into the Milky Way.

Despite my assumptions that local grapevine knowledge eventually extended its reach overseas, this... hadn't. I inhaled long and deep once again, watching the smoke rise. My parents *surely* would have texted me. One hundred per cent, they had *no clue*. I suppose it made sense; Scarlett had moved further into the Dales - very close to here, in fact - beyond the radar; no longer privy to six degrees of separation. Globalisation, that spread knowledge in the blink of an eye… met its match when it contended with a rural time frame. I loved that about this place; I really did.

It was here, set further back in the Dales, Scarlett Wilmott died.

Eight years ago.

Melanoma.

She was thirty-nine.

I was in shock, really.

Her daughter was truly beautiful. Humble, and yet, spirited. It simmered below the surface - the mirror image of Scarlett. She even bounced on the spot a little, like I remembered. I smiled at her, but, because I was somehow confusing a reunion with her mum in our twenties. One that never happened. I couldn't believe it. I literally couldn't believe it. My fingers slipped out another Kretek, coaxing it by the tip, not even half-way through my first. And after ten minutes, an intrigued personal assistant joined us; not wanting to be left in the dark, and alone in the car. After introductions, Shizz swiftly and astutely recognised my demeanour; a splattered canvas covered in soul shit. I didn't reveal… it wasn't appropriate… but she frowned as she discerned my visible wilt. Playing poker with her was a nightmare, as she easily recognised my *tell*. Here, it was handy. Deliberately excusing herself, she moved on to the King's Head to check out the beer on behalf of her incoming girlfriend. Verity had more than earned her stripes this evening.

'I have my phone with me if you need anything, Bill.' she nodded, concerned.

I called out, 'Try a Rusty Nail.'

'Whatever.'

As Serin took the worn, stone step next to me, it took me a moment to realise she had no clue what I meant.

'Your book - Her Bravest Song - really helped mum. She read it four months before she died.'

And there it was…

That got me straightaway; way too much. I pulled the cigarette further out, lobbing the first, averting my eyes to the stars. This particular novel was about a Missionary diagnosed with cancer a week before departing on her dream to help others: *brave or irresponsible* - was the philosophical question? When you delved into her family backdrop; she was definitely brave. Somehow, I felt a heightened sense of quiet around me, with no choice but to listen. Had anyone else - century after century - thought anything *remotely* similar to what I was thinking, on this hollowed perch in the middle of the countryside close to midnight?

Maybe.

'But she said her absolute favourite was Grace in Star-Spun Places, because she reckoned you based Mattie Harrison on her.'

The slight girl by my side paused a moment, unsure (maybe not wanting to hear an answer in the negative). 'Is that *really* true?'

'It is.'

I stared directly ahead, fighting the imminent descent over an emotional precipice. Robert Tipperton had inadvertently inspired my life course, and Scarlett… one of my most beloved characters. Neither knew. I had no idea *she knew*; suspected even - being handed knowledge to the contrary was hard.

'Yes. Yes, I did,' I re-confirmed. 'Your mum was *very* much Mattie.'

I could only be honest. In Hollywood, tens of thousands of dollars spent, and the awkward attrition with a psychoanalyst could never prize you apart this much. Why didn't she write to me if she knew? I had taken the opportunity to reach out to Scarlett from afar; not directly, of course. In my mind, I'd hoped she'd somehow realised it was her, and get in contact.

'That's very, very cool,' Serin said, quietly satisfied. 'She insisted she was Mattie... and told me at every opportunity.'

'Really?'

Serin nervously rubbed her hands.

'Can I ask?' I asked, changing the angle. 'How old were you when your mum passed?'

'Twelve.'

Her reply was soft, sad.

'I'm so sorry.'

'It's okay.'

There was something a little less in-your-face about Serin; more measured and wistful than Scarlett, but it could all be because her mum died. Maybe Scarlett was deep like this too; I just never got to see it.

'It must have been... horrendous,' I said, genuinely enquiring, but still in shock.

'Yeah, it really was.'

Serin nodded, her hair bouncing, and then drooping slightly as her head bowed. 'I thought you must have known.'

'I learn a lot over time,' I sighed. 'But I missed this. No idea.'

'Mum once said,' she gave the sweetest cough, 'You and her... once had a thing.'

I blushed in the dark. (Did we?) 'I...'

I took a long, hard drag. 'Yeah.'

Looking down at my packet, I felt guilty for not offering her one sooner. She accepted. I offered the lighter. She struck up and took a drag.

'Why do they light up red?'

'You won't get these in Yorkshire.'

'Tastes... different.'

'Burns the cloves within,' I said. 'I rarely smoke anymore if I'm honest... certain times, certain occasions.'

Our eyes met in silent acknowledgment, but I knew she wasn't a fan of the cloves.

'I thought you knew,' she said. 'It must be shocking... for you to hear?'

'It is.' I sighed again, letting her see. 'It really is.'

Desperate to change topic, and not crack, I recalled her pursuit from earlier,.

'Serin, if you thought I already knew about your mum, then why on earth did you follow me tonight?'

Her sapphire eyes sparked to life with understanding. Behind, her brain whirred like a sniper with a sloth in sight... and I watched the beautiful ghost of Scarlett forming in her face.

'Okay. This *will* sound weird. My mum should have been a lawyer, or a private investigator.' She stopped, hesitating, recognising we'd only just met. 'Is it okay if I continue?'

'Yeah, of course.'

'So mum became this sleuth, this - I dunno - local historian; and people came to her because she had a talent for it. She continued investigating what happened to you all and discovered things... about *that* river.'

'She told you?'

'A little, although we did live on a big, windy farm, and I didn't like those conversations.'

'I bet.'

'But aunty would tell me - at any opportunity. Well, she's not really my aunty.'

'Do you mean... Hazel, by any chance?'

'Yeah. Do you remember her?'

'Definitely.'

I exhaled more smoke in relief. She was telling me all this with perception, holding my gaze, and it was the first sign of burgeoning confidence in my presence. 'Is your aunty Hazel well?'

'Yeah, she's fine now; she works at an old peoples' home. She's actually more of a friend, if I'm honest.'

This was pleasing news. Hazel was a born carer. The tubs of chocolate butterfly buns instantly sprang to mind, and I was ruddy famished; half a roast beef and horseradish sandwich, not nearly enough.

'Serin, sorry to change your flow for a second,' I said. 'Has Hazel experienced any hassle in recent weeks?'

'From the Press?'

'Yeah.'

'Definitely, but I think that councillor bloke - Ishaq Kan - deflects most of it.'

'Good.'

'Journalists have tried visiting her at work, but an old biddy chased them away.'

This humoured me. Some sort of holy ground even the Press were reluctant to tread.

'Thanks, and sorry. So you were saying... about your mum...'

She appeared excitable. 'So, we were sorting through my mum's belongings and we found a book of articles she'd kept about *that day*.'

I jolted. 'What?'

'She kept it all in a box - she'd really investigated the Grobatards, because they... you won't know,' she blew her cheeks out in disgust, 'they pretty much pressured my grandparents into a sale.'

'Your farm?'

'Cherry Tree.'

'Really?'

'Yeah, mum knew that there was something nefarious about the whole affair. They were forced.'

Impressed with her lexicon, I patiently waited for her to carry on. I hadn't heard the Grobatard name in years.

So she did, 'Aunty Hazel explained it all more a couple of weeks ago. She said mum discovered two documents many years ago. They said the Grobatards were kinda like the Sheriffs of the area - in the sixteen and seventeen hundreds - but they were cruel ones, and people turned on them because they kidnapped kids. They got punished... and lost their land.'

Interest piqued, I let my posture prompt her further.

'But piece by piece, the Grobatards were able to get their land back. Apparently, they're all still under a - I dunno - a curse or something.'

'Sorry?'

'Yeah. I dunno.'

I rubbed my brow, trying to process. 'Serin... *a what?*'

'I know, I know…' She let her auburn curls cover her face, embarrassed, hiding. 'Sorry. I know it's bats. I don't think it's true.'

This evening had been strange enough.

'A curse?' I repeated.

Serin clearly didn't want to follow-up. She was young - and probably impressionable - but it was curious to hear anyone talk this way. I lived in America; *anything* was possible. But my first thought was: had her mum *lost it?* I wouldn't blame her in the least.

Then she blurted, 'Well, supposedly they're all cursed until their land returns to them.'

I was lost as much as I was jet-lagged. 'Which land?'

'The land the beck runs through.' she nervously coughed. 'A load of children disappeared back in the day, and a Grobatard woman was executed for her crimes.' she swallowed, anxiously looking around the deserted square. 'Sounds a bit intense, doesn't it? I'm not stupid, I promise. I know telling a celebrity this… is bloody ridiculous.'

'Usually, folk just ask me for an autograph.'

She got up, with every intention of leaving. She was mortified with herself, so I beckoned her down. 'No, no, no… it's alright, go on.'

'Sorry, I've just met you.'

She shook her head at herself, pulling her gorgeous curls back up over her brow… and she was tearing up.

'Hey, hey, hey. Your mum was great. Super intelligent. Far brighter than me. That's why I based Mattie on her. If your mum's discovered stuff… *anything*… I want to hear it, Serin. I do.'

'Sorry for shoving this on you.'

'It's lovely to hear about her, and you're… the spitting image.'

She coyly smiled, this comment clearly re-invigorating her will to continue, 'Well, I think Aunty Hazel will be able to tell it better, but the main thing I wanted to do - which is why I followed you - is to give you something mum set aside for you.'

I was blind-sided. 'Come again?'

She arched, unzipping her leather jacket, suddenly revealing surprisingly large breasts in a tight-fitting top. These grabbed my attention… until she retrieved her phone, and I diverted my eyes to the screen.

While she pulled off a glove, I caught sight of her wallpaper.

A gaunt but happy woman, sitting contentedly, head covered in a flowery beanie, resting her arms forward on a shovel planted down in the earth.

And it was gone…

Serin swiped up and showed me a photograph.

Taking the phone in my hand, I got my mind back in the game and read the writing on the screen.

A letter.

To give to William P Austin (Billy - B.A),
In the future, after I'm gone, no doubt.
Important information. Vital Information!
I hope that your money, and more importantly the passion I read, and your sense of injustice…
Will, finally, put these foul ghosts to bed.
Remember the pain.
It was so real for us all.
S. W
X

'Mum knew you'd come back, eventually.'

I read the words again on the phone, observing the contours and the strokes.

'The date at the bottom there,' Serin suddenly pressed into my shoulder, brushing her fingers against mine, enlarging the image, 'she wrote it only a few weeks before she passed.'

Her voice noticeably quivered, and I was struggling to fathom any of the last ten minutes; *Scarlett wrote this to me.*

'I moved recently,' she continued, 'and I have the actual letter in safe-keeping in a box of keepsakes. A friend messaged saying you were at Bedale hall, I didn't get a chance to get it out of storage, so I just grabbed my bike and drove in... hoping I could somehow meet you, and tell you, but I nearly wimped out.'

I remained astonished; what was even happening?

'Serin, this can't have been easy for you. Do you know what this letter's about?'

'I do, but I think you need to read it - as a whole. Some of the stuff I mentioned.'

A punter left the pub and walked towards one of the few remaining parked cars, gawking at us sitting next to each other. He was a couple of hundred yards away - but he was doing the very same thing I'd do in the same situation - checking all was normal, and in-keeping. I raised a hand of acknowledgment, as did he, satisfied there was nothing untoward in a place he knew so well.

Serin raised her hand, too.

'Back there... thank for calling me over,' she said. 'I nearly drove away, but I kept thinking about what mum would want. I knew it was my *only* opportunity; the *only* one! Honestly, if you hadn't had been driving in the direction of my home, I don't think I'd have followed you into the square. I bet you thought I was some crazed fan; a right loon.'

'I'll let you into a little secret,' I kept close. 'I thought you were a wily journalist. I'm renting nowhere near here. It's a fluke I drove this way.'

'Oh, wow.'

'I'm glad you took a risk.'

In the moonlight, warmth gushed over her face. A little blush. Kindness; genuineness. Another, larger group of patrons started leaving the pub - including Verity - and I took out my own phone.

'Can I take your number? When can I collect this letter?'

She excitedly flipped off the screen, and we exchanged.

'Serin, I'll message in the morning, if that's okay?'

'Yes please, I'd like that.'

'I've taken a lot in... for one evening.'

'Sure.'

'I'm still a bit rocked… about your mum.'

She nodded wistfully, holding eye contact. 'I understand.'

'I need to go, and come to terms with this; it's been a long night for me, you…' - I pointed to the patrons - 'And my personal assistant over there.'

'She looks glamorous.'

'I'll tell her you said that.'

Shizz was assessing us both from a distance, while being 'cracked onto' by a local. I heard her shout, *'Goodnight!'* straight in his face. Then she marched forward. Serin stood, politely acknowledging her - leaning forward to zip her jacket up - before replacing her helmet, concealing her abundant curls.

'Ride safe,' I said.

'Not far - half a mile,' came the muffled voice, 'Thank-you, William. Hope to see you tomorrow?'

'Yeah.'

Shizz stood next to me, and I could tell she was assessing, as Serin once again, gracefully mounted the scooter and zipped away.

My PA gave me a knowing look.

And I turned away.

On the ride back home, just over the bridge and out of Masham, Verity belched.

'Rate it, please.'

'Nine. Shall I name the ale?'

'We don't have beer like this in the US.'

'Well, we've had centuries to perfect it.'

'I never see you drink beer.'

'How many have you had?'

'Two.'

'Good for you. What did you try?'

'Old Peculiar.'

'Lovely pint.'

'… And two rusty nails.'

I took the car up a steep hill that stretched on for well over a mile.

'So, Mr Austin...' Shizz was a little tipsy, but I recognised an enquiring pitch. 'That was Scarlett's daughter... Serin.'

'Indeed.'

'So, where was she tonight?'

'Who?'

'Scarlett.'

'Died eight years ago.'

Shizz immediately fell silent.

I continued, 'Serin followed to tell me.'

My PA turned, staring out the window at the rolling, shadowy countryside. I heard her mutter. 'That's *really* shit.'

'Yeah, it's knocked me... quite a bit.' I swallowed. 'Melanoma.'

'And no one told you?'

'No one in my circle knew. Think she hid away in the Dales. Probably the trauma.'

She grimaced, as I made a walloping mistake, adding, 'Based Mattie on her, didn't I?'

'Mattie Harrison?'

'Yeah.'

'Your *perfect woman*... Mattie Harrison?'

I nodded, registering Shizz's shifting tone.

'Bill, level with me.' She was intently focused now. 'I did *not* know this. Was Scarlett your childhood sweetheart?'

'Never made it that far.'

My PA was a tad drunk, but this by no means diminished her powers of observation. Her brain was whirring into overdrive. Parameters and outcomes. I had to tread carefully in my replies from here on in.

'And daughter looks like mother?'

I paused. 'I guess. I didn't really thi-'

'Yes you did. And you swapped numbers, why?'

And so it began. 'I need to collect something from her.'

'*Collect?*'

'Yeah.'

'When? What?'

'Tomorrow.'

'What?'

'A letter.'

'A letter?'

'One Scarlett wrote me years ago.'

Shizz blew out her cheeks, re-kindling sobriety rather quickly. 'And you're going to collect it from Serin?'

'Yeah.'

'Where?'

'Not sure.'

'And you're going to do that in *this* climate? Desert heat. Torrential rains. Earthquakes.'

'Yeah.'

'With the Press on your tail?'

'What choice do I have?'

'Wise decision-making. That's what you have.' She frowned, furiously rubbing her glabella under her specs, not remotely finished. 'And she reminds you of Scarlett?'

'I didn't say that…'

'Your eyes did.'

I snorted. '*When?*'

She slapped the dashboard to get my full attention. 'So, you know how we all have 46 chromosomes in our bodies, and me and you are massive fans of XX on the 23rd pair?'

'I do.'

'I saw *precisely* where you were looking when she zipped her jacket.'

'And you weren't?'

'Yeah, of course, but she's too young for me, Bill. But I guess anything goes for Mr Old Peculiar.'

'That's not nice.'

'Seriously, you're nothing like my last two employers. I enjoy *not* cleaning up sorry messes after you. Well, rarely.'

'Shizz, you're the best cock-blocker in LA. I should give you a raise for the times I, ironically, can't.'

'This woman *is young*.'

'Are we really going here?'

'Don't pretend the driving is distracting you.'

I held up my left hand to stop her. 'Verity, I'm devastated to learn Scarlett's dead. I'm genuinely shocked. Hazel was on the bridge with us, but Scarlett was *only* one who saw it all with me. I missed her. I hoped one day I'd see her again.' I was beginning to break. 'But I can't... and I'm totally, *totally* devastated.'

The last words caught in my throat.

Verity gave me the grace of quietness for a few prolonged moments.

'And I do get that.' she said.

'Thank you.'

'But, I'm going to say one more thing, before we close out this shitty, shitty evening.'

I didn't respond.

'Can I say it?' she said.

I nodded.

'Frankly Bill, this is all a smelting-pot for you. You are intensely vulnerable - more than I've ever known - and if her mother's dead, Serin will be vulnerable too. Then, dashing Mr Austin appears. Handsome, suave, debonair, And she's reminded of her past - through you. You will both have *that* connection. But as you look back at her, you'll *also* be reminded of something beautiful you wanted, but didn't get.'

I clicked a button on the dashboard. 'Can you search up Radio Ferret for me?'

Shizz clicked it straight off. No messing.

'Listen to me, Bill.'

For the remaining three miles, we didn't speak.

Arms folded, Shizz silently stared at my side-profile. *The whole way back.* Channelling her essential warning with invisibly concealed, wise power.

Chapter 4

Long Lost

Sleep evaded me.

Jet lag, emotion, the events of the day… mangled and entwined in restless, disjointed dreams, and frequent abrupt awakenings. Scarlett occupied many thoughts, as did her letter. Serin, the rest.

The night hour was sprinkled with regretful nostalgia, and pointless "what ifs". When I geared my imagination to a fabricated existence with Scarlett, I saw Serin there instead. Every time. Eventually, I dozed for the briefest spell sometime after 4. When I came to, I reached over, grabbed my phone and messaged her. I waited to see if my phone would vibrate - astonished when it did - within thirty seconds.

The meet was arranged.

I lay back and stared at the timber ceiling; this was all *so* weird. A minute later, my phone went again. In the dark, I stared at the thumbnail, and the accompanying message.

"Mum wanted you to have this."

I clicked on the photo; the same wallpaper I briefly saw last night.

Scarlett was seated, the classy beanie concealing her hairless head. Till the very end, she'd dutifully performed farm work, and in this case, digging. With perspiration soaking the fringes of cloth, she was smiling - pitching forwards - resting one thin, veiny forearm on the shovel handle; the other, raised for the selfie. Behind her, trees, and a wall partly painted red. And to her side, the skeletal remains of two small mice - possibly even voles - were ready to be preserved, and possibly arranged in a picture frame. She'd set out a leather pouch for their collection. I didn't like seeing even tiny bones directly next to her, especially as this would be one of the final, probably *the* last photo taken.

She was smiling at *me*.

I put the phone down and stared at the ceiling in silence.

A couple of hours later, I dragged myself out of the bedroom, and walked into the large open-plan lounge, greeted by the welcoming aroma of freshly brewed coffee. Like me, Verity was in her pyjamas - but hers were far better - and she crossed the oriental rug before me, placing the cafetiere on the thick, oak table. She was wearing a Smurf hat, and her slippers were Smurf shoes.

'How did you fit those in your case?'

'They go everywhere with me. I thought it would be cold here on a morning. Sleep well?'

'Thanks for this, and no, not really. You?'

I poured us both a cup.

'Rubbish.'

Vigorously rubbing my eyes, I plopped down in an armchair. Shizz leaned on the edge of the table, tapping her phone.

'*Biggest author mystery since Agatha Christie*... and the blurb underneath reads: who was Robert Tipperton?'

She scrolled more.

'Then... *He was my best friend,* in quotations, followed by a subtitle: Austin's breakdown.'

She shook her head and the Smurf hat wobbled. 'There's a close-up picture of you and it's either your sex face, or you're eating a Carolina Reaper.'

She kept going.

'Author's heartbreak as bones are found forty years after friend vanishes, etcetera.'

'Are these British?'

'Yeah, similar Stateside, though.'

Sipping my hot drink, I considered the practicalities of the wedding I was scheduled to attend. Verity kept going.

'So far, the sympathy train is rolling; body language wannabees say you're genuine. I look radiant in online pics.' She raised her specs, looking my way, showing me. 'They got me, too.'

'Shame they can't see you now.'

'Added to all of this, you now have,' she coughed, deliberately building suspense, 'an *eight-figure* offer for your autobiography and requests for documentaries galore. All eighteen of your novels are back in the top thirty, three are in the top five, and the Eighteenth Lonely Chapter is smashing the top.'

Sipping more coffee, I puzzled my way through this minefield of info.

'It's fair to say,' she glanced up, 'you've never been *this* famous.'

'Read all about it.'

'Not all good though, Bill; a couple of naysayers believe you planned that dramatic entrance. You're an adept narcissist. But most reports are positive… for now.'

'We both know how this pans out.'

She nodded, adding. 'And I'm regretting using Rolly Bridgeson as your booking name.'

'Why?'

'The farmer's daughter came and knocked this morning, checking if we were settling in, and I look like a dog's dinner.'

I waited.

'And?'

'Rolly's an old man's name.'

This was bewildering; some kind of transatlantic confusion between British author and American PA. 'Your point being?'

'She asked if my husband and I were enjoying the barn. Someone as glam as me *cannot* be seen with a Rolly.'

I snorted, 'And?'

'I told her we met in Kansas and we were celebrating our ten-year wedding anniversary.'

I nodded my approval. 'Very good.'

'The hire-company called to see if the car was okay.'

'Sorry?'

'Indeed.'

'What? *This early?*'

'Exactly.'

'They can't suspect, surely?'

'There's a news segment on repeat of *me and you* hightailing it from the hall and me declaring undying love for Cassie. The company logo is visible on the back window.'

'Oh, bollocks.'

'My favourite expression... only a matter of time till we're located, Bill.'

On the arm rest, my phone started buzzing.

'I'll call Simone,' I said. 'See if he can sort us alternate lodgings through his people... independently; if this all gets too bad.'

'We should only use the car we collected from the airport for now.'

'Good thinking.'

I checked my phone.

A message from my parents saying they'd seen me on TV, hoped I was okay, and that a press-van was currently parked close to their home.

One from an unknown number.

Two from Ishaq.

Unknown numbers gave me palpitations. I'd been stalked a few times by well-meaning nutters with a skewed sense of reality, and an overly inflated sense of self-entitlement. I concentrated on Ishaq's messages. One was a "thank you" for the previous evening, and the other, a request to meet at a quiet location close by.

'Shizz, I need to go out in a bit; I have a few errands to run.'

'Sorry... *a few?*'

'A few places to go.'

'So, did *any* of what I just said, actually enter your head?'

'Yes, Papa Smurf. I promise I'll be careful.'

'You're going to see Scarlett's daughter… and then where?'

I tapped the side of my nose.

She grunted her disapproval. 'If you stupidly bring press back here, I'm going straight to that lodge and it's sayonara from me for the next ten days. All on your wage bill.'

'Deal! Trust me, this is something I simply must do.'

'Alright,' she bemoaned: a notable rise in her tone, 'Don't do anything idiotic with that girl; *just don't!*'

'I'll be as wily as a weasel.'

'Yeah, that's what I'm afraid of.'

'Ahh, you've learned about weasels.'

'Be prepared. It could get emotional. Call if you need me. I mean that, Bill.'

'Shizz, as soon as I get my head around any of this, I'll let you in on it; I promise.'

~ ~ ~

It was a decidedly remote location.

Only visited for specific purposes.

A handful of houses clumped around a triangular-shaped grassy junction, scarcely constituting a hamlet. Forests full of dark green pines and ferns encased this tiny, cloistered community, nestled in the hills. To reach it, I drove a steep, winding incline for at least a mile-and-a-half. In harsh winter months, this place would get quickly cut off, in completeness.

The largest of the houses here was a long stone building converted into three single bedroom dwellings. Serin owned the one nearest the archway which you entered to reach a gravelly car park. There wasn't a soul around. Pulling the car into a stony courtyard, I parked.

A yellow Mini Cooper, and Serin's covered scooter.

Deserted, isolated: what on earth was *she* doing living out here alone?

Serin messaged back that she'd moved here recently and I wondered if she'd broken up with someone. Scarlett was dead, but what about dad? Were things fractious, and she needed an escape? I didn't know if I'd be classed a boomer, zoomer or an end-of-alphabetter - but wherever my mindset lay - it was certainly strange that a twenty-year-old had chosen this level of solitude.

Something wasn't right.

Shizz immediately invaded my headspace.

I wondered if she had a live-in boyfriend, girlfriend? My rationale concluded: renting with a partner... but my gut suggested she was here alone. On cue, she appeared at front of a green farmhouse style front door and smiled... looking decidedly nervous. As was I. Surrounding her doormat was a plethora of ornaments, from an old iron sign that read: "Ice cream's for sale", to a massive copper peacock, and loads of hanging baskets, with colourful flowers. It looked like the entrance to a quirky shop full of nick-nacks. She stood there in the midst of this paraphernalia, hands on hips, gently smoothing down a pretty, pale green dress that ended mid-thigh. It was perfectly honed for her size and build, embracing every line and contour. This was one *gorgeous* girl, and I was immediately in a pickle. Around her neck hung quite a large, chunky necklace, finishing in a silvery crescent moon that hovered a few inches above her cleavage.

I took a good look now, so I wouldn't later.

Exiting the car, I approached, instantly receiving another snapshot into Scarlett at this age, royally correcting my ulterior motives - like a confused flagellant - for even being here. But I had a fight on my hands, now that I suspected she'd dressed up for me, or for the occasion. She was entirely scintillating, and I tried retaining Verity's fading warnings in my head. Focussing on the sobering news about Scarlett did the trick.

'Hi Serin.'

'Hi.'

'Thanks for this.'

'That's okay; would you like to come in?'

She stepped to one side, warmly inviting me.

'Yeah, sure.'

I paused, thinking about how I'd politely handled Kenzie at Simone's party, only a few evenings ago. But this felt totally different. Maybe my powers only worked in America, and the Yorkshire air was doing me big time? I felt like the old boy down his local, easily necking twenty pints perched on his usual stool, but budge him on to the next…

Shizz was correct. I *was* vulnerable. *This isn't Scarlett*, I kept repeating to myself, removing my Ray-Bans - a flimsy disguise anyway - no one else around.

'Can I make you a cup of tea?'

'Yes, please.'

'How do you like it?'

I ignored how that sounded in my mind, launching into explaining my tea preference, as we strolled into a small kitchen with terracotta tiles and cream cabinets. Modern, but nodding its head to tradition. I caught the scent of her perfume.

'Very nice,' I commentated, referring to her snug kitchen, but alluding to her scent.

'You like it? I love it here. It's very peaceful.'

'How long have you been here?'

'Couple of months.'

'Not long. You like barn conversions?'

'It was available.'

'Okay.'

She boiled the kettle, but it must have boiled less than a minute earlier; steaming very quickly.

'Did you make all that stuff outside?' I asked, genuinely interested.

I rested my hand on a small, but surprisingly thick table, with really bulbous, oak legs.

'Yes, but I mainly do carpentry.'

'Carpentry?'

'Yeah, I'm a carpenter.'

Not what I was expecting, and she picked up on this, flashing me a dainty smile.

'Yes,' she humbly waved at the contents of her quaint kitchen, 'just about anything free-standing, I made.'

I took a good look around; grateful to be distracted by other forms of physical art. *Why* was I really here?

'Wow! Was this something you always wanted to do, Serin?'

She took a moment to consider, 'No… but it's probably the one thing I'm okay at.' Her curly auburn hair seemed to dance with every syllable.

I nodded, totally relating to this, while examining the intricacy in her carvings which were profound - spell-bindingly so - hued into intricate patterns, and with expert precision. She was a professional. We made a little more small talk, and then she showed me around her ground floor home. When she led me in the direction of her bedroom, I stood in the doorway, noting a queen size bed with an indentation in only one of the two pillows. In no time at all, we were back in the kitchen, ready to engage in deeper, more pressing matters. She lifted a heavy chair away from under the table to sit closer.

I was more nervous now than seated in Bedale hall.

Nevertheless, I angled my own, so we were nearly face-on, surprised by its heaviness. Under those dainty shoulder sleeves, Serin possessed real strength, and in the corner of my mind I couldn't help myself assessing her set up again; not a single sign of co-habitation. She was by herself, at least in a non-committed way.

Three of my novels were stacked on the corner of her table, a bookmark indicating she was three-quarters through The Nearly and Mostly Shackled.

Suddenly, she leaned forward, past the periphery of personal space, while delicately stroking both her forearms. Her silver crescent moon swung from her neck like a hypnotist's pendulum, and she (almost inconspicuously) cocked her head to one side, mirroring much of my posture.

I pushed back a little… but she didn't.

Serin was doing *everything* I didn't want an attractive young woman to do. Every sodding thing. And the more she did it, the more troubled I became. Shizz was still there, a blurry grain somewhere in my mind, like ebbing static that's lost its crackle: be careful, be careful. I wanted to grab the free-standing glass, resting on the table - half full of water - and douse myself with it. What the hell was happening? This was invitational body language.

Of someone vulnerable.

'So, do you remember much about my mum?' she asked.

'Yeah, of course.'

'That's nice.'

'Shall I tell you what I remember?'

Her compliant, nodded response, was soft, yet eager.

And so I did, recounting tales of Scarlett's incisive mind, and ability to galvanise others, while placing deliberate emphasis on her wholesale goodness. I started fast, but slowed the more I calmed, embracing how rewarding and truly cathartic it was to recall all this. Good or bad, it shattered the ice between us, with Serin hanging on my every word; rivetted. Out of nowhere, a connection was forming; a chemistry. My throat was a little dry, so I finished with a sip of tea. 'I'm still in complete shock that she's gone to be honest. I simply can't get my head around it… at all.'

It was truly heartbreaking news, and I was struggling with every passing minute.

'Thank you. Those stories about mum… mean the world to me.'

Serin's ambivalence was clear - tears welling in her sapphire eyes - while at the same time, overjoyed at the power and personality I'd conveyed about her mother.

'I wish you'd been around. Look, I'm baking some scones… would you like some? Home-made.'

'They smell divine. It would be rude not to.'

(Her perfume was better.)

She smiled, delicately sliding sideways on her chair without standing, leaning out across the table and sweeping up a tea-towel in her hand. It was all done in a flowing motion, and as she did so, I caught sight of flesh, something high up on her right thigh.

A garter.

Two horizontal strips of dark leather, running parallel with one another, both joined by smaller vertical pockets and tassels. Her soft skin; perfectly smooth beneath. And I was in deep shit, right there, right then. *Deep shit!*

Serin gracefully rose, and headed toward her large stove, as I tried to force the image from my mind. Pale green dress, black leather strap, purposefully angled to reveal. My phone vibrated, and I grabbed for it in desperation. A message from Verity, like some kind of heavenly intervention. I clicked it, barely concentrating. Good grief, I needed a distraction this instant.

"Checking in. Did you get that letter? Are you even there yet? Be careful. X"

I nearly laughed out loud, and I replied that all was fine… but then immediately sent another, asking her to send a message every five minutes. She replied, '*uh-oh.*'

A homely aroma floated out from the open oven as I stared at a magazine still in its cellophane, and a single letter pushed to the side of the table, and the paisley curtains, and the terracotta tiles. My novel - The Nearly and the Most Shackled - became symbolic of the situation I faced, so I looked away.

I was absolute putty.

All it had taken was a half-second glance, and I'd already memorised the garter with its tiny pockets and tassels. So discreet. I tried concentrating on the beautiful smell of baked scones and recommenced staring at the letter and magazine on the side of the table, frantically trying to erase. If she sat down. If she moved closer…

I stared at the model on the front cover of the magazine - just about visible through the cellophane - the white, printed address obscuring her body. I kept staring like this was *somehow* a form of replacement therapy.

Ms S. Grobatard.

I read the address, over and over. Exactly the same on the adjacent letter too; none of it immediately registering.

'Another cuppa?'

'Yes, please.'

'Same strength? Is that how you take it?'

'Perfect.'

I looked again, seeing the *same* name on each... S. Grobatard.

And then a sickness spread through my heart. The most venomous of snake bites, carrying deadly sepsis, injected to every fibre of spirit and vitality. Organ collapse. Heart failure. Serin was standing at a side angle; her profile, beautiful. Grobatard? What the *hell* was even happening here? What was *that* name doing there? My mind was struggling to process anything linearly. Had she drugged the tea? Then, the sinking dread of realisation. Like being tazered, with a gun attached to a pylon.

This wasn't Scarlett's daughter.

I channelled Verity Schulenburg at that moment. I really did.

Entrapment? Duped? I *was* the idiot king. A whisker away of falling foul of the same falsely arranged situations that had reared their heads in my past: charity, and kiss and tell. So, so close, in fact. I rose from the chair, which alerted her... and she briefly looked over as she stewed the tea. I aimed for the opposing window, staring back out onto the road, keeping my back turned away. Physically, she *was* the spitting image. No question. The mannerisms - hand's down, Scarlett. This *was* Scarlett's daughter, no denying. And if this was her mail with her address - which it quite clearly was - and she was a Grobatard, then it could only mean one thing.

One horrible, horrible thing.

'Serin, did your mum ever marry?'

I asked this abruptly, keeping distance, creating an obvious separation from her, analysing every single facet of her response. She froze - with her back to me - before resuming a slower stir, and a more measured pour from the teapot.

'Yes,' she said.

My question was blunt, and deliberately suspicious. She knew it. I'd taken-in a lot in a short space of time, but I didn't want *this* dawn of horrendous revelation at all.

Then she blurted, 'She re-married a nice bloke up here called Geoff, but her first marriage was a mistake.'

I paused, assessing this; rocked to my core. 'The first man she married,' I swallowed, 'was a *Grobatard?*'

She solemnly nodded, almost ashamedly glancing at me, and away.

Scarlett Grobatard?

Scarlett would *never* marry a Grobatard; no way on earth... so what was going on? But there was no mistaking Serin's surname on the magazine cover.

'I need to give you this.'

Her fingers urgently slipped under a patterned tea cosy, collecting the envelope concealed beneath. Eyes angled down, she swiftly moved to the table, pushing it halfway to me, before beating a hasty retreat. She ever-so-slightly peeked in the direction of her mail, resting on the side, recognising the source of unexpected insight.

'My Step-father was Geoff,' she continued, nervously. 'My biological father is a man called Craig.'

In astonishment, I looked down at the letter from Scarlett she'd pushed my way. It felt... tainted. With that *one name*, things had turned exponentially worse. The envelope mirrored the photo she showed me on her phone yesterday evening. This was definitely real... but I was absolutely dumbfounded, flabbergasted.

'*Craig?*' I couldn't disguise it. 'She married *Craig* Grobatard?'

'Not a nice man,' she stared across at her mail again, 'I think I'll change my surname back to mum's maiden name.'

This was horrific. My life was profoundly altered by the beck, but to entertain this scenario bordered on impossibility, unearthly almost. Marrying the damn enemy? No way.

'Serin,' I rubbed my brow in angst. 'You told me yesterday… the Grobatards' *forced* your Grandparents into selling Cherry Tree?'

'Yes, William. They did.' She stopped, pointing. 'Mum explains it in the letter.'

'But, didn't your mother spend time in the Dales, to get away from all the trauma? That's what I heard. She never came to my secondary school, and neither did Hazel. It was too much for them… to be this close to it all.'

Serin looked a little lost.

'I-I don't really know anything about that part of mum's life after… after the river. I'm pretty sure she didn't come up here until much later.'

'Sorry.' I vigorously rubbed my face. 'So she stuck around in Leeming?'

'I believe so.'

'Really?'

'I think so.'

Right on my doorstep. All those years. A mile, two miles away? *Right there.*

'And your father is *Craig Grobatard*?'

She felt confronted, constantly wiping her hands on the towel. 'We lived on his farm when I was very young, but I don't really remember. Mum and I moved up here and lived in a cottage before moving to a farm. Cherry Tree was sold while this was happening, so we never went back.'

This *was* alien.

But goodness only knows what Scarlett would think if she heard about my aberrant behaviour in my teens and early twenties. I'd gambled away thousands of pounds at University, not even making it through the first year. With my final, fabricated loan, I boated and flew my way to Vanua Levu to escape forever, like some petty fresher fugitive. When success first called in my career, I'd pissed and snorted my way through a mid five-figure advance in about two months flat. Subsequent, higher advances, hardly quelled my sense of deferred gratification. I was *off the rails,* abundantly so.

I comforted myself by imagining an *equally* deranged Scarlett entering a marriage of convenience, desperately and honourably protracting the sale of Cherry Tree farm. Considering both our mental states, this *was* a distinct possibility, and the only one I'd entertain.

'My step-dad passed away eight months ago,' Serin said, jolting me from my stupor. 'I've sold his farm, and it completes this afternoon. I needed to get away and rent here because there were too many memories if I stayed. Mum, Geoff... I'm looking out for a place like this, but hopefully with a workshop.'

'Serin, sorry to hear that, and sorry for sounding-'

She interrupted, 'It's okay, honestly...'

This poor, poor girl.

I rightly chastised myself for my desire; she was a broken soul, probably mirroring my movements at the table because she felt supported for the first time in ages. She had someone who related.

'So, I'm going to suggest something,' I started. 'If you need anything - and I mean *anything* - and I'm not bloody joking; tell me. I know I'm sounding like some pompous rockstar here, but I mean, *anything.*'

'That's kind,' she shook her head. 'Mum said you were kind. But I'll be fine. I embrace my independence, and I'll be wealthier from today. I've had to learn on my feet.'

I held up the letter shakily.

'If your mum predicted that one day I would have *this* in my hands, then I'm a part of... all this.'

I could tell she was still in awe of me, so I pointed to my novels on the table. 'Serin, I live with the most profound guilt that I don't deserve any of this. Good people like Robert... and your mum... have passed without experiencing-'

And then I thought very long, and very carefully about how I'd end this sentence because fame and wealth had certainly not brought me happiness. I was guilty of unintentional assumptions. I sighed at myself, deciding instead on shutting the hell up. She nodded back, with understanding.

'Mum was happier in the final years.'

'Good, I'm glad for it.'

'William, I did read the letter again, last night. I hope that was okay.'

'If it was me, I'd do it. Please call me Billy.'

I could see she wouldn't consider doing this.

'There's a part in it, where,' - she tailed off, contemplative, unsure - 'where Mum's very grateful that Geoff's around for me.'

'I can try to imagine.'

'And that my dad can't find me.'

'Yeah, I met him. Understandable.'

But this shocked me. She looked puzzled before continuing, 'There's weird stuff going on in that whole family. Mum discovered it when she was a part of it all. I think they were only together for three years, and I *needed* to be kept away.'

I let that resonate in my head; picking up on the emphasis.

'Kept away?'

'Yeah…'

'From what?'

'Mum mentions it. I find it hard to talk about.'

'Okay.'

Here I was, sitting in a compact contemporary farmer style kitchen with forest on every side, positioned away from prying eyes - listening to a girl - hiding *out of fear*. I didn't push this, waiting as she took her seat again.

'So, erm… I guess I would really appreciate you looking out for me.'

'I need to read this letter, don't I?'

'Yeah. I don't think I'm being paranoid.'

'Okay.'

Her actions from the previous evening suddenly made complete sense. Not only had she subtly tailed our car to tell me about her mum - and this letter - but she'd also circled around on her scooter like a lost puppy, hoping she'd be gathered in kind arms. She presented me a second cup, and I sipped; equally good.

I said, 'There's probably a lot I can do to help here, but I am getting the impression there are deeper currents, in deeper waters.'

'Pretty much. My Aunty Hazel will tell you more, but - yes - I'm definitely staying under the radar for now. I don't really go out much anymore.'

'Really? That bad?'

'She said she texted you this morning.'

'Who?'

'Hazel.'

I put my tea down, stunned again - recalling the unknown number from earlier - immediately checking my phone for the message. And there it was: well composed, friendly; asking me to meet. My heart leapt a little; I definitely wanted to check in on her, and her message sparked an idea. I placed the mug down.

'Serin, did you give Hazel my number?'

'No, no… absolutely not.'

She was telling the truth.

'If you don't mind, Serin, I'm going to leave the rest of your tea. I need to drive back and read your mum's letter; get my head around all of this. I'm finding this all so weird. Then I'm going to pay your aunty a visit.'

She looked a little dismayed. 'Oh yeah, sure. I promise I didn't give her it.'

'I know. I suspect I know who did.'

'Okay.'

'But the press are getting ever closer… and I want to see if I can keep you safe, and remain a chameleon myself for one more day at least.'

'I get it. I don't know how you cope.'

On cue, a car pulled through the stone archway on to the gravelly car park, and I pressed the chair back into the corner. Serin looked out of the window, cheekily smiling at my wilted retreat.

'It's Cerys; she's my neighbour.'

The lady got out of her car, and looked over at mine, studying it for several seconds. She then turned and stared over at Serin's front door.

'She's a journalist,' Serin remarked.

'Oh, shit!'

'I'm joking. She owns a Tea room in Masham.'

Every muscle on her face relayed the familiar cheek I'd once experienced, and adored, and missed. Hiding in the corner of her kitchen, I approved her wit with a warm smile.

'You remind me of someone.'

The neighbour walked down the side of the barn conversion keeping her eyes on the house, her feet crunching over the pebbles. As she passed the window, Serin waved, and the woman's serious face blossomed into a smile.

'She's checking in on you,' I said.

'Yes, and she gives me discounts too; very kind.'

I listened out for a big front door to close.

'I better go.'

'Will you please stay in touch?'

'One hundred per cent.'

She rose from her chair as I took my Ray-Bans out. I was struggling with an appropriate goodbye, and she was waiting for me to take the lead in how this should happen. Leaving her standing would feel even more weird.

'I'm going to hug you goodbye, if that's okay?'

'Yes, it is.'

She smiled, purposefully positioning for a full embrace. I squeezed, and kept it brief and polite, but tender and meaningful. To my shame, for the second or two we held each other, I wanted to pull her dress up over her right thigh.

Then I remembered she was Craig Grobatard's biological daughter.

And the thought *instantly* evaporated.

Chapter 5

Memory's Garden

The back route to the underpass took twenty minutes to reach.

Two small streams ran parallel with one other.
'Huh!'
I was surprised to see this. (On and on, into the distance they flowed.) Almost purposefully aligned to run side-by-side; a potential mark of human intervention. The rest of the ground was open. Just fields... wide, open fields, and the sky above was blue, exactly like the last time I was here.

When I felt I was out of sight, I reached into my pocket and put on my Ray-Bans. Very sunny. Hugging close to an old parameter fence, I moved swiftly around the edge toward the underpass.

Before my arrival, I'd discreetly pulled over somewhere in the Dales, finding a secluded place to read Scarlett's letter. And in a fallow field, in the middle of nowhere, I embraced her message to me, while scrutinising the documents it contained. I hoped a tractor wouldn't arrive; desperately trying to digest the contents. But the more I read, the more I wrestled with the ramblings of a madwoman. Borderline conspiracy, and a complex plot far too disjointed for any novel I'd attempt.

This wasn't fiction... at least, not in Scarlett's head.

Her assertions, accusations and tireless studies... devoted to Robert's disappearance, *Serin's safety*... and the protection of children from the beck.

Oh, and the destruction of the Grobatard dynasty.

It was bewildering.

I'd been partly correct in assuming she'd married for security... but a revenge motive was here. Rather than protect her own family's farm, Scarlett had effectively secured its demise, surrendering it to a Grobatard portfolio. As I secretly walked the back way to the beck, I continually reminded myself this place *also unhinged me* in its entirety. The letter outlined the regret and remorse for her actions, and her eventual return to relative normality. How she turned informer and infiltrator while still married to Craig... as suspicions grew. The enclosed documents were stealthily lifted - and photocopied - right from under the noses of the Grobatards who (apparently) chronicled their own history. I was convinced these were all indeed genuine, but Scarlett's conclusions wouldn't pass any Ishaq 'logic' test.

No way.

Had it not been for my firsthand experience of the 'things' here, I'd dismiss this all as mumbo-jumbo. And yet, it *did* make sense in a freakish way.

I stopped, studying the forested outcrop ahead - here again for the first time in decades - at the very place Scarlett was describing in painstaking detail, but on the other side of the bridge this time. The mysterious side. My plans had changed (everything, in fact, changing), as was my perception of the area. As an impressionable child, it was *this* side that led to an enchanted, forbidden forest.

I could not have been further from the truth; no orcs or fawns here. And, in reality, it made sense why Ol' Bobby preferred to potato-pick at Ivy farm. He'd just have to *roll out* the other side of the slope, and he was already there. Drawing nearer, I heard the cars on the road ahead; but more so on the newly built motorway pushing east.

This was the same cluster of trees I feared as a kid; a dense clump of a gateway leading to a dark, unchartered world. Certainly, in 1983 this was all unnavigable, inhospitable and dangerous - now simply an aperture into my faulty infantile perception.

After the tiny copse, flat land and open pastures.

And just before it… both streams converging into one, creating *the beck* we knew - flowing under the bridge with the rampant cars above.

'Huh.'

Joining together meant more water to nourish birch saplings, allowing this abundant, wild growth. No wonder Hazel didn't even realise this was part of *her own* farm; it was more like no-man's-land.

My app was showing me an extra underpass half-a-mile ahead, connecting Ivy to Cherry Tree; for all manner of tractors to drive through. I had no idea it existed.

My thoughts turned back to Hazel.

Earlier, we'd arranged to meet at the old peoples' home, where she worked. With her permission, I'd parked at Ivy farm (still owned by her parents) before embarking on a covert trek across the fields. I was travelling the same escape route Ishaq, and I used on the day Robert was hospitalised. Going *anywhere* near her old peoples' home in my hire-car was a no-no. Press vans were driving back and forth on the off-chance I'd visit my friend. Our connection had been identified.

Moreover, I needed to face the river again, alone.

But there were other reasons for coming here. My errand. Money was ready.

Rarely would I arrange such a large financial outlay at short notice, and I estimated I'd lose at least fifty grand in the long term. But the combination of Serin's information, Scarlett's letter, and the open forum last night, necessitated an unorthodox approach. This is why I phoned the bank in the car while Shizz filmed events inside Bedale Hall.

I deliberately sought a tree jutting out over the water's edge and relieved myself. Copious volumes of morning tea and coffee allowed for a good, long stream of piss straight into the water. I was announcing my return. I was *furious,* and I wanted the bobbing boy to break the surface so I could spray his face like a hose.

But I didn't.

Not really. I clung with one hand to a tree in my tempered aggression. Would I dare do this... on the other side?

Nothing happened. So I pressed further on, pushing myself through undergrowth, using branches and trunks to propel forward, eventually reaching a small clearing, where I stood gazing at the confluence. The noise and fumes from all manner of vehicles above were pronounced, and I wondered if lurking spirits got sick of it all, and sacked it off years ago. For centuries, no automobiles to contend with. Maybe this is why they were livid.

Why Scarlett hadn't made mention of the motorway in her letter intrigued me. This was a huge deal to the locality. Grobatard stood to receive royal recompense for a road cutting through his estate. But, this fact clearly paled in Scarlett's eyes - especially when compared to the rest of the shocking content. Financial gain was an after-thought for Grobatard senior.

Reaching the bridge, with the clatter above, I stared at the spot where Ol' Bobby probably rolled into the water and drowned. I recalled how we'd discovered him sleeping, and sadness struck me.

In the river to my left, something glimmered, catching my eye. At first, I thought it was just frothy scum forming around a grassy sedge. Two faded crisp packets - from a company long-since defunct - floated in its midst, as did several wine and spirit bottles. Consumed years ago, and then chucked in somewhere further upstream.

Then I noticed something else.

By my feet, a roll of thick string, nearly, but not quite a rope.

Set back under some branches and held down with a brick, most of it, attached and wrapped around a spool. A single line had been unravelled, concealed within the grass, weaving its way towards the bank before descending into the water… where it aimlessly floated. It appeared to be some kind of primitive fishing mechanism, and I wondered if this was some undiscovered vestige of Ol' Bobby's attempts to source protein.

I sighed. It was untouched.

Turning, I looked into the shadowy underpass; the slope, much steeper than I recalled. No idea how he'd managed to sleep this way - poor guy. On the day he died, I wondered if he'd had a heart attack first, or maybe he'd slipped and banged his head, before falling in unconscious.

I looked up.

And saw something that seismically tugged my heart.

A Cupid's love heart had been painted red on the inside wall, largely obscured by shadows cast by trees and concrete.

It read:

SW 4 BA

I was blown away.

I stared at it. Couldn't believe it. Rocked to my core.

An arrow shot from the top to the bottom, in the opposite direction to tradition; an amateurish mistake for a kid, but it had been rendered with precision, and more importantly, heartfelt intent. With a slack jaw, I processed the sight some more, but I'd already reached the correct conclusion. Serin wasn't making it up - her mum, in no way ascribing her feelings through the letter - but she had here. I took a deep breath, studying it more, both fascinated and overwhelmed.

How many years had this been here?

A young Scarlett had messed up the point on the arrow, making it rounder; sending it nearly off the edge of the wall. Nevertheless, this was her depicting her thoughts towards me; gently reaching through time, stroking the lines of scars on my face once again. Sealed with a kiss - the solitary X placed inside the end of the arrowhead.

Maybe she kept thinking about me even though we never stayed in touch. Maybe she'd painted this in the weeks after Ol' Bobby died, and Rob had disappeared, hoping I would bravely return to the beck and see it. Serin said she'd never left the area. Maybe... she was waiting all this time.

Anticipating, hoping.

For me.

'Damn this.'

I half-whispered, snorting out a disconsolate laugh... which all too quickly became breathy and resigned. Then I stood there, absorbing the initials and their meaning - savouring the substance behind each brush stroke - and smiling wistfully. That weird, childhood notion of love, or a crush, didn't matter; not in the least. I always wanted one of these; to be marked in someone's heart. No one had ever drawn me one, and mine read: Scarlett Wilmott *for...*

She was *for me.*

I swallowed.

Four letters, and one number. That's all it took. An indescribable power - like no other.

I brought out my phone, taking several photos, while shaking my head again at the twisted curvature of our life-course. I came a little closer, angling it past an upright shovel Ol' Bobby had left for digging up potatoes, but no matter how many I took, I couldn't capture its perfection.

Forcing my attention back to the matter in hand - my heart still simmering in wonder - I assessed the angle of the underpass. I had to concentrate if I was going through. No matter what, I *couldn't* fall in. The steady rumble of vehicles overhead had its pros and cons. On one hand, the waters could chant their hushed mantras to car exhausts. On the other, I would hear nothing creeping up behind me. Hoisting myself on to the slope, I fully appreciated my decision to hire a demanding personal trainer in LA. This was real-world application of core strength; much more than I ever possessed as a kid.

If Scarlett's assertions were correct, Ol' Bobby had been on the money all along; there *were* Sirens in here, calling sailors to the rocks. And now - by all accounts - the boats were being sent *directly* to them. They *no longer* needed to wait it out for the summer months to lure with their hypnotic timbre.

A playground had been built on the other side, directly next to the beck.

Right where we once played.

A falsely altruistic gesture from Mr Grobatard senior himself. On this day, one of my errands was to investigate this fast-track pass to calamity.

My progress across dusty concrete was swift, assured - and I reached the end in no time - pushing my way out on to the steady decline. Then I immediately traversed the second underpass beneath the motorway (nowhere near as steep). On the other side of this, I stepped out, wiping my hands on grass. There I crouched, concealed on a slight mound, staring at the sight before me. No guard dogs here, undoubtedly on the other farms; nowhere near kids or swings. William Grobatard was conniving, not stupid.

Ahead, I saw ropes dangling over the water near the cattle bridge, and a small single slide angled down into the beck. For regulation's sake, it wasn't steep, and constructed separately to the main play area of see-saws and roundabouts. At the base, you launched through a green arch in the shape of a croc's mouth, and then plunged into the water. Every bit an intentional addition, conceived and orchestrated by a sick mind. Get ready to be devoured in every sense.

And here I was, three decades on.

It looked different - smaller - tidier, and better maintained.

Late, *late* last night, I'd read villages and planners had proposed his land as a play area. Under local council supervision, Grobatard led the decision-making, diverting council money into directly funding this endeavour. He didn't pay for a bean. Smart cookie.

He was getting paid to feed the beck.

Live bait.

With their back's turned, I watched a mother with a pushchair and toddler gently amble away; two swings in a frame of four still stirring. I sat down on the knoll out of eyesight and took a few moments to consolidate my thoughts. But the noise and fumes were getting too much, so I aimed instead for the bank next to the slide, and the delivery chute to the unknown.

Apparently, this was where Mrs Levett's son got clawed, and others sustained similar injuries. Things were still happening - beyond doubt. No such thing as time, nor common sense cooling the reputation of this place. I mentally composed once again, preparing for what I was about to do - and in such proximity to my nemesis.

The water remained calm beneath my feet.

Basil, the bobbing boy, and the angry knight could almost be CGI if they appeared right now. It felt so detached and odd, like I'd bumped into an old flame I'd once loved fiercely... now left with nothing but numbness.

'For old time's sake, I just want you to know... I have your card marked.'

Nothing responded.

The same endless trickle, century after century.

'You took from me. You tried to destroy me... but you made me.' The water continued to glide by - my voice - no more than the patter of light rain, or an occasional gust on a windy day. 'You are correct: I *am* the enemy.'

No mist, no quiet chanting, no tree house, not even a bramble bush. Only the freshness of the flow, and the oblivious push toward the open sea. On my left, I noticed a clump of white flowers; cordoned off with a sequence of old, rusty poles. Yellow and black tape had been criss-crossed over and around each.

Giant hogweed.

Deadly stuff.

Perhaps Grobatard could get sued for not adequately addressing its removal, or maybe he was playing messiah by signalling its whereabouts. Perspective, and appearances. Regardless, I had plans to throw a humongous spanner in his works.

'So, you're pretty quiet today,' I spoke down, sarcastically mocking the beck. 'Is it because you remember me, and you're afraid?'

I immediately stepped back off the bank and marched the few hundred yards toward new corrugated barns. The pigs within smelled foul, and I listened to their clattering and clamouring within their pens.

In Mr Hislop's day, this is where our game of hide-and-seek took place. But the old had gone, and the new barn's shone… and the stink was utterly deplorable. Directly ahead, between the last two outbuildings, was the large front door that led to the tiled kitchen where we once slept in fear and distress.

To the right… the track where Rob and I fought, side-by-side.

The squealing here was horrendous, as snouts squeezed and panted their way through railed enclosures on either side of me. No dogs. Not even here.

I marched straight up to the large door and banged several times, really loudly. No response, so I did it again; *louder.* Then it swung wide open, and a man who was similar age to me, answered. He was ready to swear at the insolence of a trespasser; an uninvited guest. I could tell he didn't take prisoners and his face was marked with contemptuous arrogance.

'What? What do you w-'

He abruptly stopped; experiencing the dawn of realisation. I already knew who he was, of course, but I wanted him to have 'his' moment of recognition.

'Shut up and let me in.' I scalded. 'I've come to talk business.'

He scowled. 'Are you… serious? *Like hell* I'm letting *you* in.'

'Purchasing Ivy farm is the last piece of your puzzle, isn't it?'

I let that hang…

My insight totally discombobulated him... but it only took seconds for him to reset; an unusual, odious expression forming over his face - the point of mutual understanding.

He smirked and shrugged.

'I know where your daughter is,' I said, dropping the bomb; his face, instantly freezing on his doorstep. 'I suppose I could tell you, but first, how about I buy this farm off you?'

Now, he wore the look of the contemptuously annoyed, snorting dismissively.

'How about I buy all five or six?' I said. 'Drop in the bucket for me, financially.'

I was going to keep up the metaphorical punching; surreptitiously enjoying each statement.

'Ten million for them all.'

He scoffed, 'Rich idiot. Twenty... and I'll think about it.'

'Twenty it is.'

'You're not getting these for twenty, and you know it.'

'*Well, I'll gamble* you for them. How about it?' I emphasised this part on purpose, and he knew it, especially when I added: 'Grobatard's like to gamble. The higher stake stuff.'

This evoked disdain, which gradually morphed into satisfaction before he finally spoke. 'And I suppose you're the knight in shining armour, back from his pompous crusade overseas, returning to rescue his homeland from us fiery dragons.'

'That's pretty creative. Well done.'

'Piss off.'

He went to slam the door.

'Not selling then, Craig?'

'Whatever you know... or whatever you *think you know*... you're too late.'

'Too late? Me, *or you?*'

Now, it was my turn to let something nefarious linger on my face.

I wasn't an actor, but had learned a thing or two through giving countless interviews. I could master a particular countenance for a brief spell, and in this case, I possessed the added *justification* in doing so. I let it hang a little until his hubris slightly wavered. Then, with a smirk on my face, I swivelled one eighty and walked back towards the playground.

'Get off my land or I'll call the police!' he barked.

I gave him the bird, and laughed. 'This section... is a public right of way.'

In actual fact, I was heading to the cattle bridge and over to the other side. He could call the police, or he could even call the press, but I knew he wouldn't. For certain there was *one* phone call - if he had an ounce of brain - he would definitely make. The big farm door would close and he would go and sit next to his table - and after thinking it through - something troubling would spark in his mind. And then he would reach for his phone, and make *that* call.

To discover both he, and his family, were in for a delightfully nasty surprise.

~ ~ ~

As soon as I stepped off the cattle bridge, I was treading on Grobatard land, and doing so on purpose.

Craig watched me from a distance, as I bypassed the playground, heading straight over to the other side.

I wanted him to see or sense true arrogance; to embrace my superiority even if his was a cognitive experience; not empathetic. Undoubtedly, he thought his family were kingpins - the regional Yeomen - but I was Landed gentry, dropping by to deliver him some whoop-ass. However, talking to him had given me the strangest feeling, and not only because the situation was naturally tense.

There was something off about him, and the whole vibe of the farm was decidedly different.

305

I was directly opposite his position - with the river between - when his hand jerked from his pocket to his ear. I hoped he was receiving the bad news I'd arranged, and even though my vision wasn't nearly as sharp, I swear I saw him stiffen. He was maintaining eye-contact, easy for me to return, because he was a blur from here.

So I walked on, out of view - hugging tight to the beck - along the route me and Ishaq once took flight.

Time for the next errand.

Looking down at the cool water, I considered: what if Rob hadn't been collected from hospital so early? What if his body was less resilient to countless hammer blows? Incessant, nagging *what-ifs,* forever plaguing me. And it was here, parallel with the side of Hislop's farm house, I encountered the huge white sheet.

Covering the river for a good twenty metres.

I slowed, puzzled.

JCBs were dotted either side of the beck; numerous tread marks criss-crossing below my feet. There was either some serious river refurbishment happening… or this was hogweed removal. The ping of fresh cement in my nostrils, suggested the former.

This was a *huge* undertaking.

Land was being flattened for hundreds of yards - and not only here - for a considerable distance ahead, past the tarpaulin. I was completely out of sight of Craig, so I crouched to examine, my hand touching the canvas ready to peel and peek, but then I pulled away, hesitantly.

What was happening?

It was as if something was happening *in* the river itself; some form of engineering. *Pointless* having a cover to keep the rain out of a river. Unless - and I suddenly felt jittery - *unless,* this was actually keeping something within. I felt a tingle peppered with dread, as if inadvertently stumbling upon some horrible Grobatard secret. Were they widening? Why hide it?

It was as if… they were building a dock.

A dock for what?

I briefly stared at my watch. Running late to meet Hazel. I'd missed this in my research. I'd have to study local planning later. Scarlett hadn't mentioned this. Ahead of me, the meandering river veered slightly right as I prepared to stroll memory's garden once again. Pretty much with every step, confidence growing, I cursed the river. Silently, I watched its sanguine eastward flow. Sedate, undisturbed. Maybe I *could* entertain more coherent explanations for what happened here decades ago. Certainly I knew being separated by time and the Atlantic, had brought objectivity, and at this moment... this was a placid body of shallow water, and nothing more.

But a fool forgets.

And an egregious fool stares back at time through rose-tinted spectacles, wearing a halcyon cap, allowing scant melodic memories to flood the melancholy. Drown it out? How apt? A date with the inevitable was looming closer. It was ringing like a death-knell. There was no escape, despite this escape route.

If these were Rob's bones... I wouldn't cope. Simple.

I desperately didn't want these bones to be his.

I continued my swearing tirade, letting the beck have both barrels as I moved on.

When I heard the barking, my mind instantly flashed to the hound of the Baskervilles. The tumult came from somewhere to my left, far in the distance. I wasn't unduly worried, and for the briefest second became immersed in poignant black and white, watching Basil Rathbone deducing the impossible, the unimaginable.

Taking in my surroundings, I estimated I was half way across Grobatard land, at the very outer edge. This was his original farm, one he'd owned since I was a kid.

Briefly looking north, I warily stepping away from the beck so the supernatural didn't blindside me. And I listened, while checking for signs of cameras. None. No natural positions to place any in a wheat field.

The dogs sounded excitable, almost agitated.

A healthy gap separated me from the farm house - but the clamour seemed to come from beyond, as if an unwanted visitor had driven into the front courtyard, triggering protective instincts. Surely, I'd be difficult to spot, unless someone was purposefully watching. Regardless, I kept my pace, ducking down a little. Over thirty years earlier, I'd travelled this stretch without being bitten, stomped, crushed or threatened with a twelve bore.

I had a little way to go before reaching the field with the horses (if they were even there), and assumed Craig's first frantic call would be his estate agents... occupying a considerable chunk of time. But now I could hear the low rumble of an engine, accompanying the restless barking. I instantly recognised the staccato revs of an ATV.

And then it got louder.

Maybe... four or five dogs.

'Shit!'

Old Mr Grobatard liked his Alsatians, didn't he? As did I... when they got to know me. Along with Labradors, Jack Russell's, and of course, Dalmatians, German shepherds, were the first breed I ever learned about. Specifically... handle with care.

Coming closer.

Hastily, I assessed my options. I'd given Craig *breaking news*, and now he wanted to break my body. I was close to the old people's home - but far enough away. I stared east at the forested copse we'd stumbled on as kids, the same enclosure that intrigued me and Ishaq decades ago. Even now, this was my best option; *my only option*. Get in, climb like hell, and hope for a phone signal. It was three hundred yards distant, and cordoned by black railings.

I ran.

Ray-Bans... Omega Seamaster... maybe I had tools to bribe the pack leader, or, pretend I'm from DEFRA; Hollywood branch. Gucci division.

Surely, Craig couldn't have got around there so fast...

But - from out of nowhere - things got a lot worse. Mist was forming over the beck. I rubbed my eyes, scarcely registering the inconceivable, adrenalin flooding my frame.

'What!'

That simply... cannot be. As I ran, I stared at the entire river course in palpable disbelief. I *must* be imagining this. A bright summer's day, hay-fever, too much alcohol, dimming eyes... But, it was right there, rising, in the tiniest wispy curls. I swallowed, suddenly struck by the most horrific of scenarios. A dire proposition. Hobson's choice.

I might have to jump in.

A surge of terrible fear ripped my heart. That *could not* happen.

I'd reached the south corner of a potato field - many of the crop, blighted and rotting - when the white helmet of the ATV rider appeared. At the north end, stopping their quad, opening a gate... not that it mattered; two large creatures bounding straight over it, regardless.

I went all out in a middle-age sprint, trying to reach the small forest, scared senseless on every side. The black surrounding fence appeared much taller when I was a kid. It was absolutely no barrier at all.

Drug overdose; crushed by car; shot dead naked in a hotel lobby - I was about to chart on the bizarre celebrity death list. A high, *new entry*.

I stopped, frantically searching around. The volume of barking spread down the field like a flamethrower, and I'd completely underestimated both their speed, and intent. Taking a fallen branch from the ground, I opted for defence, while pulling my phone out, calling Shizz, hitting *speaker*...

The green leaves it contained shook as my hand quivered. The irony of shaking like a leaf. *Please answer*. I'd be disposed of. No question.

'Where yo-'

'*Shizz!* I'm being attacked.'

'Wha-'

'*Shizz*, the dogs are coming. I'm getting attacked. *This* is where I am. Quickly.'

'You're *what!*'

'Shizz, I'm serious... listen...'

'*Hide, hide.*'

309

'Find me.'

I shared my location and hung up.

I chucked the useless branch, dropping to all fours, briefly considering tipping down the slim slope into some reeds. Instead, I grabbed for the largest stone I could find. The mist was turning denser. And then... the voices came, indistinguishable murmurings at first, starting at a low level, furling and unfurling; the chant steadily rising.

The ATV rounded the south-west corner, slowing to make the turn. Four dogs, one stone... and an enormous man on a quad. The Alsatians - on seeing me - boycotted the edge, pitching left, darting straight over potato furrows on a diagonal trajectory.

The end.

Raising my hands, like a terrorist covered in explosives, I shouted, 'Stop, stop. *Hey, hey...*'.

I could feel myself creeping backwards; the contour of land angling down at my heel, and I knew I was seconds away from tumbling in. Four animals of this size would maul me. Considerable damage. Slow death, painful. River or canine?

Full pelt, the lead dog charged me. And ridiculously, with bewilderingly vain hope, I stared directly at it, *willing* it stop; silent commands, forming and then freezing in my throat. And, twenty feet away, inexplicably... it did; grinding to a complete halt. The sudden braking caused it to flip once, and it landed, turfing up earth with its hind legs, before scrambling back several steps, and growling. Its three accomplices followed suit, barking in a perfect line.

My body was shaking with adrenalin, as I raised the stone, commanding arm to swing, and legs not to buckle. But now the ATV was here, launching past them, heading straight at me. Visor up, the driver expertly slammed on his own brakes. His gloved hand reached forward to take a sledge hammer - resting on the front rack - while his head jerked round to the horde. It was muffled, but I definitely heard, 'Get him!'

He pointed, clapped his hands, and pointed... again. Then he charged the ATV forward some more, taking the weapon in both his hands. The dogs repeatedly prowled the same position - backwards and forwards - snarling through saliva-coated fangs, arching their backs; poised to tear.

And I saw the flash of confusion through the slit in his helmet. He looked back at me, and then the dogs again, swearing at them.

I didn't know what was going on.

Not at all.

He *was* yelling them forward.

I'd trained hard in LA, and in a one-off with a bi-pedal, I'd fancy my chances. But not against a *sledgehammer*, nor a helmet. Nor, a farm-hand for that matter. You didn't mess; muscles meant nothing, because they tirelessly *worked* the earth, day-after-day. That was real strength.

But through the sleeves of his white jacket, I noted his arms were thin, although his waist wasn't. Dry, deep grooves savagely set themselves around his eyes. I was expecting exuberant youth, but he looked far older than me. Had Grobatard senior come out to finish the job himself?

'*Go on!*' he screeched.

Two backed away, tails between their legs, and the others cowered.

'*Enemy.*'

The word floated from behind, into my right ear.

The man continued shouting, 'You stupid dogs! *Get him!*'

… And a chill crawled my spine, slithering over my shoulders, and across my neck. The bike rider fixed me with his hateful eyes through his visor, before looking past and beyond… widening in terror.

'*Enemy.*'

Gripping the handlebars, he immediately throttled left in a half moon arc, motoring straight into the bumpiest portion of the potato field. As he ploughed into the first ridge, the sledgehammer flew off the front, landing in a trough. And, he nearly jerked off too, struggling to manage the terrain. All four guard dogs took flight. Bewildered, I stood with my arm raised, stone in hand. And then… I began to turn. Inch by inch, my mind tried overruling -

311

commanding my body to resist. Heart pounding, skin prickling. I was in mortal peril. *Do not look.* My legs remained locked - trembling - stuck fast in the earth; only my neck partially annulling compliance. But my eyes didn't obey at all... they couldn't. And out of their corner, I watched something large and dark descend, deeper and deeper. Black and ink-like, dispersing in the murky brown water; bulging below like a billowing cloud. Until there was nothing.

Millimetres above the surface of the quiet river, the mist continued to spiral.

In the distance I heard ATV powering straight through the open gate; the rider having no intention of closing. And an old familiar feeling re-emerged; one that had remained dormant since the first time I heard *this* word.

Enemy.

Scouring the beck, I searched for signs I was in the vicinity of evil, preparing to bolt, until my attention was drawn further up the river.

To the boat.

And my mind collapsed.

In an instant, shivering gripped me in a vice. The dread. A chain I couldn't slacken. It wasn't possible. A single, wooden boat with a small mast and sail. This couldn't be happening. I was older, maturer; had a better grip on things. I was richer, wiser - with celebrity status - some even considered me special. This *couldn't* be real. Just shy of a hundred yards away, pointing downstream, stationary, bobbing on a solitary spot in the water. It wasn't there before. Even though my eyesight had weakened, I could see someone lying face down inside, the soles of their shoes visible over the stern. I knew the boat, and who carved it.

And I knew who sailed it a final time.

~~~

It didn't compute. Why would it?

Error 404.

My hands were dirty from rummaging the earth, so I used knuckles instead; furiously rubbing my eyes.

There. Ahead.

An atomic plume of fear began inflating in my chest, swelling without control. It was *still* there... and it couldn't be. I stared as my limbs twitched and spasmed out of control. Fight or flight?

Neither. Falter, fail.

A moment ago the Sirens could easily have dragged me from behind, but they didn't. They wanted me to decide. Me to self-sacrifice, atone, and intentionally offer myself for his demise. I rubbed again, looked away, looked back. There was no escaping my weakness; my cowardice. Reaching down, I grabbed the same stone I must have dropped.

The boat was motionless, anchored against the current by some unseen force. Dogs, now distant. Engine noises, now diminishing in redundancy. I pirouetted, checking for signs of life; a vestige of support, an angel.

It was me, and *it*.

The river had truly heard me cursing it; no fan of wanton slander. This was the response, so I edged forwards, slammed by the morbidity of my own actions. Caught between an unparalleled *need* to see, and praying the apparition would simply vanish. Depart from me.

But, I wanted closure... a chance to rescue. Save my best friend. Furtively forward. Shivering, shaking. Erratic gait. Compelled - like a grief-ridden mourner to an open casket - I drew closer, doing so quickly. To my left, the forested copse with its black railings was now maybe twenty feet away. Baskets of red and yellow flowers hung from the tree branches within; a juxtaposition of beauty and the consuming dread firing through me. Down to my right, the boat...

With the prostrate boy inside.

Laying flat on his stomach, staring east, into the distance, and further down the river... back to where he vanished.

'God, help me.'

His neck was positioned at an acute angle. Vertebrae smashed and reset by obscene forces, sheered and then stretched out at nearly ninety degrees. I clutched my chest, panting. I couldn't handle this... Both the boy's arms dangled over the front of the bow, the forearms submerged. A soggy bandage clung to his left arm, the flimsy tail having unravelled, the cotton limply floating beneath the surface.

'Rob,' I whispered.

He didn't move. No response. A lifeless figurehead on the front of a ship... yearning, pining for the horizon... for emancipation, for Newhaven. The rest of his body alarmingly elongated within the hull, and pulling parallel now, I saw his eyes were wide, fixed on something ahead; his mind belonging to another world, if any thoughts resided within.

'Rob.'

My voice faltered, shredded... No acknowledgment, No awareness. Staring straight ahead, his focus, locked on something in the beyond. Earthly minds could not conceive what he was seeing. Stooping, I sank down - crouching - grateful for a higher elevation, and the dividing line between the living, and the *thing* below. It *was* him. The back of his head, the hair, the toned physique. Strong shoulders. The clothes.

'Rob,' I whimpered.

And then my phone erupted in my jacket pocket - closer to my ears as I knelt. The power chords of a *Metal* ring-tone sending me sprawling in shock. I clutched, answering.

'Bill... are you okay?'

'I-'

'*What's happening?*'

'I-'

'*Are you safe? Where are the dogs?*'

I didn't reply.

'*Bill!*'

'I-'

'Bill, talk to me. I tried calling 911. But it's 999, isn't it?'

'I'm with Rob. I need to go.'

'Pardon?'

'I'm with Rob.'

'You're *with-*'

'I'm *with* Rob.'

I hung up, switching to silent.

The boy below had angled his face up to his left, now glaring at me, bone twisting out of skin. I stood, unsteadily.

A neck doesn't twist like that. It just doesn't; it can't. His expression - voluminous in magnitude - conveying disorientation with dismay, and above all, contempt at his betrayal. By me. All squeezed into the centrifuge of this solitary, sickening stare. Etched in every line. Sealed in every sinew.

'Choo-Choo!' he blurted, his eyes blazing.

Then his neck crunched back into an advanced position, and he set sail.

His arms thrusting down, launching out. Rapidly paddling at an unearthly, instant speed - the boat moving faster than physically possible, beyond human exertion. Torrents of water displacing on either side of his systematic shoulder blades, pounding, driving, pounding...

The boat sped off, and I snapped out of the reverie. Let it go. Let it go.

So, I ran, trying to keep up. I couldn't let him go. I *couldn't* let this go, but he was getting further away. How was he going this fast?

'Choo-Choo!'

The edge of the field drew nearer, every single aspect of his flight defying physical law.

'Choo-Choo!'

Shouting... over and over, as I pole-vaulted the final fence, into the field where the horses once stared me and Ishaq down. I could see the main bridge ahead - the one connecting my village to the next - with the slight dip for the valley between. It was a clear path, and I had to reach him before he went into the shadows. But he was getting faster and faster, water being churned in massive waves, cascading out to the sides, leaving a bitter, frothy trail in his

315

wake. The bridge drew closer, as he pulled further away, and finally, beneath it. I wasn't running for my life. I was running for his. In turn… *my life too*. Two-thirds of the way across the field, I screamed his name, pleading for him to stop.

But he'd gone. Vanished.

Nothing stirring, nothing visible… under the bridge, the wake beginning to dissipate and dissolve, pluming out, before subsiding against the tall bankside rushes. My view wasn't impaired here. The river continued out the other side, but I could see no boat; just the vacant swash tumbling into the sides.

'*Rob!*'

I shouted, reaching the part that sloped upwards to bridge and road.

I couldn't see him.

There was no one under, or out the other side, so I tore off my jacket, flinging myself in, down through the flowery foliage, past dense reeds, and into the deep. The current was so much stronger here, and even though the water was waist high, I could feel the tug; the power. I grabbed at a sedge in the middle to halt being propelled under the bridge. My strength and grip just about off-setting the driving water, as I feverishly searched at this new level for any sign of the boat. I could see *two hundred* yards directly ahead, downstream, but no sign of anything.

There was nothing there.

The boat had gone.

I searched the bed, still visible.

Nothing.

Struggling to acclimatise to icy waters, I turned and looked the way I came. Nothing. My breath - all but snatched from the sudden impact of cold on skin - and I struggled to keep a regular flow of air to my lungs. Releasing the sedge, I angled myself back to counter the current, edging closer to another cluster of reeds. Passing this brought me closer to the archway under the bridge. That's when the woman appeared, gliding out of the watery shadows directly in front of me.

'Ad me adducere ossa.'

Something small and grey lay centrally in her calloused palm, as she pulled close. And I launched away, to the bank, mindlessly scrabbling for purchase, slicing fingers as I frantically grabbed sharp stalks, and pulled on them harder. I didn't care how much I bled.

'Ossa eius adducere me!'

Hers was a venomous hiss, screeched over and over.

I glanced back at her bloodshot eyes, her straying… withered arm, stretching to take my leg.

The boney fingers, disproportionately long, some with blackened nails… most with none at all.

I grabbed for another clump, and *yanked* myself up the slimy bank, almost immediately beginning to slip on full bodily contact, clawing at wet mud to arrest my descent. *Desperate* levels of determination saw me make grass roots a lifeline. I gripped tight, managing to bring my arm over the top of the bank, pressing down with elbow and forearm, and dragging myself over like a primordial slug.

Behind me I heard her *shriek*, this time in English.

'Take him out, take him out!'

Scarcely breathing - and in abject terror - I rolled, and rolled, jerking myself upright, clasping my jacket, and staggered away. Out into the open field now, not looking back, charging towards the end. In the distance a car rounded the corner and headed down to the bridge. I frantically waved it to get away, and it slowed - only a little - before speeding up.

'Th-there's… there's a mad… w-woman.'

I implored them to drive on with beseeching gestures. The sight of *me* - the mad man - was enough; the wailing flagellant, sodden clothes clinging to me, and water sliding off every surface and contour, dripping into my eyes from my wet hair. I wiped and turned. Looking for her; looking for the witch, the face now peering out through the reeds. But it wasn't. Because no one was there.

Imagination. Pareidolia. Fear-creations. Neither in the water, nor under the bridge.

Swivelling around, I ran up the slope; the old people's home within view ahead. The only thing that mattered was the distance between me and the beck. Periodically I turned, imagining her body dragging itself over the field towards me; too fast for me.

And, I'd been tricked.

Duped like the arrogant prick I was. The river sang... and I listened. Scarlett had explained this in the letter, and I'd ignored every component of the river's ability to enchant. In my hubris, I hastily neglected the details Scarlett wrote me about the woman, and how she came to be there. Here now, closer than ever to my very own private-public breakdown, I reached in my jacket for my phone; only stopping to use it when I reached the far side of the fence, directly next to the main road. Close to hyperventilating, my fingers were *so* cold, the adrenalin *so acute*, I could barely graze the screen... but I made sure one hand gripped the wooden support tight.

This was a day of sun with cloud; no way I'd dry off in the next few hours. With blood smearing my condensing phone screen, I finally managed to reach the number I was searching for, noting tonnes of missed calls from Shizz.

I hit dial, waiting.

'Hello.'

'H-Hazel, is, is... that *you*?'

'Billy?'

'Y-yes, it's... m-'

'Are you okay?'

I quickly glanced over my shoulder, angling myself for a fuller view.

'I'm n-nearly with you. I'll g-go around the... back. Co-could you bring me some... t-towels?'

'Towels?'

'Yes.'

'Shall I roll out a red carpet?'

'No, j-just... towels.'

I shivered my way through this request.

'Yes of course. You sound... *are you okay?*'

'C-cold.'

'It's not exactly LA out there today, is it? Towels, you say?'

'Th-thank… y-you.'

I kept my attention firmly planted on the river behind me, searching the entire visible length for activity.

'Right you are. Are you sure you're okay? How long will you be?'

'Five.'

'*Five minutes!*' she paused a moment. 'So, you meant it when you said you were coming the back way?'

'Yes.'

'We heard the dogs going crazy earlier. That wasn't you, was it?'

'P-pr-probably.'

'Okay. Tell me about it when you arrive. See you shortly. I'll make you a cuppa. Sounds like you need it.'

I hung up, but kept bodily momentum - immediately heading through an empty paddock - and gracelessly clambering another fence. Now behind houses and back gardens, a little further ahead I saw the perimeter of the old peoples' home. I couldn't *believe* how cold I felt. Through the hedgerow it looked every bit a manor house, and I quickly realised anyone peeking from upper floor windows was privy to the most bizarre of spectacles. Kind of Benny Hill, meets Blair Witch. It was clear the final fence would prove a considerable challenge. Sopping wet, cut to ribbons, shivering profusely… and confronted by thick horizontal lats, coated in wire mesh.

My slippery shoes couldn't get any traction in the small, diamond gaps, and my palms were finally registering pain. Finally, I huffed, puffed and brute-forced my way over into the gardens - grateful for a sturdier barrier between me, the river, and the woman.

There, I assessed the large slope of manicured grass at the back for signs of *human* life.

Two old ladies were sitting in separate chairs close to where I appeared, looking down at me from a loftier position. One gazed at me with great intrigue while catching her nourishing rays of sun. Quite content and cosy…

watching me in her warm, patterned blanket, pooled up on her lap. I slowly ascended, while I keeping one eye on her, and she on me. As to not appear rude, I bid her a good day as I moved past. She continued her avid study of the dripping wet merman, before reaching a hand to me. So I stopped.

'Where's my Milk Tray, then?' she said.

'Sorry?'

She smiled.

'You want some milk? I'll ask.'

She smiled even more, as I pointed to the back of the home, hoping it was a kitchen.

Moving on quickly, I angled past the second resident. Very different. Her eyes were very much like Rob's - vacant and expressionless - the pupils narrowing, behind the glasses. I wondered if she'd watched my whole escapade without registering any of it. I whispered a *hello* that didn't hit, continuing to the back left wing, where Hazel had instructed me to go in our initial exchange. As I approached the door, she appeared.

With six folded towels in her arms.

'Now I *know* why you sounded cold.'

She looked at me with mild astonishment; eyes, tracing me up and down. I smiled. There she was. After all these years. Hazel was here. I motioned over my shoulder. 'Before you comment, I've had a hell of a last twenty minutes... and there's a lady back there, who requests a tray of milk?'

'A what?'

'Milk.'

'*Sheila*?' Hazel frowned, disbelievingly, staring at my pointing finger. 'Sheila's lactose intolerant.'

'Really good to see you, again.' I said.

'You too, Mr Austin!'

'Billy please, Hazel.'

She stopped, and unfurled the first, flinging it at me while taking note of my state. 'I take it you've been in the beck.' Sheepishly, I nodded, pushing back my hair.

'Why?'

'Best not to ask.'

She threw me another which landed on my chest and shoulders.

'Here, come inside. We'll get you out of sight. Any visitors staring out of the windows,' she nudged an elbow in the direction of the roof, 'will question an author's sanity.'

'I could do with that cuppa.'

'Kettle's on already.'

'Thanks.'

Briefly, my teeth chattered. In another lifetime, I could imagine meeting Hazel again, while wearing a cavalier designer suit - swinging around into the front car park - in my open-top coupe, and taking her out for a spin. I reckon she'd decline. Refreshingly, her reaction wouldn't alter whether I was wearing designer, or my current scuba.

Hazel Pickford was in the caring profession; a woman with a job to do, and seeing her face again was a trigger for reminiscing. Your mind plugged the age-line gaps until you re-connected with the person you once knew. Instantly, I perceived the same kind face, and warmth brimming beneath the surface. Her hair was in a tidy, shiny bob and she clearly looked after herself; smart and pragmatic in appearance. She was wearing a long green pinny over a navy shirt; officious and dutiful.

You could not describe her frame as large in the least, but she was of good stock. A physical career had honed necessary strength over the years; while carefully assisting many a fallen resident.

She laughed at my watery-winnowing and cries for tea, as she turned and walked inside. As she disappeared into the office, she called, 'You must be mad to go in that river again; did anything get you?'

She was probably out of earshot when I replied. 'Nearly.'

I was utterly shaken and messed up. If I wasn't so wet, I would have hugged and clung to her.

And she probably would have shooed me away, replying with that horrible phrase I got a lot in Yorkshire growing up: "Frame yourself".

Employers and relations used to bark it at you if you weren't doing a job correctly. Of course, they'd never *show* you how to do it properly; just kept shouting until you somehow *inferred* how to do it.

I couldn't frame myself at all here in any case.

That *wasn't* Rob back there.

But even in the moment of the chase, I'd filled in the gaps and hoped it was.

The beck had struck me on purpose, exploiting the hot core of my emotional vulnerability, duping me with its parlour tricks. Close to tears, with adrenalin finally subsiding, I pulled out my phone and messaged Shizz an apology and a brief explanation.

I requested she bring two sets of clothes; a power suit, and some casuals.

All the while - as well as *framing myself* - I was wholly attempting the other impossible act of 'pulling myself together'.

Chapter 6

Bones

'I can give you thirty minutes tops, and I told Ishaq the same… so he better be here shortly.'

Hazel's terms were delivered with a broad grin, and a mug of hot tea.

'Our guests are a full-time job.'

She clarified, not that she needed to.

Playfully, I scoured every inch of the table, carelessly lifting and tipping mats, abruptly standing… boisterously checking the shelves behind her. 'That's all well and good, Hazel… but where are you hiding the tub?'

She snorted.

'You mean the chocolate buns?'

'Look, I'm not fussy, but it's the only way you'll *ever* prove you're not a journalist, an impostor.'

'Thought you'd be into millionaire shortbread these days, anyway.'

'*Ooohh*… very good!'

I applauded, and then, strangely, we shared a mutual moment of knowing silence… softly smiling at one another. Then my teeth chattered, and she laughed.

I rubbed my palms some more with a towel. I'd drawn a little blood from grabbing the reeds, but most were just long scratches. My old friend had somehow honed the art of the juxtaposed: the formidable, and the gentle. She had that *air* about her. That demeanour, *that* presence. But I also sensed she was up for a bit of tomfoolery too - every now and again.

She said, 'It's been a really difficult time for us all, hasn't it?'

I nodded. 'I've literally just had an experience, if I'm honest.'

'In the beck?'

'Yep.'

'Oh, okay,' she sighed. 'I'm not in the least bit surprised. It's still alive, isn't it?'

I wasn't expecting this. Revealing this was a gamble. For a few seconds, I thought she might even chastise me for my wild imagination, rebuking me with, "That stuff belongs solely in your books now, Mr Austin."

But instead, she was exonerating me.

She took a seat.

'One of the reasons why I chose this particular office,' she paused, considering her words. 'Is so that I can keep my eyes on the beck, and the residents too. We reinforced and panelled the fence at the bottom to stop some getting out. Never seen such determination. Not even the attempts on the front door - straight down the garden at the back. Even those in their eighties, and nineties - bee-lined straight there. The angle of the garden doesn't deter them.'

I processed her frankness; her accent, still broad, matter-of-fact.

'That explains the wire mesh; I could hardly climb over it.'

'Well, doesn't that tell you something?'

At that point, a younger carer peeked her head through the door.

'Hazel, you have a…' she bemusedly became distracted by my wet form, 'another visitor.'

'Thanks, Niamh. Send him in. Ignore this one; he's been feeding the ducks.'

'He's not the one eating them?'

'Couldn't catch a lame one if he tried.'

Hazel winked, and her colleague departed. This meant Councillor Khan was imminent, so I quickly enquired, 'Ducks?'

Hazel shook her head. 'It's not good down there, Billy.'

I acknowledged with a frown. We were in the depths of Herriot country, and all creatures great and small was taking on new meaning.

'I hate to say it,' she continued, 'but I think the river lures things… mainly people. Before we reinforced the fence, we found residents down by the bank… staring into it.'

'Really?'

'Doesn't harm them, though.' she looked up to the ceiling, 'None ever jumped in, either.'

'Thank goodness.'

She took another sip of tea. 'Mercifully, the beck isn't keen on old people.'

'As in… notably?'

'It's preference seems to be animals and kids.' She touched the wooden table. 'Considering everything it likes to grab, we've been very lucky here at the home.'

'What if it's Basil the pike?'

She warmly laughed, 'Y'know, I do still think about him - every once in a while - but apparently they don't live past ten years.'

'You wouldn't put past him.'

'Agreed. So tell me,' she looked down at my watery attire, 'Why the dip? You really should be taking your clothes off, you know. They're a bit muddy.'

'My personal assistant is bringing spares.'

'Ooohh… *personal assistant.*'

I was on the verge of revealing my saga - my heart still not quite in equilibrium - when Ishaq poked his head through the door. 'Afternoon.' Immediately, his attention was commandeered by me. I was about to share, but hesitated.

This didn't stop Hazel.

'Come in, Ishaq. Teapot's there. Billy's just about to tell us what happened to him in the beck.'

'In the beck? You've been… *in the beck?*'

Ishaq grimaced - like this was *the last thing* he needed to hear - and he moved over to the table, pouring himself a brew into a thick mug.

325

'Well, Mr Austin,' he declared, 'to use a well-worn phrase around here… you wouldn't let it lie?' He joined us at the table, adding, 'Straight from the US, and straight into deep water. By the way… thanks again for yesterday. Life saver.'

'Just look at the three of us…' Hazel announced. 'Back together again. Isn't it quaint?'

'But no buns.'

We sat together, silently acknowledging the untimely reunion. Three intelligent adults with an unwanted connection. Ishaq looked *exhausted*, but relieved. A man whose parachute *did* eventually open.

'Right, time's a ticking,' Hazel said, pointing at a wall clock. 'Now, Mr Austin… you were saying… about your ten metre swimming badge?'

I shook my head, almost pleadingly. 'Thought I saw Robert.'

Both were stunned.

Cups went down.

'In the very same boat he vanished in,' I elaborated. 'Just like we remember.'

This took some processing, Hazel eventually leaning in. 'Young… or old?'

'Young.' I hugged the towel tighter around my shoulders, 'And then he took off in his boat, and I couldn't catch him.'

Neither spoke, weighing me up. Hazel believed me, but Ishaq didn't give me that vibe. Not even slightly.

'I'm not mad; I promise.'

'You saw him *before* or *after* you jumped in?' Ishaq said.

'Before. It's not hypothermia-related, if that's what you're implying.'

'When I'm doing a night-shift,' Hazel interrupted, 'I sometimes see things moving around down there.'

Ishaq wasn't having it. 'From this distance? On a night? Really?'

'Yes, Ishaq. *Really*… and constantly as it matters.'

As if to drive home a point, Hazel lifted her hand and pointed to each finger. 'And the nurses, the residents, visitors, and gardeners… report many things. They removed the horses from the paddock as precautionary measure after one got mauled. I keep a book.'

She swiftly pulled a drawer next to her knees, and rummaged for a notebook, slapping it on the table.

'Forty-six pages and counting.'

Ishaq sighed and even this sound skeptical.

Feeling a little warmer - and concerned about Ishaq's preliminary showing - I tested him.

'Ish, you do still remember everything, right? You're not intentionally disregarding it all?'

Hazel stared expectantly.

The councillor pulled the ends of his open grey blazer back, revealing a black polo-neck, and stroked his speckled beard, slowly and doubtfully. 'Well, you've always had a good imagination, Billy.'

I sat back in the chair. 'What?'

I didn't get a chance to continue, Hazel sharply intervening.

It was the first time I'd ever seen anger flash across her face. 'So let me get this straight, councillor… You're saying he imagined this… because he became an author?' She thrust out her palms. 'So, what about me? *I was there*. I didn't imagine it.' She tapped the notebook. 'What about all my co-authors in here… and their experiences? Are they imagining this?'

Ishaq met her gaze, still unconvinced, so Hazel waved it at him. 'Most of these are your constituents. Should we be encouraging them all to start writing fiction?'

He'd cornered himself, and put his tea down, clearing his throat. 'Look, I have a hard time accepting it. Who wouldn't? We *were* young. Honestly, there are other explanations for what's happening down there.'

'Other explanations?'

I kept a monotone voice, while Ishaq pointed to the wallet, phone and my pair of Ray-Bans I was keeping dry on the side of the table.

'Wear those a lot?' he said.

I stared at my shades, confused, and he added, 'You spent a lot of time away from school in our final year, didn't you?'

At first I thought his was some subtle form of bitter status-jealousy, but he immediately focussed away from me.

'What about you, Hazel?'

'What do you mean; *what about me?*'

'You were home-schooled, correct?'

'Yes! *So?*'

'I did my first ever fast in secondary school. At the end of Ramadan, dad flew me out to Riyadh to celebrate Eid. It was the half-term holiday in June, 86, and my first time away since...' he stopped, expressly resetting. 'Very sunny in Saudi. I was hospitalised the day I landed. I couldn't leave for three weeks.'

He'd lost me, and Hazel.

As if to strengthen a point that eluded us, he pulled out his own shades.

'My parents are retired now, but they were reputable doctors. No one could figure how a boy from Pakistan - with my skin - could become photosensitive overnight. My folks, sisters... they were *all* fine. Not me. Massive immune-response... rashes, headaches, blisters... swollen eyes.'

He was impassioned, speaking with conviction, and from personal experience... as if *this* was *the* most important thing that ever happened to him.

'I was taken to see specialist after specialist, year-after-year... no joy. Mine was an inexplicable case. My parents researched my condition long and hard.'

He reached into his smart blazer, retrieved his phone, tapped in a *search,* and held out the resulting photo. We both stared at the tall plant with dainty white flowers arranged in umbrella heads.

'Giant hogweed sap contains furanocoumarin... and it can make you permanently light intolerant. The beck's had it there for years. *It burns.* If those stalks are snapped, or grazed even... by wildlife, or kids...'

I sat bolt upright, instantly forgetting the cold, recalling how Craig clutched the same plant trying to escape the bobbing boy.

He hoisted himself out, immediately clasping his hand.

'Ishaq,' I protested. *'I have never burned, or blistered.'*

'But in every photo I've seen - like the one of you in that bloke's Aston Martin - you're wearing shades. When you walked into the hall last night, you were wearing them.'

It was like being thrust through with a sword.

'He lives in California,' Hazel protested. '*Everyone* wears them.'

'This *isn't* California. This *is Yorkshire.*'

'So?'

'And you Hazel… are you a fan of the sun?'

'Take it, or leave it. Depends.'

'How does this relate to *anything* happening at the beck?' I said.

'Look, all I'm saying is…' he held his hands up in surrender. 'We don't know the long-term effects of this plant. If that sap got in the water, we might have been hallucinating.'

'Oh, give me a break.' Hazel sipped her tea, shaking her head in complete disgust, adding, 'That's a ridiculous leap. What - the sun didn't shine here at all in that time - and it took two whole years for you to discover your condition?'

'I took many day's off school, actually. As did Billy. And I bet I now know why. Riyadh was my first big trip.'

'Those pictures last night,' I said, sensing tension between them. 'Those kids had their backs *gouged, not burned.*' I stared at him long and hard, and admittedly, it felt an assertive power thing. 'To be frank, Ishaq, I'm disappointed to even hear you talking like this. I didn't get a wink of sleep last night, so I studied the plants that were mentioned. Hemlock makes you hallucinate. I don't think hogweed can. The boy - *and the woman* - I've just seen were *very* real.'

'The woman?' Hazel added, concerned.

I nodded, keeping my attention on Ishaq. His manner concerned me.

'Listen,' Ishaq retreated. 'All I'm asking of you both is to remain impartial. Keep it rational. I'm not saying…'

He didn't finish.

'What are you *not* saying?' Hazel said.

'Look,' he said, shrugging. He was back-peddling, trying to find common ground, and admit to something he didn't want to. 'I don't know if you remember that old tape recording… the one I made all those years ago.'

'I think we can safely say… we do.'

'So I listened to it again before coming here.' He swallowed, reticent to explain. 'Hate to say it, but I will; those voices certainly aren't ours. I studied Classics at University. Lots of Latin on the syllabus. There were phrases in there I'd missed as a child.'

This admission was quite satisfying, Hazel resuming her sipping - far less aggressively.

'Look, there's something I need to tell you both before the Media gets a hold.'

He rubbed his face in dismay, before producing some glasses and a folder from a briefcase he'd brought, and plopped everything on the table. Shifting his seat further in - as if he was chairing a meeting all over again - he opened the blue cover, pulling out a sheet from a laminate envelope.

'I shouldn't be doing this, but I'm going to.'

I pulled my towel tighter and leaned in.

'*This* is a copy of the coroner's report on those bones. I also sought independent advice from an old Uni pal - now an osteoarchaeologist - and another friend, who's high up in forensics.' He paused, composing himself. '*These are not Robert's bones.*'

And there it was.

Hazel looked flabbergasted.

Goodness knows how I appeared.

This changed *everything*.

I'd already began loosening my grip on a concrete paradigm, and its shattering foundations… *painfully*. I quickly disguised how I wiped both eyes at once, close to breaking, as Ishaq summoned another sheet, this time bringing out his spectacles. He cleared his throat, ready to deliver more significance.

'Both hands and fingers indicate fractures, particularly around the wrists, and also the ankles. The left hand is far more smashed than Rob's could ever have been, even after he received all those hammer blows. The skull also contains copious small fractures, but more importantly, adult teeth… and they're all ground down, indicating this person ate a course diet. They're also calcified. No fluoride whatsoever in this person's diet.' He skipped a few lines. 'Although the height of this skeleton may be similar to Rob's, it has a wider, more open pelvis - and some of my associates firmly believe these are the bones of a woman, as does the coroner.'

I couldn't speak.

Hazel was equally taciturn.

I exhaled, but I couldn't tell if this was in relief, or an involuntary response. It felt like my head was imploding; thoughts immediately turning to Scarlett's letter, as Ishaq delivered the killing blow. 'And there's more, I'm afraid.'

He went for the bottom sheet.

'This skeleton is between two and three hundred years old, and they found a brass tin containing *more* bones buried within it, at the same site. Now, this is key: the tin was found within the rib cage area - buried with the bones in the sediment.'

He looked over the rim at us both.

'Meaning?' Hazel said.

'Meaning… the tin was in her possession when she died, and when her clothing and flesh decomposed, it gradually fell through the gap in the rib-cage.'

On the sheet, I could see a paper-clipped photograph of several smaller bone fragments, lined up next to each other. He moved the photo closer, across the table, and continued.

'In the tin they found sixteen finger-bones. Pairs. Possibly belonging to *eight* children.'

Wide-eyed, and in silence, Hazel and I stared at each other.

'Initially... it was surmised she was buried with a keepsake of her own kids, but further analysis of the pelvis eliminates the possibility. The whole skeleton was largely well-preserved because it was buried in sediment.'

Ishaq took another sheet. 'Interesting one, this next one.'

I pulled the towel tighter. Digesting this, or passing a kidney stone: which was harder?

'Age estimates of the finger fragments, including phalanges and metacarpals, suggest these were young children - aged between six and eight - and it's unlikely they were hers because of the similarity in size, unless she bore quadruplets, twice in a short space of time.'

I felt Hazel's eyes bore into mine. 'Billy, *tell me* you've read Scarlett's letter?'

This startled me.

I raised my hand, still struggling to register Ishaq's information. 'No, only partly...'

'What letter?'

Ishaq made this salient enquiry, recognising the shift in Hazel's tone, and I brought my hand to my face, covering my mouth, suppressing the horror of realisation. Surely *that* was a coincidence! The beck was somehow manifesting my subconscious pain - in the form of the woman - but how did that explain *what I saw in her hand*?

I suddenly felt very, very sick.

'Now, I know I shouldn't have, and please forgive me,' Hazel started, a little agitated, 'but, I've read *all* of it, and I simply have to jump in here. Sorry, Billy, we were never sure if you'd ever return, and we couldn't guarantee the letter's safe passage overseas.'

'No. That's fine.'

'There's two ancient documents in there,' Hazel said. 'They're about the Grobatard's arrest and trial for bribing families by kidnapping their kids.'

'What?' Ishaq interrupted. '*When?*'

'End of the eighteenth century.'

'Stop.' Ishaq abruptly said, his eyes fluttering in rejection. 'Hang on. Give me a moment.'

He pushed his chair away from the table, folding his arms. And I *got* why he did this. Her allegation was completely detached from any current reality.

'I'm not saying this is true,' Hazel clarified, 'but it *is* weird.'

Ishaq cocked his head to the side in abject disbelief. '*In the late 1700s?*'

'The Grobatards were corrupt sheriffs in this area. The locals fought back against them and won. They lost land and titles dating back to William the conqueror, and were left with two farms - the one next door - and one further down the river. Their reputation was left in tatters. They once had enough money and influence to turn the whole beck into a canal.' Hazel urgently sped up her explanation, as Ishaq shook his head. 'Look, I nursed an old Grobatard here when I first started, and he told me they resumed their kidnapping spree - trying to bribe their land and titles back - but it all went wrong; tried snatching a kid from a prominent family.'

'This is conjecture,' Ishaq sighed.

'No, it's *recorded* evidence.'

'And anyone can access all this?'

'No.'

'Why not?'

'They *stole* their own records. Safeguards weren't in place back then like we have now. That's how Scarlett discovered these.'

'Listen Hazel, no one knows about this tin of bones, and I shouldn't have revealed it... so what are you *insinuating?*'

Hazel nearly growled. 'That my cousin discovered their continued criminality!'

'This is all because of your parent's farm, isn't it?' Ishaq said.

'I beg your pardon.'

'Hazel, sometimes... things come to a natural end. It's hard out there... financially.'

Low blow.

Kind-hearted, *bun-girl* looked ready to clout him a good one, so I jumped in. 'Ishaq… compassion… *please.*'

He raised a hand of conciliation. 'Yes, you're right. Sorry.'

Matronly Hazel leaned forward, arms folded, meaning business. 'This *Jonathon Grobatard* I nursed, was exiled by his own bloody family. He told me the ancient relative who instigated the kidnappings *was a woman.*'

Ishaq stood, dismissively shaking his head. But I was up before him, immediately heading to a side-window, with a view overlooking the beck. It was a few hundred yards distant, only sporadically visible through the trees. It was hard to tell if the mist was still there, or not. Then, I carefully and precisely mouthed the phrase burning in my head, before repeating it back to myself as a whisper.

Until it was clear.

Until it was exact.

It was pretty much seared, anyway; fear does that. Ishaq and Hazel were on the verge of resuming their sabre-rattling, so I turned, declaring it at the pitch I first heard it.

'Ad me adducere ossa.'

I said it again.

'Ad me adducere ossa.'

It was quite rightly met with confusion by Hazel, but Ishaq was stunned. In fact, he was now completely frozen. 'Sorry? What?' Maybe the phrase alone was enough to trigger his photo-sensitivity; he certainly became very pale, very quickly; almost ashen.

'You remember that?' he croaked.

'I'm not the one who studied Classics.'

'No, seriously, Billy…' he slowly shook his head. 'You recall that from my recording?'

'No, I heard it in the beck… about an hour ago. This is what the woman screamed at me when she appeared under the bridge.'

Ishaq struggled to reach the chair. Wide-eyed, he stared at Hazel, but more so me. He paused, processing… *Then he completely lost his shit.* 'You're both conspiring against me! Is that what this is?'

Hazel hesitated, shocked by his retort, before slapping the table in revulsion. '*How dare you?*'

'What does it mean, Ishaq?'

I watched the councillor's unsteady breathing, as he realised this was *no* conspiracy; no preordained set up. He stared at the coroner's report laid out before him as if... reading his own.

'What does it mean, Ishaq?'

Then, immediately and hastily, he folded his sheets away into his briefcase - carelessly at best - slotting his spectacles straight into his blazer pocket. So, I moved next to him, stooping closer.

'Then she told me *to take him out, take him out...* over and over.'

I pressed my hand firmly down on his briefcase lid, stopping all progress. Despite his perturbed look, I raised my palm face-up so he could see the cuts from where I'd grabbed reeds.

'I couldn't wait to leave that river,' I said.

He stared at the red lines, then angled his head up at me.

'Ishaq, how could I *possibly* remember a phrase in Latin... from a recording you made when I was nine?'

He looked terrified.

'Bring the bones to me,' he said. 'It means, bring the bones to me.'

Chapter 7

Fragments

Ishaq sat at the table in sullen silence. He'd stopped his packing.

His, was not a sulk; more an internal re-structuring. Reconciling and re-arranging his standpoint in light of irrefutable coincidences; those even he couldn't challenge… not even Mr Logic. I was glad he had food-for-thought, as did we all.

I was chilled to my *own bones* by his translation.

Something Serin mentioned in Masham town square flipped the sedentary stone in my mind, namely the Grobatard woman she said was executed.

We might have just met.

'Hazel, is it described in this letter?' I said.

'Is what?'

'The fate of this woman? I only scanned over it, earlier.'

'Only briefly, Billy, but she was definitely executed.'

I walked over to my blazer and retrieved it, taking out the photocopied documents; deliberately sliding these to Ishaq. These were trial records from the eighteenth century. Admittedly, they were blotched and blurry. Old parchment. Black quill pen and ink.

'Do you know the location, by any chance?'

Every kid in these parts was familiar with the executioner's gibbet and noose hanging by the old Busby Stoop Inn, near Thirsk. *And,* the cursed chair that once dwelt within, apparently seeing off many a drunken soul, who dared to sit. The drive home after a right royal skinful might have assisted their earthly exit, but - if challenged - I still wouldn't take it.

'Somewhere close to here,' Hazel said.

'Makes sense.'

There was a burgeoning possibility this woman was tried for witchcraft. Anyone with a penchant for collecting fingers in the Georgian era was, at the very least, pushing social boundaries.

'For such a rural area, there's been a bunch of other weird stuff.' Hazel said.

'Such as?'

Ishaq was back online, peering over the rim of his glasses.

'Oh, you're finally back.' Hazel stood, hands on hips. '*That* police constable, James Weedy. Shot dead right here in Leeming.'

'Oh yeah. The press is all ove*r* that,' he sighed. 'When was that?'

'1890.'

I was familiar with this case.

The officer's death took place - more or less - directly outside the house where I grew up, and it rocked the entire nation at the time. Murdered by a man with a hook for one arm, who was exceedingly drunk, and coincidently, not too far away from the beck. Few of the more transitory residents living in Leeming over the years, would even know about the shooting on their doorstep. But now the press were digging for sensationalism - anything macabre and mystical with an association by proxy.

Hazel spoke, reverting to the previous topic. 'The stuff about her execution isn't really described in those documents, nor Scarlett's letter. But I can certainly tell you about it.'

'How come?'

'Well, Jonathon and Scarlett were exiled by the Grobatards. They met together here before he passed. She knew I was nursing him.'

I leaned forward, intrigued.

'The Grobatards have historical events archived,' she continued, tapping her nose. 'The diary in question - the one she read - was too old and clunky for her to physically steal and photocopy. Remember the days when you thought the photocopier lid had to be closed flat?' Hazel took her seat again. 'Scarlett read it, of course, and Jonathon confirmed it right here at the home. I was in attendance when it happened; heard it all. He well and truly spilled the beans.'

She pointed at Ishaq's briefcase. 'And this certainly explains the fractures to the skull, doesn't it? The authorities part-drowned this woman on a day when the beck was flooded, and then all and sundry stood on the bank and pelted her with stones.'

'Shit, so she was trying to protect herself.'

'Sounds it.'

'The wounds... to her ankles and wrists... are abrasion wounds.' I was shocked. 'She would have been bound, struggling against her ropes.'

'Tied to a ducking stool.'

Even Ishaq was startled, surprise etched over his face. He stared at his briefcase, before clicking it back open - checking the coroner's report again.

'I... need another cuppa. Is that okay?'

Instead, I headed straight to the open French windows, for much needed fresh air. A carer was in the back garden wheeling the resident Hazel called Sheila back inside, leaving the other lady behind for some final vitalising rays.

I took deep, long breaths.

The three of us were connecting dots; accessing an unprecedented exclusive of sorts. A murderous witch from a criminal family who enjoyed harvesting kiddie bones. But how did any of this tie to Rob, and his disappearance? This woman surely couldn't still be in there? There was no way.

I shivered.

How did this explain the different languages of Ishaq's original recording? Serin mentioned a Grobatard curse - and Ol' Bobby - *a singing Siren*. For a moment, I even entertained the similarities between Serin *and Siren,* but this only caused chaos in my head. She'd unintentionally lured me… or more specifically, *I'd* lured me.

And Ol' (*old*) Bobby, and his claims to a bewildering age… Ol' Bobby; the guardian.

I broke away from the patio, thinking about the woman I encountered.

'Take him out, Take him out!'

She meant Rob.

I was convinced of it.

I went back in and poured myself some warmish tea.

Hazel and Ishaq were studying documents together. At peace. Of one accord. Finally.

'Did this Jonathon say anything else?' I asked, sipping.

'Lots.' Hazel huffed, looking at the ceiling, giving it some serious consideration. 'Apparently, this woman was intelligent. She ran one of the two farms they managed to retain. Pig farm. Further down the river.'

'Pigs again?'

'Pigs might fly,' Ishaq said.

'Shut up, Ishaq!' Hazel scalded.

'Ironic that we're talking pigs,' I remarked, 'yet, the amount of beef you two have.' I raised a calming hand at them. 'Please, Hazel… carry on.'

'Well, I gather it was this woman's idea to restore the family name by bribery, through kidnapping. The Grobatard's all agreed to it and then regretted it. They abducted one kid - and had her lock him in a pig pen.'

'Where?'

'At her farm.'

'The one further down?'

'Yes.'

'The old boy told you this,' I said. 'Do you believe he was credible, or vindictive to his family? A serious question.'

'Scarlett read their records of the event, too. Confirmed them all, independently.'

'Good grief.'

339

Hazel drummed the table with her fingers, thinking, deliberating. 'She had a daughter herself, who was taken in by the Grobatards, after she died.'

'Okay.'

She put her cup down. 'One more thing… and this is dark… Jonathon told me she had no intention of ever keeping the kidnapped children safe. She'd allowed her own daughter to be raised by the wider family, and then accused them of stealing her. She wanted to kill the kidnapped child as an act of revenge *against* her own family.'

I grimaced, recalling my encounter. 'So, she was proper bat shit?'

'I think the Grobatards realised their mistake and went to free the boy, but it was too late. When the authorities arrived, they discovered all the finger bones. According to Jonathon, she'd been kidnapping and murdering children from further afield without the family even knowing.'

'Why risk it?'

'Sicko. Angry with the locals for tarnishing the Grobatard name, and her own family for not protecting it.'

Ishaq spoke up, looking from his document to us, and back. 'Okay. I know you'll think I'm being deliberately obtuse here, but I promise I'm not.' He stared specifically at Hazel. 'I'm being honest, okay?'

He stared at the coroner's report, nodding to himself, satisfied he was interpreting correctly, rationally.

'So, they shaved bone fragments from two fingers - those found *in* the tin - and both came back centuries older than the woman's skeleton.'

I was flabbergasted. 'What?'

'Seriously?' Hazel stuttered. 'How is that possible?'

Ishaq pointed to the bottom. And he *was being* serious. 'Radio-active carbon dating. They're retesting… waiting to see if the originals were somehow contaminated, but, it's very unlikely.'

'How much older?'

He shook his head. 'Very strange.'

'Ish?'

'Each separate set comes in at a thousand years.'

Hazel and I stared at each other in wide-eyed disbelief.

'We're talking, the bones in the tin, here?' I said. 'That can't possibly be accurate.'

'That's what it says.'

'It has to be a mistake.'

'Well, actually,' he nearly smiled, 'I'll throw you both a massive curve ball, and go as far as saying, I'm siding with professional opinion.'

I coughed in disbelief. '*This* passes an Ishaq logic test?'

'Two samples tested separately. Extraneous variables eliminated.' He nodded his head from side-to-side, weighing it a final time. 'A thousand years. Yeah, agreed. These folk are meticulous in their approach. I know a couple from Cambridge. They have a reputation to uphold; they lead the field. They wouldn't possibly declare this, unless-'

He didn't complete; just quietly nodded to himself.

And there it was.

Ishaq Khan.

Extolling the incredible, and downright unbelievable. Curve-ball, indeed. Then his phone went, and he grimaced long and hard, staring at the message.

'You're both going to hate me for what I'm about to say,' he said. 'I'm sorry, but I'm under enormous pressure.'

We waited for clarification as his fingers mauled his speckled beard. 'That's from my boss.'

'Boss?' Hazel asked.

'The member of parliament.'

'Ahhh.'

'I have to tow the party-line.'

'Party line?'

I stared at Hazel, who was equally surprised. 'The party line? There's a party-line? Are we talking... this matter?' I repeated.

He nodded.

'Already?'

'I've been given a head's up. I have an urgent meeting to attend, right this instant. They're preparing to release info about the find to the public.'

He was in visible distress, raising his hands protectively, anticipating attack. 'They're angling for a woman drowning while fishing here 250 years ago, and Giant hogweed as the *definitive* cause of all the current injuries. William Grobatard will donate a small fortune of his own money removing it from the river bank.'

He let that resonate, invisibly pushing us back with his hands. 'I know, I know.'

Although I fully appreciated he was a pawn in the power game, it wasn't acceptable. However, Hazel was quicker.

'I'm telling you, Ishaq, he's getting away with it!' she hissed, jabbing her finger at Scarlett's letter. 'Grobatard knows the land's cursed because of *his* line. Hislop sold for peanuts back in the day because his farm was no longer viable. The same with Cherry Tree. My folk's farm is next... and it's the last one. He's disguising the curse, deliberately spreading hogweed, and making himself messiah for removing it!'

'Sorry, he did what?' I turned to Hazel.

'You cannot prove any of that!' Ishaq said.

'No, I can't. *But we all know.*'

'Both of you stop. Clue me in.'

'Billy, the Wildlife and Countryside Act of 1981 states anyone who knowingly *causes* continued growth of hogweed is committing an offence.'

'Okay? And how does-'

'As kids, we were playing right next to it, literally two years after the act was passed.' She threw out her hands in despair. 'It was a *new law;* more impactful. Grobatard was secretly planting it and then intimidating farmers, threatening them with wilful neglect. All our farms were struggling anyway, but he made sure it grew on ours too.'

Ishaq stood up to leave.

'Look, that's spurious conjecture, and if we're being honest; borderline slander.' He took hold of his suitcase. 'I need to go. The bone coincidence is weird and I won't ignore it, but let's forget this nonsense about a curse. We're adults. We need to get a grip!' He turned, but not before fixing on Hazel. 'You'll do well not to let anyone hear you talking this way about him.'

'So, you're not telling your superiors?' Hazel said.

'About this? About Grobatard?'

'Yes!'

'Absolutely not.'

'After *everything* we've just uncovered?'

'Uncovered? Hazel, I'm a lead councillor. He's earmarking me for a career in politics. I'm not jeopardising all this over some old bones.'

'The curse won't go away, Ishaq.'

'What *curse?*'

'Go on.' She pointed at me. 'Explain what just happened to Billy in the river. That Latin phrase you *literally* just translated.'

'I can't.' He looked across at me, apologetically. 'Regardless, this plant's bloody harmful, in of its own right, and needs removing - *however* it bleeding got there in the first place.'

Hazel thrust Scarlett's letter forward. 'So, you don't believe Billy, and you don't believe Scarlett, either? Shame on you. I'm going to tell you something you don't know, *councillor!*' she stood bolt upright, nearly toppling her chair. 'Scarlett's daughter is in grave danger right now, and I'm deadly serious. She's in desperate trouble.'

'*Hazel!*' I had to step in here.

But this stopped Ishaq dead in his tracks. 'What... what do you mean?'

'She means, this river will not rest, Ishaq. People *will* drown. And as much as I'm loathe to admit this myself, it won't rest until-' I paused, a fraction too long.

'Until we give the bones back,' Hazel finished.

Unapologetically.

Ishaq smirked.

And then he laughed. 'Wow! I think we all need a little cool-down. Super-intense. The bone thing... odd, but the rest is pure fantasy?'

He shook his head, belittling, and then turned, heading to the door.

343

'You translated it yourself.' I called. 'You can't ignore coincidence: *ossa eius adducere me.*'

I saw him nod. He could not deny this.

'We *need* that tin back, Ishaq.' Hazel called.

He slowed on reaching the exit, and even from behind, I could see the shift in motion, as if the car had run out of oil, and the engine had dried, and died. He arced his head around, revealing the confusion furrowing his brow. 'Sorry, what did you just say?'

'Pard-'

'The Latin phrase you just used.'

I held his gaze, wondering if this a last dig at our stubbornness. Backing completely out. 'Maybe I'm not saying it cor-'

'No, you're saying it correctly.'

'Ossa... ossa eius adducere me?'

'*That* one.'

I shrugged, bewildered.

'That's not the phrase you used.'

'Sorry.'

'Before, you said... ad me adducere ossa.'

'I-'

Disorientated, I stared back at him, lost in confusion. But then, like a bullet, the incident rifled back into my mind. The woman in the beck yelled *two* phrases.

'The first meant... *bring the bones to me!*' Ishaq said, pale again. 'But you just said... Ossa eius adducere me.'

The three of us stared at each other, as Ishaq's jaw hung - all elasticity departing - his face chiselled in trepidation.

'That means bring me *her bones.*'

~ ~ ~

Shizz had collected clothes and was waiting in the car park at the front. I thanked her for being prompt and messaged I'd be out in five.

Ishaq had left.

Wrapped in swaddling towels, I was - at least - physically more comfortable than half an hour earlier, as Hazel and I strolled into the sloping rear garden. Emotionally, not remotely, the case. We'd spent ten prior minutes on the patio, confirming each other's worst fears. Silently, I'd chastised myself for revealing to Craig that I knew Serin's exact whereabouts.

'Suzy enjoys her forty minutes in the sun,' Hazel said, staring at the stationary resident ahead. 'A lot of our residents like this vantage point.'

I looked across at the old lady, the one who appraised me through a veil of vacancy, and thought about revealing to Hazel my secret activities before I'd set off to meet her here; including my conversation with Craig Grobatard.

Hazel moved forwards with strength, purpose, and surety; every bit a professional.

She continued giving me more insights into the residents.

'Now the planes have calmed down a bit, the guests can enjoy this garden in peace. Kind locals bring flowers, and the horses frequently graze by the fence below... well, they used to.' She sighed. 'Sometimes they don't talk for days, but a ray of golden sunshine sometimes bursts them to life.'

The grass dropped away abruptly, and I hoped wheelchair brakes were being regularly checked. For some reason, as I looked at the lady in the wheelchair, a wildly intrusive and inappropriate thought about the cheese-rolling festival at Cooper's hill entered my mind.

I surveyed the valley and searched the fields as we closed in on Suzy - who was staring back... head turned... watching.

'And here's an example,' Hazel said.

There were too many permutations in my brain to calculate. Plotting books could be arduous, but this whole adventure was as complex as it was cryptic - and I was floundering. I could control my story-lines; their twists, their arcs... but not here: solutions here weren't rational.

Suzy looked in her early eighties and she raised a hand to Hazel.

'Aww, bless her,' Hazel said sadly. 'No one ever comes to visit Suzy.'

My heart tugged. I had nothing but respect for Hazel. She was one of life's good souls; playing the essential, understated role society was desperate for, but didn't always recognise. A moment ago, Hazel had asked if I could hire security at short notice. I could easily hire *good* security.

Entirely for Serin.

'We've got to stay in touch, and share thoughts.'

I reminded myself of the phone-hacking scandal year's ago, and so I added, 'I'll give you a different number. Use that instead.'

'If you're flying back any time soon, we'll need to do something about this… quickly.'

'Like, what? I honestly… don't know-'

Suzy raised her hand again.

'Just coming, my lovely,' Hazel smiled, and then she looked at me, concerned. 'We've figured so much out in a short space; there's got to be a way of ending this.'

'You mean *without* bringing her bones?'

Hazel looked at the old lady, warmly snug in her flowery blanket. Her eyes, somehow still fixed on me; fascinated - lips slowly, noiselessly moving. There was no way, she'd know who I was.

'She stares at the beck every minute she's here, you know?' Hazel studied the beautiful countryside unfurling around us. 'Sometimes… I let her do it on purpose; hoping she'll reconnect.'

Suzy stared at me, and pointed.

Hazel said, 'Get ready for marital mis-identification, Mr Austin.'

'I saw you playing,' she said, croaky voice.

This startled me.

'Pardon me.'

'You were playing with that boy… weren't you? You *always* play together.'

She turned, staring at the beck, sighing. 'He never comes to say hello.'

I was freaked out. She'd seen.

But, I was more fearful of the sudden rigidity in Hazel, and the fact she'd lost all colour.

I knelt close, composing myself. 'Oh, I'm sorry to hear this.' And then I smiled, not knowing what the hell I was even saying. 'Maybe... he's just busy today - and yes - I enjoyed playing with him.'

I made the mistake of glancing at the bewildered Hazel, pushing her own way down to Suzy's other ear, on the opposite side.

'*Who* did you see, my darling?' Hazel said.

'I saw them both playing together in the river... about an hour ago.'

Hazel movement was disjointed - staccato-like - as she searched my eyes.

'That's lovely to hear, Mrs Tipperton?'

Blood drained from my face.

Something departed me right there. An essence of soul, a fragment... something. Hazel graciously giving me chance to recover, as I stepped away.

'Your son and Billy here, were such good friends, weren't they?'

'That's right... Billy.'

'And you son's at peace, now; enjoying himself. Carving boats, making tree houses, catching fish and all sorts.'

'Oh, I do wish he'd come up and see me,' she said.

I took a further step away from the wheelchair and gazed out; shaken. Completely shaken.

His mother. All those years ago. Accused of crimes she didn't commit. A whole four decades earlier, I remembered being dragged inconsolably from the field alongside Scarlett. The only other thing I recall from that fateful day, was Mrs Tipperton - at her wit's end - shrieking and begging for her son.

And here she was. She'd seen me with Rob.

How, I knew not.

Maybe she'd imagined a younger version of me playing in the river; faulty re-wiring courtesy of callous dementia.

Or possibly she'd become immersed in swirling, ever-decreasing circles of never-ending nostalgia.

In this moment, ironically, we'd both come full-circle.

The old lady peered up, snug in her blanket. Deep lines and pocks covered her entire face; a thousand bird prints on a beach strewn with sand and stone. She was only probably in her mid-seventies; her frail hand beckoning Hazel closer to her mouth. My friend stooped and listened, and then slowly rose; looking puzzled, *exceedingly* puzzled.

'Are you okay?' she said. 'This must come as a shock.'

The huge expulsion of held-breath was my reply, which she acknowledged with a nod.

'This is the most she's spoken in years,' she said in genuine amazement. 'Well done, Mr Austin!'

'I don't know... how I feel, Hazel.'

'I should have warned you. Sorry. Look, she's just asked me to tell you something - but obviously it won't make any sense.'

Hazel wore the cheekiest glint, clearly preparing for something ridiculous. 'Remember, Billy...' she raised a finger, smiling warmly, then doubling-over in laughter, hands on thighs, and for a good few seconds.

'Goodness... I needed a laugh,' she said, wiping her eyes. 'Especially after this afternoon. The residents do crack me up sometimes.'

I was intrigued. 'Go on. What did she say to tell me?'

Hazel looked around, shaking her head. 'I'm not saying *this* out loud. No way.' She beckoned me, immediately stepping closer to my ear, and whispered,

'Choo-choo!'

I watched a detached caricature of Hazel as she laughed... somehow, silently in my mind... until her expression faltered... and she finally recognised the brittle, petrified statue of a man standing before her.

349

Chapter 8

Legacies

Verity Schulenburg.

PA extraordinaire. Sitting on the bonnet smoking a cigarette. I wasn't sure if it was allowed in a care-home car park, but I lit a Kretek beside her, anyway.

'So, you saw your mate... and dived in?'

I took a huge drag. 'That's... basically what happened... yes.'

'You had me scared *shitless*.'

'I've been there all morning. Honestly.'

'You're still shivering.'

I nodded.

'And the dogs?' she said.

'Saw a ghost behind me, and ran.'

'Of course they did.'

I was a big fan of the word *agog*, for it perfectly captured her current expression.

'Billy, I've heard of method-acting,' she continued. 'but not *method-writing;* are you secretly struggling for inspiration?'

'I could feed a thousand ghost-writers.'

'But not dogs, thank goodness. Can I give you some advice?'

Uh oh.

'Cancel the wedding. Get the hell out of here. Go home. They're not close relatives - send them a cheque. Those photos of kids and shredded animals: this place is just *wrong*... honestly. It's beautiful an' all, but it's *wrong*.'

A van slowly drove by on the main road - satellite dish on roof - and we brutally ducked. At connecting corner's of this old peoples' home were entrance and exit driveways, stretching for fifty yards. A solitary, low-lying hedge separated us from every vehicle passing by.

At low level, Shizz whispered, 'It worked out last night, but vultures are gathering... and we both know the sympathy train rapidly loses steam. For goodness' sake, what if you were spotted in that *damn* river?'

'I was.'

'What?'

'The old folk thought I was Michael Phelps.'

She shook her head, disparagingly, but with a hint of a brewing smile.

'Is my suit in the back?'

'Suit? *Yes.*' she looked puzzled by my choice. 'I thought you'd go comfier.'

'No, I'm in need of power-clothes.'

'Why?'

'We're taking a little trip.'

She didn't need to say or do anything; savagely scalding me through red spectacles.

Opening the back door, I took the suit, and shoes, and headed back indoors to a room Hazel had secured me.

In five minutes, I was back outside, Shizz already in the car.

She called *out* shotgun, *already* battening herself down in the passenger seat. I stooped by her side, tightening my belt, as she held her phone out the open window.

'What's this?' I said.

'That song to do with *music*, and *the day* it started *dying*.'

'What?'

'Your downfall.'

I held it to my ear.

'No, you fool,' she snatched it off me, pointing it at my face. 'Watch.'

I squinted at the dark and blurry footage, cupping the screen with my hand. There was light in the centre, and a black background. Street lamps. Night-time. It was suddenly enlarged, zoomed by whoever was recording. I had no idea what I was looking at - none whatsoever.

'Shizz, enlighten me.'

'Not mainstream. Not yet. Appearing on some gossip pages...'

'Go on.'

The video clip reset to the beginning, cutting to an enlarged still.

'Well,' she began. 'There's a big full moon, a tall memorial, and two people. A beautiful curly-haired girl, and an old, peculiar man.'

'Shit!'

She slyly added, 'I think the memorial stone's yours.'

I slapped the roof of the car. 'Who would possibly... *think* to film this?'

'So, I would say, or I would conclude at least,' Shizz surmised. 'We missed one of punters parked up in a car, waiting to collect a friend, before we arrived.'

'So?'

'Let's be fair. The game of *tag we* played with Serin's scooter probably caught their attention. To the passive onlooker, it might raise suspicion,' she enlarged the image, keeping her fingers central. 'And, if you study *really carefully*, you can see the cloves in your Kreteks light up red; and it looks like you're smoking a damn firework.' She clapped her hands. 'Mr Austin... you *truly are,* the master of the inconspicuous.'

'This is just plain unlucky.'

'Ain't it a bitch!'

I raised my head, assessing the stately appearance of the care home, and the lines of peaceable trees within the secluded enclosure. A couple of visiting guests were staring at us from a second-floor window. Despite my suit, Verity was decidedly more eye-catching. Even if I was wearing her Smurf pyjamas, she'd get the nod. Further ahead on the road, the same news van we'd spotted earlier had turned and was heading back - slowly.

Peeking atop the passenger door, I noted a degree of deliberation in its approach. Intuitively, I moved around the bonnet, diving into the driver's seat, lowering myself, as the van pulled into the entrance.

Verity was unsighted and pushed herself down, mimicking me.

'What's going on?'

'Trouble.'

Despite being sequestered in Hazel's office, a tip-off was possible. I had walked past staff at various points. People who had seen me and Ishaq on TV last night, and then watched him arrive here… might join dots.

Verity glanced over her shoulder as the van pulled into the forecourt, right in front of us.

The news crew briefly searched the parking bays, but were largely concentrating on the entrance. I had left my PA with no *other* option except to collect me in the *same* hire car we'd escaped in the previous evening; the second, still parked at Ivy Farm.

This could be over real soon.

'Stay down,' I whispered.

A member of the crew was studying licence plates, and a smartly dressed woman in the front seat was on her phone, frantically scanning everywhere. Somebody was revealing something quite urgent; possibly informing her of our location.

She suddenly stared at the adjacent car, and then ours, directly, and for much longer.

And pointed…

Yanking the ignition to life, I aimed right, and headed towards the exit, as slowly and inconspicuously as I could muster. In the rear-view mirror, I saw the woman repeatedly jabbing her finger, and slapping the back of one of her colleagues. Momentarily, I left my foot off the gas, trying to hold my nerve, but the van immediately pulled away and started following.

'Lots of Yorkshire grass. Lots of Yorkshire grasses,' Shizz murmured.

'Yeah, they're pointing at the care-hire sticker.'

I longed for my Mustang's power. Even this car could outrun a bulky van. The problem was - I didn't intend to drive too far. Slowly reaching the end of the exit driveway, I briefly looked right for oncoming traffic. Nothing.

I slammed on the gas, screeching away, with maybe two miles to shake them.

Shizz grabbed the support handle above the passenger window as the car curved left.

'I am so, so sorry, Verity…'

'No, this part's fine.'

I was normally so good at not getting rumbled in a seething celebrity metropolis, where everyone thought they were famous, but - out in the sticks - was an entirely different dynamic. The car was nippy enough to create distance, their van only just pulling onto the main road as I reached the T-junction, two hundred yards ahead.

Left, Bedale. Right, Northallerton.

Many cars were approaching and passing, leaving me no choice, but to wait. Good work was being undone, and the press made up the ground easily, moving straight behind me. A gap presented itself, but with enough space for both vehicles to slot in… directly behind a tractor, and a whole host of cars, bang on the speed limit. 30 mph.

Shizz checked her nails. 'This is exciting. Have we shaken them?'

'Well, we've got another half a mile to do that.'

'Half a-'

A thought came; one that could prove advantageous.

My arms relaxed, and I withdrew from harassing the tractor in front with my attempts to overtake. The rear-view mirror revealed excitable journalists signalling my registration plate, and I briefly considered pulling onto the approaching A1M to give Verity a more dramatic escape; my gut telling me, no.

'Can we have a break from this chase? I'm getting tired?'

I shook my head as we passed the last house on the outskirts of the village, and I saw what I assumed, was the entrance I'd been searching for. Thankfully, it was a wide space and the giant gate was open. Aerial calculations in my imagination were proving correct. I indicated in good time to demonstrate my full intentions to the news-crew… and bore left onto a white cemented track.

My personal assistant protested. 'Where the hell's this? This isn't a drive-through?'

'It's a farm. It's where they grow the meat.'

Behind me, the van followed suit, mirroring my actions.

'Shizz, stay in the car when I reach the end.'

'Why?'

'Woof-woof.'

'Oh, come on, Bill. Have you completely lost it?'

'Here's where I might find it.'

'And the press? What about them?'

'I'm giving them a new angle.'

'You're not thinking this through.'

I shrugged.

Pulling into the main part of the farmyard, two Alsatians instantly sprang from the smooth, cemented expanse - and charged us - growling their displeasure at impostors. I swivelled the car in a semi-circle towards the front door of a grand, old house. As impressive as the exterior was, the large stone itself looked drearily drab and neglected. The owner clearly couldn't care less about keeping up appearances; not in this sense, anyway. Three more dogs bolted around from the back of the property, forming an impressive barking battalion. They homed in on the larger van, and it struck me that they wouldn't shirk their duties if there was a tank in tow.

Only the supernatural gave them second thoughts.

A perplexed woman stood on a porch watching us approach.

She stood next to buckets of red and yellow flowers, and I watched her pull her hands out of the soil and shake them before cutting short her stare, and marching straight inside, as I parked directly outside the entrance. This told me everything I needed about the *reception* for uninvited guests. The dimly dilapidated building was a complete contrast to the many brightly manicured flowers she'd left behind in the lobby.

Baskets of reds and yellows, everywhere.

Suddenly, the same quad bike from before burst into the fray. The rider, clearly keen to track the flight path of the dogs: visitors, infrequent... and actively discouraged. I blasted the horn and kept my palm pressed.

Shizz covered her ears. 'What the heck, Bill?'

The man with the enormous paunch veered the ATM round to my window in an intimidating manner. He had his dogs as his protectors. Pulling up his visor, he glared like he was some kind of German Panzer commander. Suited, and booted, he initially didn't recognise me; the *same me* he'd failed to conquer. But, I'd recognised him down by the river, earlier. Even through his helmet; those eyes, that single eyebrow.

At my point of vulnerability, he clearly knew who I was back by the river... and that hadn't mattered one iota. Those dogs were purposefully released on me. But now I had caught him off guard, and *I* was calling *all* the shots. I brought my window down half-way - as one dog clambered the bonnet, Shizz cowering - and released my hand from the horn, immediately aggressively yelling in his face, *stunning him.*

'*Tell Grobatard, I'm here!*'

He was at the point of shouting back when he leaned close enough... finally recognising me.

'*I said go and tell Grobatard I'm here!*'

Peering back at the approaching press van, his eyes flashed bewilderment. I bet there were all kinds of nefarious activities occurring here at the epicentre of "the" establishment. He was wrongly assuming I was bringing the press to highlight them. I'd beaten him once as a kid, and I was now unleashing my own brand of pandemonium. And he couldn't handle it; not knowing what to do, or where to turn. Was he now a full-time farm-hand?

The woman re-appeared at the front door, closer to Verity's side. She, also started shouting at *him.*

'He wants to see the boss.' I heard him weakly say, almost apologetically.

I shouted at him, '*Come on, Dove! Flap those fat wings and make it happen!*'

I pulled my window up to block out his response, purposefully shunning him, and zipped down Shizz's window instead.

This freaked my PA out, and she shrank back, rightly afraid that a hound's slobbering head might appear. 'Don't worry.' I said.

Ignoring Dove, I engaged with the older woman in an equally assertive manner. 'Tell him, *William P. Austin* is here.'

She pretended she didn't know, or didn't care, but the news-van was clearly irritating her intensely.

I lied. 'I want a little word about the dogs he set on me earlier. My friends in the van behind would like the scoop.'

Her stature reminded me a little of Hazel's - her demeanour - anything but. She had been socialised in the dark arts of the dismissive, oozing inhospitality, embodying disdain. It was set in her face - tapering lines, refined with contempt. Commoners were beneath her; deserved fodder for the dogs. Mark Twain once said, "Wrinkles should merely indicate where the smile lines have been." He'd clearly never met a woman quite like this.

I heard her growl something at me, but zipped the window back up to shut her out, drowning out the barking dogs.

Nestled in my chest, Shizz unblocked her ears. 'Are you done?'

'I'm so sorry, Shizz.'

She sat upright. 'Right now, *Bill. Tell me* what's going on!'

'The man who lives here is holding people for ransom - and I want to send him a warning.'

'Police. *Call the police, then.*'

'Outside the law, this. Not literally holding them ransom… manipulating them.'

'Oh, great. Brilliant. Ostensibly true!' She threw her hands up. '*Who even is this?*'

'William Grobatard.'

'Grobatard?' she quit speaking a second, calculating: 'You *deliberately* led the press here, didn't you? Why?'

'Those bones they found, weren't Rob's.'

'What?' Shizz gasped, covering her mouth. 'How?'

'I heard the coroner's report... but the bones were found on one of *his* farms, exactly where Rob vanished.'

'Shit. *Who's are they?*'

'A woman's. A relative of his.' (I neglected to reveal "when.") 'I want to start... and keep drawing attention to him and this location. The press saw me shouting; they know something here angers me.'

'Okay.'

'This guy's been forcing people to sell-up for years, and he's about to do something *a lot* worse. I want to tell him *I know.*'

Shizz saw my whitening knuckles gripping tightly to the steering wheel, and softened her voice, 'Bill, please... you need a chance to catch breath, take stock... the last eighteen hours alone, have been-'

She didn't finish, instead, planting a firm hand on my thigh. Although Verity wasn't for messing with, she possessed profound abilities when it came to handling my tempestuous associates, diffusing their steel with tenderness; frequently with singular, soft insight like this.

'Bill, are you going in there with *any* proof?'

'Nope, a bluff.'

She groaned, visibly wilting.

I had conjecture - powerful or not - dependent on a convincing delivery. Nothing more than the hodge-podge of a partly read letter, written by one dead person, and an experience in a river... with another dead person. Outside, the angry-looking woman started shooing at Dove to call off the dogs. He appeared pretty useless at even this, withdrawing his helmet in the end, and driving around like a novice sheep herder to divert them away from the press. Had he not tried to kill me, I might feel a degree of sympathy. The level of leather he was wearing for a job on an isolated farm, was beyond disproportionate. I wondered if he even got paid, or he was doing it solely to be associated with the Grobatard's.

'I need to go. If the Journo's come knocking, just declare your love for Cassie and Woes Almanac.'

She shook her head. 'I am *not* winding down that window again. That smell; what the hell is it?'

'They're pig farmers.' I pointed to the truck, and huge green trailer in the yard; countless snouts poking out the sides. 'Seems, they're taking their little piggies on holidays.'

I clambered out of the car, pushed my shoulders back, and buttoned the front of my blazer. This was intentional. A full view of sophistication, demonstrating style and panache, and above all, assurance. I'd created the scene: the fracas with canine, quad, and old battle-axe.

The cameras were rolling.

Although dogs were still in the vicinity, they were being flapped away by a younger boy who had appeared from nowhere. Without exception, he was more effective in this endeavour than Dove. But even this kid looked strange, with outlandish mannerisms, and an expression born of distrust. Even the most infrequent of furtive glances he gave, revealed a covertly sinister, secretive nature.

Pushing my chin up, and smoothing down my blazer, I approached the front door, straight past the affronted woman… hurriedly attempting to give me stipulations and directives. I ignored each one and kept walking - desperate to escape the smell of pigs - *no idea* where the hell I was even heading. This was all about poise and presence. I'd studied the Dorobo tribe in Kenya - how they walked up to, and then dauntlessly stole fresh meat straight from the mouths of hungry lions - leaving them perplexed in their wake… before, nonchalantly strolling away.

William Grobatard would be in the first room I encountered, or possibly the second.

He definitely would be somewhere on the ground floor, unless he was bed ridden.

How old even was he, come to think of it?

Embarrassing Presidential stage-exit gaffes entered my head; or thoughts of me lost deep in the Winchester Mystery House again.

I strutted through the porch into a large kitchen-diner with lots of cooking space, pans, and utensils hanging from wall hooks. The Panelled tiles were small, containing pictures of wild game in some corners. Walls were painted in cream which was flaky and in need of updating. It smelt of soggy wellies and farm animals; not even remotely homely. This was purely functional; there was no soul to the decor whatsoever.

Grobatard wasn't in the kitchen, so I walked towards the furthest door, where more light was shining. I could sense the woman behind me, still on the porch, glaring. I didn't break pace as she attempted barking something; not even flinching.

Then I entered a large lounge with a copious, half-octagon conservatory at the far end, where a man with white hair was sitting. His armchair was at a right angle to me, and on the thick coffee table in front of him, were three incomplete jigsaws.

Each three quarters's finished, and all, thousand piece puzzles.

He tilted his head to me, as I confidently advanced, unfastening my jacket in a sweeping, flowing motion. The red carpet glide. As I approached, I assessed single seats that I could instantly sit upon - without invitation - or a moment's hesitation. His armchair was one of a matching pair, positioned across a low oak table opposite him.

He narrowed his eyes as I closed-in.

Cunning eyes.

His thick hair was white with specks of grey; immaculately rendered at a medium-length. Time and effort had gone into this. He looked more a wall-street CEO than a farmer. His phone was propped to his ear, paying more attention to me than the conversation.

I took the opposite chair.

'He's here,' he told someone.

Pushing my hands together on my lap, I leaned forward, fixing on him as he conversed.

Here I was. Finally, face-to-face with the lead minister in a long-line of corruption; the ruler of a tight-lipped legacy. This was a bright and airy room, but nevertheless, this was a war room; *his war room*. Grobatard Senior was a man to be reckoned with. This much was obvious; possessing gravitas in spades. The man he was speaking to was still talking when he moved the phone away, and hung up.

Placing it down to one side, he replaced it with a comb, scrupulously sweeping it through his silvery hair. He had a distinct air about him; master of the guileful plan. With his other hand, he smoothed his mane as he studied me intently.

Second, after silent second elapsed, as this strange, quite intimate grooming regime continued. I imagined he repeated this process frequently, and it made no difference who watched.

But now was the time to duel.

My internal monologue: how strong was my hand really here?

His exterior was ice cold and calm as he watched me, continuing to comb and craft, before resetting, and starting over. Like some weird ASMR for a narcissist, who would repeatedly watch, but feel too entitled to subscribe. Grobatard Senior may very well enjoy playing with his jigsaws, but I was playing Monopoly. And without his knowledge, I'd secretly acquired Park Lane. Grobatard no longer held the property cards, he assumed; not the complete set, anyway.

Did he *know* the results from the bones? Had someone informed him? How much did even *he* understand about his ancestors and the extent of an apparent curse? Did he even care...

'Look what the cat dragged in,' he said, voice smooth, accent atypical in these parts.

'Well, your dogs couldn't do it.'

A smirk appeared on his face 'What exactly can I do for you today?'

'We're here to talk business.'

'Are you buying… or selling?'

I nodded at his phone. 'I believe you've figured that out.'

There was a hint of a French accent in his voice; significantly less Yorkshire than anticipated. The phone burst to life again, and I could see "Craig" flash up on the front.

He was going to ignore it, but I instructed him otherwise.

'I reckon you should *really* take that call.'

'It can wait.'

'I can't. I fly overseas soon.'

He put down the comb, straightening it, making it perpendicular to the arm rest, before fluidly raising his phone to his ear. I listened to the entire, brief conversation - with an *exceedingly* angry Craig Grobatard - on the end of the line. His son had tried shelling my battlefield earlier, but not before I'd planted the mother of all landmines.

It had clearly just gone off.

Craig was screeching, and, despite no physical twitch on old Mr Grobatard's face, I watched his pupils dilate. His son was still ranting as the phone moved down, and the call ended. He picked up the comb again, fixing on me with a penetrative stare.

'Buying *and selling*, Mr Austin… or is it Mr Bridgeson?'

'Just buying.'

The previous evening, I'd called the bank. Platinum privileges. My idea was based on part-information at that point. I suspected I would have to make Grobatard an offer he couldn't refuse, and attempt to purchase *some* or *all* his land. My actions were designed solely to protect the general public.

But things developed quickly, as did my understanding of the matter.

Earlier, I had parked at Ivy farm and visited Hazel's parents - the elderly Pickford's - before heading to the underpass. Scarlett's letter gave wonderful insight into the property merry-go-round, mentioning her role in relinquishing Cherry Tree. Ivy farm was the final piece for the portfolio - to end a curse - and the Grobatard's took its acquisition very, very seriously.

Hazel's parents told me they were about to sell to Grobatard at a ridiculously low price. Two offers they'd received from elsewhere... had been mysteriously withdrawn. They suspected the same nefarious mechanisms that conquered the Wilmott's farm, were in play again; intimidation and bribery putting-off prospective buyers. So also were the surreptitiously planted employees in survey companies, delivering damning verdicts on properties... seeing their value spiral. The Grobatards lost land and titles, and they knew every trick there was to ensure others didn't get them.

After saying my goodbyes to the Pickfords, I went outside, and called their estate agents; a man who had clearly been *got to*.

My Hollywood investor status - as a Mr Rolly Bridgeson - with conveyancers already on standby, cash-in-hand, and proof of funds - more than reassured him. My offer *above* market value heartened him. "The Pickford's deserve it. Thank-you."

Park Lane on the Monopoly board.

My only stipulation: a box of freshly baked buns *must* be thrown in as a goodwill gesture.

Ivy farm was now mine - subject to contract. I would not need a bogus survey.

And now I wanted to watch William Grobatard wilt.

'How do you feel about this news?' I smiled at the old man before studying the gaps in all three jigsaws. 'Look...' I pointed, 'you're missing an important piece of your puzzle.'

Leaning over the table, I let my fingers hover over one of the three piles of colourful pieces, carefully selecting a double-winged cut. I took the piece, flicking it into a separate pile... pressing my hand flat, pushing the piece down, and in. Then I watched for a response; was he a sociopath about to blow? For a moment, I considered it strange that a man like this was drawn to such beauty on canvas. All three puzzles were pictures of mills and rivers, including Constable's famous Flatford Mill.

William Grobatard carefully watched my placement, not withdrawing his eyes for several seconds; memorising. Not even a flicker on his face.

'How much do you want for it?' he suddenly said.

'Nothing. I want it to be mine.'

He smirked.

'No fake-tanned honeys in bikinis here, Mr Austin. Not in Yorkshire. No beaches, promenades, or roller-skates. Only pigs, cold weather, and noisy motorways.' He waved my words away with a brisk flap of the hand, his tone unaltered. 'Surely, these actions are an aberration for a man with priorities elsewhere, in the land of fame, glitz, and showbiz.'

I fixed my gaze. (Would he suspect I knew of their supposed curse?)

'Mr Grobatard, I didn't buy Ivy Farm for its merits, I bought it for its position... next to the beck.'

Something finally glimmered in his eyes, but it wasn't anger. He nodded, resuming his surveillance of the jigsaw, and the grooming of silvery hair.

'You mentioned Serin to my son; you know her whereabouts?'

'I do.'

I'd been rash to mention her to Craig. Nevertheless, I confidently pulled out Scarlett's letter from my inside pocket, deliberately smoothing the front, keeping perfect time with his brush strokes, until only a fool wouldn't notice the synchronicity. Making it awkward. Trying to provoke, to goad.

Again, not a flicker; and this... was concerning.

Just prior to my shock meeting with Suzy Tipperton, Hazel and I had stood on the patio together, where she revealed the latter part of the letter. The curse - according to Scarlett - entailed all land returned either side of the beck, and an assumed sacrifice directly from the Grobatard's own bloodline, for the woman they betrayed.

As I listened to Hazel recount its contents, all I could think: is modernity failing us?

Hazel revealed Scarlett wrote all this in the last few weeks of her life, while her dose of pain-relief was doubled. My heart sank when I heard this. The letter was a fraught mess, words slanting far-right, increasing in size, and tipping off the page the further down you went. It was incoherent, rambling, and repetitive.

Ivy Farm. Serin. Bring me her bones…

But why Rob?

I invoked my best interview face, going *all-in* with my bluff.

'So, you see, I am tasked with protecting your own granddaughter from you. Your attempts to break the curse by buying land, and murdering a girl on behalf of a woman your ancestor's executed is futile. Once your old daughter-in-law's farm is sold, Serin will be wealthy and secure. And with my help, support, and my considerable wealth and influence, her safety will be assured.'

Now he pushed his fingers through his hair, preening and styling. It didn't appear to be a nervous response.

'And you'll bring her to me.'

'Pard-'

'You'll bring her to me.'

'Are you out of your-'

I pulled out, laughing. Did this arrogant prick hear *a single word*?

Nothing stirred in his face. 'I'd like her delivered this evening by 9.30pm. We will go down to the beck with her together.'

I snorted another dismissive laugh. Was he *for real?* Only the pitch in his tone had changed, as if puberty only partially broke his voice. He leaned forwards, as if closing-out the deal; searching my own eyes for an equal: the enlightened, the erudite. A smile of surprise and increasing satisfaction ripened his tyrannical face - like he'd figured my tell. And every millisecond of my numbed silence was becoming his advantage; I knew this. I don't know how. Something was wrong.

He wasn't breaking his focus.

I *thought* my hand was strong.

'I frequently meet folk who only hear what they want,' I said. 'Mr Grobatard, I know what the curse is.'

'And you know your friend remains there until it is lifted.' Grobatard held my gaze. 'Trapped.'

Something in me nearly gave out.

I paused, too long...

'I can keep trying to feed her, Mr Austin, I really can... but she's taking and maiming my livestock. Until she departs, everyone's in danger. The yield from my crops will never surpass sixty per cent. All our businesses have been harmed around here for decades. My beast are never rotund enough for bacon, sausages or chops. Emaciated... because she even curses fodder.'

It was his viewpoint, or bust; a blatant disregard for any social norms.

He continued, 'The play area, the low banks, and the slide... are whetting her appetite; she's making this clear. I think she's growing bored with the boy she has in there. I wonder how long he has left, and also, all those dear children who so enjoy playing there.'

I couldn't contain my grimace.

Then, he said. 'I wonder what it would feel like to have your friend restored to you?'

Pathetically, I tried feigning composure, but I was the boxer who'd gone in swinging, entirely missing... sweatily crawling to the corner. I coughed. 'You cannot *possibly* believe... sacrificing your *own* granddaughter is the solution?'

'It is. Withdraw your offer for Ivy farm.'

'Mr Grobatard I can give you my deepest, and most heartfelt assurance, I *will not* deliver Serin to you this evening, or ever.'

'Have you ever shopped in a supermarket when you're hungry?' he replied.

'Pard-?'

'Reacting impulsively. Adding more and more to your basket. More than you need… at extra *cost*.'

I waited.

'Who will *she* add to the basket in her unsated state if he isn't replaced… quickly? I suspect she'll be forced to drastic action, take even more this time… like she did centuries ago.'

He held out both hands, wiggling his fingers. 'Sometimes, solutions are painful, Mr Austin. But they prevent far greater misery.'

And there it was.

Spelled out, plain and simple. He knew about the tin.

The hall meeting last night suggested everything was picking up pace. And his claims about Rob… I just couldn't handle this at all. He'd undoubtedly clocked the total dejection I could no longer hide, not that he cared. All that mattered was he was correct, and I should learn. I needed to leave. I swallowed, audibly… noticeably.

Then he said, 'Tell me, Mr Austin, do you believe in demons?'

'I-'

He waited, and for the first time, I sensed impatience. 'Trivia for you, Mr Austin: the demons begged Christ to be sent into which animal?'

'Pigs.'

'And you can smell mine?'

'Along with everyone in this county.'

'And where did the demons go when they were given permission, Mr Austin?'

Again, I was confounded. The instant shift from tyrant to Sunday school teacher.

'Barbados.'

'Close. They ran into the sea… and were drowned.'

Uncomfortably, I pitched back in the old armchair and folded my arms.

'She doesn't want pigs,' he said. 'She wants juicier morsels… and she'll persist in her insatiable lust until the criteria are met. The deplorable… wasted land… *Vasta*. I'd chain pigs to the bank, hoping she'd enter them, but she'd bite off their legs through the shackles, leaving their bloodied torso behind.'

'You've forgotten one important prerequisite in making that workable.'

'What's that?' He looked intrigued.

'This thing Jesus had, called… faith.'

No response.

William calculated me like a savant with talent, penetrating every ounce of faulty discernment to his agenda. He sat back and started combing his hair again, watching me.

'Have you considered throwing yourself?' I said. 'I'm sure your royal blood would cure everything.'

'You are correct to recognise our legacy,' - he ignored the rest - 'to recognise our direct descent from the conqueror.'

Then it hit me. *The harrowing*. Vasta. The *wasting* of the surrounding land. The age of the finger bones in the tin, and what Ol' Bobby revealed all those years ago. The children *in* the river, killed by a King; on *his* command.

The Grobatards… *his* lieutenants.

I leaned forward, desperate not to reveal a visible sign of revelation, almost shaking in the armchair.

This man's *French* accent, and surname. The *name* and *titles* he wanted restoring. And in that second, I knew he'd got it wrong.

Completely wrong.

I'd nearly been persuaded; convinced by the capricious cult leader, but he'd *misidentified* the origin of his *own* curse. I rubbed my forehead, wanting him to believe he'd *got me*, but buying time; cementing my understanding. This mad Grobatard relative; the one his family betrayed - this thing, *this Siren* - he thought killed those children... couldn't possibly have.

The bone fragments were a thousand years old.

No one alive in the 1700s could murder someone living centuries before. These children were slaughtered *during* the harrowing by others in his royal bloodline; certainly not her. For the first time in decades, I recalled the game of hide-and-seek and the vision of the ghostly knight, and the screaming children on Ishaq's recording, devouring their own siblings in starvation. It was a knight from the Grobatard line who drowned the rest.

I licked my dry lips, staring at the carpet.

According to the *exiled* Jonathon - and Scarlett - the authorities raided this woman's farm, found bones, accused, sentenced... and then executed her. But these *weren't* the bones of any kidnapped infants. It was starting to sound like they were *planted*. Whatever was in that river was *wicked pissed*, and with good reason.

And what of Serin?

A like-for-like sacrifice. Grobatard for Grobatard. Blood for blood. Had the old man in front of me got this wrong too?

I kept my voice low, swallowing, trying to keep composure, 'Okay, Mr Grobatard, explain why Serin's death is necessary?'

'The woman in there thinks we betrayed her, so we will give her a betrayer in return. It has been settled.'

'Settled? By who... *by her*?'

But, he didn't answer this.

'How on earth could Serin possibly betray you?'

Again, no response... because when you're entitled, and it doesn't fit your fixed paradigm, another person's reason, is static.

'She was an infant when she left,' I pursued, not giving an inch. 'How can *she* be blamed? Give this *thing* someone else in your family!'

'If you don't deliver Serin, nor withdraw your offer for Ivy farm, I will keep sending the beck its gifts, until it tires of four-legged beast.'

I nodded. In this much he was correct; it *would* keep taking…

'The hogweed will be removed,' he continued. 'More play areas will be built; hollowed-out picnic bays right next to the water's edge. My maid told me you have brought the press with you.' He smiled and clapped. '*Good!* The more people who hear the mystery of this place, the better. More will flock, and I will let them. Thrillseekers *love* a thrill and ignore the risks, don't they, Mr Austin? And, I will provide a never-ending free-pass to the river.'

Not even subtle.

For this twisted man, in the worst-case scenario of life leaving the forever lemon - he'd adapt.

'It sounds like you could feasibly live with your own curse?' I said.

He responded by spitting on the carpet near my feet.

'We are a blue-bloodied family, Mr Austin,' he replied, with deliberation. 'Our name is great. Our heritage, unsurpassed. Our business dealings were once nationally known. Our name should be on every tongue in this land, not tarnished by…' he contemptuously scowled at me, '… by a serf.'

Breakthrough.

'History will forget your paltry efforts,' he continued. 'But it cannot forget out great name.'

'A name you want associated with historical genocide?' Again he ignored this, so I moved in, probing more. '*This* is the legacy you crave; a murderous legacy?' I shook my head at his psychopathy. 'If you want your name etched in memory, I'll get it in my next novel.'

'We are conquerors, Mr Austin. Assigned by the original conqueror who controlled this land. We want a separation from the weak. When this curse is over, our name will be great. You had to *work* for your name. *Peasants* work. You made it sound grand, but it wasn't bequeathed.'

I was astonished.

'Are you capable of even…' I paused, floundering at his asinine ideology. 'Of even listening to yourself? Who cares about your bloody name? Get with the times you coiffed criminal. Haven't you heard of globalisation?' I stabbed my finger towards his conservatory windows. 'The world's bloody borderless, you muppet! No one gives a shiny shit about titles anymore. You're not a conqueror, and your self-ascribed label is *lunacy*.'

Genuinely chortling, he concluded, 'This *must* be undone. It is an intolerable injustice, and you know it?'

'Oh… my… good grief.'

I stood and fastened my jacket.

'That will be all,' I declared, but not before *getting* in his face. 'You're a Bourgeois *prick*. That's what you are!'

Not a single muscle twitched on his face; nothing faltered.

Up close, I could smell the Brylcreem in his hair, and on his comb, and on the headrest of his armchair.

The comb continued to glide seamlessly, as his expression held firm.

So, I reached over with my left hand and mixed the anomalous jigsaw piece I'd taken earlier… further into its new pile. This ignited a spark of controlled contempt, his bristling cheeks pulling tight.

'Seriously… that's what pisses you off?'

I stood upright - astonished - and left, staggered that childishness was the only trigger. I was crossing the threshold of the conservatory when he suddenly asked, 'Do you not care about Robert's fate in there?'

Yeah, this part was torturing me.

I strolled into the kitchen… feeling the gathering storm behind my eyes. Serin must be protected, but so also must the locals.

William Grobatard had to be wrong in his proposed action… but I was none-the-wiser to the solution. The *thing*

371

in the river wanted something, but I'd die before it got Serin's bones.

Immediate concerns: should I fake smile when I get outside for the press? Did I have it in me? Probably not.

I needed to be alone; the jet lag was kicking in again and my beck experience distilled a lasting liquid chill.

I needed ammunition.

I prayed there'd be an essential clue in the rest of Scarlett's *rambling* letter. Her daughter's life depended on it.

Chapter 9

Gone Fishin'

Thankfully, the press were not outside - parked instead - at the end of the track, on the roadside. As trespassers, they'd been expelled, but they were shrewd; positioning themselves for my inevitable departure: one way into the farm, one way out.

Mercifully, the dogs were being contained somewhere in the back.

Verity sensed my ambivalence on entering the car.

'How did it go?'

'The guy's deranged.' I turned the ignition. 'As in bad-guy-in-book, deranged.'

'Handle it well?'

I shook my head. 'Terribly.'

The moment the nose of my car peeked out the end, the press sprang to action, hoping I would turn left so they could hug my slipstream. I hung back from indicating, but angled as if this was also my intention. Assessing my options, I waited for an ambling car travelling from west to east - the opposite direction. Then I aggressively arced the car, screeching right instead, cutting off the driver.

He slammed his anchors, giving me deserved horn-blast and bird.

I waved a sincere apology.

'Finally,' Shizz said.

Anticipation was the name of the game for journalists; their driver already preparing for this, but I knew his vehicle was too cumbersome for a one-eighty on a road this width. I opened up a sizable gap pretty quickly.

'Do not - under any circumstances - drive back via that care home,' Shizz said.

'Why?'

'The press are reporting from the river; *breaking news* about the bones.'

'That's fast.' I scoured the rear-view mirror. 'So, why on earth didn't they snitch-'

'Snitch on your location?' Shizz interrupted. 'Smaller news-station, vying for an exclusive.'

'Ahh. Gotcha.'

Right on cue, a van with a dish appeared ahead - slowing to study a brilliantly bohemian furniture shop on the corner - before turning down the same road we came; flocking like sparrows to breadcrumbs. A major detour was in order and, in truth, one I was grateful for.

Driving cleared my head. *This* countryside cleared my head, and I had a chance to settle matters with my long-suffering personal assistant; gently pulling her from my own deep water, hopefully, without giving her *the bends*.

Shizz had earned her money's worth, thoroughly deserving of the fanciest, late, *slap-up* lunch as a profound apology.

I racked my memory for the nearest available Costcutter.

'I need the restroom,' she complained. 'Getting hangry. Need food.'

'I'm going to buy you the nicest sandwich.'

Verity paused a moment, processing the offer, before picking up her phone. '+1 from the UK, right? Let me call your surgeon in Pasadena; see if we can hurry along the vasectomy.'

Our journey took us towards Northallerton. At a roundabout, we bore south, accompanied by the lush rolling hills of Hambleton.

'Can you hold for another twenty minutes, or shall I find a field?'

'I'll hold.'

She stared out at the steadily ascending peaks in the distance, quietly marvelling at the majestic solitude the moors always bestowed. An ominous garrison of cloud was gathering, painting the horizon grey from east-to-west, with occasional shards of light grazing hills of heather coated in violets and purples. It was a striking contrast; bold, dramatic shadows sent with an entourage of light from on high.

'That's gorgeous,' Shizz said.

I didn't reply. Quiet appreciation was best.

I looked out towards the North York moors, indebted to nature for forging a reality more attractive than the one I led. More rays pricked through the billowing charcoal, fiercely reminding cloud that light always burned away the dark.

Beside me, I left one of my closest friend's time to bathe contentedly in the sunlight silence.

~ ~ ~

The better part of an hour was spent rallying around.

Haphazardly so.

We had a well-judged stop at a supermarket for the toilets and *exquisite-addition* sandwiches, and then we nestled ourselves out of sight in the far recesses of a car park. Shizz and I started chatting, and I came clean about everything.

And, it was *way* too much for her to take...

'Billy, you know what I'm going to say,' she eventually said.

'A borderline horror novel?'

'No, not a borderline?'

'These last twenty-four hours have been off-the-scale for me. I had no idea *this* was going on.'

'You really saw Robert in there?'

'I was lured, and I couldn't resist. It was his form, or something mimicking him.'

It was her job to ask me difficult questions, and the tone and timbre of her voice was exceptional when it came to eliciting an accurate response. 'And you're sure you can't go to the police… not even for some of this?'

Momentarily, I revisited her suggestion, but it was like a forest path that started deceptively wide, invitingly so, before suddenly narrowing, leading nowhere.

'Shizz, I'd like to. I'd like to get shot of the whole matter. Fly home. Have the Grobatard's done for fraud and intimidation, but it's going so much deeper. The locals are in danger. The police can't do anything. They've been out to the beck countless times… for nearly a century.'

'So… a curse… then?'

She left enough in her voice that both acknowledged, and challenged.

'I don't want to believe it, but I don't know what else it can be.'

'And he'll send Scarlett's daughter to a watery grave?'

'Hell-bent.'

'The next time you record a conversation, don't leave the damn phone in your pocket.'

Brushing her specs up above her short curls, she repeatedly rubbed her perturbed brow with two fingers, and then commenced her diligent consumption of her tuna sandwich. 'If this crazy river witch gets hungry again… then what?'

'I confess, I'm not the expert on curses.'

My personal assistant was asking the *necessary* question; the only question that mattered. It was Scarlett who confirmed her daughter was in danger.

I started the engine.

Shizz caught on to something new in my head. With a cheek full of food, she just about managed: 'Where now?'

'Me? Ivy farm. Collect our other car.' I pulled out of the space. 'You? Our lodgings. Rest. Keep an eye on developments.'

'And what else are you up to?'

There was no fooling her; she sensed my planning.

'I need to read the rest of that letter.'

She swallowed. 'and then?'

'And then I might know what to do.'

Slowly, we ambled out of the massive supermarket car park, and a half an hour later, drove the dry bumpy track to Ivy farm.

Shizz commentated on the state of it. 'So, you bought this *entire* farm to stop the curse?'

'I honestly don't know.'

'More money than sense.'

'It's pissed Grobatard off.'

'But, it's not the solution.'

I shook my head. 'I just don't know, Verity. I'm at a loss.'

'So you might potentially be pro-longing it?'

I swallowed. She was completely correct. My actions were for the greater good, but I hadn't thought it through at all. The only glimmer was that Grobatard *needed* it - but I am now certain, I *was* endangering people.

'If I could,' I said. 'I'd make him an offer he couldn't refuse, and buy every farm this side of the beck. try to subdue this *thing*, permanently.'

Verity grimaced. 'How much?'

'No. I'm not going to. He absolutely wouldn't sell, anyway.'

She nodded.

I scanned the dilapidated farm on either side of us. Apparently, I owned Park Lane, but it felt more like Old Kent Road. The farm building itself looked cosy. However, the fields were neglected, and overgrown. Fencing was rotten and broken. An old stationary tractor, one with grass growing through its frame, was rusting brown with its original blue. The Pickfords were too old to care for it.

Beside me, Verity yawned again, desperately needing sleep, as did I. Despite the unparalleled urgency of everything, I was *spent*: adrenalin from earlier had subsided, jet-lag was kicking in, the previous sleepless night...

My mind was nullifying the gravity of events and outcomes, aching for slumber.

Shizz repeatedly made me promise I wouldn't do anything: stupid; rash; life-threatening; impetuous... and absolutely *nothing else* without first consulting her. If she was asleep, I should *keep ringing*. She was deadly serious; almost angry. I promised, and I intended to keep it.

Giving her the keys, she drove away, leaving me standing by our remaining hire car. I climbed in, pulling down all the windows. It had warmed up nicely in the mid-afternoon sun; almost too hot. Taking out the letter, I studied Scarlett's handwriting on the envelope. It was an immense letter - thick and bulky.

It flitted from long stretches of investigation and accusations into sections of protracted confessions about the difficulties she faced in life prior to becoming a Grobatard. And those after. She was directly telling me all of this in a personal, almost apologetic, manner.

Of course, it was like she was still right here, just a village, a cup of tea, and a natter away. Like she'd posted it yesterday, and it arrived today. Eight years ago, she was alive and strong enough to address this all to me. I traced my memories of that very same year - and the things I was doing - when she was still on this planet, and I was elsewhere. While I was sipping cocktails on a veranda, she was being intravenously injected. While I embraced mega-stardom, she metastasised.

Vividly, I could recall many events, related to career and personal matters... while she ebbed away. Tracing my fingers over the pen strokes, I admired the elegance and easy-going rapport on the front; a stark contrast to anything I'd so far read inside.

I opened it back up, at the point I'd left off, where Scarlett was becoming emotional, and incoherent... and this was concerning me. She hated the Grobatard's, but she hated her younger years more - like me. Some sections rambled; huge claims, vicious insults - scant, or little objectivity.

I sighed, pushing the window completely down, resting the letter on my lap, feeling my head drooping forward. A quick doze, nothing more - no dumb dead celebrity ending, baking to death in a hire-car - *not* when a curse could claim me. The wave of tiredness was hitting exceptionally hard now.

I was the *enemy*. Was I the river's sacrifice? Why didn't it take me?

Scarlett's words were like breadcrumbs of comfort resting near my hands. Even though she found deserved happiness with a man called Geoff, for a few private moments, she was with me. In my mind, we were young and together - sharing a Slush Puppie, through a single drinking straw. Life was easy. Life was an adventure. We were wearing silvery, all-in-one space outfits, and we were flying... to the moon in a serene and calm universe.

I looked out in the distance towards the underpass, where Ol' Bobby would sleep; largely happy to roam around carefree until the end. On a warm day, he would curl up and slumber - content with his lot. I slouched down in the car seat, angling my head towards the open window for a gentle breeze to soothe my thoughts.

~ ~ ~

You were always warned: never stare directly at the sun as a kid.

The moment you learned you shouldn't even look at it *with your eyes shut either,* was a shocker.

So, you bought your first pair of cheap, blue, American-cop, sunglasses - the kind they wore on motorbikes - and you and your friends played dare with the fiery orb.

When I came to, I thought I'd permanently blinded myself.

My head was resting sideways, dangling out the driver's window. Startled, I moved, suddenly cricking my neck, and groaning at the predictable stupidness of a self-prescribed idiot. Blinking repeatedly, I let my eyes attune to the daylight again, dark fuzzy blotches slowly melting from my vision. This brought relief, but my neck was one jerk away from a week's worth of delicate movement, so I relaxed the best I could, gently stroking the nerve until the ache subsided.

My eyes were *red hot*.

Why didn't I put on my bloody Ray-Bans?

Come to think of it…

Distinct points on my forehead felt like they were sizzling, and I explored; gently dabbing fingertips around the spot in question. I'd been well and truly out for the count, now disorientated and discombobulated. But the sun itself was shining on the opposite side of the car. Confused, I watched a solitary, laser-like line searing into my shoulder - even through the fabric - and with my wits returning, I gently moved my head, partly to observe; partly to protect.

Sunlight was reflecting from a green bottle wedged in the grassy track to my right, blazing into my body like a torch.

'Idiot.'

Something in my physiology had rightly said: quick, urgent, injury: wake the plonker up. And maybe karma was paying me back for burning ants with a magnifying glass as a curious kid?

I needed to stretch.

Opening the car door, I tentatively exited, checking for other areas of stiffness in my upper body. Fresh air was necessary. The letter needed finishing, but not here. Rubbing my tender neck, and I strolled over to the green bottle. I hated waking up to the same old problems. Taking out my phone, I checked: an hour and a quarter of sleep; no new messages. I was in a state - my blazer, crumpled and creased. With a degree of lightheadedness, I used my shoe to dislodge the wine bottle from a yellow tuft of grass; cloaked here for years, the label worn white.

Looking out across fields of variable quality - most of which I now owned - I considered Ol' Bobby. I liked the guy. My mum did too. He possibly died on the same day Robert vanished, but the tramp was nothing but a constant after-thought; not a single person asking me about him in the forum last night. Kicking the bottle completely to one side, I returned to the car to retrieve the letter. As a memorial to him, I decided to read the final part near the underpass. It would give me chance to freshen my sagging brain, and picture this world as he saw it. Decidedly dicey, though. I didn't want the river rearing its ugly head with any more supernatural visuals, so I'd hang back from the bank.

Grabbing the letter, I carefully hoisted myself over a fence, and moved in the direction of the two neighbouring streams that formed the beck. Again, I sensed nothing particularly sinister in this stretch of land. Both parallel channels were too shallow to conceal anything spooky, and I calmly watched their serene flow as I traced my way back towards Ol' Bobby's makeshift abode.

Yes, definitely nothing here. I could feel it.

Reassured, I surveyed the land and pondered Serin's welfare, staggered by William Grobatard assumption I'd deliver her by 9.30. Thankfully, I still considered she was relatively safe despite the footage of us both in Masham. Her home hadn't been revealed. At least, he couldn't get his hands on her without my help.

Nevertheless, as I approached the underpass, paranoia began to build. Grobatard could well have killed me in his conservatory had the press not been outside, and my offer for Ivy Farm would have been retracted as I hadn't signed a completion. But, he would do me away later this evening, if he could. Serin too. This was a certainty.

Clambering passed the last cluster of trees, I reached the confluence, and stared at the sloping underpass. I would remember Ol' Bobby right here. Further on, the beck seemed to *kick-off,* so that was out of the question. I looked around: these trees, these flowers, bushes, weeds and everything in between - I now owned. Did I have to manage the river on my land too? The thought surprised me.

For several stupid seconds, I thought I'd hit on the ultimate plan; diverting the river. Starve the beck and its "inhabitants" of a supernatural life (death) source. It was my beachfront, King Cnut moment, and I blamed it on tiredness, and desperation. Bonkers.

Divert it... *where?*

I grew disappointed in the false revelation and let it seep away so I could think about the real reason I was here. Stretching out a little more, I listened to the cars overhead, and watching the newly formed beck. Clasping Scarlett's letter, I pulled my mind onto Ol' Bobby, while periodically surveying the underpass. He lived here free from most of life's restraints, but with loneliness and the harsh elements as a constant companion.

More than once, the Cupid's love heart caught my attention.

Scarlett used to come here, too.

Similar contemplations, feelings - but an ocean (and now a universe) apart. Even now, the overly long arrow pointed down and out towards me. I took out my phone to check the photos were there.

My keepsakes.

Then, a thought formed from out of nowhere... but it didn't emerge from the river. Me, *the enemy.* It told me this years ago... and then again today. Why? I stood up and pushed my arms out, stretching tiredness from my muscles.

Why?

Ishaq *the* protector. Scarlett, hide-and-seek... *the* finder (finding more than she bargained for). But me... *the bleeding enemy;* plain and simple. Then it hit me. Ishaq was the lead councillor in this area; a knight without his armour. I stared at my shoes, considering all this. Representing his people, this area's interests... reluctant to entertain anything paranormal; extolling practical solutions. For a *cursed* river, why did Ishaq receive such a positive message - a title, even?

And me, such a negative one. Rob was asked to come and join them. Hazel, however…?

I took out my phone and messaged her. She never revealed this all those years ago. Surely, no trauma would prevent her from telling me now. If the thing by my feet - the *it*, witch, Siren, whatever - somehow knew I now owned this part of the river, it certainly wouldn't endear me.

I rubbed my brow, grumbling over the green bottle that had scorched me like a laser, but mainly ruing my lack of devotion to Ol' Bobby's memory. So, I headed to the slope where vehicles were louder, and fumes grimmer (but more tolerable now the motorway had diverted traffic). Perching on part of the slope, I looked out over the waters, carried calmly by the current. No wonder I thought it was deeper here. It was darker, but not necessarily deeper. The frothy scum continued to gather around the bobbing bottles in the centre.

Then I looked to my left again, noticing the line of string I'd seen earlier, slithering under cover of grass and leaves… dropping into the beck. It danced to and fro as gallons of water tumbled past.

I smiled. Ol' Bobby did like his fish, and this was a worthy way to remember him. If he could only get to them before Old Basil pounced, catching one would have given him great joy. This line was a testament to his enduring presence in this place, and it both heartened and saddened me. I traced its course over ground, from the thick spool under the tree and then into the river, expecting it to extend downstream towards the remains of a net, or perhaps a hook.

Instead, it went straight to the centre of the river.

I watched for a few moments, puzzled.

Attached.

Moving away from the slope and Scarlett's gorgeous love heart, I knelt down to examine, warily eyeing the river. It was more of a coiled cotton rope, and the bulbous spool was held down by a brick; easy to miss under the canopy. And there were two lines. One, well hidden in the grass, meandering further back under the branches to darker ground. It ended in what appeared to be a shattered bottle; certainly no modern glass - darker. And the shards were a similar colour to the one we found and smashed all those years ago; its head still fastened, the body long since disintegrated.

We will see you on the 29th of August.
If you don't see us first.
Robert.

I stood bolt upright, and stared. Recalling, it was a misshapen bottle, like the one on the floor ahead. As kids, we assumed the note was a token from a bygone era - trapped for centuries in the reeds - eventually unearthed by Rob's dock excavations. *Or,* a message sent directly to us from the spirits in the river: *We're coming, if you don't come first.* Robert. *Ol' Bobby...* the tramp we trusted, who my mother looked out for, who we sought out for advice.

He was sending *them* a message.

'Oh shit.'

I looked again at other thick line, the one I'd seen already, leading out across the water. Clasping hold of the string, I gave one sharp tug, watching and listening to the glass clinking together in the middle of the beck. A solitary crisp packet, trapped for decades, broke away from the scum and froth, and floated downstream, and I watched its trajectory from west to east pushing into the shadow of the underpass, released from binds countless years old. The collection of bottles still remaining bobbed in the river with more vigour.

I tugged again.

More glass clattered.

Slowly and carefully, I drew the rope in, dispersing many empty beverages nestled in the foamy reeds, from stout to whiskey - several, unharnessing... and floating away; emancipated. One in particular took great exception. As I pulled, it tottered and swayed, fastened by its thick neck. My heart hammered; this was mold-blown - not mass produced in a factory like its contemporaries. I brought it closer, observing a sealed lid, and a rusted iron fastening attachment.

This wasn't Ol' Bobby's fishing rope at all. Carefully, I withdrew my find from the water. It was glass alright, and quite solid at that - as wide at the top, as the bottom - the lid shut securely, and strengthened with a decaying swing stopper, close to failing. Tape had been wrapped around to secure the contents further.

Delicately, I took it in both hands.

There was something inside - like in the one we once found. This, an archaic, brown misshapen jar. What was I even looking at here? I scoured the froth once more from a distance, and then the ground, looking for anymore hidden string; nothing more presenting.

The original message had enticed and convinced Rob, luring him to the point he *utterly* accepted it. But the original invitation didn't come from them at all.

Turning it upside down, a shadow clunked against the stopper. Too dark to see, possibly wrapped in cloth. Whatever it was needed prising, and with my share of palm scratches, that left only one alternative.

I glanced up at the bridge, searching for a prankster, someone who had purposefully planted this, now watching from the overpass. Cars and trucks motored by, thundering their way north and south. No one was there. I was alone. Storing Scarlett's letter in my jacket, I stooped for the brick over the spool, and walked away from the edge, passing the cluster of trees, and out into more welcoming open pastures.

I wanted my wits about me for this.

Holding it to the sun made it slightly more transparent. Clearly, there was both something flat, *and* something bulbous within. A stem, only marginally narrower than the main body, explained the entry point for its deposits. Victorian era. And the only man who get his hands on this, if his claim to a great age was true, was the man who lived right here.

That last deadly genie we unleashed from a bottle… took Rob away from us.

Placing it down by my feet, I hovered over it with the brick in my right hand. The last time I adopted this position, I was defending myself from an Alsatian… but this was far more dangerous.

The edge of the brick utterly obliterated the glass on contact.

~ ~ ~

The letter was dated August 28th 1984.

The day before, Robert Tipperton vanished into the river.

And its contents destroyed me.

I imagined the precise moment on a drab, grey London street - during the Blitz - when the first air-raid sirens roared to life, and the prickling fear that laced the skin.

This was Ol' Bobby's last will and testament. Signed, Robert Worthington.

And for the first few moments I felt honoured to discover and read words from the forgotten man; his precious cargo in my possession - treasure in a buoyant wooden chest - floating out the side of a sinking ship.

My opinion couldn't be more wrong.

Paragraphs written in flowing, sweeping strokes; a style he'd embraced and honed in the nineteenth century, matching completely the note he'd sent down the river… trapped in the jetty. The note to them.

The note to *it*.

To whoever finds this; I'm gone.

I tried protecting many from this river, but I grow weary, and my dismay builds daily.

My Grandfather was William Worthington - old Mr Worthington as he was better known - much too old to be a Grandfather, but he was mine, nevertheless.

He was cursed, and I carried the curse in his place.

Although reputed to be a man of good standing, he oversaw the execution of an innocent woman right here in the beck. He signed the order, and on this very day, was cursed to old age. Then he passed the curse to me, getting me drunk on Barley wine as a teenager, and thrusting me into the river. That was in 1876. I was 17. He hoped my death would end his own burden. Later, my father tried to break its hold over me, by selling this land to our cousins, the Hislops. All to no avail.

I have served and documented this river for well over a century - trapped by whatever resides here; the Siren. It may be the spirit of the wronged woman out for vengeance, and possibly even children from the harrying - for I hear their anguish too. Whatever is here, will not rest. The curse itself has power. Like the Siren sings, this thing lies... mimicking appearances and manipulating its dark melody over the land, enchanting children to come, and keep coming; to feed its evil energy.

I hatched a plan to end this curse.

I hatched folly, and now I have damned the innocent in return, like my Grandfather before me.

Please forgive me.

Only recently, I learned the Grobatard's have acquired Hislop's land; they who betrayed the innocent woman in the first place, paying the price. Their actions through the centuries are wholly despicable - all in pursuit of power - originating from William, Duke of Normandy, himself. He assigned their esteemed family the duty of travelling from Northern France to carry out the harrying, and in their bloodlust they saw to it, and then settled here as overseers and cruel Lords.

387

But, these are just words. I am sorry. I cannot prove any of this. I cannot even prove my age apart from the pocket watch given me in 1926 for fifty years of loyal service.

But now I am finally dying, and I long to be at peace. In the same way the river told me my Grandfather would die, and the very next day he did, the curse is now passing to another... to the one I assigned; the one I agreed to.

If the Siren takes the boy, it may protect every child, both in and out of the river, for now, but this curse won't lift until the land is fully restored, and Grobatard and Worthington alike, have sacrificed from their own line.
Betrayers and condemners.
Having received their own curse on the day of her execution, the Grobatard's are unaware of the full extent, believing their actions alone will stop it. They have no clue that on the day she was condemned to die, in a closed courtroom - with my own Grandfather presiding as Judge - she condemned our bloodline too. I am living proof.

Of the five kids who regularly come to the beck, the children in the river call to the boy. They feel his pain. I have whispered back... and assigned him as my temporary successor; their protector.

But the Siren wants the other boy - the one with Worthington ancestry - she demands him as my replacement.

I have made a huge mistake. I hadn't counted on the sale of the land, and with that now gone, the curse will grow stronger as the end draws closer. No one will be safe. Not a soul.

I have assigned her the wrong boy. I could have ended this much sooner.

Please forgive me.

I want to see and be with my Annie again.
I must go and be with her.

Robert 'Ol' Bobby' Worthington.

I stood there, frozen... then falling; collapsing. Somehow, down. Without intent.

To my knees, bruising earth.

Mentally concussed by a calamitous trajectory. A dissident ensnared. Rocked by the revelatory.

A forbidden confession... and the most heinous of human actions - in a world where none of this should even be real.

Rob was "The wrong boy."

I was *the enemy.*

The thing in the beck had chosen me. All along.

My Granny W, who made me glossy boats from magazines. Who said I was of *good stock,* who said our family had a crest; its own coat-of-arms.

And all those years ago... Hazel, reading out names under the black-and-white photo from the newspaper headline, entitled - "Haunted river gives children a right old fright." - and asking me why my Gran's surname was different.

Worthington.

The maiden name of my mother, before she married an Austin.

And a *Worthington* condemned this innocent woman to death.

I thrust my hand into my pocket, pulling out the tiny blue and yellow badge, the one my Gran gave me in the shape of a shield. A knight's helmet, and three forks.

I was an only child. I had no children. I was the last in line.

Between me and William Grobatard... we now owned *all* the land required for fulfilment.

Both Grobatard *and* Worthington were required to sacrifice.

Together.

Tonight.

Serin's blood, and my… eternity.

Ol' Bobby's pocket watch rested next to me within the shards of broken glass; hastily wrapped in cellophane. I turned away from it in total disgust. I was one noisy underpass from the end, and three fields away from my car. And I *knew*, I wasn't grabbed earlier because I was coming later.

Except, I wasn't.

Not worth it.

I stared at Ol' Bobby's last will and testament sprawled on the grass before me. That was *his*, not mine. Mine was a life of writing… a flight back to LA, clinking cocktail glasses on Simone Chapdelaine's veranda, all in less than twenty-four hours should I so choose. I could shut it out forever, like I had for such a long time. Make the madness go.

But, visceral images of lacerated local kids tortured me, slashed as dire final warnings, and the certainty of a mad old man poised to supply more.

I couldn't provide Scarlett's daughter a permanent security detail either, knowing the next attack would kill a local kid. No question.

If I didn't yield, if I didn't provide Serin.

Inadvertently, I'd become the *buy one, get one free, in this paranormal transaction*. My innards were being ripped, torn asunder. Run, forget, self-medicate… pretend an alternate existence; embrace unbridled altruism in other ways. To atone.

There was one last slip of paper nestled in the shattered glass.

I unfolded and stared - my mind entirely blanking.

Beat you!

Seriously, prepare yourself, if you read this before Ol' Bobby's letter. (I mean… seriously.)

See the smashed bottle over there by the tree?

That's the original.

I replaced it with another in the river. I found it by chance.

I've returned here in secret today, to finish another matter.

Billy, when you fought alongside Rob on the track, it was the bravest thing I ever saw, and now I need you to *dig deep*, and be brave for me and my daughter. I only hope you met Serin first, and she forwarded you the photo. This is more important than the letter; I was heavily drugged when I wrote that. I have to be cryptic, here. I have no choice. I need to think about what I'll do if you don't come back? But, I know this curse will call to you. I'm counting on you to finish this, in my absence. I must ensure what I discovered doesn't fall into the wrong hands, and by that, I mean the Grobatards. This is imperative.

Look very carefully at the photo.

And, you'll figure it out what I've done.

My

Sweet

Heart

X

Astonished, I fixated on the hastily drawn love heart at the bottom; precisely the same as the one rendered behind me in the underpass.

SW 4 BA.

The same long, dodgy-looking arrow… hitting the edge of the sheet with a kiss inside the curved tip. I pulled out my phone to access photos, and study the image Serin sent me earlier.

Of her mum.

A cancer patient on a relatively good day. The same old Scarlett radiance, shimmering under her damp floral beanie. That *magnificent*, wholesome smile and the cheeky brilliance glinting in her eyes, and despite her advanced illness, by no means neglecting her farm work. Seated, taking a timeout… resting forward on the hilt of the shovel; one hand raised

391

for the selfie. I purposefully ignored the two boney animal carcasses to her side, wishing she'd already shoved these in the leather pouch. Instead, I focussed on a backdrop of trees, shadows, and a partial view of a wall coated in red pai-

I bolted upright… immediately staring at the underpass.

Not quite believing.

'*You smart-*'

With the phone inside my palm now bleeping, I surged forward.

The photo wasn't taken in some random field on Scarlett's own land in the Dales, it was taken *right here*.

I thrust through the trees to the spot I visited earlier, stepping over the lines of string, and stopping at the bridge; raising both photo and note, together.

She'd *purposefully* left the weathered shovel upright, and I'd angled around it repeatedly earlier, crouching for a better shot of Cupid's heart.

Then, I saw it, as clear as day - both on wall, and paper.

And it blew me away.

The elongated arrow with an 'x' in its tip, stretching way too far out - and in the wrong direction - the pointed end purposefully aiming down.

At the ground.

A minute ago, I was terrified.

But Scarlett had deliberately brought herself here, too - confronting the thing in the river. The domestic dangers she faced with Craig, and her mad father-in-law. Maxed-out on medication, in the final stages of disease; her daughter in mortal peril… And I could only stare in wonder; silently saluting her courage, her resolute determination, *her creativity*.

This painted red line, diagonally streaking down over the underpass wall, and across the heart, was never *meant* to be an *arrow*.

She'd painted a long shovel.

An 'x marks the spot' deliberately placed within the rounded blade at the end, purposefully pointing to her *actual* shovel.

'You were always smarter than me.'

I smiled, shaking my head.

I looked at her note again, nodding.

"and now I need you to *dig deep*, and be brave for me and my daughter."

She'd sang Her Bravest Song on a daily basis... mine was but a hum in comparison.

As I grabbed for the handle, I felt my phone vibrate again.

Hazel.

Five messages.

"It said, she'll betray you, like she betrayed me."

"I'm pretty sure it meant Scarlett."

"After she married Craig, we didn't talk for years. (I hated her for what she did to my aunt and uncle.) We made up when she came to visit Jonathon at the care home."

And then,

"But, when the river spoke - it meant something else, too. I'm sure of it.'

'Rob, Scarl, and Ishaq heard the children speaking, but me and you heard the woman. She terrified me, Billy.'

I replaced the phone, grabbed the shovel and commenced the dig, hitting metal in next to no time. Then, I heaved out a small tin, about the size of a shoe box, and opened it.

The note on top, read:

"I met up with Mr Hislop recently. He understands what I've been through, and let me look through and photocopy some old records he took when he moved. He stored them on behalf of his cousins. They are *Worthington* records. They owned the farm before him. I have highlighted the essential parts. LOOK CLOSELY."

Scarlett was frantic in the letter, but not here. Here, she was composed, and focussed. She was closer to death, but far more lucid.

These documents were comprehensive, so I pulled the first - studying more detailed notes from the day judgement was passed - staring at the highlights - just to say making out the perpetrators name: Maude.

And a child's name, and the phrase: children of unknown origin.

Unknown origin.

Something hooked in my head.

A place where important thoughts hang, like pulling back your clothes rail and finding the top you forgot you owned.

Her victims were being cited... but all were of unknown origin. I knew it was impossible she could have killed any found on her person, so I searched for details of her crime and sentence.

"Her own daughter testifies against her. One count of murder, kidnap, witchcraft, and several counts of meddling in this area's affairs with her spells."

I studied the words over, and over - particularly the *one count* of everything - before staring at the next highlight.

"On declaration of sentence, Maude has cursed me to old age, and her daughter will receive the strap."

Maude, clearly the name of the Grobatard woman, on the verge of execution, and it sounded like her daughter was in line for punishment too - from the days when getting lashed supposedly corrected attitude.

This photocopied document had a question mark in blue biro next to it; an addition from Scarlett who had puzzled over this herself. The daughter in question was in Grobatard care at the time, her name, short, but illegible.

And directly underneath this line.

"I desire her carrying pouch, but she has bequeathed this to her daughter."

I looked away from the document, back in the direction of the two small streams flowing side-by-side; not too far from my position. Neighbours for centuries, unaware of each other until the point of confluence, when they joined to form the beck. Unaware. Scarlett had discovered both Grobatard, and - in her final weeks - Worthington records. She'd compared, contrasted and discovered.

William Grobatard senior had no idea she'd done so.

Somehow, he knew Robert Tipperton was a troublesome appendage *lodged* in the beck, requiring removal; holding this as leverage over me. He sensed *something else* was happening here; things were off-kilter. The apparition of the woman in the river insisted: *get him out!*

Apart from land, William Grobatard had somehow concluded a sacrifice from his own line was essential. And the vengeful woman of the river demanded *her* bones.

But she didn't mean Serin's…

I now suspected whose she meant, and, more importantly, exactly where to look, to find them.

Chapter 10

Crazy Ghosts

Placing both hands on the car roof, I paused a moment, gathering my wits.

Something in me tugged at realigning normal protocols, grasping for true reality; one where you nip your skin till it pinks and hurts like hell. The reality where you pack your suitcase, drive to the airport, and fly home.

Instead, I took out my phone, and followed up on what Granny W revealed all those years ago, enquiring about a relative with extraordinary longevity.

Then, scrolling down my contacts, I clicked on Shizz-Bang, messaging her.

Hazel, Ishaq, and absolutely, Serin too; her whereabouts, the absolute priority.

I climbed in, turned on the ignition, and made my way down the bumpy farm track. Even as the arcane solution tried presenting, it was quickly obscured by a smudge. Four, maybe five blurred letters on an ancient record. And even if I deciphered, how did I extract, let alone supply? *If they were even there...*

This might just save Serin, but my own fate was in the balance. I numbed existentialism from crisis to silence, as my phone began pinging. The first was Serin: At farm. All completed! Got the keys ready. Sad though. Couple and EA on their way. (I replied, with a sad/happy emoji, and warned her we'd been spotted in Masham and to take the utmost care.)

Hazel replied she was doing a late shift. Ishaq didn't reply.

Shizz had managed a two-hour nap, and had some exciting news, but was unwilling to reveal it.

My phone buzzed again, and this time it was mum.

Hi Son,

Yes!

Your Grandma and Great Aunties used to talk about him.

William Worthington. Born 1726 - died 1876. Surely, a mistake.

There was also a rumour Ol' Bobby was somehow related to our family.

That's why I looked out for him.

Xxx

And there it was.

William Worthington's date of death, verified.

And our family link to Ol' Bobby.

It took just over five minutes to reach our lodgings, tyres crunching pebbles as I drew closer to the huge, centrally positioned windows. I stopped alongside our second hire car and pressed my forehead against the steering wheel. My thoughts were brutal. Was Rob still in the river? Was I meant to be in there all along?

The boy who had his neck so savagely twisted back - like he was clearing the pole in the high jump - *wasn't Rob*. It was some kind of deception; the irony being Ol' Bobby revealed this; the same man practising deception. For a moment, I entertained what choice he actually had, considering his own Grandfather set him up. But, I was also nearly set up.

I slapped the steering wheel one last time, grazing the horn and slumping back in the seat.

Through the barn windows, Shizz was already pressing herself against the huge pane, beckoning me inside, while mouthing, 'You okay?' condensing the glass with her lips.

The beck was going to claim more lives, of this I was certain. Exiting the car, I half-heartedly waved back in defeated acknowledgment. She was excitable in her gesturing, pushing her phone up so I could see moving imagery.

I entered via the side, kicking my dirty shoes off before I entered. My brow felt damp; afternoon sleeps neither suiting, nor refreshing me. But, I felt completely wiped, here. Jet-lag, virus, inordinate stress.

'Billy, come here.'

Shizz pointed to the welcoming sight of freshly brewed coffee with one hand, and the sofa with the other. Pouring a small cup, I flopped down in the comfy chair, rubbing my neck. She was face timing, suddenly tossing the phone onto my lap, and I stared back in confusion.

'Hello, sailor. Ahoy there.'

The voice spoke to my thigh.

I flipped it over. A pretty girl. Dual heritage. Jamaican and Haitian. Cassie Star twiddled a strand of her blue dreads while saluting me with the other hand. She audaciously winked at me while angling her mouth at an incredible diagonal, exposing pristine teeth between bright red lipstick.

'How's things on the good ship, Austin?'

'Hey Cass.'

'Rocky seas?'

'Yeah, yeah - pretty much.' I processed her blue and white attire for a second. 'Are you filming CG?'

'And a new *Woes music video*. Finishing up. On a big ass boat, right now.' she saluted again. 'Hey, sorry to hear about your friend; I had no idea how bad this was for you. It's rampant here - you're all over the news.' From the other side of the Atlantic, she pointed over my shoulder at Shizz. 'And, you have a loyal PA; didn't breathe a bloody word to me about any of this!'

'I do.' I leaned in to sip my fresh coffee.

'And you got attacked by dogs?'

'Oh yeah, that too.'

I'd forgotten about those.

'Cheer up, Chum. the press will clamour until the next celebrity has their breakdown.'

'Ain't that the truth?'

'But yours was pretty wild.'

'I don't remember half of it.'

Cass stared at me, assessing my sagging shoulders. 'You look sea sick, sailor. What else is goin' on? I can see something ain't right, ship mate?'

I looked across at Verity, who confirmed with a look bordering 'motherly' - a first from her in my book.

'Has Shizz told you the latest?' I whispered, 'And I don't mind you knowing.'

'The woman in the river? Yeah, I wanted to give you insight.'

'Insight?'

I pulled the phone closer.

'Listen, Billy, we just did *the* most amazing investigations I've ever been a part of.'

Cassie was ecstatic. Electric, almost. A film break could well be a blow break for her and the band; even on a bright, sunny Californian morning. She did say she was *finishing*. 'I highly doubt you're dealing with any ghost kids in that river,' she said.

This instantly intrigued me. 'Meaning?'

'That's what Shizz said; ghost kids, am I correct?'

I acknowledged, listening.

'Whenever we get *spirit children*,' she made an inverted comma sign with one free hand, 'it doesn't make any sense.'

'In what way?'

'Well, why on earth would God leave innocents here on earth?'

'You got this from your investigations, Cass?'

'Well, we see patterns.'

'Patterns in hauntings?'

'Mimicking spirits, Billy. Mimicking kids. On occasions, these kids are seeing angels, but not always; not if the family is getting terrorised.'

I took another sip, wrestling with her postmodern brand of empiricism, just as Shizz came in from the kitchen carrying biscuits. I raised my brow, silently appreciating her intuition; stomach rumbling on cue. Maybe I needed carbs; I felt bloody awful.

'Yeah, we get called in when things have gone south,' she continued, flipping the occasional blue and white dread out of her face. 'The trajectory is usually bad to worse.'

'Why's that?'

'Wham, bam, thank-you, ma'am.'

I shook my head. 'As in?'

'There's an emphasis on viewing figures and capturing phenomena, not cure. Sometimes… things get purposefully stoked.'

'Stoked? On purpose?'

'Yeah, if not handled correctly, we can stir up more trouble.'

From the clips I'd seen of Crazy Ghosts, her band, Woes Almanac, concluded their investigations by playing live music to the spirits. This was the show's unique selling point, making it a bit of a cult hit on the West coast - the drummer, usually the recipient of aggressive poltergeist activity.

Whatever they invoked *didn't* like drums.

'And Casper's very rare, Billy.'

'Casper… as in friendly? Why?'

'Well, if it ain't residual, then it's something trapped here on earth, and a lot are angry.'

I rubbed my brow. 'Residual?'

'Events, usually the painful ones. Crises in people's lives… powerfully imprinting on a location. No ghost, just an endless video-loop in a sequence.'

Cass wasn't comfy in her position and she hoisted herself up and walked towards a different leather chair, plopping down. 'That's better,' she purred breezily, flinging back her dreaded hair again.

'Okay, so you know about my past,' I began. 'What about rivers, and curses? Know anything?'

She genuinely gave this full consideration. 'Yeah. Traumatic events, accidents, murders… seem to pull open the veil. Curses are spoken and imprinted beyond the veil, and they can be an invitation to the nefarious.'

I leaned forward, alert. '*What's* invited, Cass?'

'Bad entities, Billy - the type that mimics kids. A location, or an object, can be cursed, and it needs breaking. Water has a very strong association with all of this.'

My skin bristled upon hearing this. 'How?'

'It seems to be a conduit. The amount of times we see taps get deliberately turned on, showers… and, of course, people vanishing near to, or found dead in rivers.'

'Sorry?' My heart leapt. 'And Verity mentioned nothing about my past? Are you sure?'

'No, I bloody didn't.' Shizz angrily retorted.

'Yeah, it's usually men, too.' Cassie jumped in. 'Noticeably so.'

'You can't… be serious?'

'Deadly.' She fixed me with her steely stare. 'In your homeland, the figures are actually ninety per cent for men who disappear on a night out.'

'What? Ninety per cent, disappear where?'

'Pub, club, gathering… straight into a body of water.'

My jaw dropped. This couldn't be true. 'Cass, that can't *possibly* be correct?' I shook my head.

'Well, eighty-nine per cent, matey. Just rounding it up. Not all drown, either. Half return an open verdict. It's as if they're all drawn to water.'

'That's alcohol, surely?' I tried not to sound dismissive; I normally respected her meticulous research, but this…

'Billy, you didn't hear me, darl; ninety per cent retrieved from water… only ten per cent on land. That's a preposterous stat. It's totally wrong to assume they're all shit-faced when they disappear, too.'

Her every syllable chilled me. I moved in, ready to further protest, but she interrupted. 'Why not dead from blood loss having cracking your head on a kerb, or found down an alley choked on vomit, or dead from exposure in an open field somewhere?' she raised her own hands in despair. 'Now, that would make more sense, surely, especially if you're staggering out the pub alone? But they all take the plunge, as if they're being pulled there.'

I swallowed, and stared out the French windows, as she asked a question that my PA immediately high-jacked.

'Billy, how many times have you been to that river since you arrived?'

'Twice!' Shizz jumped in. 'He's been twice already. Today.'

Cassie flinched. 'What? *Twice?*'

'I… yeah.'

'Why?'

Suddenly I was rationalising my motives for even being there. Why did I actually go? Scarlett's letter, facing the river…

'Billy, under no circumstances, go back. Look at me. Do you understand?' I turned, watching Cassie shift uncomfortably. 'That river is cursed. No question. It's going to do *everything* it can to summon you back. It will call to your soul, and you can't let it.'

I tried holding her gaze, but couldn't. *I* was the end of the curse.

'There's no dead kids there,' Cass continued, 'just a constant whirring wheel of evil, manipulating what it wants you and other people to see. If someone cursed it, or murders took place anywhere near… avoid, no matter what.'

I stood, still holding the phone. 'So, what breaks it?'

'No, no, no…'

'Cass, I need a solution.'

'This is centuries old, and powerful, Billy. We're talking sustained fasting and prayer, or terms and conditions fulfilled. They're the only things.'

It was the moment to feel a crushing, compressed pressure in my chest. I knew no priests here. I had good friends in America; people of faith. I rubbed my eyes, took another swig of coffee, and tried pulling my head around it

402

all. It dawned on me Cass was wearing a blue and white navy-outfit - to match her blue and white dreads - explaining all the sailor references she was throwing my way. Most appropriate.

I thought long and hard about my next phrasing, 'Cass, if a real witch was executed by drowning; why would she be carrying around kid's fingers in a tin?'

'Because she murdered them?'

I shook my head again. 'No, these bones were much, much older.'

'Spells, charms, rites...'

'What? To practice with, while walking around?'

'Yeah, she might have a brass tin at home for her charms, and a pouch for carrying them everywhere in person.'

'So, she could have found some older bones, and carried them around with her... as part of her craft?'

'For her witchcraft? Most certainly. Avoid. If we're talking *cursed objects*, you're carrying dynamite across a minefield.'

My phone started to ring on the coffee table, but it would have to wait. After vibrating five times, it stopped.

'This tin she once had... is now *out* of the river. But the thing I saw... demanded *her* bones.'

I was surprised by Cassie's retort. 'Verity, *do not* let this man out of your sight! Under no circumstances.'

'Hold on, Cass,' I paused 'You said, terms and conditions?'

'Did this woman read them to you?'

'What?'

'The terms and conditions.'

I processed some more. 'I believe she did. She was holding a single bone in her hand.'

'A single bone?'

'Yeah.'

'Sorry, Billy - that's not someone remotely presenting terms.' Cassie threw her sailor's cap off screen in despair. 'So, whose bones is she demanding?'

'I think it's her own daughter's.'

403

'And do you have them?'

'No, but I believe I can get to them.'

Cassie was frantic. 'Billy, wait... wait till I come over. I have contacts. We'll all meet and go togeth-'

'Don't worry, hon,' Shizz cut across. 'The Press will have tapped his phone by now. They'll have GPS'd the hell out of him by tomorrow. He ain't going anywhere.'

A sudden surge hit me - the need for the bathroom - right that instant. Dizzily, I stood, said 'love you' and 'big thanks' and dropped the phone to the sofa, tottering, staggering.

I heard Shizz rise behind me, preparing to speak, and then with-holding...

Lurching into the downstairs cloakroom, I willed the energy to shut and lock the door behind me before three clumsy attempts at raising the toilet seat. Nothing came out as I wretched. I felt terrible. My head was banging. This felt strange... both sudden and violently weird. Was William Grobatard dancing around his conservatory in his underwear, reciting chants, as I wilted by the cistern? I tried cooling my forehead on the stark white porcelain.

I knew precisely what was happening. More thoughts drummed brain splitting pain into my head.

All those years earlier... the bobbing boy *didn't* take Craig Grobatard from the water. It left him. Stars had to align: land, livestock, Grobatard and Worthington in unison? The conclusion - the best, my stricken mind could muster - was follow Cass' advice, and stay *the hell* away from the beck. Wait till she flew over. And, above all, keep Serin's location and identity safe. This was the *only way*.

There was a gentle tap on the door behind me.

'You okay in there?'

'Yeah.'

The soft, disembodied voice floated through the wood again. 'I really think we should follow Cassie's advice.'

'Agreed.'

My voice sounded weak.

Shizz needed to hear about Ol' Bobby's letter; how Rob had replaced him… as guardian. Was Rob trapped in there, somehow damaging things from the inside? Get him out! With an awkward, protracted grappling - damp palms against smooth surfaces - I hoisted myself up. Moving to the sink, I freshened up; moistening my lips, thinking about shaving; feeling too weak to bother. Then, I recalled how ill Ol' Bobby suddenly got in the days before he died.

Shizz was standing a small distance away when I exited, my own phone in her hand. She was waiting for face-to-face confirmation of what I'd agreed to. She looked distressed on my behalf, wearing the same motherly expression: twice in ten minutes. Times like these, you needed this level of silent support.

'Yeah, I'm not going down there. Don't worry.'

'You look *awful*.'

'Think it's stress.'

'Probably,' she acknowledged, holding out my phone, 'Your friend, Ishaq, is calling every few minutes.'

She passed it to my shaky hand. With precarious movements, I shifted my wounded body to the nearest armchair, hoping he wouldn't call again… but he did.

'Ishaq.'

'Where are you?'

'My lodgings.'

'Are you watching the news?'

'No.'

'The press know these aren't Rob's bones, and it's building a head of steam.'

'Of course.' I coughed.

'It's now an ancient murder mystery… journalists sleuthing to find records about this area.'

'I'm sure.'

My PA was already accessing news channels on TV, while reducing the volume. The first visual was a female reporter with a hedgerow and a kid's slide as a backdrop.

'Where are you?' I said.

'Hislop's old farm.'

'Are you with journalists?'

'Well, they're around, Billy, but I'm forbidden from speaking to any.'

'By who?'

'By my boss, the MP. He's taking charge of matters. I wanted to call and let you know that. I was thinking about what you said earlier, by the way, about bringing me her bones,' his voice turned into a whisper. 'What do think it meant?'

'Do you remember that creepy small forest with small stones?' I leaned forward. 'On the north side. We passed it as kids. I need to get there.'

This statement immediately alerted Shizz, who raised a finger. 'No!'

I accepted her reprimand, as Ishaq continued. 'Yeah, yeah, I remember that. Weirdly, I've heard it mentioned as a site of interest recently.'

'The Grobatard's have their own little cemetery.'

'Oh, I bloody knew it!'

'Yeah, it's like the Druid's temple in there. All kinds of weird stones, and shields.'

'You've been there? Why are you telling me?'

'I passed it, today. It's been in their portfolio for centuries.' I stared at Shizz, who was monitoring every component of our exchange. 'It's a graveyard for their own royal blood. It's got fresh red and yellow flowers hanging everywhere; they're preparing for an occasion. Ishaq, I need you to go back there right now.'

'What?'

'I need you to get across to that cemetery and take as many detailed photos as you can. Inscriptions, engravings, anything. As much detail as is humanly possible. I need you to do this.'

'Billy, I can't.'

'Hold on, mate.' I altered my tone. 'I *threw* myself under the bus for you last night.'

He paused. 'Shit! Can't I say thank you with a Sunday Roast, or something?'

'Yes, that as well. But I also need you to drive to the care home, go down the back garden, climb over the back fence and head that way.'

His whisper was now a hiss. 'I'll be trespassing. What if I'm spotted?'

'Stick your arms straight out like a zombie, claim you've seen Robert, and march on.'

'Billy, I'll do anything else; not this.'

'Why?'

He went quiet. 'I really don't want, to be there... by myself.'

'What else is worrying you?'

'Nothing, I-'

'Is it the plants? It's only hogweed, remember? You said so yourself. Just don't grab, or swallow any.'

'Oh, for crying out loud,' he profusely protested. 'Okay, okay. Explain, why I'm doing this?'

'I need you to find Maude Grobatard's daughter.'

Again, silence. Pronounced, this time.

I added, 'Maude died on October 8th, 1776. Search around that date. Photos. No matter how insignificant, Ishaq. Females born prior to this. You owe me.'

There was another lengthy pause, and I didn't like it one bit, but he eventually spoke.

'You're a tosser.'

'Wait till you really get to know me.'

He hung up, and I pounced, half scrambling on all fours, back in the direction of the cloakroom. Sweat cascading from my brow. The same kind that dripped from the delirious Ol' Bobby, shortly before he drowned in the river.

Chapter 11

The Invisible Chain

Outside, in the immaculate courtyard, I took some huge gulps of fresh air.

The green chair grated along the flagstones as I dragged it along. Now sitting, I studied the long stone wall to my right. Clumps of royal blue aubrieta clung to the top like a friendly monster's furry, thick fingers. Any moment he could peek his big fluffy head above, and smile warmly.

The sight calmed me. Innocence.

Pebbles, and a shiny new driveway, spanned the gap between the barn conversion and the main farmhouse - a mere hundred yards away. And in between, the ancient archway separated us from the main road. No doubt, countless press vans had already traversed this stretch without being aware of my location.

For now.

Peering up, I got the sense I was being watched, anyway. And sure enough, directly opposite, faces appeared and then vanished in the farmhouse kitchen window. Seconds passed before they sneakily rose back up for another glance. Quite exciting viewing for young occupants, if indeed, they finally recognised me.

Slouching over, I lowered my head, gently tipping my phone between alternating palms. I felt dizzy, and in great need of balance, before checking the messages from Serin. Looking down, I could see she'd also tried calling, and there was an unknown number. I took a deep breath, re-reading her response from earlier about meeting the buyers at her parent's farm. Handing the keys over was a chance for her to begin erasing painful memories, and gather enough capital to start afresh. I was pleased that she was actively pushing for her own closure. I read the first new message. "All fine. Last tidy up. Waiting on the couple and the EA." And the second. "Solicitor's here for the exchange. Couple running late - stuck near York."

I accessed her third; immediately struggling to interpret it.

"The press will leave shortly. Meet as planned."

The first arrived as I face-timed Cass; the final one while I was in the cloakroom.

I replied. "I'm not sure what you mean. Press? Where?"

Earlier, my phone had lit up on several occasions while it rested on the coffee table - and I assumed everything was incoming from Ishaq. Somehow, my typed response felt out of place, and I re-appraised it; not impressed with myself in the least. She'd mistakenly sent me this; it was meant for her fella, or a date, or something.

The press stuff concerned me, though. Surely, they hadn't found her? Then, I thought about the phone-tapping I'd experienced a few years back, and became troubled.

'Bollocks,' I whispered.

A missed call came after her third message; an explanation, apology, or maybe an update? And I was about to call back; but first checked the message from the unknown number.

"The press will leave shortly. Meet as planned."

Same message, different number.

I clicked back to Serin's, puzzled. Had my phone lagged with the slow Wi-Fi? Precisely, the same phrase had been shared. I swiped off, and back on, but it was still there, so I scrolled to her second message again, frowning this time, as I read it properly.

The solicitor was there for the *exchange*?

And at that point, my insides plummeted. The exchange had already happened. This was completion day... where the estate agent hands over the keys.

I clicked call and waited. No answer.

The ring eventually shifted across to her answering machine after several seconds. (Do not assume the worst, I told myself; there's no way she could be found.) I'd told her to be extremely careful. I hesitated, refraining from leaving a message as I assessed everything at lightning speed. I hung up.

Who else would she give my number to? Did she have a second phone?

My fingers hovered over the unknown message, as hope drained into the gaps in the flags beneath my feet; dissolving, seeping between pebbles. A gust of wind blew at the blue aubrieta on the wall, and the finger shapes were no longer friendly. The monster behind the wall, was now clinging to it, vexed; ready to pounce.

How much had I inadvertently revealed to Craig earlier?

I dialled the unknown number.

Four rings.

Then I heard it click and the time signature started.

Nobody spoke. Neither me, nor the recipient. A silent line for now... hidden agendas passing somewhere in the sky above. Every kid wondered how voices travelled down lines from one place to another?

Then the man took the lead, his tone smooth.

'Mr Austin.'

'Who, who is this?'

And, he laughed. 'You know. You have my messages?'

'Where's Serin?'

'With me.'

My mind rocketed, calculating distances. West Masham, Leeming, on several of his farms.

'Put her on.'

'No.'

410

'*If you've hurt her.*' I shot upright. 'Now, you listen to me, you psycho piece of shit... If you don't think I'll call the pol-'

'Ah, ah... *ahhh.*'

Shizz appeared at the open door, and the faces in the farmhouse window had multiplied.

He spoke, 'If you do that, it doesn't need to be 9.30, at all. I'll do her in now and drag her battered corpse straight to the beck. The blooded trail, smearing over cement and grass, will be a marinade for the witch to lick and taste.'

I was stunned, *somehow* suddenly seated again at a table in Vegas - having gone all in - yet, reappraising my hand. No hiding my tell; the dealer was about to flip the final card - the irony of that card being called, *the river.*

'And, of course, if you call the police, your precious friend will remain trapped in there forever.'

A flush for my low pair.

'You're warped.'

'No, I'm right.'

'No, it's just not real. *Enough* of all of this.'

I heard him say "Denial" as I hung up.

'What's happening?' Shizz was in the open doorway.

'He's got her!'

'Who?'

'Grobatard's got Serin?'

The footage of me and her together in Masham: had he gone there, waited; and got plain lucky? Then I froze to the spot; stunned by my lack of foresight. I'd told Grobatard, Serin was on the verge of wealth and security, having sold her mother's farm; doing this solely to goad him. So, in turn, he'd combined video footage, proximity, and mobilised his insiders to narrow down the search. He possessed the resources to station several men, at different farms, on the off chance, one was the correct?

My hand moved to my mouth. 'I've led him straight to her.'

'Call the police. Call the police, now! This needs to end, Billy. There's nothing else.'

'I know.'

Letting the phone droop, I thought about Rob.

Rob was dead. He died. Surely, he died. Scarlett was dead, and her daughter was close. And, Grobatard needed life behind bars, but, he was threatening to kill Scarlett's daughter right this instant. I'd stared directly into those barren eyes, devoid of care.

'Billy, we need to call the police, *right now*.'

Another message flashed on my screen.

"*You have thirty seconds to confirm, or she goes. Any police. She goes.*"

'Billy?'

'It's too late, Shizz. It's too late. *He's going to kill her.*'

I shakily responded. Quickly praying, I could manage accurate predictive text.

"No police. See you at 9.30."

A response came that was as pompous, as it was depraved. "My plans far exceed any plot you could devise."

Sick.

My PA began to chastise - at exceedingly great volume too - but I raised a hand.

'Call the damn cops!' she shouted.

'Robert might be alive, Shizz. He might *still* be alive, in there.'

Stooping to my level, almost crest-fallen, Verity grabbed me low around my waist, squeezing her head gently below my chest. 'No, no, he's not.' Then she gripped me even tighter, angling her head, staring up through red spectacles. 'No, hon... he's gone. He died. You did nothing wrong when you were young. You *couldn't possibly have* saved him. He's gone.'

'But, what if... p-part of h-him-' I completely broke; totally wept.

Shizz clung on. 'He would want you to move on, Billy. Scarlett's gone too, Billy. The best we can do - the only thing we can do - for her daughter, and her welfare, is call the police. If I *hadn't* told you this at Simone's party last Friday... If I'd kept this hidden long after the weekend... none of this would have even existed for you.'

'I don't know h-how to make this right.'

'You don't have to.'

'I'm dying.' I said.

At first, she didn't respond.

'I'm dying, Shizz.'

She compassionately shook her head, but her eyes were etched in shock. Not because she believed me...

'I have to die tonight. I know you won't believe me. I'm Rob's replacement. I'm Worthington blood.'

'We should never have come here.'

She looked away, distraught, while my mind was getting hazier, drifting all over; tuning in and out of Shizz's wisdom, and then across the ocean to my friend, Simone - a true friend - and then back to my gratitude and thankfulness group in LA. Like a tree growing taller, with more and more foliage and branches... further and further away from the dark, hidden roots, obscured at the bottom. Out of sight, unseen. I couldn't even see the base anymore.

I'd built my life back together from perpetual bricks of shit. Turned back the consuming tide of black at the very edge of a personal abyss, harnessing creativity for a reader's counsel and delight - to be stored in minds as a form of indirect self-help.

For their day-glow reading on some warm, sunny beach. A far-flung place, where bronzed skin is smoothed with sunscreen, before delicately taking hold of the book mark in the very tips of the fingers. Or, for the plump, comfy chair, positioned next to the seasonal window, near arranged flower pots - and the occasional peek over the top - watching for the gathering, bleak clouds outside, and listening to the torrential rain, in the safe seclusion of the home.

Novels to love.

But they could not see, nor even conceive, the invisible chains that tightened; constricting my throat with my every syllable, and the reasons why - quite simply - the *need to write*. It was death, and life, in every word.

But all of it really didn't matter, anyway.

Not one bit. All my novels.

Fans didn't view the shelves of my work as I saw them. For them, the colourful spines, slotted side-by-side, were backbones of support; memories to cling to, to recall like important rites of passage. For me, those same shelves were a funeral parlour full of neatly packed headstones, compactly arranged in rows, for every facet of the tragedy I felt. The consumer was buying a tailored brand of my grief; vicarious melancholy to connect to, and soothe.

'Come inside for a bit,' Shizz whispered. 'Busybodies watching us through that window.'

I felt catatonic. Speechless. Obsolete. Redundant in this world. My life was those jigsaw pieces Grobatard fit together, except - at least - he had a picture on the front. Mine were turned upside down, on the cardboard side - the grey side - with their supporting box long since discarded.

Never liked jigsaws anyway.

And this puzzle was too immense.

I was done.

'I'm done.'

I think I whispered this... to no one.

Chapter 12

Joan

Back in the open plan lounge, I flopped on the nearest chair as Verity extracted the phone from my limp hand without resistance.

'You believe helping Serin is your chance of redemption… but this isn't the way. I'm calling the cops.'

She scanned my phone, but then went quiet, fingers swooping up and down through photos and messages, studying furiously. 'The last thing you need to see are these. At least, councillor Khan's is good to his word.'

For a moment I was my old bike, cast aside in our dusty garage with a nail in the tyre. I slouched forward, like the sagging handlebars. Soul punctured, torn, and the will to live ebbing away. How I pined for the upgrade? The BMX, I received, when it arrived, was *my prize*. *But,* any love toward it died that summer, mere days after purchase. I hardly took it out after. Tainted.

Shizz started to speak, and then halted. Her eyes continued to zoom up and down, from top to bottom. I assumed she was now reading messages.

'He's *still* sending them.'

'Pass it here, please. I need to read.'

'No, no, not Grobatard. It's Ishaq. He's still sending you the photos you asked for.'

I motioned over, fractionally more alert. It seemed he'd actually done what I asked.

'Graves and headstones.' she looked dismayed. 'Most request holiday snaps from friends… but you require death.'

Shizz held one up and then thrust it screen first to me. Detective Ishaq. Sleuth Ishaq. He'd certainly made it to the forested outcrop on their main farm.

The cemetery.

No law prevented you from burying someone on your own property, providing health and safety regulations were adhered. This place probably had the added advantage of historical security; a Grade II listed memorial. Initially, Ishaq had scouted the newer plots, before making his way deeper into the enclosure. His photos were interspersed with comments about stinky pigs and the strangeness of the location. Clearly, no dogs had harassed him. My pang of guilt for not forewarning him subsided as I scrolled through the images.

"They clearly care for this place. Red and yellow flowers hanging in baskets over every grave. UR right. Seems to be an occasion."

I messaged back. "Thanks. Appreciated. Don't stop looking. Females only. Around 1776."

Almost immediately, another notification came through. A message from Hazel. I accessed it, pondering if I should confide in her about Serin. Doing so was dangerous, but it doubled eyes and wisdom on a shared adversary.

"The press will leave shortly. Meet as planned."

I stopped dead, heart rising to my throat.

I read it again.

The name on the title bar: "Hazel". The message…

Someone had aimed and launched a flamethrower, roasting my head. This *had* to be a phone error, name-stamp error; a glitch. Over and over, I went off and back on the message. How was this possible? No matter how I reasoned or resisted, the beck was beckoning me. And having sent Ishaq deep behind enemy lines, Grobatard was on the verge of taking us all out in one foul swoop. The answers died right here, tonight.

'Shizz, he's got Hazel.'

'*Grob-*'

'Yes.'

'*What!*'

Pushing Ishaq's name back on to the screen, I immediately called him. Shizz sat opposite, fixing on me with intensity, the knuckles on her hands whitening, clasping her fingers tightly together.

'Billy, I'm here. You getting those photos?'

'Yes, how did you get there?'

'The back way... like you asked... through the care home.'

'Did you drive?'

'Yeah, parked in the care home, hid my car between two ambulances, so I wouldn't be seen.'

With everything I could muster, I tried not to sound perturbed, but my heart hammered my chest.

'Did you see Hazel?'

'No.'

'Wasn't she doing her late shift?'

'Yeah. Hoped I'd see her actually, but she'd been called away. A nurse let me in through her office.'

'Called away?'

'Family emergency.' He paused, sensing something off. 'Why?'

'Grobatard's got her, and he's got Serin, too.'

Initially, nothing came back over the phone line, but then he sighed, '*Oh, c'mon, Billy! That's ridiculous.*'

'Listen... *listen to me.* He's got them both.'

'Bollocks! Absolute trash.'

'Ish, look around you. *Look* at that cemetery. Look at the crests, the emblems, the flowers. They're preparing for something important. They're all out, trying to make this happen tonight!'

'Paranoia talking.' Ishaq was having none of it. 'You're trolling him.'

'Ishaq, don't ignore what you're seeing; the man's mad-obsessed with his own legacy.'

417

'No, you're obsessed with *his!* I've heard you've even bought Ivy farm.'

'That's one reason why he's taken them.'

'So, you've obviously called the police, right?'

'No, no. He'll to kill them both.'

'He told you that?'

'Yes.'

'Oh, *get real!* Seriously, get real. As much as I respect you, listen to yourself; you sound delusional. This is getting out of hand.'

'Have you forgotten the conversation with Hazel earlier? This is what Grobatards do.'

'Their fraudsters, not *kidnappers*. The press is absolutely bloody everywhere! There's no way! Absolutely… no bloody way!'

I watch Verity shake her head, mouthing, 'He's right.'

I thought quickly, listening to echoes of him wittering sympathy about my breakdown last night. Conjecture wouldn't cut it with Mr Logic. He needed nothing short of unequivocal proof; a thing I *couldn't* provide. And though proof was in scant supply, I *did* have a compelling sequence. It wasn't exactly a smoking gun, but it was three convincing coincidences, all with time stamps.

I brutally interrupted. 'Have you heard any dogs?'

'W-what?'

'Dogs barking in front of your position?'

Ishaq paused a moment. 'Yeah, at the front of the farm… that's why I'm lying low. They're Alsatians. *And?*'

'And the press are focussing on that kids' playground, right?'

'Billy, *of course* they are. '

'On the south side of your position?'

'What's *that* got to do with *anything?*'

'They're being distracted while he moves Serin and Hazel in.'

'Bullshit.'

I whipped out my phone. 'I'm going to forward you three messages, Ishaq. Read *who* they're from, the time they're sent, and *what* they all say. All three.'

'Oh, for goodness' sake.'

'Read them.'

I forwarded.

Then I waited, letting a full thirty seconds elapse before timing the invisible cue. 'Now, *Councillor Khan*, I want you to type that *other* number into your contacts - the one that doesn't say Serin or Hazel - and see if it matches any of your constituents.'

Ten seconds was all it took. 'Oh, *shit!*'

'So, to clarify, Ishaq... he has all three phones in *his* possession. We're on the same page here, right? All three. And this can only mean he *has* their owners, too.'

Silence.

'Either that,' I continued. 'Or the four of us are besties, planning to meet in secret - waiting till the press has gone - so we can have one big orgy.' I gave him a chance to process the content. 'Meeting as planned, means meeting him at 9.30 tonight!'

'We need the police.'

'No, no... *no!*' I was breathless at the urgency of conveying this, waving Shizz down as she nodded furiously in front of me. 'Now please listen. Please let every syllable resonate, Ishaq. This is *precisely* why I need you to find Maude Grobatard's daughter in that cemetery. There isn't a practical solution here. I swear it. Shove aside any rational, fixed stuff you have in your head... and just trust me. Please!'

'Okay. No police.'

'He's got to Serin through my own stupidity, and his own dumb luck.'

'It's that bloody video footage west of Masham, isn't it?'

I sighed. 'Possibly. Probably.'

'Is there something that will stop him in here?'

I heard him shifting foliage back and forth, clearly crouching and hiding.

'I'm hoping.'

'Oh, good grief. *Hoping?*'

'The Grobatard's think sacrificing Serin will break their curse. It won't.' Even if Ishaq didn't personally believe, he was embroiled in the motivations of people who did. 'I don't think this curse can be broken with any old Grobatard, even a young female. It has to be a *specific* young female.'

'How can you know?'

'*Your* Latin translation. This woman, this *thing* - or whatever the hell it is - *wants her bones.*'

'The ones in the tin?'

'No, I read different documents. Maude's final demands as death sentence was passed. Her own daughter testified against her at the trail. She believes her family made her do it. She wants revenge on her bloodline, and she wants her back... *not* Serin.'

'Bismillah!'

'Listen, Ish, when the Grobatards attacked me earl-'

'Attacked?'

'It was Dove... remember him?'

'Yeah. He works for them... *he* attacked you?'

'Set the Alsatians on me. We don't have much time. Ish, he came at me on an ATV, close to that enclosure you're in. He saw something and freaked. Dropped a sledgehammer in a furrow close to the river. I need you to find it.'

First, there was silence, and then, 'What the hell? *And then what?*'

'Those flat stones on the ground you're sending me pictures of - they're shallow graves. They can't bury their own far down because of tree roots. You need to find Maude's daughter and smash the grave open.'

'You... are... *not*... serious...'

'Okay, just find the sledgehammer. I'm coming down.'

Verity Schulenburg, PA Supreme - loyally sitting opposite - let me know her thoughts. '*Like hell you are!*'

But, I was on a crash-course. Nothing else would do.

'Ishaq, find Maude's daughter. Use dates. Probability, logic... *anything*. I'll be there in fifteen minutes. Stay there. I won't be long.'

'Billy, that mist... it's really starting to rise in the river again.'

I swallowed. 'Is it?'

'Look, I'll do five minutes, but then I'm out of here.'

'Okay. I'll be quick. Bring the sledgehammer in and leave it there.'

I hung up, and shot to my feet, but I wasn't nearly as fast as my PA, who grabbed me by the elbow. 'I'm sorry. I'm *so sorry*. I cannot… will not let you do this.'

'I can solve this.'

'What? So, you're not dying anymore?'

I pulled away, but she bear-hugged me from behind, and she was strong; surprisingly so.

'Nope!' she grunted. 'N-not happening.'

I relented, relaxed; my energy all but depleted, anyway.

And we stood there like statues, in an awkward, decidedly weird embrace.

Finally, I said. 'Then come with me. You know you won't stop me. I desperately don't want to endanger you, but I am going, no matter what.'

She didn't tighten her grip, nor did she respond, at least not with words; letting tears grace my neck. 'I don't want you to die. You need to plot a way out. You need to use that big brain.'

In her arms, facing the other way, I nodded, raising my hand, softly wiping her cheek. 'You are so incredibly loyal, Shizz. You are under no pressure to come whatsoever.'

'All those PAs who hide mistresses in wardrobes when wives unexpectedly show. And off-set drug-hauls by stashing six-figures in panic rooms… or send helicopters from mega-yachts to the mainland, for single bottles of champagne.' Shizz stopped, wrapping me tight, and I listened intently; never before had *any* of this been revealed. 'But *my* employer…' she paused, exhaling long and deep. 'Straight for the dead bodies; doesn't even kill 'em.'

'Verity, I'm so sorry.'

'Hey, my girlfriend investigates death for a living. Go figure. I need to know you're not her next investigation.'

The embrace was becoming tender.

'Appreciated. I can't tell you,' I said.

'Good job, I thought ahead, isn't it?' she pointed back towards her bedroom. 'And packed grave-digging clothes. All the rage.'

~ ~ ~

We took the hire car, which had a handy crowbar in the boot.

Shizz had brought the largest blade from a kitchen drawer in our lodgings; more a meat cleaver, with a serrated edge. Horror movie issue.

'Rather appropriate,' she noted.

And if Ishaq had retrieved the sledgehammer, at least we had a weapon each.

'So, the plan is?'

I had no way of knowing precisely. Even if what I suspected was true, I was gambling with many people's lives. It all felt abstract, unearthly - as did I. To even be driving, while demonstrating such blatant mental and physical decline, was beyond risky.

'The plan, Shizz,' I eventually responded, 'is to find Maude's daughter, and for me to deliver her.'

'Deliver her?' My PA was rendered speechless. 'In what form? Please tell me, in a damn coffin?'

'There won't be a coffin after all these years.'

Shizz grimaced. 'Oh, in the name of everything.'

'If she's even there.'

'Will Ishaq smash open her plot, if he finds it?'

'Not a chance. I just need him to get that hammer.'

'And then, are you - and, I emphasise *you*, not me - going to tip what you find into the beck?'

'No.'

I'd frantically thought this out. Ishaq had translated two phrases in Latin. And the woman in the river could have dragged me down right there, but didn't. Instead, she'd implored me, beseeching me with three insistent demands. The final time, holding out a pertinent visual aid, imploring with a finger in her outstretched palm. This was pivotal, in no way incidental: she needed *me* to fulfil this stipulation. And despite my deteriorating health, I hoped this was the loophole in avoiding an earthly exit. Bones are what she favoured in life, and that's what I'd give her in death.

Of course, this could all be a lie; the manipulation of a Siren. Regardless, this curse needed breaking.

I gave Shizz an extended response. 'Just the fingers, Verity. We're harvesting fingers only. That meat cleaver will suffice.'

She looked down in disgust, immediately flinging it on to my lap.

We skirted the edges of Londonderry, approaching the perfect straight line of the old Roman Road; this area being steeped in history. I asked my PA to check for traffic at a triangular junction; a request that nearly tipped the American over the edge.

'Which way? What… where?'

'Sorry, sorry.' I peered over the back of her shoulders to check for trucks near the blue and white, Londonderry Lodge. Shizz then resumed with her frantic assessments based upon all the hodge-podge information I'd provided. 'So, chucking in her daughter's fingers will do it?'

'There's bound to be more to it than that.'

'Meaning?'

I thought very carefully about what I was about to admit. 'Shizz, I think I need a direct audience with her.'

'That's precisely why we need Cassie, here.' She looked utterly aghast. '*You've got to be joking!*'

'And William Grobatard, too. He needs to be present, and he's got to go.'

'Shit! As in, *get rid?*'

'Yeah, but not by me.'

'I don't believe what I'm even hearing here, Billy.'

'Yeah, so how's Yorkshire been for you, so far?'

I didn't give her the opportunity to reply; no way I could bring myself to acknowledge the fiery glare.

'When I was a kid, the river told me I was the enemy, and I learned today that someone in my own family line - the Worthingtons - signed off this woman's execution. It knows me; it knows my family. I need to face it. Whatever's in there, senses, Rob shouldn't be. The Grobatard's don't know about our Worthington curse.'

'So… your family name before Austin?'

'Exactly.'

'This *won't* end well.'

I sighed in head-splitting pain. 'Tell Simone he's welcome to make a movie.'

Shizz growled and dug her nails into the side of her own head in frustration. 'So the deal with this crazy curse is giving the crazy bitch her daughter back, and then what happens?'

'I just don't know.'

'Maybe a rainbow will suddenly appear… and you'll both ride off together on a unicorn.'

'Right now. I'd take it.'

Shizz fell silent, but only for a half mile stretch.

'Is that an air base?'

I glanced to my right. 'It is. Eighties, and nineties, Tornado F-3's day and night. Noisy.'

And as we entered the southerly tip of Leeming Village, I caught sight of the Willow Tree; a pub I longed to enter as a reclusive, self-sequestered teen. My right turn into the car park was impromptu, met with, 'Finally, common sense prevails.'

'I need to think.'

I reversed into a bay - right in front of the very tree the drinking establishment was named after. Then I killed the engine and watched a plethora of contented punters walking from the back of the pub to a field behind us. It was a welcome distraction, although I ensured my baseball cap was angled down over my brow. The locals were accustomed to familiar patrons, and despite the unfamiliar car, many smiled and politely acknowledged us as they passed.

'They don't recognise you at all, do they?'

'No, just being friendly. I vanished from here when I was eighteen. My parents moved.'

Several more people appeared from the back, carrying large cast iron hoops in their hands.

'What are they doing?' Shizz said.

'Quoits.'

The nonplussed Yank to my left-hand side shrugged, but continued watching, intrigued. 'Never heard of it. What is it? Is that how you kill wildlife around here?'

'It's a game, Shizz.'

I'd forgotten how traditions were wholly embraced and lovingly preserved in pubs like these. In the same way a willow nourished the earth with sustenance, pubs like these tenderly cultivated to their clientele; a subtle, understated art.

'Those hoops are heavy,' I said. 'You throw them across a huge sandpit, and hook them over a spike. Takes skill.'

Shizz paused a moment, and then sighed, slapping her thighs. 'I tell you what… sack this all off. Let's get exceedingly drunk - you and me - throw some hoops under the moon, and if that witch wants you, she come out of the river, drag her sorry wet ass down here, and we'll buy her a pint.'

I didn't respond. I felt trapped. Everyone outside was jovial and expectant. I wanted to harness their mood and take my PA up on her offer. Get absolutely and utterly annihilated to the point I woke in puke, and counted it a blessing.

Thankfully, Verity was also good at the sobering questions: 'So, do you think he's alive or dead in there?'

I wiped my wet brow. I was at death's door.

'They dredged the river for miles, and didn't find him. Couldn't find his boat. I don't know what reality curses create, if any? He's maybe in some limbo state.'

'And if you sacrifice yourself, you're convinced he'll be released?'

I swallowed, releasing my window partly down, and stared at the fields through my rear-view mirror. I wanted to be honest with her. She would protest like hell - grab the car keys and drive us both away - but I couldn't handle this survivor's guilt. Regardless, I couldn't answer directly.

'Shizz, I need to give Ivy farm to Grobatard.'

'Why?'

'The stipulation is he gets all his original land back.'

'But you haven't actually signed anything.'

'Correct. He'll kill me anyway, but I can buy myself time by feeding his ego. He's a pompous sociopath, so if I can make him believe I'm ceding to a superior, I can figure what to do with the bones.'

'And save yourself?'

'Let's hope.'

'Uh oh.' Verity was alerted to something on her phone; an ever present on her lap. 'That's the third in as many minutes from *different* contacts.'

'Third?'

I leaned over and stared at the thumbnail. It read *breaking news* in bright red. She clicked it, and we watched a journalist interviewing someone with their face blurred; identity concealed. After thirty seconds, it cut to phone footage.

Three boys.

Two were seated on a river bank, next to a single, stationary fishing rod to their side. I noticed a whole raft of colourful cider bottles in the background and estimated the youths to be in their mid to late teens. One was standing several feet from the water's edge, aggressively hurling bricks into the beck. His friend was beside him, filming - the recording edited and extensively bleeped - especially at the end of a provocative line, the boy kept shouting, 'If there's a witch, come on out *you b-*'

This went on for several seconds, the camera increasingly unsteady, as laughter ensued.

That was... until the standing boy suddenly became horizontal, his legs lifting from under him at eighty degrees, and he hovered - suspended in thin air - for a split second, before launching six feet across the grassy bank into the water below.

Dragged continually under the surface by nothing. Nothing visible anyway.

The news team had arranged a *still* of his face, for the moment he hung there at bizarre, unnatural elevation. Paused on an expression of utmost surprise; like the realisation your jacket was caught in farm machinery, and your body was to be hauled along a clattering conveyor and minced.

Then, it unfroze, and he flew. Over and over again, in a sequence repeated several times.

If he was alive, Sir Isaac Newton would decline to comment.

'*Shit!*' Shizz whispered.

At that moment, my own phone flashed in the central compartment.

I immediately accessed the photo.

A gravestone.

Joan Grobatard
Born 1765
Died 1782

Daughter of Maude Grobatard.

Underneath, Ishaq had added.

"The *Daughter of Maude* part was inscribed at a later date, almost as an after-thought; not by a professional. I need to go. I left the sledgehammer right here. Not getting involved! My boss is calling me. Already in enough trouble. Got to do a live interview with him supervising me in ten. A chance to atone. Good luck. Wish me luck too."

My mind raced as I covered Shizz's screen with my palm and looked her square in the eyes. 'So you see, it's not just about Serin, Scarlett and Rob. This thing's on the verge of murder.'

She nodded, as I enlarged my photo and shared.

The headstone was old and you could barely discern Joan's name and her paltry age. The accompanying inscription referring to her mother, looked far more recent.

Shizz pointed at the ignition.

'Come on, let's do this quickly,' she said. 'I've brought old covid masks I found in the case - useful if we're robbing graves.'

Chapter 13

Skulduggery

It was marginally easier to conceal a cleaver than it was a crowbar.

Thankfully, I could double it up as a clumsy walking cane for the more visually impaired in passing cars.

Roadside parking wasn't difficult (maybe a little odd in this locale), but we still had to make the journey along the slip road right by the old people's home. Then we'd hop a fence, traverse a field, and skirt the periphery of the grand building. All without being noticed.

Shizz was spooked by the river, and as we descended grassy bank at an acute angle, the fog was already rising. She checked her phone and patted me on the shoulder. 'Live footage from the river, look!'

'Where?'

I jumped, scouring from east to west.

'At the playground.'

'Okay, that's close; we need to tread carefully.'

I watched the MP for this area as he gave scientific explanations for the mist rising behind him, only hundreds of yards from our position. He was a stout man in his late fifties who wore a tailored grey suit, embodying swagger in his every nuanced response. His mission was to ensure public reassurance, and confidence - with the facts, as he saw them. The "flying boy" he was shown… had slipped on wet earth, after copious amounts of cider.

And in terms of the mist,

'Our great county is prone to weather fluctuations, and this, quite clearly, as every good farmer around here will tell you, is what happens when warm air meets cold water. Better known as *condensation* in layman's terms.'

He assuredly jabbed his huge thumb over his shoulder, in case the reporter was somehow missing what he was referring to.

'Goodness knows how cold this fresh water is, flowing down from our beautiful Dales, and with it being warmer here at ground level, in the vale...' he stopped, addressing the reporter directly by name, 'It's Karen, isn't it? So Karen,'

'It's Carol.'

'So, Carol,' he smiled, holding out his palm as if presenting a gift for all the viewers - the gift of the imperiously wise. 'Think of this as a basin - like a bath basin - with bubbles gathering in the tub, with nowhere to go.'

The interviewer then connected the mist with the day Robert vanished.

And, the MP deflected completely.

'If you have a greenhouse, like me, and you regularly mist your orchids, you'll see dew form on their leaves. That's what's happening here on a grander scale. And with the abundance of vegetation by the river, and particularly this hogsweed, Mr Grobatard is now *kindly* removing - goodness only knows how disorientated you'll become in mist like this.'

He droned on. Expertly, as he did so, running down the interviewer's time-slot.

I noted he was mispronouncing hogweed, and implying that *this* particular plant could leave you confused.

Burns accounted for the apparent scratch marks on kids, and also livestock deaths. The hogweed, combined with the subsequent (and in his words, "unusual") cooling of water, could result in rapidly falling body temperatures, hypothermia, and possibly even hallucinations.

This was all delivered impeccably. On another day, I would have believed it myself. Everything was explainable with a smile and inflated confidence.

He had a big, broad chin that jutted out slightly as he talked before setting itself back in the confines of his face. He periodically cocked his head, feigning listening, but it was obvious he was recycling responses within a rehearsed political lexicon.

Difficult questions were routinely brushed aside… with an obstinate call to embrace a "concrete" and "watertight" approach.

'Would you like to hear a new, well-used expression to describe someone like this, Shizz?' she looked up, feverishly nodding. 'It's only just come back to me after all these years.'

'Go on.'

'A pillock.'

~ ~ ~

The forested outcrop to our right was dark and eerily silent as we approached the low, surrounding railings.

There was no breeze today and nice degree of August warmth; always more of a pleasant, dry heat around here. To my left, the end of the original Roman Road, where it turned into stone crossing in the river. Two thousand years ago, this joined the opposing banks - but now - no evidence of a Roman presence - existed to the north side. This would have been one of the more developed areas in the country until the Romans packed up and left. By the time William the Conqueror stepped foot in England, this place would be unrecognisable.

In many ways, this small, seemingly insignificant village, had a hidden, fascinating history. In a vast area of forested wilderness, replete with boars, wolves, and wild bears, Romans had cleared away and designated this route, building a main passageway between the south and

Caledonia. For century after century, it remained a major connection, enhanced further by the opening of the dual carriageway in 1961.

One millennium after the Romans first entered Britannia, William 'the conqueror' fanned his men out wide outside of York, and marched north, torching the earth and all its occupants. A true road, an expertly crafted Roman Road... was a welcome sight for murderous knights. Easy, innocent pickings, and the ease of access to settlements dotted on either side. Close-knit communities lived here, working hard together, tilling the earth and tending to their animals and crops. They had no time for politics; day-to-day toil was challenging enough. They weren't rebels. But the French king didn't care.

Around fifteen years after William decimated the land, entries in the Domesday book record countless village names without a *single* resident. A blurred word, that looks like 'Vasta', appears instead.

Waste-land.

Exelby, Theakston, Burneston.

All men, women and children... mercilessly butchered by a war criminal.

I beckoned Shizz to stop for a moment and looked out over the mist as I considered a truly horrible truth I'd learned about this place; Leeming *didn't* even exist according to the Domesday book. Like the nearby settlement of Newton Picot - no longer habited to this day - there was *nothing* left. But I'd heard the voices of the children crying. Whether it was residual energy as Cass described, or the never-ending loop, or a manipulative Siren, or some demonic deception.

A settlement was once here.

I knew it.

'So, is this what people mean by skulduggery?'

'Pardon?' I snapped out of my reverie.

'Digging up skulls and bones. Finding great treasures buried with the skeleton. *Skulduggery?*'

'It sounds like it should, but I'm not sure it actually does.'

'Well, that's terrible etymology.' Verity looked very disappointed. 'So when we're eventually tried in court, providing we don't die, it won't be for skulduggery?'

'No,' I sighed, smashed by the full weight of our imminent actions. 'It just means being deceptive and underhand.'

'Ahh, a Grobatard conviction.'

We clambered over the last wooden fence, and stared into the rectangular, forested outcrop. The metal railings with the yellow and red shields, and their correspondingly coloured flowers; all hanging from the baskets over the stones. It was shadowy, and bleak in here, as if the trees themselves sucked death from the earth.

'It's very creepy.'

I agreed. 'Not a good vibe.'

'These are the same flowers that woman was planting earlier.'

Shizz was correct.

'Preparing for a jubilee, or a coronation even.'

A tarnished name, ready to be restored. Emancipation, and a skewed righteousness, re-established. The black gate was ajar, and the sledgehammer lay only a little way into the enclosure. Flat stones, almost like poorly laid stepping stones, were dotted in and around the diagonal tree trunks. These were sycamore trees. I hadn't realised in my haste before. So much of their white bark was shredded and peeling off.

We had missed Ishaq by ten minutes, but he'd faithfully left a marker.

Looking further west, I assessed the noise we could potentially be making. We were at a sufficient distance to do this surreptitiously, and our location - in relation to Hislop's old farm - favoured us. We'd be disguised and sound-proofed by trees and although you could see the building some way ahead; it was the back of it. Press vans would congregate at the front.

Further east, past the bridge - where Rob vanished - we hadn't seen any film crews near the point where the bones were discovered. The MP was the moth to the flame at a single spot, for now.

The iron gate creaked as we entered and walked towards the one 'marked' grave that mattered. My salvation was based on a gut-feeling, a chance encounter with the woman in the river, an inference from Ol' Bobby... and a document Scarlett had buried in a box. I was operating on levels of conjecture that truly mortified my rational self.

We knelt alongside the stone where Ishaq left the hammer.

Whoever scrawled the part about the "daughter of *Maude*" had done so as an after-thought. It appeared a genuine attempt to alert attending Grobatards to their one faulty member - highlighting disgust for the mother. Her name was written at a slant, and it bordered on vandalism.

Shizz picked up on it, too.

'None of the others are like this. They're old, but this looks recent.'

'Maybe this spirit was causing so much trouble they tried appeasing it by acknowledging her existence?'

'Like she would be visiting this place in the middle of the night?'

I suddenly shivered, and it wasn't from the lack of light. At that moment, Shizz stood and looked away. 'Billy, I-I, I'm sorry, I can't do this...'

'No problem.'

I stood back up, staring back down at the grave of Joan Grobatard.

Died when she was seventeen.

Then I scanned the other smaller headstones close by. And here I noticed something... curious. Keeping an ever-watchful eye, I processed the peculiar coincidence I beheld: *several* younger family members appeared to have died the same year as Joan; mere months before. She was the oldest to die that year out of them all; possibly a terrible year for tuberculous. Four children - aged between three and eight - all died in August, on exactly the same day, and Joan passed in November.

Shizz had turned completely away now, with her hand over her mouth. This was way too much for her.

'I'll be quick, I promise. Watch out for the news channel if you like? Just tell me if any press decide on heading our way, over the cattle bridge.'

'Yep.' Her face was ashen. 'Billy, I think I'll vomit.'

'Stand really far back.'

She turned to walk to the perimeter, and I was loath to ask her for what I really needed. 'Shizz... the meat cleaver...'

Silently, and shakily, she reached into her jacket and retrieved it. It was in two plastic bags now, for safer-storage. I watched her reach the perimeter before I stooped down again, hitting on a better idea.

Rather than just smash the thing with a hammer...

Taking the crowbar handle, I tried prodding the earth just to the right of the flat stone. I probed for damper ground, and forced down, looking for some kind of purchase. The soil was soft enough for it to stick two or three inches before being stopped by something hard; possibly stone. Pushing down at an angle, I could feel the clotted strength actually belonged to a capillary root system; the denizens of a spade. Wiping my brow, I realised that only adrenalin was pushing me through this morbid endeavour. I felt shocking, unsteady on my legs. I looked up, composed... breathed some more, and noticed two more smaller stones, jutting out from the base of another sycamore.

1782
Twins. Born the same day. Died the same day.
Both seven.
September.

The Grobatards were smote by disease this year, and I wondered if their entire line was nearly wiped out; Maude's curse definitely kicking in quickly. The crowbar was helpfully sticking out at a diagonal without support. Taking the sledgehammer, I gave the end a whack, sending it deeper into the ground. I stood back, astonished. On the first try, I'd pushed the metal shaft underneath the flag, and if I prized it right now, the stone would definitely hoist.

I whispered down at grave of the girl, who died when she was seventeen, 'I'm so, *so* sorry, I don't want to do this.'

In my mind, I imagined the smallest of holes, a broken coffin full of brown and dusty bones, coated in slimy dark residue. And shrunken fragments of rag-like clothing, wrapping the withered flesh of the occupant, accompanied by an odour so vile, it would cling till the day I die.

Wiping my mouth with the back of my arm, I steeled myself.

Taking the crowbar in both hesitant hands, I inhaled, prepared, and made my legs as sturdy as possible. The knife was new and ready to sever anything I found. I would grab an arm… hack off the finger bones, and not think about it, just not think about it…

I stared, swallowed, and heaved.

At first I thought it would tip completely, but at the last minute the end slid sideways, revealing a gap; a hole with more than partial visibility.

A battered, open coffin, just beneath the surface. Not six feet under.

Two feet.

With great apprehension, I examined the contents, my mind picking up speed; the power of observation refined to analyse what was only 'necessary'. At first I thought my eyes hadn't adjusted correctly, and bundled clothing was making me confuse limbs. Taking the phone, I pushed the torch option, swiping up an incoming message from Ishaq. Crowbar in hand, light in the other, I fished the hollow before me, as my eyes finally communicated to my brain.

A tiny skeleton.

Seventeen? Half that age, surely?

Withered, wasted… clothing disintegrated.

Blade marks on the bottom that had shattered the wooden base.

No hands.

Severed at the wrists.

Hacked off.

Gone.

Dropping the crowbar, I stared at the baskets of flowers, marking each and every plot. Then I fell to my knees in the memorial garden - the pretentious *Show home* for the Grobatards - sifting through remains with the crowbar. Pelvis, skull, ribs, legs - feet with toes - forearms, smashed at their ends.

'Hurry up!'

'They're gone.' I heard the combined terror and astonishment in my voice. 'They've been taken.'

'What?'

My tall personal assistant slowly made her way back inside, taking her eyes from the live reporting about a quarter of a mile from here. 'The hands?' she fired. 'Just the hands?'

'Hacked off. Gone…'

Taking the crowbar and hammer, I stepped over to a similarly sized flag and stared down. This child died when they were seven - a boy - buried further away from its adjacent tree trunk. I stuck the pointed end in the damp earth next to the stone, watching it sink with ease. Driving the sledgehammer hard against the metal wedge instantly shifted the flag sideways. Yanking out the crowbar, I hoisted up the rest of the cover, just as Shizz joined me.

She covered her mouth, staring down… and staggered away in revolt and disgust.

A musty, rotten smell broke through the seals of two centuries, and a clear skeletal body of a small infant honed into view, lying in a supine position. It couldn't be more clear.

Nor could his hands.

Where hands should be.

'Oh, Bil-'

Shizz wretched, grabbed her mouth, wobbling back to the perimeter like a new born deer taking first steps, grabbing branches on her way. I covered my own, fighting to understand; deciding I really didn't. With my heart thumping in my head, I pushed the stone back into its original place, overwhelmed by the forbidden urge to open *more*, to clarify matters definitively.

But this was the truth: *someone else* knew. They *knew* precisely what to procure.

With the smell of rusted iron and wood pushing into my nostrils, I rubbed my face in anguish. Whoever had stolen her, for whatever reason, had stolen my solution, and my absolute salvation. It couldn't be the Grobatards. Stealing Joan's fingers would make Serin's sacrifice utterly *pointless*... if they already possessed the ultimate skeleton key. William wanted his *name* restored and was of firm persuasion Serin's capture and death would solve *everything* - from legacy to increased productivity.

Betrayer for betrayer.

I stood there stunned, in complete brokenness. Mine and Serin's lifeline was gone.

'Billy, you need to come and see this.'

In total defeat, I pawed for my tools - feeling more ill by the second. No bones. Bye - bye, Billy-botch-job. The repercussions were devastating, Shizz surely knowing the gravity, but she was somehow distracted.

'We're on the north side, right?' She held up her phone, as I trudged over. 'This guy's name is William, correct? William Grobatard?'

I nodded, looking at her screen, listening to the reporter explaining they'd now "get a few words" from the landowner. The camera panned to the cattle bridge, and William Grobatard and his entourage, crossing over to the south side.

I was gobsmacked. 'This is only ten minutes from here.'

'Walking?'

'Yes.'

438

'Surely, we would have seen them?' Shizz said. 'Or, they would have *heard* you smacking the crowbar.'

'Unless,' I looked over, guessing they came from the West; from Cherry Tree Farm direction, 'Unless, they've come from Scarlett's old farm. The one they swindled off them.'

The journalist continued, 'We're still hoping to have a few words with councillor Khan too, shortly.' she looked around over her shoulders. 'But in the meantime, Mr Grobatard has agreed to talk to us about his plans for this land, and the hogweed removal.'

'Here's the thing,' Shizz started - rising concern in her tone, 'and you really don't need to be hearing this right now.' She stopped, and slowly turned, staring back into the cemetery; a look of bewilderment on her face. 'When they were preparing to interview Ishaq a moment ago,' she stuttered through her explanation, 'They went "live" with someone else instead.'

'I really don't understand what you're saying.' My head was shot to pieces. 'So?'

'I could hear the MP off screen. The mics kept picking him up.' Shizz continued to engage with a frown. 'You could hear him slagging Ishaq in the background. A journalist went over and asked him to stop swearing.'

'The MP?'

'Yeah, he kept saying, *where is that stupid wanker?* Listen, you can *still hear him* ranting.'

Pulling my fingers away from her the phone, I brought out my own. Ishaq had messaged me at the pivotal moment, and I'd swiped it away, so I could use the torch.

'Hang on a sec.'

I clicked on the message.

"The press will be gone shortly. Meet as planned. Thanks for the updates."

And I sank to my knees, smashing my chin clean down on the crowbar.

Grobatard had him… and *he had* the bones.

I was stunned by my idiocy; setting the councillor directly next to the only grave that mattered; delivering him straight to Grobatard. I knew in chess, the very best players resign long before the end; understanding - countless moves in advance - the futility of their position. Novices kept moving their pieces. Novices like me.

'They've g-got him.'

I blurted at my personal assistant, who grabbed my shoulder, and then my phone, and stared. She didn't say anything; mouth slightly parted.

'They've got him,' I whispered again.

My body boughed in the middle, and my stomach lurched - looking every bit - the outstretched Rob I'd seen close to here, only hours earlier. Then Verity's hand squeezed my shoulder, hard.

'Billy, look at me.'

I wept uncontrollably... lost, blind-sided. I'd occupied this position *all along*; first round KO, smashed in the first assault, leathered against the ropes. The ref would see my eyes rolling into the back of my head, and sack-off the ten count long before I hit the canvas.

'Billy, please look at me.'

I somehow managed to, with dignity, pulling myself upright again.

Verity Schulenberg, PA extraordinaire, gave me her unflinching attention. She let this linger, demanding me to reciprocate with full engagement.

'What if they *don't* have Ishaq?'

I went blank, gazing for endless seconds, before making some involuntarily guttural sound; a dismissively croaky protestation.

'What? You've just s-seen the mes-?'

She placed her fingers on my lips to quiet me. 'We only ever came here, because of *his* emails.'

She fixed me earnestly, with an intensity bordering on ferocity. 'How is Grobatard calling this all so perfectly, Billy... from start to finish? How can Ishaq vanish in *ten minutes* flat? He would have been spotted; he's *not* at his interview.'

I listened, my insides beginning to tug against her words.

'You always put your phone on speaker. *Ishaq* was the one who said Hazel left on an emergency. You mentioned Serin and the footage… and he mentioned *west Masham,*' she was astonished, bewildered by my shortsightedness. 'What the hell is even west of Masham? I don't even know that! You and Serin were spotted in the town centre, right?'

I felt like I'd sank to shin height, into one of these plots. I'd driven west of Masham, into the Dales, to meet Serin in secret.

She went on, 'He only knows Scarlett's letter - because of what you told him - and you've kept him updated on everything throughout.' Verity pointed into the midst of the cemetery. 'I literally heard him ask you if there was anything here Grobatard needed… and you said it *wasn't* the finger bones in the tin… it was, *her bones.*'

'Shit!'

'You asked him to use probability in finding Joan. You even gave him dates!'

I went light-headed, throat drying, realising he'd accused me of trolling Grobatard, and he knew I'd bought Ivy farm. But how could he know… when I'd bought it under an alias? Rolly Bridgeson had bought the farm; not me.

Shizz remained undeterred. 'He's been a councillor here for years. A councillor with no solutions. He wants this all to go away - just like you - for his *career's* sake. It screwed up him, like it's screwed up you, and he's tried fixing it… and *can't.*'

She grabbed my face, her eyes blazing into mine. 'Bill, are you not getting this? He's working for the Grobatards!'

Something shifted in me, and Verity grabbed my arms above the elbows, nodding at me to acknowledge, to realise, to accept. The boy, Ishaq, would *never* do this. But, the man, Ishaq… was a stricken, *desperate* man.

I knew that man. He was me.

An internal cataclysm now rocked my insides. Out-of-body stuff. The kind that sends you spinning into other realities; far away with the fairies.

'He couldn't,' I whispered. 'Shizz, he couldn't.'

'I'm so sorry, Bill… he *just* did.'

And then she pulled her phone around, catching sight of William Grobatard starting his interview. The man produced a comb and groomed himself as the first question was asked. Then he smiled; a grin of genuine contentedness. He wasn't remotely flustered when we met in his conservatory, because he was in complete control.

I hadn't seen him smile at all earlier.

'I finally get it,' Shizz said, face marked with the purest consternation. 'I now know what skulduggery means.'

Chapter 14

Tunnel Vision

High-flying parents.

Esteemed in their respective medical fields. Money in abundance; privately educating their son, sending him to Cambridge. Cultural capital was a given, as was educational and financial. Ishaq was a complete Pierre Bourdieu case study in a strong *head start*. But he was back in the village he was born and raised in. Called by the river.

Years ago.

I hadn't asked him about his current profession, the one apart from lead councillor. It couldn't possibly be property, but nothing was impossible. I wonder if his parents approved; probably not.

Ishaq was called to be the protector of this area's heritage; closely engaged with - and invested - in the welfare of hard-working people. Although he hadn't seen Rob vanish that day, he knew his wasn't a natural, explainable disappearance. Despite being absent from the horrific clamour on that fateful August day, the impact would have been sustained, and forever life-changing.

We'd only reconnected yesterday evening - not even twenty-four hours earlier.

For me, my subconscious worked by expelling broken fragments which I quickly changed, and disguised in the form of stories, but how did a rational man cope with the irrational? Staring down at continuous blown-up, glossy

443

photos of ripped-up constituents... week-after-week, month-after-month. He lived here, *within* the midst of his own life-defining moment, searching for solutions. Now - after years - solutions had evaporated. Problems weren't just mounting; they were land-sliding.

As Shizz and I hastily departed, these were half-formed, unconnected thoughts; dots joined in the twilight. I still couldn't believe he'd do this. On a hot LA's day, you could find shade under a beautiful black walnut in an arboretum, or a botanical garden. But, in Hollywood, shady characters were everywhere, in an all pervading dog-eat-dog culture. I knew the trustworthy were few and far between. But, I always thought the Ishaq of old - and the Ishaq of new - would, in no way, defer from factory settings; retaining the utmost integrity. A glimmer of hope told me Shizz was wrong, despite presenting a devastatingly convincing case. If she was; he was in mortal danger too.

The mist ascended higher from the cold river to our right, as we clambered over the fence and headed back. I considered running in the opposite direction, a mere quarter of a mile, hoping Grobatard was still being interviewed, and dramatically interrupting:

"This man has kidnapped two people! Send the police! Do not trust councillor Khan! This man here is going to sacrifice a girl... right here in the river tonight! He is going to try to end his curse!"

If I'd gained any public sympathy yesterday evening, this would kill it, with calls for me to be sectioned. Grobatard had his men positioned if I disobeyed. Blowing a whistle would be the end, of *all matters*.

Our exit up the field was anything but discreet. We probably looked like sweaty junkies in need of a hit. I needed to get away. I needed time to process. There was no time to get away. There was no time to process. We reached the track to the care home, and hoisted ourselves over the final barrier, frantically moving towards the car, and then bolting across the road to it. I throttled up without regard for seat-belts or squealing tyres, duplicating the exact route from earlier; within minutes, passing the entrance to Grobatard's main farm. I thought about driving down, performing a crazed rescue mission, but, they might not even be there.

Location, location, location.

The road took me through Aiskew into Bedale, down into the valley, over the bridge, and back up to the junction; Vasey's corner, as some locals still called it. I once bought comics there in a time of tarnished innocence, 5.20pm being my preference - ten minutes before closing. In the back was a little alcove with stocked toys and you felt more secluded and protected in there, surrounded by hope, escape routes, and the fleeting possibilities of joy. But the colourful boxes and exciting packaging would turn greyer the more I stared at them, so I stopped going.

Bearing left, we headed back towards the very same villages recorded as being wiped-out by the harrying, the road weaving and meandering all the way to the entrance of Ivy farm. I slowed. There was no point driving up the track. My purchase was pointless. So I pressed on over another small bridge in the direction of Exelby, and Burneston. Here, the Green Dragon honed into view and without provocation, or warning, I abruptly pulled into the car park, tyres kicking up gravel as I slammed on the brakes. It was 8.31pm.

'I need a drink… and I need to think.'

Shizz nodded, already exiting the car. I was past caring about being recognised, nevertheless, asking Verity to hit the bar on our behalves, while I used the gated side entrance for the beer garden. This was a hidden gem on the highway, a pub brimming with character, replete with nooks, crannies and ancient timber. Centuries of conversations, joviality and attractive glances contained and concealed within stone cloisters, seated on red leather sofas, and warmed by log-fires.

The space out back had been refurbished, planned with great forethought over two well-kept levels. I ascended the top tier - away from a few early evening revellers - closing in on an enclosed section with a summer canopy; secluded from the rest of the garden. There, I collapsed on a comfy chair and briefly watched the sun lowering in the western sky.

A family had clearly been here in the afternoon, their younger children tracing shapes and messages in the pebbles below my feet. I let my foot hover, ready to smooth the stones over, and then thought twice. It was a bit mean; I hated the sea when it wiped out my sandcastles.

I planted my foot to the side of someone called *Kelly*... who'd reached as far as the brown earth with her finger tips. Instead, I studied the low-lying table opposite, and the centrally placed wine bottle. The candle in the thick neck had burned on many a previous evening, wax cascading in bulbous streaks and pooling around the base. To its right stood a glass biscuit jar - replete with home-baked cookies of vast sizes - a pleasant touch for the peckish. A packet of anti-septic wipes was positioned adjacent to the jar for the safety conscious.

People had sat here and laughed, reminisced... romanced, and their conversations would have been easy, sanguine... a needed release after an arduous day. This was my last drink. I knew it with certainty.

Shizz would be coming over shortly with a double or a triple... tasked with procuring a whole bottle of the strongest stuff, whatever the price. Whiskey was in order, even though I couldn't stand it. However the drink came, it needed to be stiff.

Some local patrons had arrived early-doors, and through the cosy windows below I could see this part of the evening was devoted to diners feasting on succulent roasts.

446

I hadn't eaten since our late lunch, and despite the inviting aroma, lacked any desire. Poor Verity must be starving.

On the first tier of the garden I got a good view of her exiting the back of the pub carrying two large wine glasses in one hand, a metal cooler in the other, and crisps under both her arms. The Landlord had clearly rebuffed our moonshine grab.

She was staring down at the ground, clearly concentrating on the delicate art of balancing and moving, but I could see serious lines of defeat etching her frown. No whiskey. I leaned forward - careful not to scramble Kelly's name - and grabbed the wine bottle to clear a space. I tugged, and it didn't budge. Surprised, I pulled again, but it held fast, wax anchoring it down. In frustration, I yanked a third and final time, and it popped off.

Holding it aloft in my right hand, I stared at the bottle, reminded of the moment Joan's stone shifted... and then my eyes slowly descended to the kid's name, hastily scrawled between my shoes.

And I visualised the state of the grave, suddenly, fighting to understand how Ishaq and company could lift, get inside, and smash off fingers... in next to no time. I noted no sign of dislodged turf, trampled ground or excessive footprints. And the prising of a flat stone wasn't easy, especially with a thick sledgehammer. Smashing it wasn't the Grobatard way either; an unholy act in their sacred reserve.

I leaned forward again, waxy bottle in hand, musing... recalling the moment I pushed the crowbar down, and felt the strong tug and the snapping of surrounding weeds and the solid clods of dried earth, locking everything in place, as if...

As if it hadn't been disturbed in *some time*.

Crouching further, I realised right there this plot hadn't been touched recently... it hadn't been touched *in years*. Thoughts now frantic, I turfed pebbles as I hastily stood, staring at *Kelly's name directly* beneath me again.

A message, a name.

447

My brain, pounding like a pilot testing G-forces, as I realised William thanked me for updates via Ishaq's phone - but what updates were these?

Earlier, back at Grobatards main farm, Joan never featured at all in our verbal duel, nor his explication. Her hands had been removed, but not today… *not by him*. The attention to detail in the cemetery was being ramped-up for a finale, but it would never involve *her bones*.

He still had tunnel-vision.

Shizz slowly ascended to the top level, surrounded by a myriad of beautiful flowers. She peered across at me - and something flashed over her face - something bordering on shame. My PA needn't think she could do any more; she'd been brilliant enough. Her walk was tame, precise; not wanting to drop anything - slowing time - the wine bottle in the metal cooler wobbling back and forth as she approached.

Nearly dropping the lot when I shouted, *son of a bitch!*

'*What!*'

My phone was out. In photos. Enlarging. Centring on the only one that ever mattered. I zoomed in, down to the side of the seated Scarlett. "Daughter of Maude" wasn't scrawled over stone by any Grobatard family member, nor did they make any spade marks at the bottom of Joan's coffin.

I studied the beanie-clad beauty… a dear, passed soul, and the two boney animal carcasses to her side; the ones I thought were voles or mice.

'Son of a bitch.' I stared at Shizz, pointing to a spot on the ground in the photo. '*Scarlett* took them.'

~~~

For some reason, I always associated August with sunshine through to 10pm. But two months had passed since the solstice, and now, at 9.26, the skies were rapidly darkening, and solitary lights twinkled above.

As a medieval peasant, I wondered how I'd handle seeing a moon on a blue sky day, realising it wasn't the harbinger of night. Staring up at the mysteries of the universe would undoubtedly be my passion, closely monitoring afternoon clouds, hoping my night view would be undiminished. Every evening, I'd stretch out my arms, desperately trying to touch the heavenly host, marvelling at the distance and the majesty. How close, how far? And as twilight pulled near, I'd eagerly await the sun to disembark on the western horizon, watching it pulsate and sink in the most vibrant of colours.

Like the evening sun, Shizz had disembarked the car further down the track; sinking herself down, and out of sight behind a hedge.

And as I now moved closer towards the farmyard, I prayed there'd be no preordained 'look-out' hiding somewhere in a furrow, using night vision to watch my approach. But this was Yorkshire, not Hollywood. Grobatard wouldn't care less for such measures, when his own skewed omniscience would do.

The pebbly road slowly descended, as the first of the barns appeared ahead on the left. Even with the car windows tightly shut, I could smell his pigs. No more happy memories of this place resided within me.

There was only darkness here.

This place gushed and sparkled with youthful optimism for the first year we came. The mystery was there, but it never encroached. And then, the following year, it did, and everything was gone.

All gone.

I let the car coast down the slope into the yard, before turning one-eighty, parking with the front pointing forwards - ready for a quick getaway. It really did stink here, not like in Mr Hislop's day when this seemed a wholesome farm. Despite the curse reducing his own crop and livestock yields, he'd done his level best to make his venture as viable as possible.

In the rear-view mirror, I got a clear view down to the river bank, people moving about in the exact location where we'd seen the burning cow, and the knight drowning the child. Turning off the engine, and hence, the lights, I studied them all walking by, two hundred yards from my position. Not a single one looked my way.

Small groups, of maybe three or four, were heading east, disappearing out of sight at the edge of the farmhouse. I was shocked to see anyone at all, but who could tell what William Grobatard was planning? Regardless, as even more people appeared - casually strolling in from the west - it dawned on me; this was a monumental *occasion*. And, an astonished part of me fully expected this hubris man to even go as far as inviting the press, along with his own bloodline, such was his astounding arrogance. Looking around - even a cursory glance - suggested no media were stationed anywhere as far as I could see.

This would be a covert Grobatard rite. A private celebration of a legacy restored.

I swallowed, readying myself - knowing, that in a moment or two - down by the beck, I'd encounter people I cared for. For the final time, I pictured the five of us as kids, tracing the invisible outline of a memory as the fields opened out to the right. I wondered if Cassie was correct, and our collective trauma would somehow imprint, leaving a spectral residue somewhere along the bank.

I was *so done* with this place.

Now all my friends were either dead, captured, or had double-crossed me... possibly. When it came to Ishaq, I'd taken a huge gamble on Shizz being partially incorrect. My gut was telling me he was a reluctant Judas, who'd gone past the legal threshold of action without realising it, and I would muster every ounce of my power and influence to pull him back over the line. He had emailed me in desperation, with no confirmation I'd fly here. My hope vainly clung to this; I had little else.

With no intention of dying tonight, it was almost bizarre that my salvation was paradoxical - the cure - was the curse itself. A game-changer, depending on how it was handled.

It could free me, but more likely condemn me. The question, now: did I now have the upper hand in terms of *true* knowledge? Had I interpreted the situation correctly back there in the beer garden? Grobatard had beaten me to the punch at his farm earlier today, but only in respect of the undiluted terms in his faulty paradigm. This man was resolutely determined to fuel the tinder to his monstrous mission. No words would sway him, only actions. *His* actions. I was counting on this haughty oversight; an error of calamitous proportions.

Had Scarlett and I already figured this out?

She was the grave-robber. How, and when, I now knew.

Her time on this farm had given her space to investigate the whole area; the entire lineage. While her marriage was going south - she'd gone west - back to the place where Ol' Bobby made his home. And eventually, with the help of Mr Hislop - and the Worthington records - had returned to discover the cog that powered the machine. Goodness knows how many times, living directly next to the beck, she'd encountered Maude in much the same way I had.

Scarlett had expected me to return.

Letters, photos, love-hearts, bottles, buried boxes.

And together, we'd been the first to climb, and reach the fraught mountain pass. But she'd already passed on to the other side, and when I looked down, the bridge was missing. I could see her on the other side... calling to me, frantically shouting something; her voice becoming lost in the covering clouds and valley winds.

She'd left clues - safeguarding them from Grobatard hands - and I solved them all, but I couldn't take the final step.

What had she done with the bones?

I vigorously rubbed my face, racking my brains. 'C'mon, think.'

She certainly wouldn't have reunited Joan with the beck, not before the allocated time; not until the stipulations were met. These bones were her daughter's insurance policy. She'd concealed and stored them somehow, somewhere.

In the enclosure to my right, agitated pigs suddenly squealed and jostled against steel fencing; their smell, instantly more pronounced. I stared into the shadows... something, possibly a rat, disturbing the harmony of their rancid dwelling. Whatever was in there, bore no comparison to the giant rat already standing by the beck. Like me, they were troubled, pushing against the periphery, squeezing their snouts through the gaps.

Trying to get out, *trying to get away.*

They were rammed into two separate barns; brimming with pork. Wildlife and countryside, along with animal welfare acts... remained low on Grobatard priorities, and I estimated he'd tripled, maybe quadrupled, the legal allocation. The green trailer I'd seen with Shizz at his main farm earlier, wasn't transporting them to the abattoir at all. They were being brought here.

Seeing the swine reminded me.

I took out my phone and prepared the message I would hopefully send Shizz, when the time was right. I left the text in the box, ignoring *send.* We'd jointly agreed on a method of distraction, if required. If she were to receive this, she knew things had gone *badly south.*

Somehow, I managed to push my thoughts back to the love heart in the underpass.

Scarlett was happily married in the end, but she was remembering, recalling something she'd also felt when she was young. A message from another time, and universe - solely for me - to say the feelings were reciprocated. Stroking away the tear streaks, I allowed myself this last happy thought.

And then, I took the bones from the glove compartment, slotting them inside my jacket pocket.

Rabbit bones... prized from one of the picture frames hanging from the walls in our lodgings - the ones that so intrigued Shizz when we arrived - carefully selected for size, and likeness.

After visiting The Green Dragon, we'd briefly returned to our accommodation; the unopened bottle of wine now resting on the car's back seat. And if I made it through the night, I'd be reimbursing the owner for my vandalism: various frames now hacked apart in an attempt to find suitable bones.

Rabbit's legs, it turns out, are remarkably similar to a child's fingers. Mole bones were too small, and fox bones would just about do it - but the frame was stubborn. This was a gamble. A bluff. Any second now, I would approach a Vegas style roulette wheel, with a big reputation... and a blank bank account. It was fake bones and a poker face. Nothing else.

The plan I had *would* involve a physical fight. Punching, brawling; inevitable. And if I was to survive, then the anguished faces of Serin and Hazel would be my impetus to go down swinging. Back in LA, my personal trainer was an ex super middle weight boxer, with a seventy-five per cent professional win ratio. He had taught me so much physically, but mental strength was always key - as he rightly said. I had no more than one or two rest days per week, so despite my age, I was no slouch.

However, the curse was preparing me to replace Rob; seasoning my soul, searing my flesh to weakness.

And now, sitting right here, directly by the beck, I felt like death... fighting healthy farmers was not ideal. My *jab and retreat* policy would be useless against a tornado flurry of fists.

Exiting the car, I surrendered to supernatural intervention as the only vestige of providence, casting my eyes to the starry heavens. Earlier, I sent a few messages to

453

people of faith back in the US, who'd be saying a few on my behalf. I didn't know if God existed, arguing against in the main, but I struggled in making him mutually exclusive to this ubiquitous high strangeness. Regardless, I craved for cosmically ordained justice to be working in my favour.

Pain insists on being attended to. God whispers in our pleasures... but shouts in our pain.

Staring down at the bank, I soaked in the words of CS Lewis, as two more people walking east past the edge of the barn. Unlike the others, these two wore hooded cloaks.

Good grief.

This was increasingly looking more like a magic rite, especially as the mist was soaring above the river beyond. Tonight was a designated night for something to occur, undoubtedly. And the water itself, just about visible beneath its wispy, spiralling overcoat, was *unusually high*, almost flooding out over the bank. Walking down the slight decline in its direction, uneven and unkempt at every step, I tried fathoming this. It hadn't rained at any time while I was here, and the dark clouds that gathered over the moors earlier, did so without intruding further in-land. I tried to figure if there'd been a deluge of water from the source further up in the Dales, but that was impossible; not to *this level!*

Something wasn't right.

I was fully expecting a sinister welcome party, but people were ambling about like a leisurely author meet-and-greet. Two more walked by a little further ahead, like revellers attending an outdoor gig, chatting away in anticipation. They disappeared around the side of the farm house, without even noticing me. Did they know what was happening? Did I even know?

As I drew closer to the bank, large volumes of candles steadily emerged in my view, dotted all along the grass, every single one burning brightly on a breezeless evening. Ubiquitous. Under normal circumstances, this would be a nice atmospheric touch for an auspicious event.

Not tonight, damn creepy.

Turning the corner, I stared in astonishment - not remotely conceiving what I saw. Maybe it was absolute fear, maybe, bewilderment. But suddenly it made complete sense why the beck ran so straight in large sections before it reached the underpass; the two streams running side-by-side in perfect tandem. I had never - even remotely considered - how carved the beck purposefully was. My truly ludicrous notion from earlier today, tackling the curse by altering the river course... was a reality.

To my shock, I could now recall all the childhood clues that this had *once been* a canal; clues I'd completely ignored. I remembered Rob discovering the huge hinges on the inside of the cattle bridge, and the rusted, iron pulley wheels marked on the map stored inside his tree house. Hazel had even mentioned earlier in the care home, before losing their titles, they once had the financial clout and influence to build this river route. The Grobatard's were refurbishing the beck, restoring it to former glories. The tarpaulin sheets I saw earlier, now discarded on one side. This was a grand plan to connect the beck to the Swale, on the verge of being fulfilled...

Rob built a jetty; a small dock. Did he somehow sense the purpose of this entire watercourse? Was this revealed to him from below?

As shocking as this all was, it paled in comparison with the most disturbing sight of all. It wasn't even the extensive mist that stretched as far as the first restored *lock* - the whole reason for the water reaching this extraordinarily high level. Nor was it the two subjugated figures, tied, and kneeling directly in front of William Grobatard, who was pulling down his hood, and staring in my direction.

The thing of absolute horror - was the thing jutting out across the beck.

A long, thick beam of wood, set at a right angle to the river, with an old chair strapped to one end. It pivoted on a centrally placed triangular fulcrum, with three men - at the opposing end - holding and hooking a chain to freshly cemented ground; an anchor point.

A giant see-saw with one end raised, hovering precariously over the lower lock, now rapidly filling with water.

Bound and gagged, sitting at the far end, a girl.

Dangling above, as if patiently waiting for the ride to begin.

Wearing a pale green dress.

The twisted irony smacked me with its immediacy. I knew *exactly* what this was; what I was looking at. Once more, hindsight was correcting false memories, and faulty impressions. During our ill-fated game of hide-and-seek - after the thing had tapped the entire length of the wall - Scarlett had entered, shining the torch inside. I heard her mention the 'weird' see-saw next to me - the one with a rusted chain at one end, and a wooden chair at the other.

We hadn't discovered a see-saw. This was a cucking-stool. An elaborate construction for publically drowning an accused witch.

Scarlett had illuminated it as a kid. How ironic that her own daughter was now strapped to the end? As Maude once had, centuries before. The Worthingtons, as Judge, Jury, and executioners, had administered the ducking; drowning her in the beck. Then they stored away this giant contraption away, sealed, out of sight, in their own barn yard. My ancestors had constructed the very device that would return to haunt them, and me.

Hazel and Ishaq were directly in front of the old man; their hands tied together with rope.

I felt a strange relief seeing Ishaq this way, but almost immediately, caught between many conflicting emotions, I was totally overwhelmed. All I could think to do, was stumble over to William and plead him to release all; surrendering to my fate in the process.

Behind me, on the ascent, my car was two hundred yards away. The bottle of wine was in the back. Why didn't I take at least a single sip?

Run.

Behind me, more ferociously now, boisterous pigs were ramming against the steel enclosure. Unceasingly, and with far more impulsivity, and deliberation than a minute earlier. Their din was quickly becoming a cacophony, those closest to the railings, squealing while being squashed; eyes bulging wide. What did Grobatard say about Christ, demons and pigs, earlier?

Around me now, invisible currents permeating the air; strange micro-climates, all out of reach of a discerning radar. There were answers here. I knew it. Solutions. Countless times I kept tapping keys, and plots would spring from nowhere. I needed that to be a physical reality, right *now*.

In the basin between the two lock gates, the water level continued increasing; deep enough to drown.

'Mr Austin,' his voice startled me, as the patriarch beckoned, 'Why are you still standing over there? Do come over and join us for this important occasion.'

Ishaq and Hazel both looked up, desperation in their eyes. Helpless little lambs.

I raised half a hand to them. *It's going to be okay.*

Time for the power play.

Time to show those gathering my external and internal control. Power was a lie; a manipulation of perception. I marched forward, shoulders back, into the midst of the extended Grobatard family. Not a single member seemed unduly perturbed or alarmed by proceedings. Young and old alike, had gathered here for a celebration. Even those stood adjacent my kneeling companions appeared jovial and excited; desensitised to the dismay inches from their waists. It smacked of the Dupont de Ligonnes murders a decade earlier; the psychopathic French father murdering his entire family to halt the flow of his royal lineage. However, the Grobatard's were *hellbent* on continuing theirs.

Time to barter.

Time to convince my current audience.

Above all, with fake bones in my pocket; time to use my imagination.

'I thought you wanted to end this curse.'

457

I called this out, nonchalantly walked forwards, passing several clan members, not evening registering their presence. The occasional candle flickered either side of me as approached, but not much; there was no wind. More stars peeped out overhead. I felt as alert as an ill man could be.

'I have her,' William called softly in that strange pitch of his, 'And I have you. Therefore, I have everything I require.'

'Yes, whatever happens,' I looked down at Hazel, 'You get Ivy farm, but I have conditions in all this. The first is you let these two go.'

I took the time to assess my surroundings. This was paramount; attuning to my environment for a chance of survival. At this precise point, I noticed the small circular table beside him, containing a ring, a candle, and a copy of my book, Grace in Star-Spun Places - of course, a giant curving ceremonial knife, too. I faltered slightly, staring down a little too long, wiping my clammy forehead. The book mark indicated he was a third of the way through; clearly researching me, taking time to infer personality through the words.

'It's a little too… how do we say… *kitsch* for me?'

'My novel?'

'Extensively sentimental.'

'You should try this.' I reached into my jacket pocket and pulled out another. 'Here, I've signed it for you.'

Shizz always packed spares as gifts for fans on my travels. I handed him a copy of *A Fountain of Falsehood* with an excessively large *Austin* scrawled on the front cover with a black marker.

He smiled. 'You leave this world a portfolio of genuine effort.'

I smirked back, but almost immediately he picked up the signet ring, placing it on the small finger of his right hand. The old man with the immaculate hair fixed me with the same inanely sympathetic grin he'd given earlier. He pointed at Ishaq and Hazel.

'In response to your request: everyone kneeling, won't be leaving.'

'Thank you for clarifying.'

Aside from the table, the only other significant object was a flat stone set into the ground; made of marble, pristine and newly laid. Its position - adjacent to the beck - suggested a commemorative purpose. Out of the corner of my eye, I scanned it quickly.

The most glorious house of Grobatard - all your livestock will be cursed from this day forth, until our lost land is restored to the highest honour, and you bring the treacherous girl to me.

And then beneath, today's date, and a Latin phrase.
*Veni * Vidi * Veci*

His own face had been engraved at the base in white, his brow clad in a laurel wreath. I shook my head at the sight. Maude's curse for his family was etched in stone, as was the identity of its pompous custodian, and saviour of the bloodline. For the first time, I fearfully stared at Serin - the treacherous girl - elevated to around twelve feet, struggling against her unwieldy bonds.

It wasn't her. This was a mistake. Maude wanted the daughter who testified against her.

What had Scarlett done with her remains?

Time was crucial, so I reached into my jacket pocket and pulled out the bone fragments, secured in a silver cigarette tin, found in a kitchen drawer.

'The thing is, Mr Grobatard,' I tried remaining calm. 'Councillor Khan here led you straight to the solution, and you ignored him.' I opened the lid, like I was offering a Kretek, pausing a moment, adding, '*Veni… Vidi… Veci.*'

I maintained composure as the water, suddenly and inexplicably bubbled and churned to my side. Above, Serin squirmed in the seat in response.

'There you go, William,' I stayed assured. 'Even the river's giving you a sign. It knows the truth.'

I pushed rabbit bones closer, giving him an opportunity to glance, before quickly withdrawing.

'Thanks for leaving the sledgehammer where I asked you to.' I patted a silent and subdued Ishaq once on the shoulder. 'It meant I could bring the *correct* betrayer to the party.'

Ishaq momentarily angled his head at Grobatard. 'I told you.' He immediately turned away again.

High to my left, I sensed Serin fixing on me, desperately trying to communicate through her gag; words, constricted and caught in cloth. The water in the lock was now three quarters full, cascading through the open door to the left.

I needed time.

I was flying blind.

Why didn't Scarlett leave the bones in either the buried box, envelope, or Ol' Bobby's bottle? *What had I missed?*

William looked away from my tin and across to the water's edge; a bemused flicker on his face. There was something ominous in the timing of the river's reaction, but now it had calmed.

'And what exactly are you showing me?' he said.

'The end of this curse. This is what Maude needs. Her own daughter's bones. The daughter your family stole from her. Fingers are the magical currency.'

He contemptuously scowled. 'She wants a *worthy* sacrifice.'

'No, that's what *you* think she wants.' I clicked the tin closed, casually replacing it in my jacket. 'Without these, your curse stays.'

'Nonsense.'

'I guess the closest comparison… is… a *missing* piece of your puzzle, right?'

I let that resonate, hoping he'd get the reference to what I'd surreptitiously done sitting opposite him earlier.

He *ignored* it. 'Look down there and read that stone again, Mr Austin. With your death, all this land is back in our hands. The treacherous Grobatard child is high above you now, penitently preparing in her remorse. Today, our eminence is restored.'

'*Nothing* is restored.'

He swept his hands around poetically, like someone assured victory by a massive margin. 'And you *should* be grateful, Mr Austin… because I alone, will finally liberate your poor friend from his entrapment. This sacrifice, and your very own, will ensure completeness.' The old man smiled - confident in his own hand - before snapping his fingers: 'Let's put this matter to rest and see who's correct?'

Nodding at the three men holding the chain at the end, they released it from the floor hook.

'*No!*'

With a muffled scream, Serin pitched down into, and under the surface of the water. I thought she might temporarily float on impact, but the weight of the plank was immense. Straight under.

Two men grabbed at me as I launched at the twisted patriarch. I cleaned one out with a hook, but missed the second. We grappled, and I managed to slither round to his rear, grabbing him in a headlock, resolutely choking him. The three other men left the opposing end of the beam to tackle me; hate lining their face. My reactionary plan was terrible… I needed *them* to pull Serin back out, so I immediately released my victim, who fell to the floor, grasping his throat.

I raised my hands. 'Pull her up, *pull her out!*'

I thrust them higher in surrender - and the tin - not secured within my pocket, dropped, spilling boney fragments. I tried covering with my shoe, but it was obvious. '*Get back and pull her out.*'

Serin remained submerged.

I had to think fast; I had to solve this *now*. Scarlett, clues, *anything*. I had nothing to barter with.

Except *me*.

There were too many people here to physically contend with.

'*Pull her out!*'

The men ground to a halt in front of me, so I turned. 'William, *listen to me*. I need to *talk* to Maude. Without me, this curse won't end. You have no idea that Maude cursed *my family*, too.'

461

Impatience flickered on his face. 'Oh, Mr Austin, please… have some dignity.'

'You don't know *who I am*, do you?'

His expression was fixed. In his arrogance, he hadn't figured his link to my family, so I bawled down at Ishaq. 'Ishaq, *tell him* what the river called me when we were young!'

Ishaq's head moved fractionally, but not nearly enough.

'If you want your ass and career saving, Ishaq, *tell him* what it called me!'

The councillor cocked his head, only slightly, whispering. '*Enemy*. It called him… enemy.'

Their eyes met.

'That's correct. *I'm* the enemy, here! *Not Serin.*'

Hazel was crying, rocking on her side, pulling on the ropes tied around her back, trying to shuffle sideways to the bank.

A chink of intrigue flashed on Grobatard's face, and I needed to get this next part absolutely correct, urgently.

'You see me as inconsequential don't you - just some writer - earning my name, fame, and success through effort. You think I'm an insignificant peasant - but you don't understand *why* I have all this in the first place.'

I thrust my hand into my trouser pocket, pulling out two small objects, pinching them tightly together between forefinger and thumb. I showed him the first side; the tiny blue and yellow badge.

'This is my family crest. Recognise it?'

For the first time since meeting him, his face faltered; eyes widening in burgeoning realisation.

'Mr Grobatard. *I* am your enemy.'

I flicked my hand over to the other side, revealing the jigsaw piece I didn't mix in his other pile at all… *I stole it, instead.*

'*I am* the missing piece you need in all this.'

From astonishment, to lust. He stared at his piece like a dog with raw steak in the food bowl, a dog I was now commanding to *wait*. But then, he waved me away. 'This is nonsense.'

'Really?' I repeatedly jabbed myself in the chest. 'I am successful because my *Worthington* name and lineage has bestowed it all on me.' I pointed at his copy Grace in Star-Spun Places resting on his little table. 'And if you still don't believe me who I am, *read the inlay* of that book right there; read *who I dedicate it to*.'

He gawked in bewilderment, as I finished. 'So, in case you skipped my dedication, go figure what the "W" in "Granny W" stands for, you contemptible dickhead.'

Forty-five to fifty seconds had elapsed. A life-time. That's how long Serin had been under. I held the crest side out in my fingers (knowing he wanted the other side back).

'*Pull her up!*' I barked.

I couldn't wait a moment longer, but Grobatard was mildly staggered, not responding.

Eventually, with practise, you could hold your breath well over a minute. But *not* when your body is shocked by frigid cold; every sinew stunned to rigidity. Her instinct would be to breathe on immediate contact; body over-ruling the very thing you shouldn't do. Incredibly, he jolted, *but* immediately pulled out his comb and smoothed down his hair, his eyes not leaving the piece I had pincered between thumb and forefinger.

'Grobatard, *Pull her out!*'

Mine was a surprise far too complex for the heartless machine to process; the comb... seamlessly gliding.

Hazel was shrieking and begging him by his feet.

'*If you don't pull her out this instant...*'

But it was too late...

Time had passed.

She would be gone.

One of the two men I assaulted stood between me and the beck - so I gave him an uppercut - shoved him sideways, flung my phone down, and dived into the mist-laden lock as more water jettisoned in.

Instantly, I submerged in blackness; the cold nearly wiping me out.

Blindly, I pushed as close to the cucking stool as I could predict - my brain shocked numb and frozen - pitching to where I hoped Serin was seated. I had to save her; I had to save Scarlett's daughter.

Fighting debilitating electrocution of icy waters, with every vestige of will, I connected with something hard, and in some parts... soft. The lock was filling faster - four feet from the brim - so I grappled under the surface for something solid to hold, desperate to get purchase. With water now way over my head, I crouched, taking a second handhold to push up from. It was conceivable - it was an arm or leg - no way of telling. My fingers grasped some floating fabric, and a rugged cylindrical object that felt secure.

I heaved on the thick plank with all my might.

Water's natural buoyancy, my strength. Inch by inch. Even if I could only push her partly above the surface, or, break the chair away.

My feet slipped on the slimy, solid bottom, but I wouldn't stop my exertion. *I could not.* Things moved up in their entirety, at least as far vertically as I could exert. I straightened my arms, aware that by saving her life, I was saving my own. Elbows locked, I couldn't hold *this weight* long, calculating that I'd *surely* taken her above surface. Despite the adrenalin, I was already slipping, losing grip; lungs busting, arms burning.

Give her chance to briefly breathe, if that was still possible.

My life-response systems commanded: *drop, drop, drop...* as I felt my body's insane default drive to self-preserve. Ten, fifteen seconds up there. If she could have, she would have gasped air by now.

Slowly, I began to release - lowering, hoping that she was alive - and had taken another deep breath.

Then I just let go.

Everything I could muster evaporated, and I tried darting away from the heavy apparatus that could pin me. Pushing up, I hit the surface, greedily sucking air like it was the only thing I'd *ever* want in life again. I was light-headed, filled with terror and panic. Serin was above me. The three men now holding the beam, slowly bringing it horizontal. I tried grabbing for a bank without a handhold, wiping my eyes, staring up at her...

Her dress, and skin, saturated.

Her neck, lolling to one side.

Diagonal streaks of hair lanced her lifeless face. The curls had all gone - and, in the half-light - I'd swear it was a pale mannequin, or an impostor with straight hair. The style of green dress was similar, but it was at least three shades darker.

I tried to support myself by the side but the refurbished walls were smooth.

Water continued to slice down the four lowest corners of the chair as the mannequin sat perfectly still. She was within reach, and I launched back to her, reaching up, grabbing and shaking her slippery thigh, yanking and screaming.

The human will to survive, can be *quite something*.

Over a minute and a half had passed, when Serin explosively inhaled... spluttering, coughing water from the far recesses of her soaked lungs. She drew the biggest gulp of air, immediately recommencing the wrestle with her binds. The same Scarlett fighting-spirit imbued in her brave daughter. The gag had come loose, pushed part way over her forehead like a bandanna.

If I hadn't had intervened, he would have left her.

I realised, at precisely that moment, that William Grobatard - in every single sense - was a murdering bastard. And with all the power I could retain, with all resolve and determination - if I could extricate myself from this sinkhole - I would do anything to see him dead tonight. Shivering insanely, I drew closer to Serin, patting her calves.

'You're okay, you're okay. Breathe.'

Underwater lights had been switched, illuminating the lock, and more importantly, Serin herself, as she coughed and heaved. I wondered at first if she'd suffered catastrophic brain damage. Something wasn't right. Her eyes were moving wildly like cognitive function was impaired, as she carried out an inane and silent surveillance around, and below me.

'Serin.'

She was wide-eyed. Scared stiff.

'You're okay, Serin. Breathe. Concentrate on breathing.'

Her head started to jolt backwards and forwards, as I heard voices excitedly talking at the brink of the bank, echoing down into the chamber. The water was rising, and I knew it would eventually take me to the rim, if I could just keep afloat. Grobatard had bought what I said - or *enough of it* at least. I continued reassuring Serin some more, checking her binds for weaknesses, so I could unfasten and loosen rope. She was a little way above, and it was exactly here, I noticed something black... dripping down her calves.

Eight jagged furrows, above her knee, bubbling out a substance; now smeared with clear water on her skin. Casting my eyes to her thigh, I watched the deep grooves oozing blood, dripping from many angles, the four lock lights below, highlighting the expanding maroon cloud now ballooning out; pluming, like a paint brush dipped in a fresh glass jar.

'Billy, she's... she's *down there.*'

I stared at her.

Listening to her fearful whimper, watching her contorting face.

'*She's down there.*'

Noise was increasing in the lock; noise I'd mistaken for the crashing torrent, or the glowering crowds gathering above.

But they weren't. As the more water gushed in through the gate, the echoes were coming from within the clouded chamber. I swivelled, looking down... and then around.

And there, on the opposing side, through the densest spiralling mist, no more than fifteen feet away, I caught sight of something below the water. In the midst of vast white spray, and bubbling deluge, only someone at my level would ever see her.

A face, floating fractionally below the surface. Jet black hair stretching out around her.

Dreadful in appearance.

Slamming myself against the stone wall, I glanced again at Serin's injured thigh; claw marks made from jagged nails, ferociously tearing flesh with ease. I turned and stared, watching the woman's contours become more distinctive: dark eyebrows; sharp nose; lifeless eyes.

'*Good* Jesus.'

A call to providence. A new fear, and belief in God. If Grobatard didn't instruct this beam to be pushed any higher - *this instant* - Serin wouldn't be protected.

'Billy… *please…*' she gasped. 'Take it off my leg!'

I couldn't process this cry. *Break the chair? The rope?* I went to grab at the cucking stool; to push her further up, or smash wood with my fist. Anything.

'*Take it off my leg!*'

In a frenzy, I kept pushing at the stool, not understanding.

Then I caught sight of it.

The garter around her thigh, the one I saw this morning.

Two thin strips of leather joined in the middle by criss-crosses, full of buckles, tassels, and tiny pockets. Bloodied scratch marks tearing the skin, on either side. Nowhere else on her legs, or body - only here. The garter clung to Serin's thigh, with flesh gouged away, as if something had forcibly tugged it down to her knee. It rested partly on an angle, with something white - almost off-grey - hanging from one of the tiny leather pouches.

'Billy, she wants the strap. *Give her the strap.*'

And I got it. Right there, I understood. Now, so clear. Crystal clear.

Scarlett, the complete genius.

What if I *never* came back? What if I had *never* returned to England… to receive the photos, find her buried box, the bottle, or her painted love heart. Who could *truly* protect Serin from this vicious curse? No one could.

So, Scarlett did it herself.

She'd read the documents - understanding it all - opened the grave, and snatched Joan's fingers. But not before first looking down at the skeleton, and seeing the strap attached to the remains - and, right there - with the Worthington records firmly in mind, figured *precisely* the type of *strap* Maude commanded her daughter receive. Nothing to do with punishment; *her own leather strap* - containing charms and trinkets - that William Worthington, himself desired at the court hearing. Maude's own leather garter passed down to Joan, and buried with her when she died aged seventeen.

Directly in front of my eyes, small fragments of bone jutted out of the tiny compartments, and pouches.

The remains of Joan Grobatard.

What I mistook for being a sexy garter was anything but. Maude's garter… *her witch's garter.*

Behind me, the dark-haired woman came forwards, arms extended, fingers outstretched. I thought quickly, grabbing at the tiny buckles.

'Mum, made me *swear* to always wear it.'

Serin was frantic, crying. One buckle had been torn off already; leaving an extensive wound directly beneath.

Despite my cold, slimy fingers, I wrenched off two more; one remaining intact. My actions hurt Serin, who tensed - almost whistling through gritted teeth - but no matter how I tried, the last one wouldn't budge. So, I reached into my jacket, clawing through my wet shirt for my own insurance policy; the cleaver I had concealed there. I'd aimed for an opportune moment to use it on land, freeing the captives, but this was desperate.

To my horror, my almost frost-bitten fingers failed in getting purchase on any part of the thick blade, *stuck fast* to my wet chest. Tearing at buttons proved wholly futile - as around me - the lights grew with sudden intensity, floating around the bottom of the immured gully. I left it as long as possible, thrusting my arm back out, and turning to the woman, now, somehow, gliding at waist height above the water towards me. To be this tall, at this depth, was impossible. Looking down - in complete dismay - I saw she was yards above the lock bed, as if the water wasn't even there; pacing the invisible platform.

No resistance to her flight.

None of this mattered; *she* - the embodiment of the curse - *owned* the river. And in a place like this, in these moments, anything supernatural *owned* science like a bitch.

She had her sights fixed on me, the closest thing to her condemner from centuries earlier; a direct ancestor of the Worthingtons. I cowered in terror, recalling fairy stories… witch's biting entire faces off.

Chapter 15

Under

I felt heavier.

Getting my hands on something small and rusted, like an iron support - pushing up. The old wood on the chair began to crack with my furious exertions, but my intention wasn't to free Serin - it was to get her *as far away as possible*. Instantly, I thought I'd made the wrong call, glancing at the garter dangling by its one stubborn buckle. I reached out to yank it off - forsaking the agony I'd inflict - but this proved entirely fruitless, as Serin was suddenly thrust even further up and away.

The cucking stool was now angled high over the beck.

She was as safe as she could be, for now.

And now there was only me.

My thoughts launched to self-preservation, frantically searched for safety or shelter. But, refurbished walls were rendered with smooth new stone, finger grips were non-existent. And then I felt heavier again, as I stared up at Serin, calculating her safety. Voices and whispers, swirled all around me in separate patches, and clusters... inexplicably changing direction, and source: a sentence started in one place... finished in another.

And she was coming.

She was closer.

At first, I thought my panicked thrashing had pushed me into a sedge of reeds; the long, sinewy stems encasing my thighs and waist. My mind stopped complying; ceasing to grasp the logical course. Surely, adrenalin would see an easy escape, but for some reason, no matter how I pulled, I could not break free. It was life or death, no time for pathetic, nuisance binds. I began to wonder if giant hogweed was paying me an ironic final visit, sealing my final demise for mockingly dismissing it. I prepared to grab and yank the stalks that shackled me.

Several tiny hands clung to me.

Dirty, broken finger nails clinging to my belt, and my lower shirt. They neither pulled, nor tugged - just held me fast. In terror, I shoved myself away, but every single time the fingers gripped tighter - relenting only when I quit exerting. I kept yanking, failing, sinking... feeling downward momentum as grey, smooth limbs slowly descended alongside me. Their force could not be resisted; diametrically opposed to my ability to remain buoyant.

Children's faces appeared just below the surface; silent expressions frozen in time.

Is this what Rob saw?

A millisecond before death, I realised fear hits a sensory peak, elongating somewhere behind your eyes. And then you experience this weird, extended second of revelatory acceptance; your body shrugging its shoulders, just saying, "*Oh, well.*" And, it hits like a bullet, at the point marginally past; *well, I guess... this is it.*

I let them take me down, away from her.

I couldn't recall taking a final, deep breath.

And it became so exceedingly dark, so rapidly, but not as cold as I expected. Deeper I went - down into ocean trenches - or, so I perceived. Until radiant pin-pricks began forming in my peripheral vision, surrounded by countless deep-sea fish showering me with unearthly luminance.

A tiny picture forming larger.

Watching it approach in its every nuanced detail, expanding in a consuming panorama, while retaining the majesty of its intricate precision. I felt warmer.

Children in raggedy clothes; begging with all their might. Language barriers. Afflicting agendas. Only *one* ever prevailing in this situation.

Quivering infants... with scant to no understanding of the shouts from the part-armoured men; let alone, their deliberate actions without constraint. When they awoke that morning, it had been cold, but sunny, and the crisp sky was blue. Winter's earth stood solid and unwieldy, as it had for months.

Now, they watched on - as one by one - the litter of piglets they so adored, had their throats slit, before being slung in the frigid beck. Dying creatures sliding over the ice-covered surface, twitching to lifelessness at the end of their red slipstream.

Then, the men turned on family members - young and old alike - without discrimination; enacting an ending to life, as brutal as it was, merciless. The children stared, barely comprehending the butchery, as grimacing loved ones slowly fell forever silent.

The sky above remained just as blue. It had been a normal start to the day.

Somewhere near York, further back on the road, days earlier... the knights rationalised their orders. They diligently awaited for the grizzled, rabid rebels to appear... a clear, visible justification to slaughter. As always, it took the psychopathic soldiers within the contingent to get the ball rolling: the first torched barn, the first screams for mercy, the first dead child.

They were all memorable.

Physical cues in the perceived enemy were rapidly being revised: reimagined in heads, and superseded in hearts. They were all pretending to be innocent. Besides, these were *different* children than those they'd fathered in France. They killed, raped and pillaged for mile after mile, before reaching the villages near here. Time enough to hone a blank and empty conscience, build a routine - treating it as a form of social experiment - exploring who could push atrocity the furthest. Shut *that* part of the brain down, and a job is a job.

They drowned each child in turn - self-analysing all the while for remnants of goodness, wholesomeness - finding none. Head first, cracked against - and then through the thick ice - before being submerged for consecutively longer periods of time; the pre-surface screams no longer connecting to a conscience. Noises, and contorted faces became an irritation.

It led to an unusual inner conflict for the knights; kill faster to get it over with, or kill slower - and see if compassion is triggered. It was winter, too bloody cold to dally, so they settled on the swiftness of the former. Burning barns and people kept them warmer.

I watched and felt it all.

A burial.

Ground consecrated; ground blessed.

The river - cursed by murderous actions - now being *blessed*.

A holy man, and his companions, travelling on foot - mile-after-mile - in the barren wilderness to find, and lay to rest. They had a duty; performing it diligently. Men, in brown animal hide, retrieving as many bodies as they could. They prayed, asked for forgiveness, and they buried. I felt their heart's desire; their conviction and such sorrow of soul… such dismay at the world.

With each spadeful of earth, they pushed over the deceased - and in direct contrast to the knights - their own hearts broke. They erected wooden crosses, in a small burial site, and prayed long into the night. Some had purposefully fasted; some had no choice… there was scarcely any food around, anyway.

A woman's hand touched me.

I felt long nails trace their way down my neck, all the way to my chest.

She was telling her daughter *not to* play with the bones. It had made her angry. The young girl, in turn, listened…

studying the contours on her mother's face, assessing shifts in tone, calculating the cause and effect of how this invoked a physical consequence. But she felt *nothing*. She fully understood she'd receive physical punishment - but sensed great power in the buried bones, *purposefully* unearthing them in this holy place. After receiving her *discipline*, shrewder, more covert tactics would be employed in avoiding getting caught in the future. Remorse was non-existent; lessons in right and wrong were an opportunity to refine physical responses suited to a particular audience.

What she wanted in return was to punish, to punish the woman who loved her...

And use the finger bones for *real* magic, to control people, for power. But her mother angrily rebuked her as they sat together in the midst of unearthed soil. While her mother yelled, the smirk could not be contained. Her mother's anger made her happy.

I felt it all.

The same girl, now standing in court; bold as brass. Eleven years old, and accusing her mother of killing many children.

She'd led the authorities - and particularly a man of regional repute - to her own mother's pig farm. She no longer lived there herself; attracted to the power in the wider family... enablers, for her own agenda. Once there, she'd shown authorities the many finger bones, mixed in with the dirt, trampled by pigs. The girl herself had secretly extracted the bones from the Christian burial site close by, planting them at night.

I was impressed by her conviction and clarity while placed under oath - having sworn on the Bible - a star witness of sorts. She told the wardens of the witch's garter, strapped to her mother's thigh, to the gasps of those in attendance.

Then I heard Maude weeping, "Why are you doing this?".

I felt the kindness she'd freely given her daughter, and in return, the false accusations of neglect and abuse.

Falsely accused, and now condemned to death.

The young girl craved power and promotion. Her own blood-line, she'd drawn allegiance with, would give her all this. The powerful family, in turn, had marvelled at the child, believing her every lie. As a final chance to win her daughter back, the mother had reluctantly agreed with her family to hide the kidnapped boy in her smallholding.

For a period, until a bribe was paid.

Kept there on the pretense she'd be given back her Joan, whom she loved dearly. And for a few days it looked promising... for the duration of the kidnapping, the daughter returning regularly to see her. The mother was happy, but conflicted. To compensate for the guilt, she'd purposefully cared for and consoled the terrified boy, desperate for the day he would be released.

He was only nine. He had his father's name.

On the third night of capture, the daughter purposefully removed finger bones from the burial site - the one the monk's consecrated. Then, she'd cursed them again, and planted them on her mother's farm - at the dead of night - near the pigs. First, she'd paid a visit to the terrified boy hidden in the small enclosure, watching with no emotion, as he bled.

Later that night, she'd ran back to the powerful family and told them, "Come quickly."

I watched, and I felt... and I lost faith in humanity.

The woman stood alone in front of the man.

He was in a place of authority; life and death, in his hands. He had loved his son. He wanted justice and he forcibly let his scruples override his emotions - his heartbreak; his distraught devastation - pushing it aside, supplanting his need for vengeance. Something told him the woman was *telling the truth*. A seed, now wrestling with his anger. Records revealed this powerful family had kidnapped children before, but the sentence of death had already been passed.

Now, it was just her and him; accuser and condemned. She told him that she'd looked after his boy.

How she was a healer using the powers of the earth to help; that she wasn't a witch. She had great power, but she used it to help, only agreeing to this endeavour to win her daughter back. Her strap was convenient for carrying herbs, and she only prayed to the Lord above. She admitted to having visions and hoped God would reveal their meaning.

And despite his despair, he started to believe her.

He was astonished at how her own daughter had spoken so powerfully against her own mother; he'd never known a child do this so convincingly. The words, flowing like honey for the listeners; truly spellbinding.

Something about the eleven-year-old girl troubled him.

After the trial, the young girl immediately asked him - outright - if she could have the garter. Her mother had just been sentenced to death. This concerned him; it was *all* she wanted.

He sensed an empty, depraved soul.

But, Maude - the woman standing here - had just cursed him and his family-line to restlessness until justice prevailed. He spoke, clearing his throat, and told her that her daughter requested her garter. The woman, the mother, solemnly nodded, and agreed she should be *given the strap*.

Maude Grobatard wept, strapped tightly to the cucking stool.

In her last moments. Joan approached her, tenderly touching her mother's arm, looking long into her eyes. Her mother had long since accepted her own betrayal as, at least, partly her daughter's doing. Still, the touch was reassuring. She forgave her daughter and whispered her love. Her daughter smiled back and patted her chest.

She then slid something hard and metallic down the front of her blouse.

It felt small and cold, like a tin.

"Some for you, and the rest for me," the girl had told her.

This was a confusing statement.

But then the young girl slightly lifted the hem of her own dress to reveal the garter now strapped to her own thigh - with bones sticking out of the tiny pockets - where there was once were herbs.

"When those Monks buried those bones, they broke the knight's curse. I want it back. Your death will make it happen."

"What's... what's, in the tin?"

"You're taking the children back into the beck where they belong."

Joan continued to smile, but it wasn't a nice smile.

Not even remotely a nice smile.

Right there, Maude knew her daughter was beyond redemption. She screamed with all her might to have someone take the tin from her, but nobody listened as the beam was flung out over the beck. She thought quickly; making a counter-curse. Maude had always sensed and possessed the power, but used it for good, but now she had to bring an end to this. So she cursed everything: livestock; land; the Grobatard name, and above all, her own treacherous daughter. The river would not rest until her own treacherous daughter was reunited with her in the river.

On contact with the water, the stool broke off, and floated east.

People in the crowd lobbed stones at her.

It had rained and flooded the area in the weeks prior, nobody attempting to follow the drowning woman in the seat, carried away by strong currents. It was assumed with such a volume of water she would float as far as the Swale.

And, William Worthington watched from afar.

He instructed his closest followers to replace the seat for the future. He also ordered them to keep a careful eye on Joan Grobatard; regretting giving her the strap.

And in the interim years, it was clear the girl had upgraded its function, no longer using the garter for storing herbs and medicines. Six years on, children were mysteriously vanishing again - particularly from the Grobatard line - and the girl, now seventeen, had been spotted, standing on the river bank at the dead of night. He may have to deal with her shortly; sensing in his soul that a grave injustice had been miscarried. Now, at 56, his vision was the best it had ever been, and locals complimented him on his darker hair growth, and increased muscle tone. His mind was sharper, less forgetful... and while this was the case, he'd pay careful attention to preserving the record of Maude's execution.

~ ~ ~

This was the final snapshot. The children, the woman. The curse, manifesting all of this. There was nothing continually sentient here; everything, confused and detached from the other. This curse was like a residue. An imprint in the heavens, bound and sealed on earth. An album full of photos, taken in different eras, with many cameras.

And then, there was Rob.
Sitting in front of me at the bottom of the lock.
He was neither alive, nor dead. Neither physical nor spectral.
He was still trying to escape the pain of his own family's betrayal, and society's... just like Maude. Ol' Bobby had allowed him to become obsessed with the beck, and Rob had sensed the pain in the currents, in the children, in Maude. He completely related to the kindred spirits in here, and the beck, in turn, became infatuated with him.
Such horrendous, incalculable injustice drew one to the other.
I sensed confusion in him, part of him at least; still aiming to navigate the waterways to reach his Gran in Newhaven. Part of him fed off the river, in turn, the river

feeding off him. It learned from Rob that centuries had passed, and in the moments of conscious thought, the occupants had realised this limbo needed to end.

The strongest entity was the thing closest to Maude.

In Rob, she'd come to see him as the kidnapped boy, stored on her farm. She wanted him freed. She wanted him out!

Minutes ago, it had sensed the small bones in the garter around Serin's leg. The curse had nearly smoked itself out.

It sensed the end.

I looked at Rob once more, sitting there with his legs crossed, staring back at me.

He was neither here nor there. His mind was in some place, and no place. He had brought clarity to the river.

Crying underwater feels very, very strange.

~~~

I broke the surface, gasping; the hands that had pulled me down, now departed. I scanned the lock for the woman, certain she'd be right here to finish me off. But she was on the other side of the chamber once again; face, submerged from the nose down.

She'd told me what she wanted - waiting for the girl above her to be ducked - so she could take, and find peace. And if that meant, drowning Serin in the depths to get her own daughter's back, so be it.

I thought I saw her nod.

I knew what I needed to do.

Touching my chest a moment ago, she'd confirmed she knew I was a Worthington: *the enemy*. It had sensed me as a kid, wanting me in there. But, I'd been afforded the truth, and more importantly, *accepted it as such*. My family line had brought grave injustice, but I could restore justice. My sickness and faintness lifted immediately; no longer from the line of condemners...

And I had to release the garter from Serin's leg and give it back. The water was rising and nearly on a level with the bank.

As swiftly as three men dragged me out, their blades met with my throat. They were perturbed to be holding a wet peasant so closely; this I could tell.

'Mr Austin, why on this earth didn't you save yourself by swimming to the other side?'

I eyed the patriarch, not responding at first; grip, pain, and fear leaving me incapacitated.

'Speak up,' he said.

Unmoved, he stared instead at my saturation, as I checked on Hazel and Ishaq. Had he not seen Maude? Then, his eyes moved to the dislodged jigsaw piece mashed up in a pocket turned inside-out; now a soggy, congealed mess. Immediately, an irrepressible rage sparked across his face; a revolting outcome he couldn't remotely accept. He looked down and away, several times; the lead weight breaking the camel's back.

One piece short of a thousand could be my demise... finished off by Constable's Flatford Mill.

So I bluffed, earnestly buying time: 'I had no intention of escaping, Mr Grobatard. We both understand, with a name like mine, I have no need to run. In fact, I have come to administer justice.'

William took his comb out and continued grooming, slowly preening as he analysed this statement.

And then, to my right, and slightly behind, came an audible commotion; a disagreement between two parties.

Craig and Dove had arrived together - and despite being afforded only the briefest glance - they were clearly arguing over the pigs in the enclosure, and their distressed state. Dove was royally getting blamed for this. On seeing me, they stopped dead.

At first I anticipated I'd harmonised matters between them.

'*Why didn't you wait for me?*'

Once more Craig's dad ignored his son; instead addressing me. 'I'm tiring. I'm losing patience with you.' His eyes diverted to the bones I'd spilled on the bank, pure condescension lining his face now, like he only just missed treading on dog shit. 'You think she wants these… *bones?*'

Then he stared down at my phone; extrapolated before flinging myself in. Actually, *the last thing* I wanted him to look at.

'Tell your men to let me go, and as the two esteemed names here, we'll end this together.'

'I don't think so.'

Events were escalating at lightning speed, the crowd growing unsettled around me. At first, I assumed this was born from disgust: how *dare* Wat Tyler address the King in this manner? But, the gasping, murmuring and pointing was aimed over my shoulder, as they all began shrinking back from the water's edge towards the farmhouse wall; those closest to the beck, more earnest in persuasion.

'Grobatard. This needs ending *now*. I *know* how to end it.'

'You know nothing.'

Candles toppled in their retreat, several rolling over, and extinguishing.

My own private captors sensed this shift in mood, turning in shock, their grip seismically slackening as priorities altered: obedience, versus preservation. I knew she'd surfaced - no need to look.

They'd all seen.

Seizing my opportunity, I yanked with force, momentarily freeing myself, causing all three men to lose footing. Crouching, I grabbed at my phone and pointed up - face-recognition failing me - pass-code page appearing. Stabbing at the numbers, I got plain lucky, the screen shooting straight to messages. And I only needed to hit 'send' - get the prepped message away - but damp fingers failed me. In no time, I was grabbed - pulled further away - from the woman, rising from the depths behind me, her clawed hand stretching out on to the bank.

481

Phone still in hand, I pawed for the button, flicking to camera instead. I had to get this to Shizz.

Jostled away, I watched William toe-poking the rabbit bones and staring at the apparition in the beck.

His mouth sagged, as he stared, aghast.

For all his pomp and ceremony, he was finally facing the true power in his blood line, as I was brusquely forced past him, but managed to angle my head, studying every inch of his expression, while gripping my phone tight with all my might.

He suddenly roared down into the chamber, '*Why didn't you take her? I gave you an unblemished sacrifice.*' Then he kicked at the dusty rabbit bones, sending a couple into her face and saturated chest. 'You want these *filthy rags? Here, take them. You disgust me!*'

Anger chiselled his face. '*Is my sacrifice not good enough for you?*'

The woman in the water would not acquiesce, not even acknowledging the plopping bone fragments, sinking before her. Instead, she rose to waist height, directly facing him, propelled higher by unseen forces.

'Bring *him* back here,' Grobatard turned, barking at his men, before looking to Ishaq and Hazel. 'Bring them *all* here!'

Instantly I was catapulted down at the edge of the beck, closely followed by my friends. Out of the corner of my eye, I could see Serin - higher than any of us - grinding her leg against the chair, trying to relinquish the garter. To onlookers, she was futilely struggling to break her appendages. I saw the rope was slackening.

'*Why didn't you take him when you had the chance?*' William scalded Maude.

The woman with wet black hair remained impervious, unmoved...

So he puffed out his chest like a peacock, and with spittle coating his lips, jabbed his finger at me. '*His* family line brought our misery, *and your own sickening betrayal...* led to our downfall.'

Incandescent with rage now.

Maude didn't flinch.

'I have brought you *everything* you wanted. *Now take it...* and restore to us our rightful place.' He brutally kicked most of the remaining fragments at the uninterested apparition. 'Well, take them! *Take your dust!*'

Large, coarse hands held me down, but she didn't want to feed on me. I carefully eyed Serin, in need of buying more time, and despite my own imminent execution, goading this psycho might afford me some. 'Grobatard, you *should have* listened... you can't end this without me.'

He stooped, glaring in my face. 'Paupers fetch me *nothing*, unless I demand they do.'

There was something about his level of proximity, the hoarseness; the damp, stale breath - triggering the deep well of the *reactionary* within me. 'So, get in the river *right now* and barter!' I screamed. 'And prove yourself a true Grobatard. I guarantee she's in the mood.'

Maude was done staring him down, her eyes slowly shifting to Serin, to the garter.

And he noticed.

So I spoke quickly to distract. 'I know why you brought every one of your pigs here tonight, Grobatard. If you're going to release them, do it soon. She's cursed your livestock, hasn't she?'

This was a test - conjecture - but I suspected I was correct. Regardless, he'd amply noticed Maude's new line of enquiry, so I *hollered* for his attention. '*C'mon, old man!* It's a fresh start for the Grobatards. Canals or swine; which is it?'

Earlier, I'd learned from the trapped river children - the residue - how they'd cared dearly for their litter of piglets; both livelihood, and sustenance. The *curse* had commandeered all this; now grabbing any stray, wandering hog at any given opportunity. And William had noted this.

Now, he raised his hand to quiet me. 'She will get them... when I'm good and ready.'

He was intently studying Serin's wounded leg. Mercifully, he was *also* triggering his own son.

'Are you *kidding?*' Craig looked astonished. 'The pigs? Is this a joke?'

483

His father didn't reply.

Craig's mouth dropped. 'Is that why we've transferred them here?'

No reply.

'What are you doing to *our* pigs?'

'Told you it wasn't me,' Dove pathetically defended himself in the background.

'Shut-up, you idiot!'

Ignoring his son's protestations, Grobatard gave me his full attention, giving me license to rile him more. 'That's the curse, Craig,' I shouted. 'all your livestock was cursed. Look at that stone plaque in the ground. This is their final destination before you get a new role… as a cabin boy.'

'Tell me he's lying.'

His own facial contortion, was weirdly akin to a pig's snout - revulsion sweeping every corner - waiting on an ounce of his father's acknowledgment. But nothing came.

'Dad, tell me he's lying!'

I got another dig in. 'Look, Craig… they're squealing and shoving against the railings. They're ready to go. They sense their duty.'

Craig's nostrils flared, as he warily walked towards his father - keeping a wide berth from the spectral woman. He pointed at his father, and then back over his shoulder. *'That's a quid per kilo… back there. We can't afford to lose any more money.'*

'Exactly, exactly.' William pitied his own son. 'One pound profit, per kilo. Every other pig in this nation is commanding two-fifty at least, right now. We give, to get back *an abundance.'*

'No. They'll get better once that poisonous plant's completely removed. You said so yourself.'

'I lied.'

'What?'

Finally, William took his son with an arm, wrapping it assuredly around him, holding him tight.

'Look at them, my boy - every one, ravaged, emaciated - remaining in this putrid state until all is fulfilled. I have told you *much*, but the gold I have withheld you, until now.'

He held Craig closer, his demeanour switching instantly.

But Craig chastised him, 'You said it was *land* and *her alone* that would end all this.'

'Oh, it's more *for the glory.*'

An incredulous Craig stared up at Serin - his own daughter - valiantly struggling above. No love lost. No tender bond between them; pure, undefiled hatred. As she jolted even harder on the chair, wood shifting, finally splitting... she was beginning to prevail; wary not to topple into the beck. Maude below, prowled the surface, watching the bait above with lifeless eyes. On seeing her, Serin frantically started grinding the garter - flinching in exceptional pain - her furious momentum spilling a single bone from a torn pocket... into the water below.

That's when I knew it was over.

The physical embodiment of the curse, the woman, reached out her gnarled hand - clasping, then cupping her prize in a pallid palm, moistening it below the surface - and then sliding it down her throat. And the old man, who had been gently consoling his son, stopped doing so... abruptly withdrawing, diligently studying the wounds on his granddaughter's thigh once again.

And he realised.

Briefly, he poked his boot over the remnants of rabbit bones I'd dropped on the bank, launching the last couple directly at Maude; who was unfazed, undeterred. Then he looked up again, returning to Ishaq, patting him lightly on the shoulder. 'Oversight is such a curse, even for the very best of us. It appears what the councillor informed us was correct.'

'What's going on?' Craig demanded.

'Maude was a witch, and her garter is currently strapped to your daughter's thigh.' He turned back, watching the last of the rabbit bones sink. 'We have called Mr Austin's bluff.'

Then he shouted to his men, at the end of the beam. 'Unchain and send her down.'

Two hands, initially pressed hard against my shoulders - now, with the supernatural distractions - losing their force. No time left; the cleaver clung to sodden cotton on my chest. I needed it *out*. Thankfully, my hands had warmed. About to warm a lot more.

I dropped further, grabbed two candles, and flung out hot wax - enough connecting - the men instantly recoiling, clutching faces. Tearing through buttons and cloth, I yanked the blade partly out from its tip, and charged Hazel's way, deliberately tumbling into her.

'Take. Hide.'

I stood back upright, slamming my phone to my face, waiting... hitting send.

Serin was screaming. '*She wants to kill every one of you! She told me under the water. She kept me alive to tell you. Get this strap off me!*'

Father and son turned, her volume and pitch causing tremors of confusion all around. At the same time, I received a real farmer's punch; a proper Houdini. As I keeled-over, I saw Hazel shuffle over the cleaver, like a hen, an egg.

'Stop!' Grobatard commanded his men, while pointing to an older member of the family. 'Arthur, can I borrow that a second, please?'

The old man graciously nodded, handing over his walking stick, and William took it, immediately marching along the beam towards Serin. A seamless procedure - so fluid. 'Insolence.' He repeatedly smacked her around her shins and calves with the crooked pole. 'I will do this until you fall silent, and *then* for an extra five seconds, *whore.*'

Initially, she shrieked louder.

So he belted her even harder.

Until her eyes widened and the scream turned more staccato, pushing its way to the back of her throat, becoming a faltering drone. He threw the cane to the floor in disgust - and with a click of the fingers - I was summoned. 'Bring me the serf,' he pointed up. 'And, *for goodness' sake,* one of you put that gag back over its mouth.'

Sturdy men dragged my frame to my feet, while a more nimble lackey took care of Serin; clambering on to the plank, yanking the cloth from her forehead, down over her lips. The combined weight of two people hoisted aloft, now stretching the chain taut against the huge hook; the huge wooden implement creaking under the pressure.

Grobatard senior waited until this task was complete, before switching to me. 'You haven't handled this remotely well, have you now? *That poor Tipperton boy, you've abandoned.*'

Below, Maude - or the thing that was once Maude - was singularly focussed on Serin, fixing on her bare, reddened legs.

William nodded at his men. 'Squeeze him.'

I could have laughed - not even *torture him.* But the pain was horrendous, especially from the thicker fingers crushing nerves in my neck. Grobatard smirked at my contortions, studying my silent gaping mouth, before turning his attention to the Siren in the beck. 'You don't deserve *any* bones, you piece of filth.'

Maude only had eyes for the cucking stool.

'Oh, you can't even look at me when I'm talking,' he sneered.

Then he waved his extended family forward, beckoning them… gently encouraging the cowardly and reluctant; his dialogue, majestic. 'I can only apologise that I am larger than this curse. Come, together, let us commiserate this pathetic woman.'

He was a false prophet - a master of Machiavellian ceremonies - tapping into false beliefs, wrapping the broken Grobatard name in a pretty bow. And as the family drew nearer, the excited chatter increased; a couple even haranguing the apparition. Maude Grobatard paid them no attention. The new, exotic animal, constrained for the safety of others; the top freak in a banned sideshow.

For tens of seconds they all gawped, then someone shouted, '*They're gone!*'

Hazel and Ishaq.

Two separate pieces of pooled rope. Magnanimous of Hazel, to say the least.

With a solitary hand, Grobatard brushed it away, 'No matter; they won't reach anyone in time.'

The mesmerised crowds were now huddling in a tight pack, staring out. Everything felt disorientated. These were priceless seconds, and I prayed Ishaq had seen sense, and they'd bumped into Shizz on the track. She'd recognise him from the open forum, and probably punch him.

Finally, William Grobatard reduced the insane element of his ranting; his body movements calming. He took his comb in his hand. 'I'll put her in the river for me, not for you. I decide.'

Above, Serin exploded back to life, thrashing harder, fighting with everything. She was a carpenter by trade; shifting heavy lumps of wood was standard. When she finally smashed her right arm off the chair with the rope around her wrist - I was hardly surprised - tussling with all her might, knowing this was her last stand. And as the seat began to shake… something cracked along the entire length of the supporting plank - far past the fulcrum - straight to the chain hooked to the ground.

The chair was new; the surrounding wood wasn't.

The original instrument of torture: rotting in the barn for centuries - long before we discovered it as kids - now, splitting before my eyes. Serin momentarily stopped, realising she'd be *sent down,* anyway. The beam was teetering on disintegration, a gaping hole forming horizontally; the first dive in 250 years, it's last.

His men might not even need to unchain. Serin looked over her shoulder, resuming her frantic mission. Hers, was now Hobson's choice.

And then the inexplicable occurred.

The hovering, undulating mist - anchored in its ethereal position - immediately, and forcibly sucked from the surface, sprawling out over the bank, roaring past his family like a wind funnel. All standing Grobatards, young and old alike, toppled in the tumult; the cloud hammering through gaps in arms and legs, battering into the side of the old farm house. And there, the crisp white clung to the stone - candles flickering, but not extinguishing - as it sought an exit, the mass steadily tipping around the corner - sand, slowly spilling from an inverted timer - before cascading at volume. Out into the darkest of farmyards, leaving only lingering vapor trails as it vanished into the black of night.

An eerie vacuum was left in its wake, a ringing in the ears... a palpable, prolonged silence.

Grobatard walked over to the table, grabbed the ceremonial knife, and marched over to me. '*Hold him tight!*'

Bye to planet earth.

'So I gather, you have no children,' he said. 'No descendents. And a name... a mere smudge in the annals of... somewhere. No heir.'

Halfway through his discourse, I heard the angels.

Their heraldic chorus rising out.

So I looked up, smirking, fixing past the crooked blade, staring directly into his eyes. 'Speaking of heirs, William, your royal bloodline comes direct from the conqueror himself, correct?'

'You are correct.'

'Remind me again.' I held my glare. 'In history, *isn't* William also known as... William the Bastard?' I let it resonate, as he slowly started shaking with rage. So I eye-balled him more, letting my own fiery intensity pierce his soul. 'And your family name - *Grobatard* - doesn't that translate in French as... *fat bastard.*'

Pole-axed, numbed to his core. The offense was great, but it quickly dissipated - as he attuned to the sound of *drumming* over the earth.

The text had been sent.

A thousand-drill thudding of catastrophic proportions. No melody; only power... and incessant pounding. Closer. Loud. Relentless.

A colossal swarm of swine, released from dank, oppressive enclosures... pitching around the corner of the house, flooding towards the only available light. Squealing, jostling, covering every inch of ground - endlessly marauding forward - aiming for the river bank. Ample space, now rapidly dwindling... as they ballooned out, brainlessly charging hell-for-leather with no brakes; *no concept of braking.*

Strong grips on my shoulders weakened, in alarm.

Two older family members fell, getting trampled, while two others inadvertently stepped back, tumbling into the beck. They screamed in fear, and splashed, slamming palms against water. Grobatard's lock had generated quite the current.

And the pigs continued pushing and cajoling as they fought for the straightest path down; dirty trotters colliding and bustling into, over one another, as they caught sight of their destination.

'Not yet... *Who* released them?' Grobatard screamed.

I had.

Shizz specifically.

Waiting in the shadows on the track.

I'd hoped their release would be distracting enough for me to free the captives. *It was so much better.*

Bizarrely, William Grobatard was smiling, unable to contend with a new emotion; the guilty laughing in court at the seriousness of their own crimes. But now he, and his entire family, faced the firing squad, *hundreds* of pigs - flying like bullets - ramming humans into the water. Men and women screeched, trying to retrieve their fallen, before being battered in themselves. The cane-less old man - Arthur, his name - tumbled in with no hope of reprieve.

Completely released, I sprang up, and charged at the ducking stool, pole-vaulting a rabid pig. Serin's executors had momentarily stopped, staggered themselves by wave-after-wave ploughing through the upright.

For a second, I caught sight of the bubbling waters, *and froze.*

The reason why *no one* was getting out.

Dozens of tiny hands thrusting up from the deep, gripping, securing the fallen in a drowning choke-hold. No matter how hard they tugged back, the harrowed children were taking down the knights of Grobatard. They sensed their own imminent release from a thousand year entrapment.

None were letting go.

'Send her down!' William commanded, in that high-pitched screech, but his sentries had long since deserted their post. His victory was being snatched in an inconceivable instant - beyond the realms of his pompous planning - and he was no longer smiling, because he could very well *die here, a*long with his family name.

I hoisted myself on the beam, as it groaned under my weight. Serin had broken two arm straps, and I smashed the remaining chair legs with my elbow to release the others. The huge planked couldn't hold at all, fracturing again near the fulcrum; two new horizontal apertures, appearing and widening.

She pulled up the gag. 'I can free the strap,' she reached down, grasping the last buckle, '*What the hell is in it?*'

'It's a witch's garter. It belongs to the woman down there. Maude. Your mum made you wear it.'

'*Why?* She made me *swear* to wear it.'

'She made you wear it for protection.'

'*For prot-*'

'Your mum's discovered a part to this curse - no one saw - not even me. She knew you'd only *ever* be kidnapped and brought here by your *own* family. That's what she wanted.' I untethered, pulling the last remaining rope apart. 'Maude wants this garter, and the ghost kids want you dead.'

'What? *Why? This is madness.*'

'You're a Grobatard by blood, and your bloodline murdered those kids centuries ago.'

Serin looked aghast. 'I haven't done a thing.'

'It doesn't matter. Everything down there's in direct, confused conflict with one another, but this strap insures you against both. You *have* what the *other* wants, so there's a stand-off. Maude wants the bones, they want your blood.' I held the rope aloft; she was free. 'In the melee, your mother's arranged your family to gather, to take them out in style. That's why you didn't drown.'

Serin had no time to look puzzled, bending forward to grab my shoulders.

'The pockets... *have bones in them?*'

'Did you ever look?'

'No, mum made me swear.'

'Yep, you've been wearing a dead person for years.'

She scowled, holding out the leather strap, but then immediately screamed. '*Billy, behind...*'

A large frame smashed me.

Pigs were absolutely everywhere, filling the entire bank side - pitching people into the beck - before launching themselves in pink, hairy bodies crashing down onto shoulders and faces.

But what smashed me was no pig...

I tumbled off the beam, bear-hugged by Grobatard. It was enough to partially wind me, as he strengthened his clasp, garroting me with his fat fingers. 'What have you done, you pathetic man?'

He hammered my ribs with his knee once more, and despite wedging my arms under his forearms, his insanity was governing his level of power. Such was his blood-lust, pushing was useless. Over his shoulders, I saw Shizz, Hazel and Ishaq arriving at the corner of the farmhouse.

Their mouths, agape. Too far away, and too many dead, and littered obstacles.

Carnage reigned around us. Complete pandemonium. More and more of the clan were being sent into the river, concussed, knocked unconscious, and dragged down by children's hands. More pigs launched on top of them. And more pigs over them. The Grobatard leader was aware of the calamity.

He'd see me dead, if nothing else.

So, he pushed me back towards the river parallel with the beam, grunting with exertion.

I couldn't do a thing.

But, Serin could - both legs - now freed.

And she used her right one, despite the pain of purplish bruising, to kick him square in his temple. Her height was perfect, as was the point of her shoe; swiftly and powerfully connecting. His grip departed, and he staggered, his legs giving way. Something kept him upright - desire, demons - I don't know, but it looked like he'd toppled drunkenly onto a wedding reception dance floor, too inebriated to care.

I took full advantage.

In a sweeping movement, I reached up, grabbed the garter from Serin, and darted behind him.

My adversary was powerless, as I wrapped the leather tight around his neck and buckled two catches. He stumbled forwards, clutching his neck, trying to relinquish the hold, but the hefty hit had rendered him senseless. He made a choking sound, despite sufficient slack for him to breathe. It made me despise him even more; such a drama queen.

And his strength wasn't returning, however, Serin's was... in spades. As was her vitriol; and a strong sense of injustice. Down from the stool now, and slapping him repeatedly, screaming her disdain in his face.

She clenched her hands into a ball and pounded him.

Ironically, we were safer here with our backs against the ducking stool - as a continual flurry of pink crashed the last few family members into the beck. The thrashing and splashing was astonishing. A kids' pool party on speed. More pigs than people littered the surface, as their volume and weight pressed people under. I watched Dove trying to swim to the side, and a solitary pig dive straight into his face, knocking him cold.

Only Craig had escaped the throng, making his way back to farmhouse wall, next to the last standing candles, virtually all being scattered around the lawn.

'*Billy!*'

I swivelled, seeing Ishaq, who'd made it to the *chain end* of the beam.

Friend or foe? Heinous, or helpful? I swallowed, but, he'd been trying to hold the wood in place all along, while Serin disembarked.

'Stay there!' I shouted.

493

Blood covered Grobatard's lips. I grabbed Serin's hand, 'Stand aside.'

She looked appalled at my request, but she needn't have been. I took a long look for the ghost of Maude, but in the frenzy, couldn't see her. That wouldn't stop me; she'd find him. I grabbed William Grobatard around the front of his chest, propelling him backwards, quickly gaining speed… aiming straight for the beck.

'This is for Scarlett *Wilmott*.'

I threw him over the edge.

Fewer pigs occupied the waters to the lock's east side, and the patriarch went straight down like a sack of shit. Freezing waters snapped at his senses, and he rose to the surface, gasping for air; less than two metres from the edge. Shock etched his face, as he struggled against the frothy wake, buffeting him to and fro within the chamber.

High above him, I looked up at the broken chair still partly attached to the thick wooden beam.

Then I heard the scream, and swivelled - Ishaq and Craig fighting - Craig prevailing, securing a choke-hold.

I charged back.

He'd blindsided me as a kid, as I fought to help Rob, and then kicked me repeatedly in the head, so I made sure I landed an instant left hook, splitting his eyebrow. This was on. He released the councillor as I followed in with a right - and semi-uppercut that part-connected with his chin, slipping more onto his nose. Instinctively, he swung a curler, an all-or-nothing, but it was wild - missing by a mile - so I winded him with a knee to the gut.

Ishaq backed away towards the wall, grabbing his own throat.

Hazel, however, was on the scene, advancing. Hunched over, Craig broke away and staggered in the direction of the river to help his father. But Hazel was on him in a heartbeat. 'That's for my *best friend*.'

An instant, swift action… causing his shift to a lurching movement. Reaching the centre of the cucking stool, he tipped sideways propped up by the fulcrum; the cleaver sticking out his shoulder blade at an angle. The tip was too broad to slice straight in, so she'd shelved it in his back.

Hazel accompanied him with his every jagged step, shouting obscenities, declaring his sins of mistreatment. For a moment he stopped, his own eyes widening as Hazel screeched right in his face. There was no point him even reaching round to extrapolate the blade. *He couldn't*; recipient of the perfect rotator cuff injury. It was sticking.

'You okay?' I turned, checking on Ishaq.

'Bil- I-I thought… if I led him to the bones, he'd release Serin. I didn't know until you called… he said it was only *ever about the land*.'

I nodded, but that's all I did.

Satisfied of no lasting damage, I headed towards the river to rejoin Serin. Hazel had left Craig flopped against the frame, hugging the plank with his one working arm. William thrashed in the water below. He was enraged, commanding Serin to help him out; the patriarch, facing the bank and pulling closer.

And that's when the wooden beam split in its entirety.

No longer capable of supporting the weight of Craig - the straw on the camel's back - nor its own decrepit age. It tore asunder above the fulcrum, smashing Grobatard junior straight under his chin, launching him skyward. And at the other end… over a thousand kilos crushed the head of Grobatard senior in a gargantuan impact. As the beck swallowed the wood, he went straight under again, like a python slithering in a hole.

Further and further he sank, trapped under its hellacious weight.

I knelt and studied his descent; amazed… until he was obscured by black. All around, the noise slowly subsiding. *Surely*, that was it.

But then he broke the surface in a pool of red, right in front of me, head split from brow to crown; blood pouring from the crevice, broken skull, and pinkish chunks. He reached out gargling, spouting complete gibberish, eyes still shining with that bespoke madness. *But, this was madness.*

On my knees, I stared at the deep gash, into his crazed face, as he clawed for the bank. And, then I realised, he didn't want help out… he wanted *me in*. His fingers made a grabbing motion, as he punched them out at me, clasping at thin air - nowhere near. So, I stared at his calamitous wound, reached down to the grassy bank, immediately to my left…

And handed him his comb.

'That's quite the centre parting.'

Temporarily, he stared at it - nestled in his palm - conflicted, and instinctively drawing it to his hairline, to preen, to beautify. And for the briefest millisecond, unbelievably, he considered this was his intention all along. Then, he dropped the comb over his shoulder. So, I stretched across the bank for the mashed up jigsaw piece, raising it slightly.

'*This?*'

Again, his eyeballs widened; whites of which, I'd never seen the size of, in such brain damaged confusion.

But then he started to choke, and I noted Serin stepping away, closely followed by Hazel - as a gnarled hand emerged from the waters - its cragged nails immediately snaking their way under the leather strap secured to his neck… *viciously* wrenching it.

The half-dead man, froze in time a moment more; perhaps experiencing genuine terror, or maybe *real* pain… possibly his own sense of skewed injustice, right till the bitter end.

And then, slowly, spluttering every inch of the way, he was dragged completely under.

At first, I studied the clumps of hair, clotted blood, and severed flesh floating to the surface, like some frivolously decanted Merlot - with fragments of cork - but then the waters settled, leaving only the occasional air bubble.

Everything fell strangely quiet.

And then, something bluish, whitish… flashed the entire length of the river, from west to east. A sudden light, no one outside this location, bar nighttime fishers or riverside campers, would even register. Motorway drivers would attribute it to a clicked *full beam* from oncoming traffic.

After this, all that remained, was death.

Shizz stood by me now, her hand covering her lips. Voices enquired after one another, before silence resumed again. It was a time to take stock; to stop and wonder... with a backdrop of bodies, and toppled candles. I turned, and stared at the snapped cucking stool, Craig lying prostrate to one side, the impact, clearly breaking his neck. Then, a warm hand reached over my shoulder, securing me with soft, perfectly manicured nails.

'You okay, Bill?' I took hold of it fully, gratefully so, as Verity stared at the chaotic aftermath, slowly shaking her head. 'I can't... believe what I'm seeing.'

Wide-eyed, in stark disbelief, my PA's mouth hung loose alongside mine, for many, many seconds, until she finally muttered. '... public-relations disaster.'

I nodded. 'Saved my bacon, Shizz.'

She quietly waited for me to substantiate on the idiom while I squeezed a thank-you again into her hand.

'Releasing those pigs,' I said.

'Pardon?'

'Perfect timing.'

Again, she paused, giving great consideration to my statement, 'Bill, I did no such thing.' She rubbed perspiration from her brow.

'What do you mean?'

'I didn't release any. I was waiting on your message.'

'My message?'

'Yeah. You said you'd send me a text.'

I looked up her long arm, into her face, showing her my confusion.

'Telling me when to let them out,' she said. 'You said you'd message.'

Blown away by the surrounding devastation, I nearly let this go. The scene, the duel... all so nuclear. So much had happened, and I could barely piece together the last minute, let alone the preceding ten. The river was absolutely shambolic; rammed with torsos and torn clothing, strewn between each lock gate. It all appeared so alien, like we'd stumbled on the aftermath of a cult massacre. My knuckles hurt like hell, and my heart hammered. Nevertheless, I reached over to my phone, discarded on the grass, face recognition bringing it straight to messages, and the *action* one I'd prepared, and sent.

But the writing was still in the box.

Unsent.

I puzzled over this as Shizz clarified. 'After I bumped into Hazel, and punched Ishaq on the track, we came down the slope, and they were already out.'

'What?'

'Well, more than out… the gates had blown clean off.'

I stared up. 'Are you serious?'

'Yeah, and those gates are *huge.*'

'Tell me.'

'Well, they were blown right to the other side, past your car.'

I was on the verge of enquiring further, when Hazel said, 'Billy, can you hear that?'

She was listening for the source, staring up and down the length of the river.

'I can, too.' Serin concurred.

It was easterly. A low level whistle, or hum… gently generated by the beck. At first I was puzzled, as the intensity and pitch grew and grew. I'd shakily clambered to my feet, just as Hazel exclaimed a lengthy, emotional: '*Oh my… look.*'

And so I did, and there it was.

A solitary boat.

Moving… steadily floating up the river, wholly against the current, and the laws of physics.

I stepped away, although I wasn't really experiencing fear; far too desensitised to the surrounding carnage. But the sense of wonder, and foreboding now hit somewhere deep in my stomach. I rubbed my eyes, but it was still coming, still approaching. Two hands drooping over the hull on either side. Wet wrists, fingers.

As Shizz looked on in horror, shit suddenly got very real for me. I found myself turning away; realising I couldn't *possibly* look.

'We need to call the police... immediately,' Ishaq declared.

This from councillor Khan.

Hands went to phones, and screens, and simultaneously pressing the same lower right digit.

I wanted to be sick.

The boat stopped in front the lock's east gate; a clear mound of clothing concealed within. And as the strange flash came a final time, the hands gently slid down from the side of the hull and disappeared inside.

A vessel, three out of the five of us instantly recognised.

Invisible forces moored it to the spot.

Chapter 16

Hand Me Downs

Medics kindly brought blankets.

Warm, and shiny.

A major incident, where the survivors are identified by their silver reflectivity… and plastic cups of tea appear from the back of ambulances. The four of us congregated around the back of one, taking it in turns to sit on the ramp. Plenty of ramps, on plenty of ambulances to choose from, but a consensus was made to stay by one furthest from the farm track, and incoming media, nearest the broken cucking stool.

Our fifth, and most severely injured member, was inside being treated.

Verity rightly instructed us all to take photos of our various wounds. A surprisingly lengthy process, adrenalin masking a lot of swelling.

Hazel and Ishaq had been assaulted before even reaching the bank, and tied by Grobatard's henchmen. No wonder Hazel had absolutely lost it with Craig. At this juncture, we all compared notes and quietly aligned Hazel's account. I'd brought the cleaver in the first place to release them all, hence a serrated blade, and she was protecting Serin when she stabbed Craig from behind.

His was the first body to be removed. Ironically, a combination of blunt force trauma from the beam, and splinters in his neck finished him, long before the knife ever could.

Within an hour, helicopters were flying overhead.

Police at first, then press.

Abject horror and undiluted perplexity lined the faces of *every* emergency services member attending. Multiple times, we explained the sequence and order of events. So much so, Shizz coined a phrase that provided a welcome context for the police. 'Just think, Jonestown meets Peppa pig.'

Ishaq and I were the most recognisable.

Hazel gave him daggers as he talked about his own initial capture, but having the local councillor explain matters acted as a buffer, especially in such a visceral location. He had his *own story* to get straight; very much dependent on our goodwill.

Regardless, shock was setting in for us all, and there were genial discussions between medical and police professions about our general mental state, as much as our physical health. Unprecedented confusion reigned amongst them, throughout: this was a scene like *no other*. Where do you begin?

I heard them repeatedly whispering Shizz's analogy as they fought to process an ounce of what they saw.

Around the side of the farmhouse, back up the track, I knew unprecedented levels of satellite vans would either already be here, or on their way. So, it was jointly agreed that Hazel, Serin and Ishaq be transferred to hospital - under police guard - and me and Verity would stay and field questions, helping with enquiries. Shizz was the perfect foil in scenarios like these.

In many ways, I should have been the one whisked away first.

But, there was another matter to attend to.

I noticed slight variations in regional dialects as it became clear this farm was sucking personnel from far and wide. Shizz showed me some red-bar headlines on her phone. It had taken thirty-six minutes for this to become: "Breaking News: Major Incident declared in North Yorkshire."

Over her shoulder I saw the police divers arrive, some sucking on coffee temporarily as they kitted up. An hour ago, they were fast asleep, but their call to attend was imperative. Discussions surrounding safety were paramount, and the lock gates were rigorously checked.

The detectives were courteous and professional, though incredulous looks appeared within fifteen seconds of our event depiction - particularly, the supernatural component - which consistently raising eyebrows that stayed firmly *aloft*. It helped that pigs were piled about six feet high above the surface of the water in the lock. In terms of incredible, unbelievable scenes, this sight alone made the inspectors pay careful attention to my every word.

Shizz and I were brought a sandwich each. She had her first ever roast beef and horseradish and loved it. I didn't think I could stomach it, but as soon as it touched my lips, I was absolutely ravenous. Coffee was being supplied regularly. Then, wise - plain clothes people - appeared around us, who were clearly some kind of trauma counsellors, and despite their own astonishment, they were high on empathy and professional in conduct.

Hours passed.

I began to feel completely drained.

Things were now sinking in for me... one thing in particular.

And Shizz rested her head on my shoulder at frequent points, comforting me.

'Is this your girlfriend?' one officer asked.

'Yep,' I replied.

'Yeah... we met through the cult,' Shizz said, too tired to argue.

Eventually, it was agreed that, to follow the necessary protocols, we both should be taken to hospital too. The wounds on my neck had been examined, and all seemed well, but precautions needed taking. As we hopped into the back of the ambulance, we watched carcasses being unloaded on the grass.

Bodies would be coming up next.

I didn't want to see those.

I was helping my exhausted PA into the back of the ambulance, when a young detective caught me off-guard and tapped me on the hind leg. 'Sorry, Mr Austin?'

She had questions about *the body in the boat.*

None of us had gone near, when it first sailed upstream, and positioned itself. With all the bodies floating around us, it was potentially *one more for the law* and health professionals to deal with.

But, it wasn't. It never was. Not for me.

It was the end of a dream, the end of my nightmare… the final glimmer of a ridiculous hope, evaporating in a heartbeat. I'd seen him under the water earlier today, but, I hadn't seen *him.*

Before departing to the hospital for their check-up and monitoring, the last thing Hazel agreed to do, was formally identify the bundle. My courage failed me. Hazel stood a distance as she did so - at the edge of the beck, with a police officer and a torch - and then she immediately headed to a designated ambulance, a little away beyond us. I couldn't speak to her, but she was walking rigidly; her face, ashen. She repeatedly tried catching my eye - to confirm - but I looked away on every single occasion. Hazel was nodding a lot at someone who may have been a pathologist.

Confirmation.

Nevertheless, it blindsided me when the young detective - standing by my calf - asked me: "If I knew the *deceased's mother?"*

'The deceased?'

'Yes, Robert Tipperton.'

'Ahh, okay.'

A hand slid over my neck and shoulder from behind me. Shizz was alert and attuned to any thunderbolt nuances heading my way. In times like these, you needed a discerning friend, high on emotional intelligence, and Shizz-banger was bang-on in every regard. My heart was broken.

'Robert,' I repeated, looking down at the ramp. Then, I registered the gravity of her question above my level of pain. 'What do you mean, the deceased's mother?'

'The old lady on the opposite side of the river.' she pointed to the cattle bridge. 'She claimed she was his mother. Do you know her?'

I paused for a second, and then stood up and stretched, trying to peer over copious amounts of people at the bank's side. Spotlights shone down into the waters; everything on the other side, rendered as black as the night.

'Sorry. Whoever it was, couldn't possibly have been his mother.'

My own voice sounded croaky. The detective was in her twenties, formal, but possessed an intuitive glint in her eyes. She stared down at her notebook briefly. 'Oh, okay. She mentioned she was a resident in a care home. One of our officers just escorted her back there. It's nearby, isn't it? In Leeming?'

'Yeah, over there.' I pointed north-easterly.

'Yes.'

'Yes, that's right. Rob's mother's in there. In a *wheelchair.* She has dementia. Not mobile, sadly.'

The young detective immediately frowned. 'Suzanne Tipperton,' she said.

'Yes, that's correct.'

'*Not* mobile?'

'Absolutely.'

She stared down at her notebook. 'Well, the dementia explains a lot.'

'What, over there?' I pointed, the unusual nature of this, snapping me more awake.

'Yes.' She turned and pointed directly across the river. 'We're not sure how she got here, or how she even knew about all this?'

I turned to Shizz. 'Did you see an old woman?'

'No.'

'She said to call her Suzy, and that she knew you,' the detective said.

'I'm sorry, you are?'

'Detective Inspector Courtney.'

'Yes, that's correct. Suzy... Suzy Tipperton.' I was knackered, and slightly bewildered. 'But the home's half-a-mile from here. There's *no way* she could get out, and cross fields like these at the dead of night. Not in her state.'

DI Courtney nodded in agreement. 'Well, that's what puzzled me and my colleague. She appeared from nowhere, said we'd found her son, but she didn't want to identify him formally.' The young woman cleared her throat. 'And she specifically asked we pass on to you a sincere, *thank you.*'

Shizz's hand froze on my shoulder.

The detective continued. 'She claimed her son paid her a little visit tonight, not too long ago, and her boy was back to his old self.'

I was speechless. 'What?'

The detective was struggling to understand this herself. For her, this didn't fit the sequence of events we'd been discussing: kidnapping, ducking stool, mad men, mountains of pigs...

'It's just,' she started up again, pausing... wrestling with the next line, 'Mr Austin... you've previously claimed that Robert Tipperton disappeared in 1984, aged nine. That's correct, isn't it?'

Everybody knew this.

Everybody had heard my testimony. This had been extensively investigated, documented, unearthed and repeatedly analysed - particularly of late. She wasn't doubting what I said, just confirming it.

'I'm sorry, detective. Please be plain with me. Is there something else happening?'

'The deceased hasn't aged... *at all.*'

'Pardon? I'm sorry?'

Hazel alone had approached the beck, identifying his body. The woman before me waited, registering my bewilderment. 'I'm so sorry to tell you this. *I* don't understand how it's even possible myself; I wondered if you might have any ideas.'

I was flabbergasted, understanding the expression for the very first time. Breathless, winded; *no clue* how to respond. 'I-'

'Mr Austin, let me read you these, okay?' The young detective quickly checked her notes, pointing to lines with a pen. 'Suzy… *Mrs Tipperton*… said she was proud of her son for helping the children… that he'd agreed to go in there… providing he could sail away to his Grandma's later, in Newhaven.'

She stopped, pulled her pen to her lips, and studied me, wearing a baffled expression. 'Do you know, what any of that means?'

My chin was stubbly, and I rubbed it, flummoxed by every syllable; the combined crash of confirmation, and mystery.

DI Courtney gave me a little time to tackle the information. Out of respect, she'd wisely reconsidered her full-on approach. Then she reached into her pocket.

'Here,' she said, 'this is the final thing; no more questions for now. His mother - if this really was - his mother, asked me to give you this.'

With her note pad in one hand, she went for her pocket, immediately struggling to remove something. 'Suzy said… that when her son visited her in the night, he'd given her this to pass on to you.'

Finally, she extracted it, leaving her pocket half hanging out.

And placed the object straight into my palm.

A blue and yellow ribbon folded carefully together, attached to a metal star. A medal. I just… held it there, staring. Right there in my open hand.

In the centre of the star, the word: Winner.

I rolled it between finger and thumb, letting the ribbon unfurl, and delicately sag in my hand. Time seemed to condense into a solitary point of revelatory meaning.

Winner.

Then I flipped it over; an equally good and bad idea. Something was engraved on the back. It was small, and it was jagged; a kid's handwriting - hastily composed - possibly using the sharp point of a school compass. I pushed it up to the ambulance door light poking out from the top, studying it intently.

Thanks for fighting with me.
… You deserved this victory.

I flipped it back to the front side once more, clasping it firmly in my fingers.

The medal, mistakenly given, the night I beat him at table tennis.

I stared down at it some more.

The fabric, the stripes.

Two distinct, juxtaposed colours… matching our family crest.

I turned to look at Shizz, who held my gaze.

'You're about to go, aren't you?'

A flood of emotion crashed through me.

Chapter 17

Just In Time

My stay at my relatives' wedding was brief.

Service, reception, food, speeches… and then I departed. No fuss. That side of the family completely understood.

A lovely day, and welcome respite: a change in scenery, and mood. I wondered if I'd ever learn to celebrate as whole-heartedly as this ever again. It felt good to experience others' joy so soon, albeit vicariously.

I came back to my lodgings and met the farmer who owned it. He'd popped in for a natter and was determined to keep my location a private matter. And he'd also added traffic cones on his grass verges outside the arched wall, just in case. I was so grateful for this, and promised to compensate him for the many broken picture frames.

This was my final evening with Shizz before Cass arrived and they headed to the Dales. So, she'd extensively studied and ordered a wine purchase that afternoon. Slapping back the red with her was far more fun than keeping company with connoisseurs and dignitaries, who constantly bragged about their honed taste buds.

Six bottles of Shiraz, and a bottle of ale, awaited in the open plan lounge.

Shiraz - because my PA insisted it was named after her - and some Old Peculiar for me (as a reminder).

I was half-cut when I took a video-call from Simone Chapdelaine later that evening. A true friend indeed, he was painstaking in highlighting the merits of at least three States where he owned 'escape' homes from the ensuing the media frenzy. He was concerned for my welfare and mental wellbeing, avidly following events.

He wanted to make a movie about it, and use my newly purchased farm as a base for his film crew..

'Yeah, not just yet.'

I'd been in constant touch with Hazel, Ishaq, and Serin, over the last three days, between copious police interviews..

Messages flew back and forth, and even if it only came via a screen, I wanted to catch up. Ishaq and I needed to lay it out straight, at some point. Hazel, meanwhile, was suffering incredible remorse for her actions, but I reminded her that Craig was heading in Serin's direction, when she intervened. The knife alone wouldn't have killed him. To get her mind off things, I'd called her up; arranging delivery of a box of Milk Tray for Sheila. Then I enquired about Suzy, told her about the detective, but most of all, I wanted to discuss Rob.

The line fell eerily silent as soon as I began.

Eventually, she spoke. 'Sorry, Billy, but that's not possible on several fronts.'

'I literally have the medal in my hands, Hazel.'

'Not possible.'

'Well, the police interviewed her, and one brought her back.'

Again, everything went deathly quiet, on the other hand.

'Hazel, is it possible that someone wheeled Suzy down to the other side, and left her there for the cops to discover?'

'After midnight?'

'Yes.'

'No.'

'Well, how else could she get there?'

'She died at 5:50pm.'

My jaw dropped in utter disbelief. 'That… can't be.'

'I have a head's up on this, actually. It's already been mentioned by the duty staff working that evening. I've also already checked the CCTV. You can see the nurses meeting the officer by the front door, and immediately he starts turning in full circles. He's asking them, if they've already taken her inside. He goes rigid when they tell him, the news. If you check the driveway camera, when he initially pulls in... he's by himself. There's absolutely no one in the passenger seat.'

I stared down at the blue and yellow ribbon in astonishment.

'Then, how did I get this?'

'We've had our fair share of the bizarre, for years, Billy,' Hazel clarified, intrigue rising in her tone. 'It's another case, of letting it lie. One for the campfire.'

It turns out, the oddities didn't end there, either.

I'd face-timed Ishaq for more inside info from his end, but not before setting the record straight. He'd realised too late, what was going on. He thought the location of Joan Grobatard... would close the matter. It was the first time I'd seen him weep. Rob's disappearance had wrecked him from the very first day. His attempts to atone, driving him to the edge of irrational thinking, and perceived solutions.

I changed topic; getting him on to William Grobatard.

According to Ishaq, he'd been dragged from the river headless, and his left hand was missing; completely severed from his body. It was a grisly, grotesque image - but befitting - Maude not even bothering to loosen the buckles. The left hand, though? It seems he also had various *deep* bite marks all over his head, and at first I wondered if Maude - or whatever it was - had tried chewing his whole face off in revenge.

'No, not from a *human mouth*, Billy...' he mysteriously replied. 'These were bites from a predatory fish.'

'Sorry?'

'Yeahhh,' he teased, 'like an over-sized... *pike* or something?'

'A pike?'

'Ring any bells?'

'Oh my goodness! *Basil?*'

His eyes twinkled with intrigue as he stared into my own. 'Maybe he was caught in the curse too? Who knows?'

'Maude gone. Hogweed, nearly. Basil… the new king of the beck. Brilliant.'

Every member of the Grobatard clan had perished that evening, all except one - an older teen, trapped between pig carcasses and bodies - in a spot close to the west gate of the lock. They'd found an air-pocket, by all accounts. I wondered what this kid's take would be, when they were finally in a position to be interviewed.

'And there's something else, that's got me intrigued,' he added. 'Not sure if you can help.'

'Go on.'

'All those bone fragments in the tin were tested. There was one anomaly.'

I stared at the exhausted councillor over the screen. 'Okay.'

'All the finger bones were a thousand years old, except for two.'

He waited for me to look surprised, but I wasn't.

I'd been thinking a great deal about my immersion at the bottom of the lock. The water, a conduit to a set of sensory mementos; segments and events in the curse's chronology. I'd drawn many inferences, and I raised a finger to stop Ishaq from continuing. 'One pair matches with the age of Maude. Am I correct?'

'Yes!' He was staggered. 'How on earth could you know that?'

I recalled William Worthington's heart-wrenching pain as he stood before Maude. My family tree could have ended right there. I sighed. 'The voices of children on your tape recording. We heard Olde English, *and Latin, remember?*'

He waited, fascinated by my reference, eager for me to explain, but it had become a personal matter, so I kept it brief, and purposefully vague.

'An educated boy was sent into the river with Maude.'

511

'What?' He wore his consternation incredibly well. 'So, *she did-*'

'No, no.' I raised my hand to stop him again. 'No, she didn't kill anyone.'

'So, was he a Grobatard?'

I shook my head slowly, sadly... and he could tell I was done speaking on the matter. 'No, Ishaq. Sadly, he wasn't.'

Later that particular day, after another conference call with Simone had ended (about a potential sequester in his remote residence in Northern Montana), I met-up with Serin in a secluded spot in a cafe-garden in Masham.

Serin said her mum *insisted* on revisiting Ivy farm, two-ish months prior to passing. Then she *absolutely insisted* on returning the following day - with a spade this time - despite Serin and Hazel's protestations.

She told Serin she had a "pivotal duty to perform. *No bones about it.*"

'Is that the exact phrase she used?' I laughed, sipping from a teacup in a pretty, flowered courtyard.

'Yeah, she kept repeating it, too. Had a twinkle in her eye, every time.'

I wistfully, nodded. 'I bet she did. Your mum arranged a huge game of hide and seek for me, but left the biggest clue in plain sight.'

'Well, hopefully not too plain,' she coyly smiled, flicking her curly hair. 'So, you figured out I was secretly wearing the strap all along? You're smart.'

I pulled out a Kretek, offering her one from the packet, before flicking the lighter. I took a long drag, staring down at the cloves. 'Yep. Very smart.'

'She prepared me for it, y'know; the week she died. Made me swear every day... and then, the morning she passed, revealed it. I thought she'd be giving me some old necklace; an hierloom.'

'Must have been a shock.'

'Yeah, it felt weird wearing it. I didn't like it, but I kept my word.' She shook her head, muttering the last part to herself. 'So glad I didn't look in any pockets.'

I flicked ash in to the tray. 'Yeah, I can only imagine. How's your leg?'

She lifted the hem of her cream dress to reveal the bandage. 'So, *so* sore… but better than being dead.'

'Give it a few weeks. If the scars bother you, I know people.'

'No, I think I'll keep them as a reminder. By the way, I've been meaning to ask: I've still got mum's gardening gloves. They've got paint all over them, and I always wondered. Do you know anything about that?'

I had *no* clue. 'What do you mean?'

'Was she secretly defacing Grobatard property?'

I laughed. '*With paint?* I'd *love* that to be true.'

'Yeah, it's something me and Hazel often talk about… from that second morning she returned from Ivy farm. She'd taken a tin of red paint, and a brush. I always thought she'd gone the under the bridge, and vandalised their farm. In the photo she kept back for you, you can *just to say* make out paint on a wall somewhere. I don't know where it is.'

I thought about this a moment, the satisfying smile steadily forming on my face.

'You know your mum, Serin,' I coughed, and studying the pretty sunflowers in the courtyard. 'Put all her *heart* into everything she did.'

Much later, deep into our final evening together (with Shiraz being renamed Shizz, and Shizz, subsequently renamed, *Sizzled)*, I'd taken myself off to my room. But not before first drunkenly crashing between an open door frame… for what seemed an eternity. I felt like a silver powerball smashing between right and left flippers in a pinball machine. This made my wonderful PA roar with laughter; my last memory of the pissed Smurf for that night.

I was merrily grateful for Shizz's company one last time on this trip. Where would I be without her?

In bed, in the dark, I flipped open my phone again and studied the photo I'd taken.

I would keep a careful eye out for Serin, through thick and thin.

Extending the screen, with a dearth of coordination, I studied the initials within the Cupid's love heart. The effects of the wine pleasantly surged through me, causing erratic flight paths of fantasy in my mind. One happy thought led to another, even though they weren't remotely fluid.

I was *compos mentis* enough to consider the painting though.

This was a message from beyond the stars, a communication of love from a bygone world. Most of all, Scarlett had wanted me to recall something *good* about those days, something that transcended all the terrible memories. Something *real*, that she'd *also* felt. I was so happy she'd eventually found happiness in her short life, but, selfishly... in another universe, we were always together - and I knew this with *absolute* certainty. And life was *pretty good* between us. Sure, she was properly feisty and obstinate, as I was selfish, and a tiny bit sulky... but we had this golden, enriched understanding, forged in the right way... in the *forever* way.

Scarlett had inspired Mattie Harrison, my beloved character to so many, and I was glad she'd figured this. And, in return, the Scarlett from my past - the Scarlett who'd richly supplied us from a land beyond - had become my very own...

Grace, in Star-Spun Places.

The End.

Printed in Great Britain
by Amazon

39549620R00284